Praise for the historical fantasies of Judith Tarr

Pride of Kings

"An eerily beautiful, sometimes frightening undercurrent to this engrossing, thoroughly satisfying novel. . . . Tarr smoothly blends a dazzling array of characters from both history and myth. . . . A totally credible delight."   —*Publishers Weekly* (starred review)

"A new tapestry of myth and magic. Gracefully and convincingly told."   —*Library Journal*

"*Pride of Kings* offers decisive proof that heroic fantasy can still be more than an exercise in fancy dress and moonbeams."   —*Locus*

"Heavy mist from the ruby heart of swords and sorcery."
                                                      —*Kirkus Reviews*

"An epic fantasy work of alternative history that thoroughly enchants the reader with powerful drama, mystical and earthly intrigue, and vivid pageantry."   —BookBrowser

Kingdom of the Grail

"Tarr spins an entertaining and often enlightening tale."
                                                —*The Washington Post*

"Eloquently penned mythical history. . . . Drawn with depth and precision, Tarr's array of characters are as engaging as her narrative is enchanting."   —*Publishers Weekly*

"Enchanting. . . . Ms. Tarr weaves fresh magic into the strands of one of our most beloved legends, crafting a mesmerizing tale guaranteed to hold lucky readers absolutely spellbound."   —*Romantic Times*

"A master of historical fantasy . . . Tarr makes the blending of medieval legends, often attempted by lesser writers with indifferent success, into a worthwhile addition for most fantasy collections"   —*Booklist*

"A lyrical and exciting story . . . richly woven narrative."   —*VOYA*

"With her customary artistry and feel for period detail, the author of *The Shepherd Kings* weaves together the legends of Camelot and the *Song of Roland*, creating a tapestry rich with love and loyalty, sorcery, and sacrifice. Tarr's ability to give equal weight to both history and myth provides her historical fantasies with both realism and wonder. Highly recommended."   —*Library Journal*

continued . . .

"An exciting story . . . The key to the plot is Ms. Tarr's uncanny ability to make her primary and secondary players seem so real that both the fantasy elements and the historical perspective appear genuine. The novel will charm fans of the Arthurian and Roland legends and medieval epic of adventures."   —BookBrowser

"[*Kingdom of the Grail*] is fun and exciting and was the first Arthurian related tale that I've enjoyed in a long time."
—*University City Review* (Philadelphia)

The Shepherd Kings

"Never one to gracefully deposit the reader at the beginning of a new story, [Judith Tarr] starts this one with a bang. Tarr has once again created a powerful female character . . . with the brains to match her beauty. [She] brings all her research skills to the fore as she dramatically describes the final battle. . . . *The Shepherd Kings* has more excitement, color and spectacle, undiluted sex, intrigue and adventure than one ordinarily finds in several novels by less talented storytellers."   —*The Washington Post*

Throne of Isis

"In this carefully researched, well-crafted novel about Antony and Cleopatra, Tarr weaves . . . a marvelously entertaining tapestry."
—*Booklist*

"Tarr's historical outline is unexceptionable, her wealth of cultural detail impeccable."   —*Kirkus Reviews*

Pillar of Fire

"A book that can be savored and enjoyed on many levels—perfect for beach reading, what with its lively portrait of enduring love between two who can never publicly acknowledge their commitment, and for such higher pleasures as those afforded by finely wrought characterizations and insights into the minds and hearts of the mighty."   —*Booklist*

"With her usual skill, Tarr combines fact and fiction to create yet another remarkably solid historical novel. This is a highly entertaining blend of romance, drama and historical detail."
—*Publishers Weekly*

King and Goddess

"A dramatic tale."   —*Publishers Weekly*

"Pleasingly written . . . provides fascinating insights into Egyptian history and daily life. Readers lured by history in general and Egypt in particular will enjoy it."   —*The Washington Post*

"This historic fiction brings the turbulent era alive."
                                            —*St. Louis Post-Dispatch*

The White Mare's Daughter

"Culture clashes, war and goddess worship set the stage for Tarr's well rounded and lively prehistoric epic. Tarr's skillful juxtaposition of two vastly different yet spiritually similar societies give a sharp edge to this feminist epic. [Her] fully fleshed out characters and solid, intricate plotting add depth to an entertaining saga."
                                            —*Publishers Weekly*

Queen of Swords:
The Life of Melisende, Crusader Queen of Jerusalem

"Tarr vividly portrays the contrast between the self-righteous, primitive Crusaders and the cosmopolitan, sophisticated residents of the sun-blasted land the Franks call Outremer."
                                            —*Publishers Weekly*

Lord of the Two Lands

"Her prose is lean and powerful, and she exerts admirable control over an impressive cast of characters, some imaginary, others not."
                                            —*The Washington Post*

DEVIL'S BARGAIN

JUDITH TARR

A ROC BOOK

ROC
Published by New American Library, a division of
Penguin Putnam Inc., 375 Hudson Street,
New York, New York 10014, U.S.A.
Penguin Books Ltd, 80 Strand,
London WC2R 0RL, England
Penguin Books Australia Ltd, Ringwood,
Victoria, Australia
Penguin Books Canada Ltd, 10 Alcorn Avenue,
Toronto, Ontario, Canada M4V 3B2
Penguin Books (N.Z.) Ltd, 182-190 Wairau Road,
Auckland 10, New Zealand

Penguin Books Ltd, Registered Offices:
Harmondsworth, Middlesex, England

First published by Roc, an imprint of New American Library,
a division of Penguin Putnam Inc.

First Printing, October 2002
10 9 8 7 6 5 4 3 2 1

RoC REGISTERED TRADEMARK—MARCA REGISTRADA

LIBRARY OF CONGRESS CATALOGING-IN-PUBLICATION DATA:

Tarr, Judith.
   Devil's bargain / Judith Tarr.
      p. cm.
   ISBN 0-451-45896-6 (alk. paper)
   1. Richard I, King of England, 1157–1199—Fiction. 2. Crusades—First,
1096-1099—Fiction. 3. British—Middle East—Fiction. 4. Middle East—Fiction. I. Title.

   PS3570.A655 D48 2002
   813'.54—dc21   2002069716

Printed in the United States of America
Set in Galliard
Designed by Ginger Legato

PUBLISHER'S NOTE
This is a work of fiction. Names, characters, places, and incidents either are the products of the author's imagination or are used fictitiously, and any resemblance to actual persons, living or dead, business establishments, events, or locales is entirely coincidental.

For Harry Turtledove

It's all your fault.

PART ONE

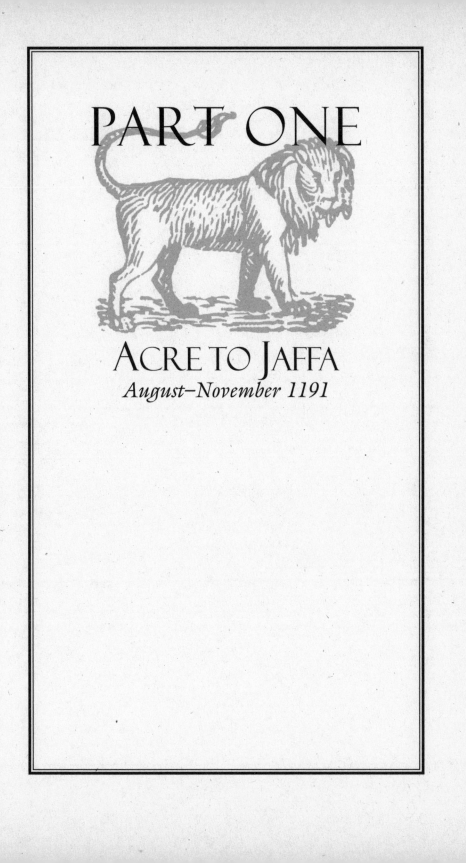

ACRE TO JAFFA
August–November 1191

CHAPTER ONE

The sun beat down on the plain of Acre. The heat was like a living thing. The battered walls, the loom of the siege-engines, shimmered faintly like an echo of the sea. Some of the engines bore the burden of names in the tongue of the Franks: Bad Neighbor, Wicked Cousin, God's Own Sling. They were silent now, their power gone still.

Just after sunrise, the army of the Franks had marched out of the city. They spread now over the plain, as thick as flies on a carcass, but as silent and as eerily motionless as the engines that had broken the city. There was no wind to stir their banners; the horses stood with heads down, hipshot, asleep. They stood in battle lines, in battle array, but made no move to charge against the army of Islam that held the hills.

Al-Malik al-Adil Saif al-Din, born Ahmad the Kurd, sipped sherbet in the shade of the sultan's canopy, high on a hill above the plain. The sherbet was somewhat sweeter than he liked it—the servants never could understand his taste for lemon barely tamed by sugar—but it was snow-cold. His brother's goblet languished forgotten except by the servant with the fly whisk, who kept it clean until the sultan should remember it.

Salah al-Din Yusuf was scowling at yet another book of accounts, though he refrained from venting his ire against the clerk who wielded it. "Sire," the man said, "it's all very well to be a saint of generosity, but the king of the Franks wants his ransom. Unless you raise a new tax or find a new benefactor, you can't both pay your troops and pay the king what he asks."

Saladin, as the Franks called him in their slurred fashion—just as they called Ahmad Saphadin—was pulling at his beard as he only did when he was at wits' end. "There's no help for it, then. I'll have to put him off."

The clerk held his tongue. Ahmad should have been as wise as that, but he could not keep himself from saying, "Malik Ric is not a patient man."

"He shall have to be," Yusuf snapped. "This ransom, to which I never personally agreed, is extortionate. Three thousand men taken captive by the king of the Franks—they could be three thousand kings; I'd buy them back for less."

Ahmad would have replied to that, but something, some shift in the air, set his hackles to bristling. He laid down the half-emptied cup of sherbet and lifted his head. All that day he had been uneasy, but he had ascribed it to Yusuf's ill temper and the predicament in which he found himself. Foolish, that, and blind. This war ate at them all; it dulled Ahmad's senses, which should have been keener than this.

Something was stirring within the walls of the city: an embassy, one could hope, come to demand the ransom on this day of reckoning. That had been prepared for: the sultan's messengers were waiting, his guards at the ready, prepared either to escort the envoys to their lord, or to beat off an attack.

With a blaring of trumpets, the gates opened. A company of knights rode out. The man at their head was unmistakable: scarlet surcoat embroidered with golden lions, golden horse prancing beneath him, golden crown on his great helm. One hardly needed the lion banner to recognize the King of the English, the terrible warrior, Malik Ric—Richard of Anjou, who was, rumor said, a devil's descendant.

Behind his company rode a guard of men in the garb of the fighting monks, Templars and Hospitallers. They escorted the garrison of Acre, three thousand strong, roped together like slaves on their way to market. They were naked, many of them, stripped of their turbans, their armor, even their dignity.

The knot in Ahmad's belly turned to stone. His brother sat rigid, as they all did, all within sight of the field.

The prisoners marched in silence. The army of Franks was a wall of steel, hundreds deep. Those on the outer edges turned as the prisoners advanced, facing outward, shield to shield, bristling with spears. Those within raised swords and spears, axes and maces. The prisoners could not slow as they ran that gauntlet of steel: the guards behind drove them relentlessly.

When the last of them had passed within the armored lines, those lines closed in, and the killing began. It had been inevitable since the army of Christendom rode out of the city, and inescapable since the prisoners appeared outside the walls. And yet the shock of it was like a blow to the heart.

The sultan's men waited for no command, for no drum or trumpet, but flung themselves headlong upon the army of Franks. They died as their kinsmen died, hacked in pieces by Christian steel.

Saladin made no move to call them back. The prisoners were dead, cut down to a man, a welter of blood in the midst of the Frankish host. His soldiers were dying. He seemed transfixed. The whole weight of war was on him.

Something was there beyond mere bloodlust: something in the earth, that hungered. Blood fed it. Terror swelled it. It drank every drop of blood that was shed on that field, and every scrap of horror in the hearts of those who watched. It reveled in the darkness that drove the Franks to murder.

Ahmad had no memory of falling, but he was lying on carpets with a servant fanning him, laving his cheeks with clean water. No one else had collapsed, however great the shock of the massacre, but no one had moved, either. They were all bound by the thing that fed below.

He staggered up. The servant, a young mamluk as fair as a

Frank, offered a sturdy shoulder to support him. He was not too proud to accept it. His brother was still spellbound, though others had shaken free. He called to the one who seemed most lively. "Fetch the trumpeters. Bid them sound the retreat."

The man dropped in obeisance. In an instant he was on his feet, running to do Ahmad's bidding.

Saladin shook himself. His eyes were alive again, and burning with anger. He inclined his head toward Ahmad: all the thanks he would offer, but it was enough. "There will be vengeance," he said as the trumpets began to bray. "God will exact His price. And I—" He shuddered, hard and deep. "I will sweep every man of them into the sea."

The royal ladies heard the trumpets from the palace of Acre: first the fanfare that rang the king out of the gate, and not long after that, the distant, alien cry of the Saracen horns. In between, the Lady Sioned knew such a horror as she had never felt, even in the darkest places of Gwynedd where she was born.

She had known that something was afoot, but she had been too captivated by the wonders of this country to pay attention. That there were prisoners, and that they were a matter of contention, she knew. Richard had set a ransom that, his spies assured him, would place the sultan in difficulty. Saladin, unlike the King of the English, was not a practical man. Not only were his armies enormous, he was generous to a fault. Any wealth that he won, he quickly gave away. He was more true to the Lord Christ's teachings in that respect, if truth be told, than most of those who had taken the cross against him.

The ransom should have come in today. But the army of the infidel had not moved, and no embassy had come from it to offer gold or beg for indulgence. Richard had betrayed no surprise, and no impatience, either. He had sent his armies out soon after dawn. Late in the morning he followed them.

Sioned was on the wall when he rode out. She had been in the newly restored market, searching rather desultorily for herbs and simples to add to her store of medicaments, but a quiver of unease had drawn her toward the city's edge. Something was stirring, something new, and there was nothing in it of either justice or mercy.

It was a darkness in the spirit, a power in the earth, but deeper, stronger than any she had known before. It craved the blood of life. And Richard fed it. He sat the golden stallion that he had taken from the conquered lord of Cyprus, and watched unmoving as his men destroyed the hostages.

Sioned gripped the mended stone of the wall. War was ugly, and holy war was ugliest of all. But this was different. Infidels the prisoners might be, but they had been men. This thing that drank their blood had swallowed their souls. There would no Paradise for them, no heaven of beautiful maidens, no bliss of their God. The dark had taken them.

She had no memory of leaving the wall or of turning back through the city. Maybe she had not traversed those ways at all, but stepped directly into the ladies' solar of the palace.

The sun shone through the high windows, casting a pattern of latticework on the tiled floor. A fountain played; roses filled the air with sweetness. Richard's sallow little queen, Berengaria, sat side by side with his sister the Queen of Sicily, leaning close together, the dark head and the red-gold, stitching an altar cloth for the cathedral. The little princess from Cyprus, taken with the rest of the island's booty on the way to the Crusade, played on a lute and sang in her sweet tuneful voice. It was a song of flowers and spring, so innocent as to be almost vacuous. The queens' maids listened as if they had no other concern in the world.

Indeed they might not, since the third of the queens—and by far the most terrible—was not there. Queen Eleanor, it seemed, had chosen to entertain herself elsewhere.

If Sioned had been wise, she would have found a corner and slipped into it, and striven for the same willful ignorance that protected all of these noble ladies. But the horror of what she had seen was sunk deep in her heart.

Eleanor had something to do with it. She knew that in her bones where the magic was, and the knowledge that was born in her of the old blood of Gwynedd. What she could do about it, there was no telling, but neither could she sit by in silence.

The queen's most trusted servant met her on the stair to Eleanor's apartments. Petronilla was not a demonstrative woman, but she crossed herself at sight of Sioned and said, "Lady Sioned! Thank the saints. Where is your bag of simples? Never mind, I'll send the page for it. You come with me."

It was like being swept up in a whirlwind. Sioned allowed it: it took her where she had wanted to be in any case, and under excellent pretext. They passed the guard almost without waiting for him to open the door.

The room beyond was dim, the shutters drawn. The air was thick and close, with a faint scent of burning, like hot metal. Sioned made her way through a clutter of furnishings to stand over the bed in which Eleanor lay.

She was neither asleep nor unconscious. Her eyes were closed, but Sioned could feel the heat of her awareness. The hot-metal scent was strongest close by her, as if she had been riding all day in the sun, sheathed in armor. But Sioned knew for a fact that she had not left these chambers since yesterday.

Her hands were cold. There was no strength in them. She breathed shallowly. The black-eyed beauty of Aquitaine was long gone, but those bones were still elegant, the face still pleasing in its long lines and clean planes.

Sioned was warded; she would never go near that great sorceress otherwise. But wards could not hold back the storm of the Sight, which seized her and engulfed her before she could stop it.

She walked in Eleanor's memory, in a place of shadows and whispers. On an altar of crumbling stone lay the carcass of a black goat. Its blood was hot on her hands, cooling slowly.

A shape hovered above the altar, light in the air as a spirit is, but there was that about it which spoke of greater substance elsewhere. She addressed it in French, in the liquid accents of the south. The shade spoke in a man's voice, deep and rather harsh, in Arabic with a strong flavor of Persia. In the way of mages, they understood one another—not perfectly, for that required a true meeting of minds, but well enough, all things considered.

Sioned strained to see the one to whom the queen spoke, but he was remarkably resistant to the Sight. He resolved himself at best into a blur of white and pair of eyes that opened on darkness absolute. Only one part of him was clear: the dagger that he held in his shadowy hand. Its blade was black, with a sheen on it like oil on water.

The queen's voice was soft and deceptively gentle, the voice of a woman who knew well her own power. "You ask why you should bargain with me? Because, lord of knives, we can be of great use and profit to one another. Your enemy is our enemy. If we destroy him, it serves us both."

"I know the honor of the Franks," said the shade. "An oath sworn to an infidel is no oath at all."

"My honor is the honor of our art," she said. "I swear to you by the honor of mages that whatever bargain we strike, I will keep to my half of it."

There was a pause. The shade coiled like smoke, thinning and fading about the edges. Its voice when it spoke was still strong, though with a hint of an echo. "The honor of mages I will accept—for if you betray it, it will destroy you. What would you have of me, then? And what will you do in return?"

"We would both see the Sultan of Egypt and Syria destroyed," she said. "Will you aid me in that, once we come across the sea?"

"If you come across the sea," said the shape above the altar. "Your son the king is idling about infamously, hounding Byzantines and conquering Cyprus. Your son the prince is closely warded in a stronghold far away, but he may be devil enough, or clever enough, to escape. Then the king will go roaring back to rescue his kingdom, and there will be no Crusade at all."

"Cyprus may prove to be of great use to us," the queen said, "and to you, too, perhaps, with its riches and its trade. As for my sons, the younger is guarded with all the strength that I can bring to bear, and that is considerable; and the elder is the best man of war in this age of the world. He will win this little skirmish here. Then he will engage the sultan's armies. Once that is done—who knows? Perhaps a shadow with a knife may dispose of the sultan."

"Ah," said the shade. It bent over her, fixing her with those black pits of eyes. "You fancy that I have no power of my own to stand against his?"

"I know that you have tried and failed. He knows you. Of me they know little or nothing, and I will see to it that this ignorance persists."

"You could," the shade pointed out, "simply send your own artists of the dagger, and never trouble yourself with me at all."

"So I might," she said. "But I prefer a web of alliances to a multitude of enemies—and you, lord of knives, know your country and its powers as I cannot hope to do."

"Very well," said the shade. "Now tell me what I hope to gain besides a few baubles from the market and the death of an upstart Kurd. What will you give me, queen of the Franks? How does it benefit my order to see a Frank again on the throne of Jerusalem?"

"Freedom," she said, "to do as you will, provided only that you refrain from harm to my son or his Crusade. Let him take what he has sworn to take, and keep your bargain with me, and we will do nothing to interfere with your nets and intrigues in the House of Islam."

"And in the Kingdom of Jerusalem? May I be free there as well?"

Her eyes hooded. "That will be for my son to say. Only remember: no harm to him or to the Crusade that he leads."

"I can hardly forget," the shade said in a dry hiss. "I will think on it. When you leave this island, look for me. This will be concluded then—for good or ill."

The queen did not like that; her lips tightened and her cheeks paled with anger. But the shade had melted into the air above the altar, vanishing with a sigh, as if in relief. It could have little pleased the lord of daggers, the Master of Masyaf, the

Old Man of the Mountain, to be summoned to such a place, even for such a cause.

Sioned fell back abruptly into her own skin, her own mind and memory. She had an unbearable desire to scrub herself inside and out, to be rid of the stink of blood and carrion that enveloped any working of the black arts. She wished desperately that she had not seen what she had seen.

Queen Eleanor had long since sold her soul for her son's sake—of that, Sioned had no doubt. But the final bargain had been struck and sealed on the island of Cyprus, three months past, round about the time when Richard swore his grudging marriage vows to Berengaria. More and more now in the rigors of this Crusade, the queen paid the price for what she had done. What she had raised on the plain of Acre was a great ill thing. If she was wise, she would not tax herself so severely again.

As long as it had seemed since the Sight took possession of Sioned, in the world's time it had been but the hint of a stumble, the blink of an eye. Petronilla seemed to have noticed nothing at all.

The page bowed before Sioned, breathing hard from his noble sprint, and held up her bag of medicines. She took it with a murmur of thanks, struggling to steady herself.

For what Eleanor suffered, there was little that herbs or potions could do, but such as that was, Sioned did it. She laved the brow and cheeks and the cold fingers, and lifted the queen so that she could drink the tonic mixed in wine. She gasped and choked, for the brew was strong; her eyes flew open. "Girl! Are you trying to kill me?"

"Good," said Sioned calmly. "You're awake. The cooks are preparing a broth. When it comes, you'll drink it. Then you'll rest. Your heart is strong, lady, for the years it's been beating, but it won't beat forever."

"I'm well aware of that," said Eleanor. She allowed Sioned to lower her to the pillows again. "Thank you. You may go."

But Sioned was not so easily to be dismissed, even by that of all queens. She saw the broth's arrival, and saw that Eleanor drank it. Then she sat on guard while the queen rested.

Eleanor endured, if not quite in silence. "I'm not your mother. Why do you care for me?"

"I took an oath as a physician," Sioned said.

"Henry always indulged his bastards," said Eleanor, "and I tolerated them, because I had one thing that none of his lemans had: I had power. Real power. I had Aquitaine."

"You still have it," said Sioned with composure. She was not a Christian; she cared nothing for the forms of Christian marriage. Among her people there was no shame or taint of bastardy. The gods cherished every child whom their blessing had brought into the world.

"Is your mother still alive?" Eleanor demanded of her.

It was not a casual question. "Alive and well, lady," said Sioned, "in Gwynedd where she was born."

"She let you go."

"I gave her little choice. I wanted to see the world. My father offered to send me to Sicily in Joanna's train. My mother was anything but happy, but she was wise. She gave me leave."

"Henry said of her," said Eleanor, "that of all the women he ever took to his bed, she was the least submissive, except for me. She used him, didn't she? She wanted to make a child, and he was the best that she could find."

Sioned did not answer that. That much was true: the king's daughter of Gwynedd had taken the English king to her bed for the use that she could make of him, and the child that would come of it. But it was not his worldly power that she had wanted. She had wanted the blood that ran in him, whom some called the devil's get, and others the descendant of old gods. She wanted the magic, which he had never acknowledged or learned how to use.

She had had the child she prayed for, but it was not, after all, the child she had wanted. That child would have been content within the borders of Gwynedd, where she was royal born of a line of enchantresses, and not seized the first opportunity to run wild in the world.

Sioned would say none of this to her father's wedded queen. She let the conversation sink into silence, as Eleanor slid into sleep. King Henry was dead in any event, and Gwenllian was at home in Wales, praying for her daughter to come back to her and take up the duties of her blood and breeding. It would be a long while before her prayer was answered, if it ever was at all.

Sioned would not trade that for this, even now—even knowing what Eleanor had done. Henry had been the Devil's get, but Eleanor was his devoted consort.

"The captives were only infidels," Sioned heard her say, or think of saying. "Their souls were lost already. I merely sent them where they were destined to go."

So she must tell herself, if she was to live with what she had done. Sioned held her tongue. It would have taken more courage than she had to betray to Eleanor what she knew and had seen, still more to offer judgment upon it.

Chapter Two

Richard lingered in Acre only long enough to see the prisoners buried and the garrison secured. Then he began the march toward Jaffa. If he traversed those two dozen leagues through the armies of Islam, defeated those armies and took the city, he would rule the coast; then, with the strength of his fleet in back of him, he would drive his own armies inland and the sultan's ahead of him, until he took Jerusalem.

This would not be a march for women or camp followers. The queens remained in Acre, secure in the palace, and the lesser women—ladies or otherwise—were given quarters in the city.

The men were considerably less than delighted to leave their life of luxury, but Richard bade them remember why they had come to this country. "You think this city is rich? You thought Cyprus was loaded with loot? You haven't seen Caesarea yet, or Jaffa, or Ascalon. You haven't seen Jerusalem. Come with me and we'll take them all, and you'll be richer than kings. God's arse, men: you might even be richer than I!"

That won a roar of laughter. He grinned at them. His looks were marred by the sickness that had felled him when he began the siege of Acre; he had been as bald as an egg for weeks, and his hair and beard were still hardly more than stubble. The effect above those massive armored shoulders was rather alarming, and rather imperfectly human.

And yet, thought Mustafa, any man in that army, in that moment, would have followed him anywhere. Even the French troops whom he had bullied and cajoled into staying when their king sailed home in a snit, and the Germans who had survived their emperor's death and the onslaughts of the Turks to come so far, were captivated for once, and their differences put aside.

It was a gift. The sultan had it, too, but without the Frankish king's sheer physical authority. Sometimes in the king's presence Mustafa could not breathe, it was so strong. Still he kept coming back, because he could not help himself. He had been the king's slave in more than simple fact since the day Richard caught him spying on the camp during a raid outside of Acre. One look at that big ruddy face, one roar from those giant's lungs, and he was conquered as thoroughly as any city.

The march began in the dark before dawn. Richard could dally about endlessly, but when there was a prospect of battle, no one was quicker off the mark than he. And maybe, Mustafa reflected, he was not sorry to see the last of the women for a while. Richard was deeply fond of his sister Joanna and he worshipped his mother, but they wore on him—especially since he had married that whey-faced princess from Spain. Her he could forget, for the most part, except when his mother forced him to visit her, but the others flatly refused to be ignored. They were at him day and night: do this, do that, look after this, look after that, and above all, incessantly, put his body as well as his mind to the production of an heir.

Once he was safe in the manly world of war, with his farewells all said and the half-ruined, half-rebuilt bulk of Acre dwindling slowly behind, Richard heaved a long sigh of relief. His head came up, his shoulders straightened. The light came back into his eye.

Mustafa did not hang about hopefully like a dog looking for a bone. He left that to Blondel the singer. He amused himself with riding up and down the column, admiring the beauty of the king's plan.

They had no baggage train, no endless lumbering ranks of mules and oxen, packhorses, carts and wagons—there are not enough of those to be had in Christian hands. Instead the foot soldiers carried the baggage. There were two armies of them: one marched free but marched a mile or two inland on rough and tumbled tracks under constant attack from the enemy; the other marched laden, along the shore, with the fleet to guard them from the sea and the cavalry to guard them on the land. The two lines curved together as night drew on, and camped together; they took turns from day to day, so that neither half could claim to be more burdened than the other.

On the first day, the beasts of burden were the king's own, his Angevin peasants and his sturdy English yeomen. He knew he could trust them to do their best for him, and they were making a game of the labor: vying to see who could carry the most without collapsing, and passing bawdy verses from company to company.

They greeted Mustafa with fair good cheer. They called him Richard's dog, meaning no insult by it, and they seemed to find him tolerable, for an infidel. He had been learning their different dialects for amusement; words were his pleasure and languages his delight. It was a grand game to address each man in his own accent—startling some of them into making signs against evil, but then they laughed, because everyone knew that the king's dog was harmless.

When that amusement palled, Mustafa rode his little Arab mare between the land and the sea, splashing through waves. The spray was cool on his cheeks. It was very hot; the Franks wilted as the day grew brighter, and their singing and chaffing died to silence. The only sound was the clash of arms on the road above, and the shrilling of the enemy as raiding parties fell on the lines again and again.

They never did much damage; their purpose was more to

vex and harass than to wreak mass slaughter. But they were a great nuisance, and now and then they killed a man. They could afford to lose a dozen, a hundred, maybe even a thousand, but Richard who had come from across the sea—Richard needed every man he had.

It was a crawlingly slow march. The road had been built by the Romans a thousand years ago; it was crumbling badly. The feet of so many men broke and tore it, and turned it into a wilderness of shattered stone and treacherous slopes. Then, before they had gone an hour out of Acre, the attacks began. Swift onslaughts fell down on them from the heights to the eastward, raiding parties of Turks that swept in, emptied their quivers of arrows, wrought what havoc they could, then retreated as swiftly as they had come. They avoided the ranks of crossbowmen and the armored knights, striking at gaps in the ranks and driving wedges of steel between portions of the long winding column.

The rear guard had the worst of it, between the broken road, the thick clouds of dust, and the slowness of the advance. But Richard had foreseen that. He had begun the march in the van, marching under his standard on its great iron-sheathed mast; by full morning he was in the rear with a company of picked knights. The dust that trapped and confused his rear guard also served to conceal him from the raiders, until he loomed out of the murk and fell on them with a lion's roar.

"Clever as well as ruthless," Ahmad observed from the vantage of the hills. The clangor of battle was faint, the fighters like chess pieces on a board. Richard in scarlet and gold was as unmistakable as ever, but today Ahmad was taking count of the rest of the army, reckoning the banners and the men riding under them. Templars in the van, Hospitallers in the embattled rear. English behind the Templars, then the French with their banner of lilies, and the men of Outremer behind, divided between their rival kings: Guy whose folly had given the kingdom into Saladin's hands, and Conrad whose strength of will had sustained what was left of it until the Crusade should come.

"He's only one man," the sultan said, "however strong a ruler he may be. If he wavers or fails, the whole war collapses."

Ahmad raised a brow. "Would you do that? Insure that he was disposed of?"

His brother's glance was sulfurous. "Not in this life. This is holy war—honorable war. We do not use the weapons of dishonor."

Ahmad sighed faintly. He had known what the answer would be; he knew his brother. But it had to be said. "You know that he won't be so honorable."

"Do I?" said Saladin.

"Franks have no honor, even to each other."

"That one does," the sultan said. "His servants, his kin . . . no. But that one is true to himself. I want you to understand him, brother; study him. Know him. Use that knowledge to help me win this war."

Ahmad bowed without speaking.

That should have been enough: he was an obedient servant. But Saladin searched his face with care. "You may refuse," he said. "I won't force this duty on you. There are others who can do it, though none as well—none with as finely honed a sense of what is fitting. I'll make do with them if need be."

"You know I won't refuse," Ahmad said. "I'll serve you in this as I always have."

"Good," said his brother. "Good. We'll give him time; wear him down. We'll prepare a battlefield. But if we can win this without excessive bloodshed, I pray we may. War is holy, but peace is holier. Remember that when you speak with him."

Ahmad bowed lower than before. This time he was not given leave to refuse. He was bound—but then he always had been, by bonds of blood and kinship.

CHAPTER THREE

However terrible the armies of Islam might be, as the march went on, the soldiers of the Crusade came to an inescapable conclusion: the land was worse. Blazing heat by day, so that the army could only march in the cool of the morning and must lie gasping in what shade it could find from midmorning until dusk. Blessed cool by night, and God be thanked for it, but men were not the only creatures who came out to bask in the darkness.

People called them serpents for their poisonous sting, but Sioned had seen them crawl out of holes in the sand: huge spiders, bristling with hair. There were armies, legions of them. They crept into cracks in armor and slid beneath shirts and leggings; their bite was fierce, if not usually deadly. As soon as the sun had set and the dusk fallen, they went hunting, and too many of them tried to dine on manflesh.

There was little the doctors could do for the great swollen bites; ointments and poultices did nothing for the itching, and bandages only made it easier to claw the swellings bloody. Some enterprising soul, driven half mad by the infestation, found a cure: an ungodly clamor of noise that drove the spiders—and everything else within earshot—into retreat.

Master Judah was in as much comfort as anyone could be: his tent was thickly floored with carpets, and he had blocked his ears with balls of cotton so that he could rest for an hour or two between onslaughts of stung and bitten soldiers. Sioned, whose tiny tent adjoined his, had gone there near midnight of the second night to fetch a bag of herbs; it was all she could do not to crawl into her blankets, stuff the ends of them into her ears, and give herself a few moments of blessed quiet. The clangor of cookpots and steel blades, hammers and anvils, spears and shields, rolled in waves up and down the army, interspersed with cries and curses.

As she came out of the tent with the bag in her hand, she collided with an all too familiar figure. Richard had put aside his gold-washed mail for a yeoman's leather coat, and covered his head with a cap. He grunted as they crashed together, caught her with effortless strength and set her firmly aside, but then paused. He could hardly have recognized her in the dark; he had no such senses as his mother had. He stooped, peering close, and said, "I'm looking for Master Judah."

"He's asleep," Sioned said. She gave him no title, since he did not seem to be claiming one. "Is there something you need? Have you been bitten? I can—"

He shrugged her off. "I'll live. Go, wake him for me."

"No," she said. "He's been awake since the army left Acre, stitching wounds and salving bites. He needs his sleep. What can he do that no other physician can?"

Richard hissed. His anger was up, a swift flare, but he neither knocked her flat nor stamped off in a temper. "I need something other than useless potions or this God-awful racket," he said—from the sound of it, through clenched teeth. "I need the arts he has. For the last time, will you wake him or will I have to pull his tent down?"

"I will not wake him," she said. "I can tell you what he'll say if you try. There isn't an herb or a potion that will protect a whole army from the children of earth."

"Can't you just ask the bloody things to leave?" Richard demanded.

"We have asked," she said. "So have the men—loud, long, and to no lasting effect. They've declined to oblige."

"They're as bad as Saracens," he muttered. "I don't suppose you can exorcise them, either."

"They're not devils," she said. "They're creatures of this land. They're no more evil than the heat or the stones."

"Those are evil enough."

"You can pray," she said. "Isn't a king's prayer stronger than any common man's?"

"So they said," he said without conviction. "Is that all you have to offer? What use are you, then?"

That stung her. She lashed him with the magic that was in her, little as he would ever notice or understand it, and said with a distinct edge, "You could at least try."

He shuddered all over, a deep quiver in the skin, and growled in his throat. Her heart clenched, but he did not denounce her for poisoning him with sorcery. He turned, almost stumbling, and went away, back toward the camp's center.

He would use the gift she had given him, of comfort and of healing. She had given it in full knowledge and acceptance of what he was; she had set strict limits on it. It would not serve his baser self or work to his royal advantage, except insofar as it made his men more fit to wage his war. But it had a life of its own, and a will that she had laid on it. Richard would do his kingly duty in spite of himself.

Sioned's knees gave way. She sprawled for a while in front of her tent, conscious and aware, but altogether incapable of moving. She was only glad that no children of earth came to sting her; the sand was cool, empty of inhabitants, and she was not at all uncomfortable. She had given Richard most of what she had in her after two nights and a day of labor among the physicians. It would come back; the earth was feeding it already, a trickle of strength to fill her emptiness.

With a grunt of effort, she thrust herself up. There were men to tend, not only those bitten and stung but those struck down by the heat of the sun. Even without her gift of magic, she had skill enough to smooth on ointments, lance boils, bathe bodies burning with fever. She found her packet of herbs where she had dropped it, and turned toward the physicians' tent.

In four days of brutal marching, the army traversed little more than three leagues. The dead were already reckoned in dozens; heat killed them far more often than infidel arrows. Richard buried them where they fell, and sent the most severely prostrated of the survivors to the ships, so that the enemy would not guess how badly this climate had weakened them.

After the fourth day they rested for two days, and Richard acted on the lesson he had learned from this bitter country. His men could not both march and play at being pack mules. He ordered them to abandon anything that could be abandoned; to travel as light as they could. The road in their wake was like the aftermath of a tempest, treasures both greater and lesser dropped wherever they happened to fall.

They traveled a little easier after that, but still with crawling slowness, and still beset by mobs of shrieking Turks. Richard rode up and down tirelessly, exhorting them, bullying them, putting heart into them. "Don't break ranks. Don't break discipline. That's what he wants, the infidel sultan. If he can divide us, he'll conquer. We'll never see Jerusalem."

They had a litany as they marched. *Caesarea—Jaffa—Jerusalem.* Every night the priest with the loudest and clearest voice chanted a single prayer: "Holy Sepulcher, defend us!"

By God's grace, as the priests declared, they came safe enough to Caesarea, the old Roman city on the edge of the sea. The Saracens had been no more trouble to them, if no less, than the spiders in the sand.

But beyond Caesarea the road went from bad to worse. The infantry had been taxed enough before, but on this steep, rock-studded, thorny track, the cavalry found themselves forced afoot more often than not. Through thickets of clawing brambles, slipping and sliding, slowed and too often halted by lamed and staggering horses, they fought their grim way onward.

The Saracens took to target practice here, picking off horses with abominable ease. A knight unhorsed was a fair-to-middling useless thing, and the great warhorses that were such a terror in open battle were clumsy and near helpless in this forest of thorns. Nor, unlike the enemy's own little quick horses, could they be easily replaced if they were lost. This country did not grow such beasts. Each of them was worth a barony, even before it was brought at great cost from England or Germany or France.

"Dinner," said a soldier just ahead of Mustafa on the track, as a scream and a crash farther up marked another destrier down.

The young knight behind him looked ready to burst into tears. He had lost his horse a day or two ago and was struggling gamely onward in his armor, dragging his lance, with a flinching gait that told Mustafa his feet were a mass of blisters. Mustafa was not the happiest of foot soldiers, either, but he had given his horse to a man with an arrow in the foot. It was an act of charity that Allah would no doubt reward.

Meanwhile, he walked. After a while, an hour perhaps, the thickets of brambles opened up; he could see through the trees how the land sloped downward to a river of reeds and sand and sudden sharp patches of stone, that smelled less of sweet water than of the sea. The king's banner rose on its bank, and a camp was taking shape around it.

With respite at hand, the pace of the march quickened. Rumor traveled back through the lines. The king had reason to suspect that the sultan wanted to sue for peace. "He's been chasing and chasing us," the story went, "and we just won't break. His troops are getting restless. They want to go home."

"And so do we!" someone roared back.

That won a gust of laughter, even as the rest of the word came back from the camp: "The king's sent Lord Humphrey to ask for a parley. He's to bring the sultan's envoy back, and they'll talk. Who knows? That could be the end of the war."

The greater idiots whooped and cheered. Mustafa was a

more jaded spirit. No war ever ended that easily. More likely the sultan had a plan, and that plan included a delay while he drew up his troops in the forest that lay beyond the river.

By the time Mustafa reached the now much enlarged camp, the young lord Humphrey had come back with his guard of Templars, escorting another, equal guard of turbaned infidels. The man who rode in the midst of them was a deceptively simple personage, a slender man in good but unostentatious scale armor, mounted on a mare whose plainness of face was no doubt more than matched by the quality of her spirit.

Mustafa did not need to see the banner to recognize one of the sultan's brothers, the lord al-Adil, whom the Franks called Saphadin. He had shown himself often enough in the army of Islam, commanding strong forces in the sultan's name. But Saladin had numerous kinsmen and a good number of generals. What he had much fewer of were men of magic—and this brother of his was a rioting fire of it. If he was here, then Saladin had something momentous in mind. Mustafa still did not think that it was a treaty of peace.

The lord Saphadin paused on the edge of the camp. Either Richard had been waiting, or some signal passed that Mustafa was not aware of: he came out with a few of his lords and squires, and welcomed the sultan's brother with open arms. Saphadin's smile was wide and apparently sincere; he closed the embrace with no sign of reluctance.

As Mustafa moved in closer, he caught another doing much the same. What the Lady Sioned was doing so far from the physicians' tents, he did not know, but she was there in the crush of men, in her veil and surcoat. She was indistinguishable from any number of young *pullani*, the half-blood whelps of the nobles of Outremer, but Mustafa would always know her by the magic that was in her.

Maybe that had called her out. Magic called to magic, and she seemed transfixed by the sight of the sultan's brother. As his escort pitched a small camp of his own outside the Frankish camp, with a pavilion of saffron silk in the midst of it, Sioned edged closer and ever closer. The color of her magic was changing, brightening; Mustafa almost could not keep his eyes on her.

The council of king and prince was mortal enough on the face of it. Neither called out sorcerers, or even a priest or an imam to invoke the powers of heaven. Lord Humphrey served as interpreter—ably, Mustafa conceded; his Arabic was fluent and nearly without accent. With his fine dark features and his wide-set dark eyes, he could have been a man of Islam himself.

He was quite beautiful, for a shaven Frank, but Sioned had no eyes for him at all. Mustafa doubted that she saw anyone in that place but the man who sat opposite Richard, drinking sherbet made with peaches and mountain snow, and making it clear soon and unambiguously that he had not come to sue for peace. "If you turn back toward Acre," he said, "we will offer no resistance; we will even provide such aid as you need, to return to your ships and sail back to your own country."

Richard burst out laughing. Saphadin was neither startled nor visibly offended, which was well, for the king seemed unable to stop once he had begun. At length, wiping tears from his cheeks, he said, "My lord, you have a wicked sense of humor. What in God's name makes you think we're likely to turn back?"

"The weather," Saphadin said. "The road. The armies that infest it. The inevitable truth: that this is our land. Even if you win as far as Jerusalem, how will you hold it? As soon as you sail away again, we'll take it back. You are this Crusade, King of the English. Without you, it has no one strong enough to lead it."

"There are a fair few lords of Outremer who might beg to differ," Richard said with remarkable lack of temper. "You speak hard words, lord. But they say I'm a hard man. I've sworn oaths; I intend to keep them. I won't stop until the Holy Sepulcher is back in Christian hands."

Saphadin rose. He was smiling, but very faintly. "And we will do everything in our power to stop you."

"You can try," Richard said, as exquisitely polite as his mother could have been. "I'll even give you peace—if you will go back to your own country. Do that, and swear never to wage war against us again, and I'll honor my half of the bargain."

Saphadin turned on his heel without a word. The shock of his rudeness startled even his own men; one or two of Richard's knights lurched forward, ready to throttle him where he stood. But Richard held them with a glance. "Let him go," he said. "He wants a battle as much as we do. Will you stop him from getting it ready?"

They yielded to that. Saphadin, who was not known to speak the dialect of Anjou, ignored them all. He sprang into his mare's saddle without touching the stirrup. Even as he settled on her back, she was off at a gallop.

CHAPTER FOUR

S ioned had come to see the sultan's embassy not for any
power or prescience, but because she was curious. There
were no sick or wounded to look after just then, and she
was still too restless from marching to retreat to her tent. She
wandered toward the camp's edge, expecting nothing in particular. Saracens were all too familiar a sight by now, with their
dark faces and their beards and their turbans. They had faded
from the exotic to the almost commonplace.

In that idle frame of mind, she saw the doubled guard of
Templars and Turks and the lordly ones they protected, and was
transfixed.

Magic—true magic—was everywhere: in the earth, in sea
and sky, even in the works of men's hands. The world was full
of it. And yet in mortal men it was not so common at all. Mages
were as rare as jewels in the earth.

She was bred to magic, raised and nurtured in it. Her knowledge was not what she would have liked it to be. She was a
young mage, more promise still than fulfillment.

This lord of the Saracens was a mage of beauty and power.

There were handsomer men in the world, though this one was hardly ill to look at: a narrow face, fine-drawn but strong, and a body like a steel blade, slender and erect. He had a beautiful seat on a horse. He was not in first youth, but old age was years away yet. He carried himself without arrogance but as one who had been born to rule—like a prince, as indeed he must be.

A long sigh escaped her. Princes were seldom mages; when they were, they could be deadly dangerous. She had only to think of Eleanor, left behind, thank the gods, in Acre.

She could sense no taint of darkness on this one. There was a flavor to his magic that she recognized from elsewhere: a richness and depth to it that spoke of the ancient lore of Egypt. The sultan had been lord of Egypt before he was sultan of Syria, and this one of his brothers had ruled it for a goodly while after Saladin went on to Damascus.

What she felt was lust, pure and simple—to know what he knew; to match her magic to the living fire of his. She had never known a yearning so strong or a desire so irresistible. It was all she could do to stand still, be quiet, watch and listen. This was no time or place to indulge the cravings of her magical self.

As he rode out with that light arrogant carriage, as if daring one of the crossbowmen to put a bolt in his back, she thought for an instant that he paused; that he glanced toward her. Her heart stumbled to a halt, then began to beat very hard.

The moment passed. He did not seem to recognize her after all, or to see what or who she was. He rode away, back to his brother and his side of the war.

The forest beyond the river was called Arsuf, which was also the name of the fortress on the other side of it. It was a freak of nature, a forest in an all but treeless country, but few men from the western forests found any comfort in this one. There was no easy way around it: on the right hand it stretched toward the sea, and on the left it spread through a torn and tumbled country, too rough for an army this large to pass. The only practical way was to go through it, and try to angle toward the open land beside the sea.

Late the day after Saphadin came to Richard's camp, the Franks marched with deep relief out of the wilderness of trees. They had had a grim time of it in the forest, marching in terror that the infidels would set the wood afire. But Richard's will had held them to their ranks. Now they had come to the mouth of a river not far from the sea. The forest loomed behind them and spread in a dark shadow along the hills to the east. There was open land ahead, a waste of sand and scrub, blessedly naked to the sky.

They slept under stars in tents huddled close together under heavy guard. Tomorrow's march would be hard, but there were walls ahead, and the protection of the stronghold, with its gardens and orchards to feed them and give them rest. The cantor's call soared up: *Holy Sepulcher, defend us!* Then silence fell, and the swift dark.

Mustafa was having an interesting night. Richard's scouts were idiots, in his estimation; either they trampled so loudly that half of Islam could hear them, or they lost their way and stumbled headlong into the sultan's own scouting parties. Mustafa, on the other hand, could move as soft as a shadow when it pleased him, and he could track a man by the memory of his passing in the air. There had been many such passings not long ago—an army's worth, and not a small army, either.

When the king's army camped by the River of Salt just beyond the forest's edge, he went back into the wood, hunting the sultan's men. He had a feeling in his bones; that uneasiness drew him out and sent him spying when, like the rest of Richard's servants, he should have been asleep.

The army of Islam was somewhat closer than he had expected. The sultan's sentries were alert: he nearly fell afoul of a party of scouts. The snort of a horse warned him; he scrambled into the feeble cover of a downed tree.

In daylight that would have been useless, but in the dark

they rode past him. He caught a snatch of conversation, a mutter of Turkish dialect. It was only a few words, but it guided him along the way they had come.

The camp began just over the hill, spreading far out under the trees. Mustafa made no effort to count the fires. There were too many. The whole army of Islam was here, the massed strength of the jihad.

He should have left as soon as he knew that, gone back to the Frankish camp and told Richard what he knew and taken his well-earned rest. But it was barely midnight, and Mustafa had a desire to see how far the camp extended. He did not doubt at all that by morning it would have melted away, and the sultan's army would be up and in arms, awaiting the signal to destroy the Franks.

He crept toward the camp, moving as soft as a breath of air through the trees. At a sudden clatter, he froze.

His senses were at fever pitch. A stone had rattled on another. A twig snapped, as loud as a shout. Two burly figures paused at the summit of the hill, silhouetted against the starlit sky, before continuing with their efforts at stealth.

Franks, of course. They advanced at a crouch, catching every twig and stone, and when that failed, rustling in the undergrowth. Mustafa could have stood upright and walked in his normal fashion behind them, and been both quieter and more difficult to detect.

The sultan's sentries caught them beyond the first ring of campfires. Once more Mustafa melted into the darkness. The prisoners would be taken into the camp, he supposed, and held until there could be an exchange, perhaps after the battle. He would wait a little while, then conceal himself in plain sight, walking in his turban and his coat of scale armor among an army of men who looked and dressed much the same as he.

The sentries bound their captives and flung them down roughly, and without a word exchanged among them, hacked the heads from the men's shoulders. They left the bodies to bleed out in the forest mould, and took the heads with them into the camp.

Mustafa lay for a long while with the stink of blood and death in his nostrils and a coldness in his heart. Why he should be so startled, he did not know. War was brutal, and the sultan's men had not forgiven Richard the massacre of prisoners at Acre. These two were poor recompense, but they were a beginning.

When he could trust his knees not to buckle, he rose. His face was turned toward the camp. If he was caught, he would die as the Franks had. He cared—a great deal. But he could not seem to do anything about it.

Curiosity was his besetting fault, and would be the death of him—but not tonight. He walked calmly, without stealth, among the lines and curves of tents.

There was no wine in this camp, unless it was very well concealed, and no carousing. The men slept in comfort, well fed and well supplied with water. Those who were awake were praying in a murmur of holy words.

The sultan was awake, and with him the fire of magic that was his brother. They held a late council with a handful of emirs who had come in to complete the army. The flap of the tent was up, the only wall the curtain of gauze that kept out the night insects. Lamplight glowed like a pearl behind it.

Mustafa crept so close that he lay against the tent's wall, deep in shadow but almost within reach of the light. The sultan's guards watched the front, where the light was, but never thought to circle round into the dark.

The gathering was nearly finished. The cups of sherbet were empty, the emirs shifting, clearing their throats, hinting at dismissal. The sultan took pity on their weakness: he said, "Go, sleep. It will be an early dawn, and God willing, a victorious day."

They took their leave with barely concealed relief, but the lord Saphadin lingered in the glow of the lamplight. "This isn't Hattin," he said. "There's no dithering fool leading the Franks now. The Lionheart is a general, and he'll be ready for whatever we can fling at him."

"Thirty thousand of us?" The sultan sighed and stretched, wincing as his bones creaked. He was not a young man; he had lived a life of war. He was wise with his years, but tired, too. "We'll take him in Arsuf, and put an end to his Crusade."

"I do hope so," said Saphadin.

The sultan shot him a glance. "What is it? Have you had a foreseeing?"

Saphadin did not answer directly. "You're well guarded as always. I'll set wards when I go. By your leave, of course."

His brother frowned. "Is it *that* one again?"

"Not tonight," said Saphadin.

That was all the sultan was going to get: Mustafa could see that he knew it. He was not happy, but he yielded to the inevitable. "Don't forget to protect yourself while you protect me," he said.

Saphadin bowed, but promised nothing. Saladin sighed with a touch of temper, and let him go.

Mustafa should have left while the sultan and his brother were speaking. There would have been time to slip away, to melt into the dark. But he was too greedy to hear it all. The lord Saphadin came out of the light, murmuring words that raised the circle of protection about the sultan's tent. Mustafa was caught before he could move, held in bonds that would not yield.

He would die. The Franks had been victims of the sultan's revenge, but a deserter who had thrown himself at the Lionheart's feet . . . his death would not be either easy or slow.

He did his best to still his hammering heart, and gave himself up to his God. Skeins of prayer drifted through his head: bits of the Koran, scraps of the daily devotions, fragments from his childhood in one of the lesser Berber dialects. The memory of the words comforted him, spoken in his mother's soft voice, with the lilt that was all her own.

She was long gone, cut to pieces in a raid, and the rest of his family with her. The pain was old, like the scars of battle and then of slavery. He was whole now, as whole as he could be; though that would not last much longer.

The lord Saphadin stood over him, looking down at him with eyes that saw clearly in the dark. To Mustafa's sight he was a shape of shadow limned in a faint silver shimmer, as if he had bathed in moonlight. Mustafa was not afraid. He was beautiful, as the angel of death was said to be. Maybe after all he would be merciful.

He stooped and raised Mustafa to his feet. The wards held, so that Mustafa could not either drop or run. He could not hide his face, either.

Saphadin looked him up and down. "A Muslim dog in a Frankish collar," he said. "You stink of pork."

Mustafa said nothing. Defiance might gratify him and quicken his death, but he could not grasp the words long enough to speak them.

"Go back to your master," said Saphadin, "and tell him that Islam will abandon this land when God Himself forsakes it."

Mustafa swallowed. Go back? He was to live? But—

Saphadin laid a finger on Mustafa's brow between the eyes. The touch was light, barely to be felt, and yet it was like a dart of fire piercing his skull. "And tell the other one," Saphadin said, bending close, speaking softly in his ear, "the great one, the prince of mages, that magic will negate magic. We do not fight in that way here."

At last Mustafa found his voice. "But there is no—"

"Go, betrayer of Islam," Saphadin said with no rancor in his voice, "before the guards find you. Not all my brother's servants are as softhearted as I."

The bonds were loosed. Mustafa could move. He hardly needed Saphadin's encouragement to bolt for freedom.

He came back to Richard's camp well before dawn, to find it already stirring. He was limping: Saphadin's dismissal had included no protection, and he had met a spy much like himself, skulking about the edges of the Frankish lines. The man had landed a blow or two before he died.

It was not cowardice or weakness that brought him to the

physicians' tent rather than the king's. Richard was asleep and his guards were grimly determined that he not be disturbed. Mustafa reckoned that by the time he had acquired a salve and a bandage or two, the king would be up and about and willing to hear what Mustafa had to tell.

The king's physician was awake and overseeing the rolling of bandages and the packing of medicines. Master Judah was always a bit of a surprise—not only a Jew alive and whole in an army of Englishmen, but a young one at that, tall and strong. Mustafa had reason to know that sometimes he walked about in the garb of a Christian, and people took him for one of the knights.

In this very early morning, he wore the skullcap and the loose gown of his people, moving with easy grace among his assistants and apprentices. They were almost done; the boxes and bags were packed, the beds folded into bundles that men could carry. Already some of them were moving to strike the tent.

The master himself gave Mustafa the salve and the bandages, working quickly and deftly, and offering no commentary on the nature or provenance of the wounds. He only said, "Keep the bandages clean. If any of the wounds festers, come back to us."

Mustafa bowed. Master Judah had already forgotten him.

Sioned had not been among the physicians. Her tent was already struck and packed in the baggage. He found her baking bread in the coals of a campfire, sharing it with a pair of wolfhounds and a squire or two. The boys were more wary than the dogs as Mustafa squatted beside her. They were ill-raised and ill-schooled children from some remote northern castle, to whom every man in a turban must be a devil, and all Islam was a nightmare of hell.

Sioned was paying them no heed; nor did Mustafa. He said to her in French that the boys could understand if they tried, "I bring you a message from the lord Saif al-Din."

Her eyes widened just a little; it was hard to tell in firelight, but he thought a flush stained her cheeks. "Saphadin? Al-Malik al-Adil? But—"

"He thought you were a prince," said Mustafa. "He said that magic negates magic. They don't fight that way here."

"What way is that? And why—"

"I don't know," Mustafa said. "Maybe he meant the king's mother instead? She wasn't there, but if I can see what she is, then surely he . . ."

She shook her head. Her face, usually so mobile, was perfectly still. "He saw me. After all. And thought—" A breath of laughter escaped her. "He gave me far more credit than I deserve. Did he seem angry? Annoyed? Frightened?"

"He seemed calm. As if he were instructing you in the law. Which I suppose he was. Do you think sorcerers actually fight wars somewhere in the world?"

"I'm sure it's possible," she said. "Master Judah says that if there's a law against it, you can be almost certain that people have done it. Probably a great deal of it, too, if it's particularly tempting."

Mustafa snorted softly. "That almost makes me want to study law."

"I think I'd go direct to debauchery," she said.

The bread was done: the fragrance of it reminded Mustafa that his stomach was empty. She retrieved the flat loaves from the coals, shook off the crust of ash, and divided them among them all, even the wide-eyed and speechless boys. Their conversation was an earful, Mustafa supposed, if one were innocent and unlettered and bred in some dank castle far away.

They were in love with her, or they would have turned tail and fled. She treated them as she did the dogs: with amused tolerance and a pat here and there.

"He really did remember me," she said, sitting with her breakfast half-eaten in her hand. Her face darkened. "He must think we have no art in the west, as well as no honor. To take me for a master of the art—does he reckon us all fools?"

"I doubt he knows what reckoning to put on you," Mustafa said. "He couldn't even tell that you are a woman, and that should be obvious to a blind man."

"Magic tricks the eye," she said, "and clouds the mind. He has a great deal of it. Maybe he has too much. Too much magic—can you imagine that? Even that is extravagant here."

"It seems he won't be using it in tomorrow's battle," Mustafa said.

She was just finishing her bit of bread. She ate the last of it, chewing deliberately, and dusted her hands over the embers of the fire. Then she said, "It is tomorrow, then."

"Thirty thousand of them, the sultan said. Waiting in the wood, to fall on us as we march toward Arsuf."

"Have you told my brother?"

"He's asleep," said Mustafa.

A smile curved the corners of her lips. She was a delectable thing, like a damask plum: dark and round and sweet. He did not think she knew that she was beautiful. She had none of the preoccupations that obsessed her sex; she took little notice of her appearance except to be clean and more or less tidy, and he had never known her to blush and giggle over a man.

"I'll beard the lion in his den," she said. "You go, and get what rest you can. If there's fighting, you'll want to be near the king."

He pondered that for a moment. Then he nodded. He was not afraid of Richard, even new-waked and snarling, but he was a little tired. As for the fact that Richard most likely did not know she had been riding with the army . . . well, he thought, she was old Henry's daughter. He would give her even odds against her brother the Lionheart.

CHAPTER FIVE

"Thirty thousand?" Richard asked. "He's sure of that?"

"He heard the sultan say it," Sioned said.

Her brother had roused instantly at her touch, neither startled nor dismayed to find her bending over him in the dimness of his tent. His squires were deep asleep near the walls, and Blondel the singer snored softly at his feet.

She did not tell him how she had got in past the guards, and he did not ask. Still less did either of them mention that the last he knew, she had been safe among the ladies in Acre. It would have been belaboring the obvious for her to point out that there was no sending her back now—she would have had to ride through the whole army of Islam.

She would pay that piper later, she knew very well. For now, she was safe. She sat on her heels beside his cot. "They're in the wood," she said, "waiting for the dawn."

"And then they'll surround us," Richard said. He ran hands over the soft new growth of his hair, frowning. "There's the sea—we can use that. If we keep formation—if I can keep the hotheads from charging too soon . . . the Hospitallers are a little less headlong than the Templars . . . if I set them in the rear . . ."

He had forgotten her existence. She left the same way she had come, ghosting past men who never saw or sensed her. There was not much time now; if she knew Richard, the trumpets would call within the hour, and the army would begin to move.

They left the river in close formation, marching through the sand, as close to the sea as the land would allow. The knights of the Hospital held the rear in their black cloaks and white crosses. The Templars, who were considerably less amenable to discipline, led the vanguard, supported by the Turcopoles: mounted fighters from this country, armed and mounted very like the Saracens, on small swift horses that could match the enemy's mounts stride for stride. The nations of the Crusade rode or marched between: men of Anjou and Brittany, Poitou and England and Normandy, then the knights of France, and last of all, ahead of the rear guard, the battle-hardened knights of Syria. The infantry marched in ranks beside them within a wall of crossbowmen, thickest and strongest in the rear, where the enemy could be expected to strike hardest.

Richard for once did not rove the lines, looking for a fight. The Duke of Burgundy and the pick of the knights took his place. They were not such fools as to waste the strength of their destriers so early in the day: they rode up and down at an easy trot, saving the force of the charge for later. Richard rode in the center under his great standard, patient as he never was except when he rode to battle.

Master Judah had dispersed the physicians as Richard had the fighting men, by nation and company. He was riding not far from Richard in a coat of mail and a light helmet, as Sioned was—for safety's sake; he carried no weapon. She had a sword and a Turkish bow, made for a boy's hand, light and not too difficult to string, but strong and with an impressive range.

She had seen fighting enough—one did, in this world—but

this was her first march to battle. Her heart was beating hard. She could see very little from where she rode, except the king's standard and the banners of the knights and the infantry companies. The ranks were so close that she rode knee to knee with Master Judah on one side and one of the king's clerks on the other; others pressed behind, and her mare walked with her nose against the tail of the horse ahead.

Sometimes a horse took umbrage; a squeal and a curse, and now and then the thud of a kick finding a target, broke the near-silence of the army as it advanced. Trumpet calls and swift-riding couriers told the king what he needed to know: that the divisions were holding together, that the men were keeping formation—and, as the sky greyed with dawn, that the enemy had begun to come out of the forest.

They fell on the rear guard first, as everyone had expected. The Hospitallers were ready for them. Richard had given strict orders: no knight was to break formation until the trumpet rang the charge. They must be a wall and a moving fortress, bristling with crossbow quarrels. The enemy could batter himself senseless upon them.

The ranks held, all of them, from van to rear. The advance was steady, step by step. Now and then an infidel arrow arced overhead. Burgundy's knights picked up their pace and began a series of short charges. They meant to draw out the enemy, and they succeeded: a horde of shrieking, galloping Turks swarmed about them, beating against them with sheer force of numbers.

"They're holding," Richard said in the almost eerie quiet of the center. He had an ear cocked to the various trumpet calls. "We'll make Arsuf by terce, at this pace. Then the real fighting will begin."

"This isn't real fighting?" one of the clerks muttered. Fortunately for him, Richard did not hear: he was absorbed in colloquy with a courier from the young lord Henry, who commanded the Syrian knights in the rear. From that vantage, though sorely beset by the enemy, he could see the line of the army, both cavalry and infantry.

"Tell him to keep on holding," Richard said to the courier.

"We'll need to draw up even closer just ahead—the sand's slowing down the Turks' horses now, but when we get in below the hills, they'll have the high ground and the faster footing. Saladin will wait to catch us there."

The man ducked his head in respect and wheeled his little Arab horse about. As he spurred her back down the line, his glance crossed Sioned's. She started a little. It was Mustafa, in the dress and armor of a Turcopole, but with no cross of Crusade on his shoulder. She would have expected him to keep close to Richard, but it seemed he had decided to follow Richard's nephew Henry instead.

It had a logic of sorts—Mustafa-logic. He was protecting Richard, and fighting the war in his own way.

So was she, if she stopped to think. She made sure her sword was loose in its sheath, and her bow and its string were close to hand. The sun was climbing, and the heat with it. The hills rose on the left hand, swarming with Saracens. Somewhere up there, Saladin was standing—and, she was sure, that other. The heat that surged in her had nothing to do with the sun.

Grimly she thrust it aside and made herself think clearly. More and more of the enemy were pouring out of the wood and swooping down from the hills. The fortress of Arsuf was close—the van had nearly reached the gardens and orchards that surrounded it. They were pitching camp: she knew that bright shrilling of trumpets. It was a physical pain to think of cool airs and greenery, water that did not taste of leather, and peace—no swarms of arrows, no hordes of Saracens.

The urge to break free of the crush, to gallop into the open, was almost overwhelming. Couriers came again and again from the rear—Mustafa only the once; she prayed that he was still alive. They brought steadily more desperate word: "The enemy is relentless. Let us charge! If we can but break him—"

"Stand fast," Richard said, implacable. "Hold for my signal."

When even Sioned, a small woman on a small horse, could see the trees of the orchards ahead, a massive figure rode up from the rear with a lone squire for escort: the Grand Master of the Hospitallers himself. He barely bowed to the king, and never paused to take off the great casque of his helm. His voice boomed out of it. "Lord king, we must charge! They're killing the horses. If we don't break the line soon, there won't be any of us left to do it."

"Patience, my lord," Richard said. "I need you where you are, and I need your strength. Hold on just a little longer."

The Grand Master snarled in his helm, wheeled his destrier and lumbered back down the line in a hail of Turkish arrows. One or two caught in his mantle and tore it, but he took no notice.

The advance had slowed. The enemy smote the rear again and again, striving to separate it from the rest, and so annihilate it. The arrows that had flown against the Hospitaller were forerunners; a horde of archers descended from the hills. The air was black with arrows; they buzzed and swarmed.

The whole of the army was beset, but the rear most of all. The last courier who came to Richard gasped out, "The infantry are marching backward—the Turks are everywhere. Lord king, we can't hold much longer!"

Master Judah was there to catch him as he collapsed, and Sioned with her kit for field surgery. Richard's guard closed in, raising shields above them. Arrows rattled like sleet.

The shields blocked the light, but Sioned was not fool enough to resent them. She tended the boy's wounds by feel. Judah, assured that she had matters in hand, had left the circle of shields. She hoped that he was safe without the guards' protection.

A roar made her start and nearly miss a stitch. The Hospitallers' line had broken. It was too soon for Richard's plan, whatever that had been—but she heard him call out: "Sound it. Sound the charge!"

It was like a great undulating wave, a long whiplash of flesh and steel. Ahmad on the hill, commanding his division of the sultan's army, saw how it broke. Two knights began it, a Hospitaller in black and a secular knight in eye-searing green. They sprang out from the massed ranks of the rear guard and fell on the warriors of Islam. The rest of the knights followed, man by man: hundreds, thousands of them.

There was a terrible beauty in that charge, a deadly glory. Even knowing the inevitable, the fall of the hammer upon the anvil, Ahmad could admire the splendor of it. He had no power to stop it.

He tried, though he knew it was futile. He could sooner stop the surge of the sea as this tide of men and metal. The power that could have stopped it would have cost him his soul.

It was a rout, swift and devastatingly complete. Ahmad stood as long as he could, though the earth shook and the mounted mass of the knights came on him like a mountain falling. Other and wiser men had long since fled. His brother was gone, the golden banner streaming far away.

Calmly, almost leisurely, just before the first rank of knights swept over him, he gathered the remnants of his guard and gave his mare her head. She laid back her little lean ears and snapped at his foot, so that he would be well aware of her thoughts in the matter; then she sprang into flight. The others scrambled to follow.

The army of the Crusade shattered the army of Islam that day at Arsuf. Most of the infidels simply fled, but some of them stood and fought, and they fought hard. Men died; knights fell, hacked in pieces, fallen over the bodies of the men they had killed. The Franks pursued the infidel to the eaves of the wood, but there Richard called them back. They came like hounds to heel, some willingly, some snarling and dragging their feet, but they were obedient. Even through the haze of bloodlust, they bowed to the king's will.

The surgeons' tents were pitched in the green and coolness of the orchards. Master Judah's tent stood amid a grove of oranges. The fruit was green, but here and there one hinted at ripeness.

Sioned's task that day was to judge the wounded: which could be healed and which should be given a comfortable death, and of those who could recover, which was in greatest need of tending. She stitched and bandaged between waves of flotsam from the battlefield. It was a great victory—glorious. The men were drunk with it, even before they got into the wine.

"Lady."

She looked up in mild startlement. She recognized the man, or rather boy; it was one of Richard's squires. He was blushing furiously, which those children had a habit of doing in front of anything female.

"Lady," he said, "please come."

Her heart stopped. "The king?" she said.

The boy shook his head. "No. Oh, no, lady. There's not a scratch on him. But he wants you to come. Bring your bag, he said."

"Of course he did," said Sioned with the sharpness of relief. The flood of wounded had slowed to a trickle in any case; she could leave the others to it, if the king insisted. She slung her bag over her shoulder—ignoring the boy's attempt to carry it for her—and after some small negotiation, persuaded him to lead her to the king.

She had been thinking as she went, that if it was not Richard, it did not matter who else it was. But when she came to the gaudy pavilion that must have been looted from an emir, and saw whom Richard cradled in his lap while he made order of the battle's chaos, she nearly lost her composure.

Mustafa was alive. He was not maimed, though the sword slash across his cheek would leave a scar.

"He's damned near bled out," Richard said. His face was red, one might think with fury, and his bright blue eyes were burning dry. "He's cursed lucky the man who found him recognized that face of his and didn't toss him in the pit with the infidels."

"He's luckier he wasn't taken for dead," she said. "Are you going to let me tend him or are you going to protect him until there's no need of my services?"

Richard blinked rapidly. There was a bed, elaborate with silks and cushions. Sioned rid it of most of the silks and all of the cushions, and waited with little enough patience until Richard laid Mustafa in it. A basin was already waiting, and water meant for the king's bath. She appropriated it and the two squires who looked after it, and sent one of them to fetch cloths and bandages. The other she kept to fend off the curious—of whom Richard was the most intrusive—and to lift where lifting was needed.

Mustafa was unconscious, which was well; he would have been appalled to lie naked under all their eyes. But she needed to see the whole of him, to count his wounds and then do what she could to mend them. He was green under the warm brown of his skin—bled out for a fact. He looked as if he had walked through a whirlwind of knives, with the odd arrow for variety.

"And yet," she said to her brother, who was still there in spite of the half-dozen messengers hanging about with varying degrees of impatience, "none of it, in itself, is deadly, or even particularly serious. It's the sheer number of them that flattened him."

"I can see that," Richard said. "Tell me what really matters. Is he going to die?"

"I hope not," she said. It was not what he hoped to hear, but it was the best she could do.

"Make sure he lives," Richard said with a hint of roughness. He did not touch the man on the bed, but his expression told Sioned as much as she needed to know.

It was nothing she had not known already. That her brother did not love women was clear to anyone with eyes. That the Saracen slave was bound heart and soul to the King of the English, the whole camp knew. It took very little wit to understand how matters were.

Richard, having confessed more than he might have wanted, finally answered her prayers and went to be king of a victorious army. Sioned settled to the task of mending the battered body. Darkness fell while she was doing it—she barely noticed, except to call for lamps.

She poured a small cupful of clean water from the jar by the king's bed and sprinkled in it a bit of powder from her store of medicines. She coaxed it into him drop by drop, murmuring as she did so, words that her mother had taught her.

The fall of night made the spirits stronger. They crowded beyond the light, drawn to the blood of battle, feeding on carnage.

A handful of them had the same scent that she caught in the blood of this man, such of it as was left. She cleansed the point of her little dagger in the flame of a lamp, and pricked her finger. Blood welled, rich and red. She sang a sweet winding song over it, a song that named and bound the spirits she had chosen, and lured them into the light.

They drifted like smoke, coiling about one another, murmuring in their eerie voices. They strained toward the promise of blood. As the first of them stooped to drink, her free hand darted out.

The spirit fluttered like a bird, chittering too shrilly for mortal ears to hear. She pressed it to Mustafa's heart and sang the blood out of it, all that it had drunk on the battlefield. When it was empty, pallid and sad, she let it sip from her finger, but lightly—it would not feast here.

Three times she milked spirits of the blood they had taken, and three times she paid them with the blood of her own heart. Then she set them free. They would have lingered if she had let them: blood was a bond, and the blood that was in her was simmering with magic. It was sweetest of all, they sang, and most beautifully alluring.

She raised the wards to ban them. In stillness empty of spirits, she bent again over Mustafa. The green tinge had left his skin. He lay in healing sleep, his heart beating strongly, his wounds beginning already to mend.

She covered him with silk and sat on her heels with a sigh. This magic had not exhausted her, but she needed a little while to recover. She caught herself wondering: did he suffer from the body's weakness as she did, or were there arts and expedients to lessen it?

He—the Saracen, whom her brother had defeated. He had been walking in her dreams since she saw him, two days ago now. No man had ever done that to her. She did not know if she liked it, but neither could she bring herself to resent it. If she could see him again, speak with him, learn a tiny fraction of what he knew, she would not be content, but she would rest a little more easily.

She thrust herself to her feet. There were still wounded to look after, and a long night ahead. She left Mustafa under guard, mending as he slept, and went back to Master Judah's tent.

CHAPTER SIX

The march from Arsuf to Jaffa was a canter in a meadow after the long hard road from Acre. There were Saracens, but they were less troublesome than the stinging flies. Saladin, defeated, had slunk off to lick his wounds.

He would come back; that was inevitable. For the moment Richard was content to strengthen the fortifications of Jaffa, while his army took its ease in the orchards and vineyards and the famous groves of oranges.

He usually had Mustafa with him, limping a little and bandaged here and there, but steady enough on his feet. Mustafa had seen the face of the angel of death; he had been within a breath's span of Paradise. But when he woke from oblivion, it was to Richard's big ruddy face and an all too mortal assortment of bodily discomforts.

He was weak then: he let himself throw arms about the king. The king had allowed it; he had even returned the embrace. Maybe something would have come of that, but someone came with a message, and that was the end of it.

Mustafa could not have said he was sorry. The king's dog—

he could be that, and happily. The king's lover was a chancier thing. He saw how the singer watched him, the ever-present and ever-watchful Blondel. There was one who would be quick with a dagger between the ribs, if the occasion presented itself. He did not mind a dog overmuch, but if Mustafa presumed to be more, Blondel would exact the price for it.

What the two of them did together in the nights, Mustafa did not know or want to know. After the first night in Arsuf, Mustafa went back to his usual place by the outer wall of the tent. A barricade of squires and a clerk or two divided him from the king; and that was as it should be.

The third day in Jaffa, Sioned faced the reckoning. She had hoped to delay it longer, expected to suffer it sooner. She had been changing a soldier's bandages; the man's sudden stillness told her who had come to stand behind her.

She let him stand there until she was done. When the deep sword cut was salved and wrapped in clean cotton, she washed her hands in the basin and dried them with a cloth, and turned to face her brother.

Richard was not scowling, which she took for a good sign. "Master Judah says you're indispensable," he said.

"I would hope so," she said.

"He also says," said Richard, "that you have the best hands and the clearest eye among the surgeons. Is he by any chance in love with you?"

"Have you by any chance met his wife?"

"His—" Richard glared at her. "Are you mocking me?"

"A little," she said. "No, he is not in love with me. I've won my place by my merits, brother. Is that so difficult to imagine?"

"It's damned inconvenient," he said. "I can't be nursemaiding you all over Syria."

"Who said I needed nursemaiding?"

His face darkened from its usual sunburned red to a remarkable shade of crimson. "Are you contradicting me?"

"What do you think?" she shot back. "Would I agree with

you? Why do you care where I am, as long as I'm making myself useful?"

"God's *feet*! This is a war we're in. I'm no Saracen, to take the whole harem on the march with me."

She forbore to point out that as far as she knew, none of the Saracens at Arsuf had had women in their tents. "Since when was I a harem? Half the men think I'm a boy. The other half wouldn't dare lay a hand on me for fear of you. Face it, brother: I'm not going back to Acre."

"You'll go if I say you go."

"Why? Just because I insist on staying?"

"You impudent little—"

"Sire." Master Judah's voice was soft and drumroll-deep.

Sioned was in no fear of Richard's fist, and she was none too grateful for the rescue, either. Master Judah fixed the two of them with a grim dark eye. "Wage your war as you please," he said, "but do please wage it elsewhere. This is a house of the sick, not a battlefield."

Richard sucked in a breath. Sioned clapped a hand over his mouth. She had to reach high to do it. Astonishment held him rooted; his glare had a perilous edge of laughter.

"I'm staying," Sioned said. "I'm indispensable, remember?"

He growled. For a moment she thought he might bite her hand, but he pried it loose instead. "You'll stay," he said, "but I give you to Master Judah's care. You obey him in every respect, or I'll send you packing. Do you understand?"

"Perfectly," she said. "I keep on doing what I've been doing, and you stop pretending you can send me away. That's fair enough."

He showed her his teeth, but for once he was wise enough not to argue with her. When he had gone, she looked up into Judah's face and blanched a little.

"So now I'm to be your keeper," he said. The mildness of his tone was rather disturbing in combination with his bland expression and the lids lowered over his eyes.

"I'm perfectly capable of keeping myself," she said. "It's only my fool of a brother who insists that I'm still a toddling child."

"Granted," Judah said, "but do recall that if any harm comes to you, it will be on my head. Not that I care for myself, but Rebecca and the boys . . ."

She could hardly object to that particular burden of guilt, since she had brought it on herself. She bent her head, as difficult as that was, and said almost meekly, "I'll be careful."

"Do that," he said.

The day after matters came to a head with Richard, Sioned found occasion to explore the herb garden that hid in a corner of the citadel. Whoever had planted and tended it had had a clear eye for the mingled beauty of leaf and flower, and a predilection for the rarer and more magical herbs of the east. Aloe she knew, and there was a myrrh tree in a pot, but she did not recognize the young tree that grew near the wall. The leaves were most unusual, like smooth green fans. "That's ginkgo," a voice said. "It comes from Ch'in. There's great virtue in it."

She looked up. She must have been asleep on her feet, not to sense his coming—and blind and deaf not to know he was in Jaffa. There had been a rumor of embassies and treaties; it should not be surprising that the sultan would send his brother once more, who had so many more arts and skills than were evident to the mortal eye.

That still did not explain what he was doing here, all alone, regarding her with a touch of bemusement. "It was you," he said. "You were the prince of mages that I saw before Arsuf."

"Such as I am," she said. Her tongue had a mind of its own, and much greater self-possession than the rest of her was capable of, just then. "Did you think I would be raising armies out of the earth to fight you?"

"It did seem that if your king had you, he would use you."

She blinked at that. "Yes, it would seem that way, wouldn't it? But this is Richard. If he believes in magic at all, he's the last man who would stoop to using it."

"He doesn't believe in it? And yet his family is notoriously gifted with it."

"He says," said Sioned, "that if God had meant him to be a magician, He would have made him one. And that's the most attention he'll give to the matter."

The lord Saphadin laughed, quick and light, as if it had been startled out of him. "I see I have much to learn of the Franks," he said.

"And I," she said with beating heart, "have much to learn of magic."

"Are you proposing a bargain?" he asked her.

She lifted a shoulder in a shrug. "An exchange, perhaps. Knowledge for knowledge."

"That could be arranged," he said. "But wouldn't your king disapprove?"

"My brother may not believe in magic, but he does believe in diplomacy—and there will be councils in which he needs an interpreter he can trust. If I occupy myself in perfecting my Arabic, he'll be more pleased than not."

"He is your brother?"

"That surprises you?"

His brow arched. "On reflection, no. There is no physical resemblance, but beyond the physical . . . I do see it."

"It's the temper," she said. "The black heart of Anjou." She paused. "Unless of course that alarms you; then I'll assure you that I'm as demure as a maiden ever should be."

"Ah, no," he said. "You needn't strain the bonds of truth for me. Shall we agree to terms? I'll teach you nothing that will endanger my people or the holy war; I'll grant the same consideration to you, and ask to know nothing that will threaten the course of the Crusade."

"That's a fair bargain," she said. "Does one seal it in blood?"

"The clasp of a hand will do," he said.

She flushed, though she raged at herself for it. It appeared that he did not see. He took her hand and bowed over it. His touch made her tremble. She could feel the splendor of his magic; when she looked into his face, it dazzled her.

All too soon, but mercifully quickly, he let her go. "I have a distressing number of people waiting," he said, "one of them a king with a choleric temper. But when duty is done, I'll send for you. Are you often here?"

"I'm usually in Master Judah's tent," she said, then added quickly, "The king's physician."

"I do know Master Judah," Saphadin said. He bowed again in the graceful manner of the east and smiled; then he was gone.

She stood for a long while and simply breathed. One would think, she thought rather crossly, that a woman of her breeding, who had eluded any number of attempts to marry her off, would be more in control of herself than this. She was as silly as one of the maids.

That would have to pass. She had a bargain now with the sultan's own driver of bargains. If she meant to keep it, she must have discipline—both to face him without collapsing in a fit of girlish stupidity and to learn what he had to teach. Magic was discipline. Her mother had taught her that. If she had no discipline, then her magic was no more than market tricks and foolish charlatanry.

He did not summon her that night, or the next morning, either. She steeled herself against disappointment. He had matters of great import to address—and if those were pursued on the hunt or in feasting at Richard's table, then that was the way of embassies. Through frivolity and seemingly aimless carousing, enemies came to know each other. He would remember her when he could, which might be days.

She had no fear that it would be never. He was a man of his word: that much she was sure of. She had ample to occupy her; she could hardly sit with folded hands and wait upon his pleasure.

On the morning of the second day, she was fletching arrows in the sunlight outside her tent—an art she had learned when she was a child in Gwynedd, which sometimes proved useful here. The messenger wore the shape of a small bright bird, one of many that flittered among the branches of the orange grove; but this one wore a crown of fire and spoke to her in Arabic.

"Lady, if you would come, my lord will begin to keep his bargain."

She suppressed the urge to leap up and run where the bird led. That would not set a proper precedent. She finished the row of feathers that gave the arrow its wings, and put her tools away, tidily, while the bird hovered, singing to itself. She had gambled and won: the creature would wait.

She considered putting on clothes that would be suitable for a royal audience, but that would put her in too much of a flutter. He of all people would be accustomed to the sight of a woman in Turkish trousers with a veil over her hair, though she had no intention of covering her face as Muslim women did. If that caused him to reckon her wanton, then so be it.

The bird led her through the orchards and past a vineyard stripped of its grapes. There was a house beyond the vineyard, small but well kept, with a neat kitchen garden—miraculously untouched by the marauding armies—and an arbor of roses. It had a wall, but it seemed more fit to keep cattle away from the roses than to keep soldiers from attacking the house.

As she drew closer, she began to understand how it could stand intact where the Frankish armies had been and gone. The light was subtly different there, the air imperceptibly altered. If this house had been here even as early as this morning, she would have been amazed.

The bird delivered her to the rose arbor, loosed a trill of pure breathtaking sound, and vanished in a blur of jeweled light. For a long while there was no response. The house was still; no one stirred inside it. She debated going in to be certain, but the air was soft and the scent of roses ineffably sweet. She sat under the arbor and let herself simply be.

CHAPTER SEVEN

Ahmad had not meant to keep the king's sister waiting. When he called forth the bird of his spirit and sent it to find her, he had every intention of being in the summerhouse before her. But as soon as the bird had flown, a messenger came with a matter that could not wait; then when he had seen to that, the Frankish king summoned him for a council that, though brief as such things went, was still tediously long.

It was late in the day before Ahmad could escape the press of duties. The spell held: the summerhouse was still where he had set it, invisible to any but those who were meant to see it. The sweet air of Damascus wafted over him as he passed the boundary between worlds; he paused to breathe it in.

She was still there, which was rather miraculous. He could trace her by the memory of her passing: how she had lingered for a long while under the rose arbor, then wandered through the garden and the courtyard, pausing by the fountain, then exploring the house. He found her in the room that was his favorite of them all, the gallery of light in which he kept the chests and cases of his books. They were not all that he owned, nor the greatest treasures—those were kept safe in his house in Cairo—but some of them were rather interesting.

She had curled like a cat on the divan under the dome, basking in light, with a heap of books about her. She was deeply absorbed in them; even as strong as her magic was, she did not know he was there.

That was a Frank, he thought. They had a remarkable innocence about them, a conviction that nothing in the world could truly harm them. And yet they were strong fighters, with a crazy courage that put even Bedouin raiders to shame.

Not that she looked like the common vision of a Frank. She bore some resemblance to the women of his own people: thick blue-black hair, cream-pale skin, sweetly rounded features. She wore no paint or kohl, and her trousers must have been purchased in a bazaar; they were serviceable but hardly elegant. There was no pretension about her at all.

Her magic had drawn him to her, but the rest of her was hardly less captivating. He allowed himself to make a soft sound, to feel the sudden force of her awareness. She looked up into his face with those eyes that were not precisely blue; that were the color of evening. She was quite an extraordinary beauty, and quite unconscious of it.

She smiled at him without affectation, and said in her softly accented Arabic, "Your library is wonderful."

No recriminations; no impatience. She was a marvel among women. "I am glad that you find my books interesting," he said. "If you will accept my apology—"

"My brother waylaid you," she said. "He does that. I've been well entertained."

"And edified, too, I should think," he said, lifting the book that had been in her hands. It was a treatise on the gods and demons of Egypt.

"Every country's spirits are different," she said. "I wonder, do the people of the country change them, or do they shape the magic of a place?"

"I think a little of both," he said. "You can see them, then?"

"Can't all mages?"

"Not in our part of the world," he said.

"Where I come from, magic is often called the Sight," she said.

"Here it's called the Art or the Craft."

"A learned art or tricks of the mind?"

He inclined his head. "Spells of words and names, and invocations of powers."

"Knowledge transmuted into power," she said. "We're less learned in my mother's country. There's lore, there's wisdom, and some of it is very great, but there's so much more to be seen and known and understood."

"You have a hungry heart," he said.

Her eyes sparkled; her cheeks dimpled. "Starving," she said.

"And a stomach to match, I'm sure," he said, "if you've been here since morning. Magical feasts, alas, give no nourishment, but there should be something earthly and edible in the kitchen."

"I found a wheel of cheese and a jar of dates, and there was flour—one could make bread."

"One could," he agreed.

She was on her feet, standing not as tall as many of her countrywomen, but tall enough. He, who was often dwarfed in the company of Franks, found it pleasant to face one who was half a head shorter. She had a light free stride, unconstrained by idleness or indolence; her carriage was erect, her movements strong, so that one might in a quick glance have taken her for a boy—but on closer inspection, there was nothing masculine about her.

The kitchen was not too ill stocked, all things considered. Besides the cheese and the dates and the flour, there was a jar of honey and a loaf of sugar, a bag of onions and a box of herbs and spices, and a lidded basket that proved to contain a sack full of lentils. She sent him to the garden for a basket of roots and greens, which when he returned, went into the pot that was already bubbling on the new-lit hearth, sending off the beginnings of savory smell.

By the time the sun had set, they had a feast: lentil stew, and bread baked with cheese and herbs, and a cake made with dates and honey and a whisper of nutmeg and cinnamon and cloves. There was pure water from the spring in the garden, and a bit of lemon and honey to flavor it; and when they had had all of that, he brewed the treasure from the stores, kaffé ground thick and fine, sweet with sugar and pungent with cardamom.

She had not had that before; her eyes widened at the taste of it, and she grimaced, but not entirely in dislike. "This is decadent," she said.

He laughed. "And the rest of it wasn't?"

"That was simple," she said.

"Simple magic. I didn't know that kings' daughters knew the arts of cookery."

"They don't," she said. "I used to plague the cooks in my sister's court in Sicily. They'd teach me this or that, to get me out of the way. I'm terrible when I want to learn something; I won't let go."

"Is that a warning?"

Her eyes glinted at him in the light of the lamp. "If you wish to take it so."

"Then I shall consider myself duly warned," he said.

He watched her sip her little cup of kaffé, growing more accustomed to it with each sip, though she declined a second cup. Night had fallen while they ate; the stars were out, soft with summer. Muted flutterings in the garden might have been birds or bats, or spirits drawn to the light of magic that filled the house. None of them would threaten those within; the wards were up, and all dark things banished.

After a long quiet while she said, "This place isn't anywhere near Arsuf. Is it?"

"No," he said. "It's a house of mine in the gardens of Damascus."

"Is it, exactly? Is it in the world at all?"

He regarded her in somewhat greater respect. "It is real. It has earthly existence. For this day, while the spell lies on it, its caretakers are occupied elsewhere, and passersby are prevented from passing the boundaries."

"That's a strong magic," she said.

He lifted a shoulder in a shrug. "It has its complexities."

"It doesn't drain you of strength?"

"Not unduly," he said.

Her eyes fixed on his face. "How?"

"Tell me why it concerns you."

"Strong magic has consequences," she said. "Or it does in my country. The stronger the magic, the greater the price."

"Indeed," he said. "That's one of the great laws."

"Then how—"

"Art," he said. "Knowledge. Alliances with the powers of the elements, favors won and given."

"Magic is commerce? You *trade* for it?"

"Are you appalled?"

She opened her mouth, shut it again. Her eyes were wide. She mastered herself; she drew a breath. "It's . . . an instinct," she said.

"Perhaps you should think of it as diplomacy. There are wars and alliances; powers combine forces for and against one another. They'll avoid battles if they can, as even your royal brother will do."

"Battles are wasteful," she said as if to herself. "Still, how does it not cost you, to work such a spell as this? It comes from your own power in the end."

She was tenacious. It made him smile. "I'll teach you to spend your magic as if it were copper instead of gold," he said. "Much of it is a knowledge of spells and potent words, in which one sets a seed of one's power, but not the whole root and branch of it."

"Learned Art," she said. "I must seem terribly ignorant and headlong to you—like one of our brawn-brained fighting men."

"Oh, no," he said in all sincerity. "You're young; it's no

more than that. When I first discovered this thing that was in me, I nearly consumed myself before a wise teacher taught me to be frugal."

"You were never as foolish as that."

"Truly I was," he said. "I had always had a gift to see what no one else could see, but I made little of it. My kin are warriors, not sorcerers. Then we were in Egypt, and the power of that land fed me—thousands upon thousands of years, magic so thick that the earth seethes with it and the nights are crowded with spirits. It filled me so full that I came near to bursting with it."

"Yes," she said. "Yes, that's how it is. Gwynedd, where I was born—the worlds of spirits touch closely on it. But I left it before I became a woman; before the fullness of the gift came on me. In France, even in Sicily, there were memories enough, spirits, powers, but they were dim and feeble beside the deep wells of magic that I had known. Then I came to the east. The lands here, the spirits, the memories . . . they woke in me powers, possibilities . . ." Her voice trailed off. "I always wanted to know; to use what I had—but I never found anyone to teach me. Spirits will answer questions, but they're made of air or fire. They can't focus for long, or keep much in their awareness, unless it's very strong or very important to them. Human mages are so few, and those are mostly mountebanks, or singularly unwilling to share what they know—particularly with a Frankish woman whose breeding is somewhat too uncanny for comfort. I've been desperate to learn, but there's been no one willing to teach me."

"I am willing," he said gently as she paused in her spate of words.

She blushed like a rose in the lamplight. "I'm sorry! I don't usually babble like that. I don't know what got into me."

"Desire," he said. "It's a need, isn't it? To learn; to know. To grasp the realities of magic."

"How strange," she murmured as if to herself, "to find such understanding in an enemy."

"We may be enemies in the ways of war and the world," he

said, "but in the ways of magic we are sworn allies." He rose and held out his hand. "Come."

She hesitated. "You don't have to—I'm not insisting—"

"No; but I am." He smiled, but with an edge of command. "Come with me."

She bent her head, as a pupil should to a master, and laid her hand in his. It was a gift of great value; a gift of trust.

Outside in the garden, a stair led up the side of the house to the roof. One could sleep there under canopies of netting; those were put away now, but the pots of jasmine bloomed extravagantly, filling the night with fragrance. Ahmad stood in the midst of them under the vault of heaven, and threw his head back. "Look!" he said. "What do you see?"

She did not answer at once. He glanced at her. Her eyes were full of stars. After a while she said, "I see infinity."

A smile tugged at his lips, but he kept his voice cool, expressionless. "Indeed? What do you mean by that?"

"I see the dance of stars," she said, "that began before the world was made, and will continue beyond the world's end. I see supernal fire. I see . . ." Her breath hissed softly as she drew it in. "I see how small the world is, and what a mote I am—and yet it makes me glad. It lets me see what this magic is, this spark in me. It's in the stars, too, and woven through all that is."

"Yes," he said. "Yes, that is so. Magic is in everything. The ability to see it, and more than that, to command it—that is the art of mages."

"Seeing is easier than commanding," she said.

"Not always," said Ahmad. He had made a decision while he waited for her to discover the purpose of the lesson. "You should go now, and sleep. Soon—maybe tomorrow, maybe the day after tomorrow—I'll send another messenger. Then your proper teaching may begin."

He saw the quick flash of disappointment, but she mastered it almost as soon as it began. "I know," she said before he could speak. "Patience is one of the virtues a mage must cultivate. I shall be a patient scholar—and a grateful one."

He stooped on impulse and kissed her hand that rested still in his, and held it for a moment, smiling into the starlit glimmer of her face. "Soon," he said.

CHAPTER EIGHT

Sioned came very late to her bed. She had taken pains not
to be seen; she had tried a thing that suggested itself to
her, drawing the night about her like a mantle. She had
learned a great deal from those hours in the lord Saphadin's
house, reading, waiting, cultivating patience; then sharing his
company. It was a subtle teaching, but neither difficult nor particularly obscure. She cherished her memory of it.

And, she admitted to herself as the stars wheeled toward
dawn, her memory of him. She was not a silly schoolgirl to squeal
and giggle over any man who cast his eye on her, but this one . . .

She sighed. He was more than twice her age, he was sworn
to drive her brother and his army from this country, and she
had no doubt that somewhere, in Damascus or Cairo or the
gods knew where, he had a flock of wives and concubines, and
children innumerable. Her magic had drawn his attention, but
she doubted rather strongly that he had noticed the rest of her.
He could have the pick of the women of the east; old King
Henry's bastard daughter was hardly worth his notice.

She was not unduly cast down. A teacher was a rarer beast

than a lover, and one who could teach magic was as rare as the phoenix. She would thank the gods for what they had given, and ask nothing more.

Although, if they should be inclined to give more . . .

She rebuked her heart for wickedness, thrust down the thought and set her foot on it, and willed herself to sleep.

The messenger came on the morrow after all, and rather early, too. It was a very young Saracen page, as black and shiny as an olive, with a turban nearly as big as he was, and a sweet lisping voice. Master Judah was not visibly delighted to lose Sioned for another day, but when she glanced at him, he sighed vastly, shrugged, and turned his back on her. That was as close to his blessing as she would get.

He had no great need of her now; they were in between battles, and except for accidents and injuries and the worst wounded from Arsuf, there was little for the physicians to do. She knew a pang of guilt for the men who would have to do without her, but the master himself was looking after them. They were as well cared for as anyone could be.

She followed the page with carefully controlled excitement. He was human, she had assured herself; magic had not made him, though magic was woven about him. He regarded her with bright curiosity, but he had been well trained: he asked her none of the questions that a child of his age might have been expected to ask. He resisted her smile for a goodly while before he broke out in one as enormous as he was small. When she offered her hand, he took it; his clasp was warm, tugging lightly, leading her through the trees of the grove.

She had more than half expected to pass from world to world as she had into the lord Saphadin's house, but they stayed in the orchards of Jaffa, making their way toward the Saracens' camp. It had grown somewhat since the first day, gained a second circle of tents within the first. These faced inward, with a veiled look to them, as was fitting: there were women in them, wives and concubines of the lord and his escort.

Sioned could not have said what she felt. Disappointment? Not exactly. Excitement? Not as much as she might have hoped to feel, if she had been going to the lord's tent and not to the one that stood in the center of these. Maybe he was inside—maybe he would seize her and bind her and make her his concubine.

Not that prince of Islam. If he had been a great deal younger and a great deal more foolish, yes, it might conceivably have been possible. But that would have required that she be a much more splendid prize than she was.

She had mastered her errant fancy by the time the page led her past the black eunuch guards—his kin, she supposed—and into a place that quite profoundly astonished her. She knew what the harem was like: she had seen the women's quarters of enough princely houses, in Sicily and Cyprus and in this country. She had expected a world of shadows and whispers, cloying scents and coiling intrigue and stultifying boredom.

This was a clean and almost empty space, remarkably well lit: the back of it was open on a sort of court surrounded by tent walls. Most of the furnishings were rugs in heaps and rolls; there were chests, three of them, along one wall, and a table with a silver kaffé service, and behind curtains, what must have been a bed. Maybe the more usual accouterments of a lady's tent were hidden behind those draperies; she caught no sound or scent, and sensed no presence there, human or otherwise. She was alone: the page had bowed to the rugs that covered the bare earth, and left her wondering whether to stand on guard or to sit at her ease and wait for what would come.

She elected, after a moment, to sit. The rug was comfortable as such things went. There was great pleasure in the quiet, the clear light, the unexpected solitude. She was meant to learn from it, she thought. It was like the house between worlds, a place of peace.

She was deep in the calm of the place, emptied of either anxiety or expectation, when she looked up into the face of a woman who was perfectly a part of the quiet. She was older than the lord Saphadin, though younger than Queen Eleanor: a woman past the years of bearing children and well into the age of wisdom, with long dark eyes and a clean-carved face the color of old ivory. She must have been strikingly beautiful in youth; she was striking still, in a way that Sioned had not seen before. But the air about her, the light of magic in her . . .

"You come from Egypt," Sioned said—rudely, she supposed, but she could not help herself.

The woman inclined her head. "You see clearly," she said. "I am called Safiyah; I am first wife to the lord Al-Adil."

Sioned's stomach clenched. It was ridiculous; absurd. Yet she was suddenly and viciously jealous of this woman who was at least a decade older than her husband.

Even through her foolishness, she could think. She understood more than the lady said. Safiyah was not the name she was born to, nor did it bind her with its power. That much of Egyptian magic, Sioned knew: that it wielded the power of true names.

Her throat was tight. She forced words through it. "Are—are you to be my teacher?"

"If you will have me," Safiyah said.

"I had thought—" Sioned broke off before she betrayed herself.

From the glint in Safiyah's eye, Sioned suspected that she already had. "I was his teacher when he was as young as you," she said. "He was a gifted pupil, but as he himself would admit, he never quite managed to surpass his teacher."

Sioned's cheeks burned. "I . . . am honored," she managed to say.

"You should be," Safiyah said. "I seldom leave Egypt, but he asked for this particular favor. I find that I am willing to grant it. He says that your Arabic is excellent. Do you know the old language at all?"

"The old—of Egypt? I know a word or two, maybe, as written in a grimoire, but—"

"You will learn," said Safiyah. "You have duties, obligations to the Frankish king, yes? Those will continue. But in the mornings, you come here. Be awake, and be prepared to learn."

Sioned nodded. Her eyes were wide; there were no words in

her at all. She had met whirlwinds enough in this world, and
Queen Eleanor not the least of them, but this quiet power overwhelmed her. It was much stronger, much deeper than at first
she had thought. There were wards within wards, shields within
shields, and such a depth of knowledge and wisdom that if she
had not already been speechless, she would have been reduced
to silence.

She had been bitterly disappointed, a moment ago, that he
would not be teaching her himself. Now she began to understand just how greatly he honored her. This was everything she
had prayed for—here, in front of her, regarding her with a
steady dark stare.

She scrambled herself together. When she spoke, it was with
no diplomacy at all. "He married you for that. For what you are."

"Magic is my dowry," Safiyah said, "and my inheritance
through ages of my ancestors. I brought it to a rarity, a phoenix
among the falcons. Does he not shine brightly? Is he not beautiful?"

Once again, Sioned's cheeks were flaming. "I didn't
mean—"

"Of course you did, child. Magic can sustain youth for a remarkable while, but the cost of that is higher than I was ever
willing to pay. And yet when he first saw me, I was not ill to
look on."

"You were beautiful," Sioned said. "You still are. But he sees
differently. I think, to him, if a woman has no magic, it doesn't
matter what her face is; she has nothing to attract him."

For the first time that great lady smiled. The warmth of it,
strangely, cooled Sioned's blushes. "Magic calls to magic, and
spirit to spirit. We know one another, we of the Art, however
foreign our origins may be."

Sioned bent her head to that, and made what sense she
could of her confusion. She had entered into a world more different than she could have imagined; its laws were strange, and
its commonplaces were vanishingly rare in the mortal world in
which she had lived for so long.

She could excuse herself; she could turn away from the bargain. But she had wanted it for too long, and come too far, to give it up now. She drew herself up and breathed deep, steadying her mind and heart. "Teach me," she said. "Make me wise, if you can."

"Wisdom comes in its own time," Safiyah said, "but knowledge I can give you, and somewhat of the wherewithal to be its master. There will be oaths, some sworn in blood; there will be sacrifices. No magic is without price—and your weakness of the body, that is the very least of it."

"I will not sell my soul," Sioned said quickly.

Safiyah raised a strongly arched brow. "Are we merchants? Do we trade in souls? You will give of yourself, to the soul indeed, but there will be no buying or selling. Not with us."

"There are those who trade in such things," Sioned said.

"There are," said Safiyah. "But not here. We do not follow that path."

Sioned had not known how strong was the tension in her body until it let go. Somehow she kept her feet, and faced the prince's wife, too, as steadily as she could with her knees trying to turn to water. "I have never been drawn to that way, nor to those who follow it."

"Good," Safiyah said, "for I would have nothing to teach you if you had."

In the event, there was ample to teach, and more than enough to learn—in days that filled to overflowing, between Master Judah's tent and the lady Safiyah's. Sioned never saw the lord Saphadin. He was engrossed in his embassy, and uninterested in the teaching of the king's sister, now that he had found the means to honor his bargain. She supposed that she kept her half of it by simply being herself, and by answering such questions as her teacher might ask, of her country and her people and the magics that they practiced.

She had been Safiyah's pupil for a week and more when the first stragglers came in from Ascalon. Saladin had not been nursing his wounds after all; he had been rendering the city into rubble. The outcry reached her even in the sanctuary of Safiyah's tent, a roar of rage in a voice like her brother's, but magnified a thousandfold.

She paused in her study of a language so ancient that the words themselves embodied magic. For an instant they burned in her awareness, taking shape in the tale of a city in ruins; then they dissipated into the sunlit air. She sat blinking, feeling nothing yet but wonder and a distant sense of urgency.

"My brother needs me," she said.

Safiyah said nothing. If she had spoken even a word, Sioned would have lingered, but she was silent. Sioned bowed in respect, tidied her inks and brushes and papyrus as quickly as she could, and returned with a physical shock to the world of men and their armies.

No one was fighting yet. Her brother's captains had the army in hand, calming it as quickly as the rumor spread.

There was no one to calm Richard. He was just back from a dawn hunt, still with a string of waterfowl at his belt; they dangled bonelessly as he paced and snarled in the hall of the citadel, shedding an occasional feather. A man less brave would have retreated long since, but the lord Saphadin sat calmly in a shaft of sunlight through a louver in the roof, sipping from a silver cup. Mustafa sat at the prince's feet, serving as interpreter, as he often had before. His face was carefully blank, as if he had made himself no more than a voice, without wit or will of his own.

Sioned should have gone direct to Master Judah's tent, where the newcomers would be receiving care and tending. The heat of Richard's temper had drawn her to him instead, and the banked fire of the other's magic bound her irresistibly. She was attuned to it; focused on it.

That was her own doing. When she had given Richard the gift of healing, after Arsuf, part of her had gone with it. She had not thought of that when she did it, nor had it troubled her unduly since. But with knowledge of magic had come power, and with power had come sensitivity. What had been barely noticeable before was painfully obvious now. Saphadin's presence made it immeasurably stronger.

The two of them were like words on papyrus, all their thoughts drawn as clear as if with brush and ink. Richard would have the other captured and held—with no animosity toward him, but in retaliation for the sultan's trickery. "You were a diversion," he said in a low growl, stopping and spinning to face the lord Saphadin. "You blinded me with pretty words while your brother wrought havoc."

Mustafa's voice was soft and characterless, rendering the French into Arabic. It did nothing to weaken the force of the king's words.

Saphadin set down the cup, folded his hands, and said in the same doubled fashion, "If I truly had meant to blind you, I would have seen to it that no word of my brother's actions reached you until the city was ground into the dust. Surely you expected something of the sort?"

Richard's only answer was a snarl, which Mustafa forbore to interpret. People were standing about as they always did in the vicinity of kings, but none of them was doing anything useful. Either they simply stood and stared, or they gathered in clots and clusters, arguing ferociously. They all kept well away from the king.

All but one. Hugh of Burgundy was as close to a king as the French still had in Outremer. He left a knot of his countrymen, none of whom appeared to take notice of his absence, and approached Richard with care but without shrinking or flinching.

Richard rounded on him. He stood his ground. "Sire," he said. "If you're thinking of riding off to Ascalon—"

"Of course I'm thinking of it!" Richard snapped at him. "That's one of the great port cities of this kingdom, and the infidel is pounding it into the sand."

"Certainly he is, sire," Hugh said, "and that keeps him busy while we fortify the rest of this country against him."

"Are you saying we can afford to lose Ascalon?"

Hugh's expression remained calm, but Sioned thought she saw a flicker of relief. "I am saying, sire, that if we let ourselves be lured out of Jaffa before it's fully defended, he'll likely come round behind us and drive us into the sea. From here we can make the assault on Jerusalem; that should be our goal. We shouldn't let him turn us aside from it."

"We need the coast," Richard said, but his growl was considerably muted. "We'll need Egypt if we win Jerusalem—and Ascalon is the gate of Egypt. But—"

"But, sire," said Hugh, "first we must win Jerusalem."

"We do need Ascalon," Richard said. "But he can't stay there for long, can he? He has to try to defend the Holy City. We'll let him do as he pleases with Ascalon, until we force him to face us in Jerusalem."

All the while the duke and the king spoke, Sioned watched Saphadin. He was deliberately silent, watching their faces as Mustafa spoke the words in his own language, but offering no commentary.

Maybe it was true that he had done nothing to prevent Richard from discovering what Saladin was doing, but Sioned would not have wagered against his influencing the duke to play the voice of reason. Richard, it seemed, had the same thought: he turned abruptly, fixed a fierce blue glare on Mustafa, and said, "Out. Take him with you. Now."

Mustafa bowed to the tiled floor. The lord Saphadin raised a brow but betrayed neither surprise nor offense. He bent his head to the duke and bowed to the king, and took his graceful leave.

CHAPTER NINE

"No magic?"

The lord Saphadin was startled: he stiffened visibly, and his hand dropped to the hilt of his dagger. Sioned had followed him quietly out of the hall, then up to the top of the tower, where he stood for a long while, deep in thought.

Sioned knew a moment's guilt for shocking him out of his reflections, but he was an infidel in an army of Christians. He should be on guard.

"You warned me to use no magic in the waging of war," she said. "You said the laws of the Prophet forbade it. Have you decided to live by a different rule? Or do you call this waging peace?"

He did not try to pretend ignorance of what she meant. "I did nothing," he said, "but encourage a man to say what was in his heart."

"It served your purpose all too well," she said.

"Naturally," he said. "Can you fault me for helping my cause as I can?"

"Only if you allow me the same latitude."

His brow rose. "So: was it you who saw to it that the news would come to your brother?"

He was baiting her. "You know I had nothing to do with that."

He shrugged slightly. "We all do what we must. Your lessons—they go well?"

"It seems they do," she said, though her lips were tight. "Are you trying to turn me against you? Is this your way of saying that you have to leave, and I have to stop?"

"Not at all," he said. "I will go, yes, for a few days, a week—not much longer, I don't think; just long enough for the king's anger to cool. But that needn't alter anything for you. If you go to the grove as always, you'll find your teacher there, as always, no matter where in the world she may actually be."

Sioned's heart stopped, then began to beat hard. "Why?" she demanded. "Why give him a weapon against you?"

"Are you a weapon?" he asked her.

"I am if I must be."

His smiled his sudden smile. "So you are. I haven't forgotten our bargain. There will be time for you to keep your half of it, and I will continue, gladly, to keep mine. My lady Safiyah speaks very well of you. She's seldom had a pupil so diligent, she says, or so talented."

"She flatters me," Sioned said.

"Safiyah never stoops to flattery," said Saphadin.

"No," Sioned admitted. "I don't imagine she would."

"Be at rest, then," he said, "and have no fear: I'll be back before you notice I'm gone. We'll go on trying to avoid an open battle as we can, and I'll be my brother's voice in your brother's camp."

"Why?" she said. "Why do you keep your bargain? What profit do you gain from teaching me to use magic against you?"

"Is that what you're learning?" he asked.

"The more I know, the more I can oppose you."

"That is true," he said without apparent anxiety, "but you're a greater danger if you remain ignorant. Power needs discipline; magic requires knowledge. Talent festers if left untended."

"I know," she said, relaxing suddenly, letting go the prickles of her temper. "Gods help me, I do know."

He leaned against the parapet, as if he too had released a deep knot of tension. "I think you see how it is here," he said. "Many newcomers don't, and some never do. Nothing is as simple as friend and enemy, Christian and Muslim, believer and unbeliever. The lines blur; the distinctions fade. Alliances form and re-form."

Sioned stood very still. Did he know of Eleanor, then, and her pact with the Old Man of the Mountain?

If he did, he said nothing of it. He sighed and stretched, flexing a shoulder that moved a little more stiffly than the other. "For now we are allies, and I confess I'm glad of it. I hope we may never be such bitter enemies that we cannot take joy in the magic that we share."

She bowed to that, to the grace of it, and the perceptible goodwill. He was a consummate diplomat, and maybe she was blinded by her own foolishness, but she thought—hoped—that he meant what he said.

He was gone for rather more than a week, but as he had promised, the path through the grove continued to lead to Safiyah's tent and Sioned's lessons. Sometimes Sioned heard odd sounds without, and had a strange sensation, as if she sat on both solid earth and the rocking, swaying bed of a wagon. Her stomach did not like that at all; but there was an exercise to settle it, a small magic that worked well and was simple to maintain.

"Living in several worlds at once," Safiyah said, "can be disconcerting to say the least. But one grows accustomed to it. You already see with the eyes of men and spirits. Now you see how we lay world on world."

"Not so much see," Sioned said wryly, "as feel it in my rump. How many senses did you say there were?"

"Why, infinite numbers," Safiyah said, "but for now, the mortal six will do well enough. Six senses, seven souls. You'll master those. After that, we'll see."

She could be infuriatingly cryptic, but Sioned was learning to read her, a little, and to know when it was wise to be patient. She bent to the book that she had been reading, and willed the world to be steady beneath her. When she was done, she walked out of the tent into a grove of oranges outside of Jaffa.

Richard did not go to the rescue of Ascalon. Saladin continued to pull it down at his leisure, then went to Ramla and proceeded to do the same again. Richard sent scouts to spy on the sultan's depredations, but himself stayed in Jaffa, fortifying it and plotting the campaign against Jerusalem.

The army, having rested and celebrated its victory, was growing bored. Pilgrims were flooding the port below the newly strengthened citadel, demanding to be fed and guided and entertained—and the ships that brought them proved irresistible temptation to homesick soldiers. A remarkable number reckoned that, having won Arsuf and taken Jaffa, they were done with their Crusade: "What's Jerusalem to us? We fought a good war. We did our bit for God's country. If we sail now, we'll be home by winter, and well settled in by spring planting."

Just when the trickle of deserters showed signs of swelling to a flood, a ship sailed in from Acre. It bore the usual cargo of foodstuffs, trade goods, and pilgrims, but it also carried a rare and deadly treasure: the king's mother. She had his sister with her, and his queen, but they were dim and clouded stars to her great burning sun.

Richard, who had been out pursuing his favored pastime of hunting Turks, rode in at a headlong gallop with half a dozen heads jostling at his saddlebow. She had declined to set foot on shore until her son was there to offer her a proper greeting. He, who knew her well, brought his golden stallion to a rearing, clattering halt at the very end of the quay, vaulted from the saddle to the deck, and dropped to one knee in front of the queen.

A month in Acre had refreshed her remarkably. There was color in her cheeks and the faint curve of a smile on her lips, as she stood looking down into her son's face. "You look well," she said.

"And you," he said, grinning up at her. "You look splendid. When did you decide to come? Why didn't you send a message? What—"

"All in good time," she said, still smiling. "I hear you've rebuilt the citadel. Is there a place in it for me?"

"Always," he said, taking her hands and kissing them. He sprang to his feet. "Come and see!"

He would have taken her on his horse if she would have allowed it, but between age and dignity she declined. He greeted his sister with a strong embrace and barely glanced at his queen, calling in a battlefield bellow for horses, litters, and escort for their majesties.

Sioned felt Eleanor's coming like the approach of a fire, a searing heat on the boundaries of her magic. That great queen took in the prospects with a basilisk eye, had the clerks and the quartermasters summoned, and set to work contending with the army's troubles.

Richard heaved a sigh—of relief, one could suppose. Sioned was considerably less glad. The desertions would stop and the army would find means to pay its troops; that went without saying. Eleanor's iron will would make sure of that. But what else it might do—if she discovered what Sioned had been doing since she came to Jaffa . . .

For the moment the queen was thoroughly occupied with her son's affairs. Sioned hoped to be as invisible as poor meek Berengaria—assisted by her duties in Master Judah's service. But there was one meeting she had to see; one risk she had to take.

The lord Saphadin was gone nearer two weeks than one—time enough to see Eleanor arrive and settle in the city. He came back in no more or less state than he had been keeping since he became his brother's particular envoy to Richard. His camp was pitched in the grove outside the walls, where

Richard's men could watch him and his own men could mount their defenses. He raised his banner over his gold-tasseled tent, and came to Richard in the hour before the day's meal, bringing with him a train of gifts for the queens as well as the king.

Sioned noticed those gifts. A pair of desert falcons for the king, and a pair of hunting hounds to match them, with gilded trappings. For Berengaria a bolt of silk embroidered with flowers. For Joanna a dozen golden pots in which grew roses from Damascus. And for Eleanor a necklace of gold and lapis and carnelian, hung with images that Sioned recognized. They were amulets of Egypt, charms against the evil eye, against demons, against curses and ill-wishings.

It was a beautiful thing, not vastly endowed with power, but he met the queen's eyes as his servant presented it in its box of carved cedarwood. The fire of magic in him was heavily damped, so that if Sioned had not known better, she would have thought him a mortal man with a faint—a very faint—hint of power. Perhaps Eleanor suspected something: she searched his face as she accepted his gift, sitting in silence while the two queens and their ladies exclaimed over the pendant images of silver and gold and copper. He regarded her with a carefully bland expression, the expression of a seasoned diplomat, pleasant but opaque.

She lowered the lids over her eyes, bowed her head a degree, and said coolly, "I thank you for the gift, sir infidel."

He bowed as a prince should to a queen. Richard, oblivious to the undertones, sprang up from the throne in which he had been holding audience. "My good friend! I'm glad to have you back again. Shall we give these gifts of yours a run before dinner, then? Come, let's see if they're as closely matched as you claim!"

He swept Saphadin away with him—with relief that was palpable, and grand good humor. Sioned had meant to efface herself as well, but curiosity held her there among the anonymous faces of the court. She was watching Eleanor.

The queen had moved to dismiss the page with the box, but in midmotion she paused. She beckoned instead, and took the box into her lap, examining the charms and amulets one by one. The stones gleamed as she turned the necklace this way and that. There was something . . .

It was a message. The little sparks and flickers of magic strung together into a sense as clear as words. A warning: *Dare no dark magic here. Serve the light if you must serve any power. We are on guard against you.*

Did she understand? That she understood something, Sioned could see. But she had not seen what Saphadin was—he had made sure of that.

She said nothing, gave no sign that would tell Sioned more. She beckoned to the page again and said, "Take this to the king's treasury. Put it with the rest of his jewels."

The boy obeyed her with alacrity, as pages learned to do under Eleanor's tutelage. Sioned followed him, but not to retrieve the necklace. She had thinking to do, and questions that she meant to have answered. Richard would engage the lord Saphadin for the rest of that day, but Saphadin's eldest wife would be where she always was when Sioned went seeking her. She would answer; that was her duty. Was she not a teacher?

Safiyah was not in the grove. The path that Sioned had walked every day led to a row of trees laden with ripening fruit. There was no sign that a tent had ever been pitched here.

Sioned refused to give way to frustration. The lord Saphadin's camp was protected, which it had not been before. She could pass; she knew the spell that let her walk through without breaking the wards. They sang below the threshold of hearing; they would send word to the one who had cast them that she was in the camp.

There were no women here. Nor was there any message, any track that she could follow, to find her teacher.

Sioned considered the number of things that she could do. The most sensible of them was to return to the citadel and join in the daymeal. The most dutiful would be to seek out Master Judah and place herself at his disposal. That in the end was her choice, not because she was a saint or a loyal servant, but because it would engage her mind. Grinding herbs, mixing potions, seeing to the odd soldier or servant who came wandering in with a sore eye or a cut hand or a toothache, absorbed her completely.

Darkness took her by surprise. Her sight had been dimming for some time; someone had lit lamps, but they were not near as bright as daylight. She squinted as she wrote out the label for the last pot of salve. When that was done, she set the pot on the shelf with the rest of its fellows, cleaned the pen and put away the ink and straightened, stretching out the kinks in her neck and back.

Her stomach growled. She had completely forgotten dinner; there would be nothing but leavings now, but one or two of the cooks had been known to set a dish aside for her.

She had been working in the portion of Master Judah's tent that was closed off from the rest but open to the air, and she had been alone since she began. When she came through the back of it into the larger space, there was a lone physician making the rounds of the sick—dysentery, mostly, and recurrent fevers—and a cowled monk praying over one who was dying. She drew no notice to herself, but slipped out softly into the scented night.

It was no longer summer, though a westerner would hardly have called it autumn. The days were still breathlessly hot, but the nights had begun to cool perceptibly. She shivered a little, less with cold than with the pleasure of air that did not sear the skin like heated bronze.

Any camp of soldiers was a redolent thing, but the physicians tents' were upwind of the privies, not far from the sea. The fragrance here partook of earth and greenery, ripening fruit, and sea salt, and only a little of overcrowded humanity. Master Judah taught cleanliness by example; soldiers who came here, drawn as much by the absence of stench as by the need for a physician's services, often went back to their companies with a somewhat less jaundiced attitude toward the necessity of bathing. Some even ventured the eastern luxury called soap, and found it remarkably pleasant.

Sioned found the cooks still up and about. Master Jehan, who was an artist with a stewpot, had saved a bowl of his latest creation for her. With the last of the day's bread and a lump of pungent cheese, it was thoroughly satisfying. "New spices?" she asked as she savored it.

"New undercook," Master Jehan said. "He's half a Saracen. He claims they eat like this in Africa, where the king's black-eyed boy comes from."

"Mustafa?" she asked. "I should ask him. This is lovely."

Master Jehan shrugged. "It's not bad. It could use a little more savory and a little less sweet."

She forbore to argue. He was the master, after all. With a full belly and a reasonably contented mind, she turned toward her solitary bed.

He was waiting for her. That was altogether unexpected—so much so that when she saw the lamp lit in the smaller tent that she had so lately left, and the turbaned figure sitting by it, she wondered what had brought Mustafa there at so late an hour.

But it was not Mustafa. This was a taller man, somewhat, and considerably older, and although she had no complaints of his looks, he was not the hawk-faced desert beauty that Mustafa was. He had a book in his lap, one that she had borrowed from Safiyah, but he was not reading it. He was gazing into the lamp's flame.

When he raised his eyes to her, the flame burned in them, clear and steady. His smile was a part of it; it warmed her immeasurably.

She had all but forgotten that she had been hunting for him earlier. The urgency was gone; it seemed vain and faintly foolish now to take him to task for giving Eleanor a gift that would arouse her suspicions and possibly turn her magic against him or his brother. Even his wife's absence—need that signify anything but that Safiyah had other concerns than the teaching of a single thickheaded pupil?

Sioned needed sleep. Tomorrow she would be passionate again, and indulge in indignation. Her tent beyond this one, the bed that waited, lured her irresistibly. But he had drawn her, too, back among the shelves of salves and the boxes of bandages.

She greeted him politely, bowed to the dignity of his rank, and said, "My lord. Are you indisposed? Is there some medicine that you need?"

"I'm well, lady," he said, "and I ask your pardon for keeping you from your rest. It is only . . . I have a thing to say, and it seemed best to say it soon, and not wait for a more proper time."

"About Eleanor?"

He lifted a shoulder in the suggestion of a shrug. "I know I don't need to warn you against her. But are you wary enough?"

"I would hope so," said Sioned a little stiffly.

"I've insulted you," he said with what seemed to be honest regret. "I didn't mean to do that. It's only . . ."

"She is subtle," Sioned said, "and I'm terribly young yet. I know that. She's dangerous. But she doesn't know what I am—I've kept my head down where she is, always, and let her pass over me. It seems safer somehow."

He nodded with perceptible relief. "Yes, it is safer. I . . . should greatly dislike to see you harmed."

Her cheeks were warm, but her heart was cold. There was something she should say—but she could not. She could not tell this man what bargain Eleanor had made.

This was an outlander, an enemy. And yet it was a sensation close to pain, to keep silent; to let him go away in ignorance of the plot against his brother.

Magic drew its own lines, created its own bonds of nation and kinship. The magic in her did not want to see this man as an enemy. He was of her own kind—her heart's, her magic's kin.

Still she did not speak. She protected her true enemy and concealed the truth from her true friend. She would pay for that.

Chapter Ten

Time was when Mustafa without a war to fight would have been a lost and useless thing. But since he came to Richard, his gift for languages had served him remarkably well. Richard trusted him, Allah knew why, and kept him close through all his interactions with the folk of Islam. He was notably more preoccupied now than he had been on the march, kept at his translating from dawn until long after dusk. When he was done, he had no thought for anything but to fall asleep—it hardly mattered where.

Richard's servants looked after him, kept him clean, saw that he had fresh linen in the mornings and a bath every evening. They were all handsome boys, big and fair as the king was said to like them. Sometimes Mustafa wondered where that left him: dark, slight, dwarfed among all these foreigners. The deserts of Morocco bred beauty, but seldom endowed it with size.

Not, to be sure, that he wanted to be a great hulking creature like these nobles of the Franks. He was more than content with himself. And so, it seemed, was Richard. He used his servant ruthlessly, but Mustafa never felt that he was a mere and mindless instrument. Richard would add a phrase or two, or a glance or a smile, to the speeches that Mustafa rendered into the languages of the east: Arabic of course, Greek, Turkish, Armenian, and the odd dialect of Egypt or Syria or the Arabian desert. Richard knew what he had in Mustafa, and was visibly glad of it.

A day or two after the lord al-Adil came back from his prudent retreat, Richard went hawking in the hills above the sea. It was a very early morning, up and out before dawn, and he took only a few hardy souls for escort, reckoning to be back in Jaffa by full morning. He did not need Mustafa for that, but Mustafa had been unable to sleep.

So, it seemed, had the singer Blondel. Richard did not raise a brow at either of them, but Mustafa was aware of the chill in the air, which was more than early autumn in this part of Syria could account for.

It did not matter to him. He had a favorite hawk, a desert falcon, small but swift, which the king's chief falconer was so kind as to look after for him. It was good to see the fierce little creature again, to feel the grip of claws on his gauntleted fist before he bade it shift to the padded perch on his saddlebow. He took a place not too far from the king, but not too presumptuously near. Blondel, with his lute in its case but no falcon to hunt for him, rode just behind Richard, defying anyone else to displace him.

No one did. Newcomers would cross him, but anyone who had been with Richard through the Crusade had learned to let the singer be. He was Richard's and only Richard's. He cared for nothing and no one else.

The hunting was good—so much so that they had gone rather farther than they had intended, out of sight of the city and into a stretch of tumbled hills. They dismounted there to drink from a spring that bubbled up from the rock, to eat such provisions as they had brought in their saddlebags, and to share a brag or six. No one troubled to post a guard. Mustafa thought of it, but fast riding and fresh morning air and the rising of warmth with the day made him lazy.

Richard, having eaten and drunk with good appetite, spread his cloak on a flat stretch of ground and lay on it. Blondel tuned his lute. The others gathered to listen, or were already snoring in the sun. The horses, hobbled, nosed about for what grazing they could find. Only the falconers were honestly awake, tending the birds in a curve of rocky hillside, sheltered from the wind.

Blondel's voice was sweet, whatever one might think of his disposition. Richard smiled as he drowsed. Mustafa took note of the words of the song, which were in the language of the south of France, swift and liquid, with a hint about it of strong sunlight and thyme-scented hillsides. Someday he would see those hills, he thought sleepily. Someday he would—

Sleep broke asunder in a thunder of hooves, a chorus of shrilling howls, and the clash of steel on steel.

Turks. Seljuks, shrieking out the titles of the Almighty in barbarous Arabic. Mustafa bit his tongue before he sang them back. The Franks would never understand. He leaped up, whirling his sword about his head, eyes darting until they found Richard. The Lionheart was on his feet, laying about him with his great sword and bellowing like a bull.

None of them was in armor; they were only armed with swords and knives and here and there a hunting spear. Those who could get to the horses at least had the advantage of weight and speed—even the Franks' palfreys were heavier than the eastern horses, though never as fast on their feet.

Mustafa hacked two-handed at a shrilling Turk, hauled him down off his horse and vaulted into the saddle. The horse wheeled, shaking its head, ears flat back. It snapped at his knee; he dealt it a vicious kick in the jaw, which subdued it handsomely. It was still a hard-mouthed, dead-sided, evil-tempered ravenbait, but it had one sterling quality: it had no fear at all.

The way was open—all the Turks had fallen on the Franks, leaving Mustafa alone and seemingly forgotten. He could make a run for it and maybe reach the outskirts of Jaffa in time to fetch reinforcements.

And maybe not. There were a good half-hundred Turks and fewer than a score of Franks. The Turks were in full battle gear. The Franks were dressed and armed for a hunt. And—

They knew Richard was here. They called back and forth in Mustafa's hearing: "One of them has to be the king. Which one? The biggest? The one with the reddest face?"

"The one with horns and fangs!"

One of them spat a curse. "Bloody Franks all look alike. How in Iblis' name—"

Richard, thank Allah, could not understand them. Mustafa's heart ached to fight at his back, to defend him, but if these Turks had in mind to take prisoner the dreaded King of the English, then he must not be singled out. He was dressed in plain hunting garb, with no coronet on his light helmet, and nothing about him to mark him as any higher in rank than the rest of the knights in his company.

They were all beset. Mustafa seized the advantage of his Muslim face and turban, and rode through unresisting crowds of Turks. He caught such of the king's men as were less preoccupied at the moment, and to each said the same: "They're out to capture the king, but they can't tell which of you he is. Don't let them guess!"

These were seasoned fighting men, and deeply loyal to Richard. They wasted no time in argument. Those that had been gathering about the king stopped their advance and stood in place, letting the Turks come to them.

Blondel had been cut off from the king and driven back toward the falcons. Of them all except for Mustafa, he was least likely to be mistaken for Richard. His white-fair hair marked him as a different breed of Frank than the famously ruddy king. He had a sword, which he wielded well enough, but chiefly in defense of his lute; there could be little doubt as to what he was.

Mustafa could hope that he would have sense enough not to betray his king, but it was all too clear that he had only one thought: to fight his way back to Richard. As ill luck would have it, one or two of the Turks had realized that Mustafa was not one of them; they began to turn on him, and all the more fiercely for that he was obviously a Muslim. *Traitor* was the least of the words they laid on him.

He could not come to Blondel, could not beat sense into him. He saw Blondel's mouth open, knew with sinking heart that the fool would call the king's name. And Richard would turn, would hear, because Blondel's voice was trained; it could carry across a battlefield.

Just as Mustafa struggled to hold off a grimly determined Turk and to muster himself for a shriek that might, if Allah was merciful, overwhelm whatever Blondel could say, a great voice lifted up above the clamor of the fight. "Let them be! I'm the king. I'm Malik Ric!"

That was not Richard's voice, even if Richard had known enough Arabic to say such a thing. It was one of the knights— William, his name was; he was holding his own against half a dozen shrilling horsemen, as far from Richard as the battlefield would go. He did look rather like the king, not quite so big and not quite so broad in the shoulder, but massive enough, and the bristle of his beard was more red than gold.

The Turks abandoned the rest and fell on him with howls of glee. He laughed as he fought them off, even as they overwhelmed him, bound him and carried him away.

He was gone before Richard understood what had happened. The Turks barely paused to take up their wounded and their dead; they rode off as swiftly as they had come, and left the hunters in stunned silence, bereft of a battle.

Of fifteen men, half were down. Five of those were dead, and one was lost, taken prisoner in Richard's name. Richard stood leaning on his sword, blood dripping from it. His boots, his hose and tunic, were spattered with scarlet.

He lurched into motion. The horses were still tethered in their line, the falcons still on their perches. The Turks had found a greater prize, or so they thought. "Mount!" Richard commanded his men who survived. "After them! We'll get him back."

None of them moved except to take up the dead and bind them to their horses' saddles. It was nothing so blatant as disobedience.

They simply failed to hear him. When the hale and the wounded were mounted, they turned not toward the departing Turks but toward Jaffa.

If Richard had galloped off to rescue William singlehanded, Mustafa would have followed him. For a long moment Mustafa expected him to do just that. Then his face stiffened, paling from the crimson of rage to stark white. He stooped and wiped his sword on the trousers of a dead Turk, and thrust it into its sheath with just a fraction more force than was strictly necessary.

When he turned, Mustafa offered him the rein of his horse Fauvel. He offered no gratitude, snatched the rein and sprang astride. The stallion squealed at the unaccustomed outrage of spurs dug viciously into his sides, reared, bucked, and bolted in pursuit of his fellows.

Mustafa held his tongue. He had let go his conquered Turkish horse and retrieved his mare. She fussed, objecting to being kept behind while the rest of the horses ran for home. But something was troubling him. Someone was missing from both the count of the dead and the number of the living.

Mustafa found him under the body of a huge Turk, a mountain of a man who had died with a dagger in his throat. Blondel's fingers were locked about the hilt.

He was breathing, if shallowly. Mustafa found no wound on him. His lute was crushed by the Turk's weight, but the giant in falling had done no more than knock him senseless.

Mustafa bade his mare kneel. She was skittish, snorting at the stink of death, but at heart she was a sensible beast. She lowered herself to the ground and held steady while he heaved the singer onto her back. Blondel hindered him by waking and beginning to struggle. Coldly and quite without compunction, he sent the idiot back into the darkness with a well-placed blow to the head.

When Blondel roused again, he was tied to the saddle and Mustafa was walking beside him. It was a long way back to Jaffa on foot, but Mustafa sighed and endured and tried not to regret the horse that, too hastily, he had let go.

"Why?"

Mustafa looked up, mildly startled. It was rather impressive that Blondel could speak while lying head down across a saddle. He creaked as Mustafa untied him, and groaned when he sat upright, then sagged suddenly and relieved himself of everything he had eaten since the day before.

He straightened painfully, still gagging on emptiness. Mustafa handed him the water bottle. He drank in sips as a wise man should, and did not gorge himself. His cheeks were still more green than white, but he no longer looked half-dead. He repeated his question. "Why?"

"I should have left you for dead?"

"Why not? Everyone else did."

Mustafa shrugged. "They had their own friends and kin to fret over."

"We are neither."

"That's why," Mustafa said.

Blondel stared at him with eyes as pale as a corpse's, set deep in bruised skin. "*He* forgot that I existed."

There was pain. Mustafa was not the one to ease it.

"Don't expect gratitude," Blondel said in his silence, "or a reward, either. It would have been better if you'd left me to die."

"Probably," Mustafa said, "but he would miss you sooner or later, and I rather like your songs."

Blondel's expression was pure outrage—at Mustafa, and after an instant at his own rebellious stomach. It was some while before he could speak again. "You," he gasped. "You—"

Mustafa ignored him. The next hill would bring them in sight of Jaffa; then it would be a mere hour's walk to the edge of the Frankish camp.

It was too much to hope that he could complete that walk in silence. "God knows what he sees in you," Blondel said. "He's not a man for your kind at all."

That so perfectly mirrored Mustafa's thoughts before the Turks attacked that he laughed. Blondel took a very dim view of such levity. Mustafa had no hope of redeeming himself, but he did feel obligated to say, "I'm useful. I can think in two languages at once."

"Braggart," Blondel muttered.

Mustafa made no effort to suppress the smile.

"You are pretty enough," Blondel said, "for a desert rat. What are you, Bedouin?"

"Berber," Mustafa said. He was careful to keep the edge out of his voice. Bedouin, indeed. That was worse than a rat, and he did not doubt that Blondel knew it.

They were not going to be friends. Mustafa had never expected that they would. He shut out the rest of Blondel's chatter, until it faded and eventually stopped. He wished the singer would sing; that would at least have been pleasant to hear. But Blondel saved that aspect of his voice for his art. Silence was a relief, even with the barbed edges that Blondel put in it.

Blondel was pale again and clinging blindly to the saddle when Mustafa brought him to the king's sister. She had heard of the king's hunt; both camp and city were buzzing with it. It was a grim tale in itself—so many dead for so little cause—but William's capture had struck a nerve.

When she saw Mustafa, the flash of relief warmed his heart. Her brow rose at sight of his companion, but she wisely refrained from comment. Blondel was ill as men sometimes were after a blow to the head; they could die of it. "Not this one," she said, seeing clearly into his heart as mages—and women and physicians—could.

He was glad, not for Blondel's sake but for the king's. Richard had not forgotten his singer—he had thought the man safe with the falconers, and only discovered his absence when all the rest were back in Jaffa. After Mustafa had left Blondel in Sioned's care, he found the king in a dangerous mood, ready to ride out again and find Blondel, then win back the captive knight with the whole might of his army.

Mustafa passed a delegation of French nobles as he came into the citadel. The Duke of Burgundy led them; his face was thunderous. Whatever had passed between them and the king, it had not ended well. The air in the hall was still thrumming.

Mustafa judged it wise to hang back and wait until the audience should end and he could speak to Richard alone. But the king had seen him. "Mustafa! Thank God! I'd given you up for dead."

"Not quite, sire," Mustafa said, sliding out from behind two hulking Englishmen. He suppressed a sigh. Now they were all staring, whispering among themselves, waiting for the next turn of the entertainment.

Richard fed their hunger for gossip by calling Mustafa to him and pulling him into a tight embrace. Mustafa seized the opportunity to murmur rapidly in the king's ear. "Blondel is well. He's with the Lady Sioned—he had a knock on the head; he won't die of it."

"Good," Richard said. "Good indeed. You have my thanks." He let Mustafa go. "I'm trapped here for now. Go to my rooms and wait. Ask the squire to give you what you need—a bath and food, I'll wager, and a bed, too, from the look of you. Are you wounded?"

Mustafa shook his head. "Allah was kind to me. And you?"

"The Devil looks after his own," Richard said without levity. "Wait for me. Sleep if you can."

Mustafa would not have thought that he could sleep. But a thorough cleansing in a proper Muslim bath, then a meal of cheese and bread and dates washed down with sherbet, left him loosed in every muscle and blissfully replete. He lay down at the servants' urging, closed his eyes for a moment, and opened them on Richard's face.

Lamplight limned it. Night had fallen. Richard was wrapped in a scent of wine, but he was steady on his feet, his cheeks only slightly flushed.

Mustafa tensed inside of himself. But the king did not touch him. He sat on a stool beside the bed and said, "They say you walked back to Jaffa."

"My mare won't carry two," Mustafa said, struggling against a yawn. "He needed her more than I did."

"He loves you less than he ever did, now."

"I didn't do it to make him love me."

"No," Richard said. "That's not something you would do."

"I didn't do it to make you love me, either."

Richard's mouth fell open. It was a moment before he laughed, a light, startled sound. "I hope you're not asking me to understand you."

"Franks can understand us," Mustafa said, "but once that understanding comes, they're no longer Franks."

"They're what? *Pullani?*"

"Easterners," said Mustafa.

"With all due respect," Richard said, "I'd rather stay a Frank."

"I also would rather you did," Mustafa said.

"Why? Would I make such a terrible easterner?"

"You are a glorious great brawler of a Frank," Mustafa said.

"Out there they're calling me a fool," Richard said. "I lost too many men; there's a good knight taken prisoner, and God knows what will become of him once they find out he's not the infamous Malik Ric." His fists clenched. "God damn their hides! He'd be back here with us, roaring over the jest, if even one of them had been willing to follow me."

"I was willing," Mustafa said quietly.

Richard did not choose to hear. "We'll get him back. They'll pay the blood price and the thieves' price. I'll give them good reason to regret their day's work."

Mustafa refrained from asking if Richard intended to be wiser in his pastimes after this. Wisdom was not in Richard's philosophy.

He would not have wished the king to be otherwise. If that made him a fool, too, then so be it. Like Richard, he could not be other than he was.

CHAPTER ELEVEN

Wright illiam came back at the lord Saphadin's order and as his gift, alive and more or less unharmed. Saphadin asked no ransom in return, and nothing but the king's goodwill. There were many who whispered that he had conceived the whole of it, both the abduction and the return, but Richard closed ears and mind to them. The rumblings swelled to a low roar, then dropped away again as summer gave way to the relative cool of autumn—cooling tempers with it, somewhat, and turning men's minds toward newer scandals.

William's return altered the relation between Richard and Saphadin. What had been a game before, a pastime of princes, shifted and changed until, almost inadvertently, Richard found himself seeking a means other than battle to win this Crusade.

Eleanor was remarkably, almost ominously quiet. She sat in the councils, but she spoke little. She made no move to oppose anything that her son took into his head to do. One might have thought that the old she-eagle was weary at last and ready to surrender to the weakness of age, but Sioned was not that great a fool. Eleanor was waiting for something; her patience, when she had need of it, was infinite. When the time came, she would flash into motion, as swift as an arrow piercing its target.

Sioned's lessons continued, but they had shifted from the grove to a house in the city. It was not far from the market, where she made occasion to go every day; it was always deserted except for the room of blue and white tiles in which Safiyah received her.

Sometimes Saphadin came there as well, and conversed with her of anything and everything. He was learning, he said, and she was a splendid teacher, although she had no sense of delivering instruction. She answered questions, that was all, and told stories, and taught him a little of her mother's language. In its beauty and complexity, it was rather like Arabic, although otherwise they bore no relation to one another at all.

"It sounds like you," he said one afternoon when, for the first time in longer than she could reckon, the sun had veiled itself in cloud and a thin rain was falling.

It was surprisingly chill, that rain. A brazier warmed the room, but the day's lesson had been in summoning fire. Sioned was as warm as she would ever need to be. Even so, the brazier was pleasant, the coals glowing brightly in the grey light. For amusement, and as a test of her skill, she had kindled sparks of witch-light that drifted round the room.

Safiyah seemed to have slid into a dream or a magical trance. It was as if Sioned had been alone with the lord of Islam. He had bidden her call him Ahmad; although it still came uneasily to her tongue, she liked the sound of it. It was not as harmonious to the ear as Saphadin, but it defined him somehow. It was his name as the other was not. That was a title, a mark of office; it did not touch his innermost self.

"Your mother's tongue and you," he said. "They fit one another. Strong, but with hints of sudden softness. Intricate and rather mysterious."

"I'm no mystery," she said. "Whatever I'm thinking is written large on my face."

"Ah, but can every man read it?" He smiled at her. That smile melted her knees.

Well for her, then, that she was sitting on a heap of cushions, half-reclining in the manner of the east. She need have no fear of falling, or even of betraying that waft of weakness.

It passed soon enough. They were sipping kaffé, she by now with as much relish as he. He bent forward over his cup and brushed her lips with his—lightly, quickly, and altogether without warning.

She astounded herself with her own response. She should have been furious. And yet there was none of that in her at all. There was only heat like the fire she had learned to wake within her, but most intensely and potently centered. She wanted to leap across the space between them, cast aside the low table with its silver kaffé service, and take him by storm.

Of course she did not. He had returned to his place. But for the torrent of heat spreading inward and downward from her lips, she might have thought that he had never kissed her at all.

But the fire in her found its image in his eyes. Was he as startled as she? She could have sworn that he was, even in his age and experience—and in front of his wife besides.

That mattered remarkably little. Safiyah's presence was a blessing. If she was either jealous or offended, she concealed it masterfully. Sioned might almost have thought that she approved.

They were foreign—how much so, she had been tending to forget, because so much about them rang in harmony with her own heart. Their world was not hers. They did not see as she saw.

And yet as she looked into those steady dark eyes, it made no difference at all. Her magic knew his, perfectly. Her heart had found its place.

She took his hands in hers. They were narrow but strong, with a warrior's calluses and a tracery of fine white scars; their touch was light, a horseman's touch, attuned to the nuance of bit and rein. Her magic uncoiled through the medium of that touch, weaving softly with his, shaping a pattern that partook of both.

It was a deeply intimate thing, and almost unbearably sweet.

Part of her wanted to take flight, to run all the way back to Gwynedd and hide in a hermit's cell. But that was folly; even her most cowardly self could see it.

He was not as strong as she might have thought, or as steady, either. "Have you ever . . . ?"

The words were out before she knew she had spoken them.

He shook his head. "Never. Not like this. Though I've heard—there are stories, legends—"

"No stories," she said. "Nothing like this, not in my part of the world."

"Plato," he said. "The two halves of the soul. The Greeks knew, though if any of them was a mage, he never admitted to it."

Words were a veil, a defense against truth. She silenced him with a finger to his lips. "Don't talk," she said. "Be."

His eyes were wide. He looked young then, younger than she. Great master, great lord of mages—had he never learned to silence his heart, to hear what was beyond mortal hearing, to open himself to the currents of the world?

It seemed he had not. His magic was an art, and not a sense of the body.

She rode with him on the tides of power, in a sea of light. Its beauty was familiar and yet never tedious. His presence altered it, made it more beautiful.

It was almost physically painful to return to the world of the living. Safiyah was asleep, sitting upright, lost in a dream. The sun had only shifted a fraction, although Sioned would not have been surprised if days had passed. Her fingers were locked with Ahmad's.

They drew apart in the same instant, with the same tearing reluctance. He drew a shuddering breath.

She spoke before he could begin. "Will you forgive me if I go? I promised Master Judah that I would take his place for an afternoon."

"By all means you must keep your promise," he said.

"I will come back," she said. "Will you be here?"

"Call me by my name," he said, "in your heart where I am. I will come."

Her hand went to her breast. "Always? You promise?"

"I promise," he said.

She barely remembered the rest of that day. People did not seem to notice her abstraction: no one said anything, even Master Judah, who could not abide that sort of silliness. Her mind was a perfect blank. He was in her heart, cultivating stillness.

Was she in love? It seemed too commonplace a word for so ineffable a sensation. Did her body want him? Very much. But the desire of the body had never been the greater part of what she felt for him. It was everything—all of him; all of them both.

She was aware of the passage of days. She had duties, obligations. There were lessons—Safiyah had become more exacting and the lessons more complex. She never spoke of her husband, nor did Sioned ask after him. He was engrossed in his embassy, but his heart was hers. She felt it beating warmly under her breastbone, matching pace with her own.

She woke from that long half-dream with a shock like a dash of icy water to the face. Richard, insofar as she could notice him—and he was more noticeable than most things in the world, these days—had been nursing some great and cherished secret. Even Eleanor could not get it out of him, which had caused a rare ripple in her cultivated calm.

On the day after the feast of St. Frideswide, which some of the English had celebrated with suitable ecclesiastical pomp, Sioned happened to be in the citadel when the sultan's envoy arrived for his daily conversation with the king. It was another day of raw rain; rather than brave the weeping sky for a hunt or a ride about the gardens of the city, they met in the solar of the castle.

Their meeting was not open to any who happened by, but neither Sioned nor Eleanor was a casual stranger. Eleanor was received with grace and given a chair by the fire. Sioned was a shadow, and shadows on this dark day were so common as to be invisible.

The chill of Eleanor's presence lingered, but Richard was too full of his grand plan to let it trouble him for long. The lord Saphadin and his emirs waited politely for him to finish pacing and gathering his thoughts. Mustafa, seated at the foot of the chair in which Richard must have been sitting, was perfectly still.

At length Richard stopped and turned. "Suppose that we could solve this without continuing the war. Suppose," he said, "that we can agree on a division of lands and treasures. What if we seal it in the best way of all? I have a sister, my lord, who is widowed and wealthy—and a beauty, too. You have dispensation in your religion to marry as many wives as you can support. Why not take her, my lord, and make her your wife, and make an alliance of the two worlds? West and east, Christendom and Islam, queen and prince: you'll bring the two together and make them one."

He ended his speech with a flourish and stood beaming at them all. It was a splendid, a glorious solution, his expression said. Was he not brilliant for having conceived it?

The silence was enormous. Even Saphadin's eyes were on Eleanor. She wore no expression at all. When she spoke, it was only to inquire, "Have you spoken to Joanna about this?"

Richard's face fell, but only slightly. "I'll talk to her. She'll be glad, I'm sure. She'll have a knight and a gentleman, a prince of renown, who admires and respects us of the west."

Eleanor arched a brow. "Indeed," was all she said.

Sioned did not stay to hear what the prospective bridegroom thought of Richard's offer. He had voiced no objection. Why should he? Joanna was a queen, and the dowry that Richard would give her would be wondrously rich. The impediment of religion could be dealt with; even as she fled, she heard Richard say, "We'll send to the Pope by the next boat, and get a dispensation. He'll give it to us if it wins us back the Holy Sepulcher. Unless of course, my lord, you would consider converting to our faith . . . ?"

Not in this lifetime, she thought. It was not wishful thinking. Wishful thinking had been her dreams of the past days, her moping and mooning about, sighing like a silly girl.

Certainly he found her pleasant to the eye. He was much intrigued by the nature and strength of her magic. The rest she had built into a palace of air, and peopled it with dreams.

This was cold reality: the policies of kings. In that world, a queen of legitimate birth was infinitely preferable to a king's by-blow. Sioned had no wealth, no rank but what her brother gave her, no place that was her own by grace of birth and breeding. What she had had in Gwynedd, she had left to follow her father's will and ways. She was of some use for her healing skills; if she left to make her way in the world, those would provide her with a living. Quite a good one, if she chose.

That was all very cool and practical, just as anyone would have expected of her. Yet her heart refused to listen. It had gone from shock to anger, a flare of temper as fierce as it was unreasonable. She did not want it to be reasonable. She wanted to indulge in a good and proper fit. Then she could rage at her idiot brother, and not at her idiot self for dreams that had never been more than empty fancies.

"I will not."

Joanna measured each word in drops of ice. Her shock at first had been as great as Sioned's, and her anger if anything was stronger; but not for the same reasons at all. So great was that anger and so deep the shock that it turned her cold. "I will not be sold in slavery to an unbeliever."

"It's not slavery," Richard said with remarkable patience. "It's marriage—and a very good one. The man's a king's brother, he's as powerful as a king himself, he's rich, he's cultured, he's a knight and a gentleman. What does it matter what he calls his God? Maybe he'll convert to our religion. Maybe he won't. The Pope will give a dispensation, you needn't worry about that. I've already asked Mother to see to it."

"And she agreed?" Joanna asked coldly.

"She didn't disagree," Richard said.

"She knows it will never happen," Joanna said, "because I will not marry that man. Not now, not ever, not if he were the last man alive."

"Oh, come," said Richard. "What objection can you possibly have to him, except the one?"

"The one is enough," she said.

"That's ridiculous. What is it really? That he's not as young as some? He's not old, either. He's strong. He's a splendid fighter. He's got a clever tongue on him, and a good voice—I've taught him some of our songs, and he sings them well. Any reasonable woman would be delighted to have him."

"Then I am not reasonable," she said, "and I will not ever be. I will not marry him."

Richard's face darkened to crimson. His eyes were bright and searing blue. His voice was quiet—a soft growl, barely to be heard. "You will not? Even for your king's command?"

"You are not my king," she said, "and you will not command me to do this."

"I'll force you."

"Try that," she said, "and I'll take the veil. The Church will shelter me. I, a Christian queen, forced to marry an infidel—I'll find asylum wherever I go."

He curled his lip. "You, a nun? You'd go mad in a month."

"Never mad enough to marry that man," she said.

"Do you want to bet on it?"

She met his glare with one just as blue and just as sulfurous. "I'll bet my life."

"Do that," he snarled. His voice rose. "*Do* that, you damned bloody woman! Do it and be damned to you!"

"Oh, no," she said. "Damnation is this marriage. I will not marry him."

"You are out of your head!"

"*I* am? I never proposed to hand my sister over to the Devil's own!"

"That is a better man than half the knights in Christendom, and every blasted one of the priests."

"Blasphemer!"

"Bitch!"

She drew herself to her full and considerable height. "Better a Christian bitch than an infidel whore."

Richard's hand flew up. Her eyes dared him to strike her. He spun and stalked away from her.

CHAPTER TWELVE

Joanna had won the battle and the war. There would be no
wedding of Christian and infidel. The whole army knew
every word that Richard and Joanna had said to one another, embellished and re-embellished until it had become a
legend and a song.

Sioned heard that song everywhere she went, until she was
ready to take a mule and her bag of medicines and ride to the
world's end. She was still angry, abidingly so—and never mind
how foolish it might be. Her heart knew neither wisdom nor
reason. It only knew that it was wounded. She had not gone to
her lessons since the day Saphadin had failed to put a stop to
Richard's folly.

When she was not playing physician, she was pacing the
streets and alleys of Jaffa. The darker, the narrower, the more
dangerous they were, the better.

She was in the darkest and dankest alley she had yet found,
near evening of a day some untold number of days after Joanna
had refused to marry an infidel. A footpad lay gagging and
clutching his privates, some distance behind. He had thought

to find easy prey in a woman alone, and discovered all too quickly that not only did she know exactly where to hurt a man most; she was completely ruthless in the doing of it.

It was not like her at all to so indulge her temper. And yet she could not control herself. Was it not just? Was it not, after all, fitting?

That was a hazard, Safiyah had warned her. Mages were so strong in so many things, that God had given them a weakness to balance all the rest. It was dreadfully, deliriously easy to give way to the dark side of the soul.

And for such a reason, too—it was absurd, if she ever stopped to think about it. But she refused to do that. She wanted this darkness. It was better than facing reality; than admitting that she had let herself fall in love with a man. Love was not for the likes of her. She should have known that from the beginning, and built walls against it.

The alley in which she had been stalking, nurturing the swelling bloom of her anger, came to an abrupt and stony end. At first she thought it a blank wall; then she saw how it bent round a corner, and marked the faint outline of a door. It was a postern, tiny and hidden, but to her surprise it was unlocked.

This must have been a mosque when Jaffa was in the hands of Islam. It was older than the first Crusade, though not as old as Rome: she could feel such things, it was one of her smaller magical gifts. There were marks of fire on it, up near the dome, and broken tiles along the arches. Rats had nested in the rugs that heaped the floor, all hacked and fouled as they were.

Yet this was still a holy place. The air held a memory of incense; the light of day blessed the faded tiles of the walls. The lines of sacred script that flowed over the arches and the doorframes were hacked and broken, but she could read a fragment here and there, and one intact near the *mihrab*, the niche that faced toward Mecca: *There is no god but God.*

Spirits lived here. Sunlight made them shy, but she caught glimpses of them in shadows. At night they must come out in force. A deep thrum came up from below, a throb of sanctity. God, or gods, had been worshipped on this circle of earth since long before Muhammad proclaimed himself the Prophet of Allah.

Sioned knelt in front of the *mihrab*, not in worship, not exactly, but because it seemed appropriate to kneel in such a place. There was peace here, such as she had not felt in much too long.

She did not want peace. She wanted anger. She wanted the dark that came up from the earth. She wanted—

Eleanor.

As if the thought had been a conjuring, she saw in the *mihrab*, framed like a painted image, the queen in her chamber in the castle. Eleanor was dressed in black as she always was, but this was not her wonted fashion; it was a long robe without belt or girdle, and her hair was loose, unveiled, thick and gleaming, flowing down her back like a river of snow. Hers was a cold stark beauty, but beauty it certainly was, like a stone of adamant.

As she had done in the shrine of Cyprus, she spoke to a coiling shape of nothingness. It was stronger than it had been. Because she was closer to it? Or because all this war and blood had fed it, and given it space to grow?

It spoke in a voice so deep it rumbled in the bones. "Now?"

"Not yet," Eleanor said. She did not waver, nor did she forsake her icy calm, but Sioned could feel the strength of the effort that kept her so steady.

"We have a bargain," the dark one said. "I would keep my half of it."

"You will do so," said Eleanor, "in the fullness of time. Are you not well enough fed? Has not my son kept you sated with blood of Turks? Is it another battle you require? Surely we can arrange a small one. There are always skirmishes; men are men, and they will fight, however feeble the cause."

"A holy war is feeble?"

"Come now," the queen said. "Your faith is not the one that moves the sultan, nor is your worship any that he would approve of. You serve another power altogether."

"I am a power in my own right," said the dark one, "and he rankles at the core of me. Let me dispose of him now."

"No," she said. "It is not time. My son is managing him well enough for the moment, and these illusions of peaceful negotiation are serving us well. When his fall will destroy all that he made, when my son is so placed as to fill the void of his absence, then you may take him."

The dark one hissed, but forbore to strike like the serpent it just then resembled.

"Patience," she said to him. "You will have your prey."

Maybe he trusted her; maybe not. She dismissed him with an incantation that raked claws through Sioned's bones. He vanished. Eleanor sank down in a pool of black robe, as if all strength had abandoned her.

Yet when she lifted her head, her eyes were burning. Her hand, upraised, drew letters of fire in the air: wards, bound to Richard's name and presence. She was wise and she was wary, and she knew her ally—who was also the worst of her enemies. He would not attack her son while he fancied that she was too weak to stop him.

The wards rose in a searing shimmer, closing off Sioned's vision of her. Sioned made no effort to call it back.

Here was a way, if she would take it. Here was a path that she could choose. She could take the darkness to her; become both its ruler and its servant. It would possess her in the end, but then so would the light. Every living thing died; that was the price one paid for life.

It was a potent temptation. She knelt in the empty mosque, in the fading daylight, and all about her the spirits gathered: jinn and afarit, wrought of essential fire. They were no more purely of dark or light than any human creature. They too had that gift and curse: they could choose which power they would serve.

They swarmed above her, thick as a migration of swallows. They darted, swooped, wheeled. Some of them sang in eerie voices. When there were words that she could understand, those were words in Arabic, verses of the Koran and praises of the All-Merciful. Of course these would be good Muslim spirits, since this was a Muslim place, however faded and forgotten.

Laughter bubbled up in her, sudden and altogether unexpected. It had an edge to it, the cut of irony, but it was honest enough. In the giddy swirl of the spirits' dance, she had found, not peace, not exactly—but a degree of sanity. She was still angry, but with some vestige of measure and restraint. For the first time in a long while, her mind was clear. She could think. She could make a choice.

Not the darkness now. Later, who knew? For the moment she remained in the light, though the shadows were a fraction deeper than they had been before.

She remained there into the night, resting her spirit in the dance of the afarit. When she left them, they sang a long, rippling note: bidding farewell for a while, but not for always. She sang it back to them as best she could. Those that were nearest to solid form and substance bowed before her, not entirely in mockery, and one or two followed her through the midnight blackness of Jaffa, seeing her safe to her room in Master Judah's hospital.

PART TWO

ASCALON AND TYRE
January–April 1192

CHAPTER THIRTEEN

The rain that had begun in the month of October continued almost without interruption for the whole of that
winter: month upon month of raw damp and bone-
numbing cold. The season of Advent gave way to a wet and shiv-
ering Christmas—and few enough of Richard's men had any
shelter as dry or warm as the Lord Christ's manger in a stable.

At the New Year, Richard marched on Jerusalem. But
Jerusalem would have none of him. At Beit Nuba within sight
of the holy city, he could go no farther. There the rain turned
to sleet and then to a blinding blast of snow. The men could not
march; the horses, those that had not fallen to cold or sickness
or Turkish arrows, were never enough to carry an army.

"Face it, sire," said the Grand Master of the Hospitallers.
"We'll get no farther this winter. The men have had enough.
Their armor is a mass of rust, their shirts are rotting off their
backs, they're eating more mold and weevils than bread. Even
if they'll follow you to Jerusalem, what can they do when they
get there? They're too weak to storm the walls, and too few to
hold the city even if by a miracle they should take it."

The king's council had gathered in Richard's tent, which if not exactly warm and not exactly dry, was warmer and drier than the storm without. Even as the Hospitaller paused, a blast of wind smote it, rocking it on its moorings; the sides groaned in protest. But the tent was made in this country, and it was well anchored. It held.

They all drew a sigh of relief. Only the king had taken no notice. His eyes were fixed on the Hospitaller's face. "Are you saying we should give up?"

"I am saying, sire," said the Hospitaller, "that there is excellent reason why the infidels send their armies home in the dark of the year."

"That's why I kept mine on the march," Richard shot back. "Because there's no more than a garrison to defend Jerusalem. We can take it. We're still stronger than a few hundred Turks and Kurds."

"Are we, sire? Listen to the wind! It's blowing straight from the walls of Jerusalem. The harder we fight it, the more powerfully it drives us back. We can fight men—but can we fight the wind?"

"Wind stops," Richard said. "Storms end. We'll wait this one out, and march before the next one hits."

"Men must eat, sire," the Hospitaller said. He was as stubborn as Richard, and he was no coward, either. "Our supply lines are dangerously thin as it is. If we go any farther away from the sea, we'll starve."

Richard's expression was alarming. Some of his lords looked as if they would have preferred to brave the storm than face the king's wrath. But the Templars were as bold as any Hospitaller. Their Master scowled at the Hospitaller, but he said, "He's right, sire. As little as I like to agree with him—he's telling the truth. We can't wage a war under these conditions. If we go back toward the sea, toward Acre or Jaffa or Ascalon, we'll be warm, dry, fed—and we'll keep our troops until spring. They're dying here. They're not an army now, sire. They're a mob of invalids."

"That is true." The voice was not one that spoke often in the king's councils, but the ring of authority silenced any protest. Master Judah did not either rise or come forward; he sat still until all their eyes were on him. Then he spoke again. "My physicians and surgeons are working night and day, and they can't keep up with the number of the sick or wounded. We've used up most of our medicines; men steal the bandages to wrap their feet or hands against the cold. If even half your men are up to fighting strength, I'll be astonished."

Richard shook his head obstinately. "I can take Jerusalem now. I have enough men for that."

"You do not," Master Judah said. "Even the hotheads of the Temple are telling you so. Will you listen?"

"Give me a map," said Richard, biting off the words.

One of his clerks had one to hand. Richard snatched it with little grace, sweeping wine cups and bits of bread and moldy cheese off the table that stood in the center of the tent. He spread the map there, glowering at it, muttering as his finger traced the lines of road and hill, wall and gate.

His eyes flashed up. "We have to go on," he said. "Don't you understand that? If we turn back now in sight of victory, we lose it all—and I take the blame."

"If you go on," said the Hospitaller, "you will lose. You can live with a bit of blame now in return for a chorus of praise later. And consider this, sire—I hear the men talking as I walk through the camp. They are convinced that once they come to the Holy Sepulcher, their service is over. They can lay down the cross; they can leave. There will be no one to hold the city once you've taken it, and no hope of keeping it past the first blush of spring. The Saracen will come back, and he will destroy you. Jerusalem will lie in unholy hands once again; all your Crusade will be for naught."

"That won't change," Richard snarled, "whether it happens now or half a year from now."

"Maybe not," said the Hospitaller. "Or maybe, once spring comes, new forces will arrive from the west, and the forces that are here will remember their strength and devote themselves fully to the defense of the Holy Sepulcher. The air itself resists them now. In spring, when winter's cold is forgotten and summer's heat is no more than a promise, they'll learn again how to fight for their faith."

"Stirring words," Richard said, glaring at the map, which told him exactly how far he had to go through a cruel winter, without water or provisions, to take an impregnable city. "I'll hold you to them, damn you. And damn you again, for making too bloody much sense. We'll wait out the storm. When it lets up, we'll march."

The Hospitaller bowed his head in respect. "Where shall we march, sire?"

Richard rolled up the map and flung it at his clerk. "Ascalon. We'll build it up again. That will keep the men warm, and give them something to think about besides running for home."

"And," said the Hospitaller, "the ships can come in with provisions from Cyprus and the west, and our men will be fed and dry for the first time since we left Jaffa."

"Dry feet," someone sighed. "Ah, God! A dream of bliss."

Great wit it was not, but it struck them to a ripple of mirth, an easing of tension that had gripped them all. Only Richard did not join in the jest. He stood stiff and still as they took their leave, not flinching from the lash of wind and snow through the open tent flap. The Hospitaller was the last to go; he looked as if he might have paused, but the snow was deepening inside the tent. He thrust forward into it, turning to wrestle the flap back into place.

The wind had blown out the lamps. Richard turned in the dimness, moving toward the nearest, but Mustafa was there already, striking a spark from the flint off the steel of his dagger. Richard started a little. "You! Where did you come from?"

"I was here, lord," Mustafa said. He lit the other lamps from the flame of the first, taking his time about it. Lamp oil at least they had enough of: one of the quartermasters had intercepted a caravan to the holy city, and its chief cargo had been oil for eating and for burning in lamps.

"You're as quiet as a cat." Richard flung himself onto his

cot, arm over his eyes, groaning aloud. "Damned bloody cowards! Every pox-infested one of them."

Mustafa held his tongue. The brazier needed feeding; he fed it with care, until the coals were burning steadily, sending off a blessed wave of heat.

Richard sat up abruptly. "You've been out, haven't you? What have you found?"

"That the Master of the Hospital is right, sire," Mustafa said. "And that this storm will grow worse before it dies down."

"You don't think it's—"

Richard would never speak directly of magic if he could avoid it: strange, considering what his mother was, but perhaps not inexplicable. The son of so strong a mother might prefer to resist her rather than to give way to her.

In any event, Mustafa could answer him honestly. "If it has been . . . assisted, it's still a natural storm. This is the land itself raising walls against you." He paused. "Maybe, sire, it does this to give you time. If you take your army back to the sea, and let it rest and recover, in the spring it will be much stronger and more willing to fight."

"Are you the council's tame ape, to mimic all that they say?" But Richard's rancor lacked its usual ferocity. "Do you know where the singer is?"

Mustafa rebuked his heart for sinking. "I saw him with the men from Aviègne," he said. "They had a fancy for a song or two."

"So do I," said Richard. "Go and fetch him, will you? Then find a dry place and rest. Whenever this storm of hell stops, we're marching—even if it's the dead of night."

For Richard, that was kindness. Mustafa braced himself against the cold and the cut of the sleet, wrapped his mantle close about him and the end of his turban about his face, and set hand to the tent flap.

He paused. Richard was lying flat again, eyes shut, sulking mightily. It was no ill Mustafa could cure. But Blondel, however waspish his temper, had his lute and his sweet voice. He was the medicine that the king must have. Wise Richard, to know the physic for his own sickness.

Mustafa found Blondel still singing for the French soldiers. They objected not at all to surrendering their entertainment to the king. Their mood in fact was remarkably light, for warriors of Crusade who were about to withdraw just short of the Holy Sepulcher. They were all singing paeans to the great dream of the army that winter: warm hands and dry feet.

Almost Mustafa followed Blondel back to the king, but a faint glimmer of wisdom restrained him. He sought another sanctuary instead, a small tent, empty just then, but sharing the warmth of the greater tent beside it. He curled like a cat in the corner, and like a cat, seized the opportunity to sleep.

Sioned was weary to the bone. The flush of satisfaction she had felt since she attached herself to the army yet again without a word of objection from her brother was long gone. Victory over Richard's will was no small accomplishment, but this was as wretched a campaign as even the most seasoned soldier could remember. She actually found herself envying the ladies in their cushioned prison in Acre. It would have been a stupefyingly long winter of gossip and embroidery and court intrigue, but it would have been warmer than this.

The storm had begun in the dark before dawn. Now it was almost dawn again, and the wind showed no sign of slackening. Snow heaped against the sides of tents; those whose occupants were not diligent in keeping the tents clear had collapsed, with much cursing and struggling to get them back up again.

She had been tending frostbite and physicking winter rheums since before the storm began. There was not a tent in the camp that was free of a chorus of coughing. When a man began coughing up blood, he came in search of the physicians. Sometimes he found them before it was too late. Sometimes he died on the way.

Too many men had died today. Richard's retreat came none too soon. Later there would be carping and blame. Now there was only relief.

She stumbled to her little bit of tent to snatch an hour's rest. The shape curled in the corner aroused no alarm. Mustafa came here as often as not; he said it comforted him to sleep in the light of her magic. Sometimes if there was time or if she had strength left, he taught her to sing in his Berber tongue, or to dance with knives the way his people did—the women, he said, even more fiercely and flamboyantly than the men.

There would be no dancing or singing tonight. She fell onto her cot as if into deep water; sleep took her before she touched the blanket.

She had dreamed of Saphadin often enough that winter, and dreamed that her lessons with his wife continued, night after night. The dreams of him were only dreams; those of Safiyah, she was less sure of. She remembered every word of them when she woke, and as often as not, the magic in her was different; it had grown, changed, become something other than it was when she went to sleep.

There were no lessons in this early dawn. Her dream was full of snow, but it was not cold; it had no edges that cut. It was like a cloud of feathers, white and soft, suffused with a silver light.

She had a dagger in her hand, but its blade was silver rather than steel. The hilt was in the shape of a silver swan, its eye a ruby, red as blood. Because this was a dream, the eye was alive, alert with intelligence. It sparkled at her as she turned the dagger in her fingers.

The veil of snow parted. She looked through it into a room dim with lamplight. It was a beautiful room, with walls of many-colored tiles in patterns of leaves and flowering branches, and a floor heaped thick with carpets. A golden lamp hung from the ceiling, shedding soft light on the curtains of a bed. It was not an extravagant bed despite the beauty of the room; there were few cushions, and the coverlets were almost plain. They were wool and cotton, not silk; yet they seemed warm.

He was asleep within those coverlets. She had not seen him before without his turban; he looked more ordinary so, a slender man, fine-featured, with short-cropped black hair barely touched with grey, and a neat beard.

No one shared his bed, nor was there any memory of a woman in that room. If he did his duty by his wives, he did it elsewhere. This was his own place, his sanctuary. There was a great air of peace in it, and of warded protection.

She could feel the wards about her, sliding like water over her body, but they did not drive her away. Indeed they welcomed her; they guarded her as they did him, within walls of air and light.

She drifted down beside him. He smiled faintly in his sleep—not at her presence, surely, but at some pleasant dream. She remembered that she was angry, and she remembered why, but without the flesh to feed the anger, it seemed dim and rather distant. In this place she was simply glad to see his face, to know that he was well—and yes, to see him alone.

They had not spoken since Jaffa. She had no craving to hear his voice now, but neither was she in great haste to leave him. She sat at the foot of his bed and tucked up her feet, and watched over him for what was left of the night.

CHAPTER FOURTEEN

The hope that roused Richard's army to march away from Beit Nuba turned quickly to rancor. The roads were abominable and the weather worse. Storm after storm battered the land and the sea. There were no supply lines from the ports: the ships had to put far out to sea or be dashed to pieces on the shore.

One morning not far from Ascalon, after a grueling march through a morass of mud and icy water, the army woke to find itself reduced by half. Duke Hugh and the French had packed up in secret, gathered their belongings and the loot that they had won, and left in the night.

Some said they had gone to Acre, others to Tyre. "Either way," Richard said with as much good cheer as anyone could muster, "that's all the fewer mouths to feed. Up, and march! The sun's out, for once; we'll make good time today. Maybe we'll even dry out by sundown."

Mustafa heard that as he came back from scouting the road to Ascalon. The sun was a pleasant change, to be sure, though it was not what he would have called warm. If anything it was colder than the storms had been before. There was a thin film of ice over the mud of the road, and his breath was a cloud of frost.

He was not eager to bring Richard the news that he had gone to fetch, but soonest done was soonest over. His little mare was a bony shadow of herself, but she had a spark in her yet. She consented to carry him along the columns as they dragged themselves into place, and to fall in behind Richard's squires.

Richard would come when he came. He was seeing the sick and the wounded into the carts himself, and giving them such comfort as they would take.

The army lurched into motion with a now-familiar step and drag, accompanied by the sucking sound of feet or hooves in mud, and the groaning of wagon axles as the wheels strained to turn. The oxen lowed in protest, and the mules brayed harshly; the drovers cracked their whips and cursed. The men marched in grim silence. No one laughed or sang.

They would have even less occasion for mirth when they heard what Mustafa had to say to Richard. It was midmorning before the king came to the center. His golden stallion was as bony as the rest of the horses, and the beast's winter coat was like a filthy fleece, but he had enough strength even yet to arch his neck and offer improprieties to Mustafa's mare. She flattened her ears and snapped. He was barely chastened.

Richard slapped the woolly neck and grinned at Mustafa. "Good day, my friend! I've not seen you about. I was almost starting to fret."

"That was kind of you, my lord," said Mustafa.

"I'm never kind," Richard said. "So, out with it. Where have you been?"

"Ascalon," Mustafa answered him baldly. He had learned some good while since that Richard had no patience with indirection. When he wanted a report, he wanted it clean: short, sharp, and to the point.

Richard read most of it in his eyes. "Bad?"

"Worse," said Mustafa. "It's razed to the ground. There's not one stone standing on another."

Richard nodded slowly, without surprise. "Did he take the stones away?"

"No, my lord. They're scattered everywhere."

"Good," said Richard. "Good. We've got something to work with, then." He paused. "There's something else. What is it?"

Mustafa could not take his eyes off that windburned face. It was raw and red; the cheeks were peeling. Small dags of ice hung from the mustache. There was nothing beautiful about it at all, except the bright blue eyes. And yet Mustafa would not have traded this man for the loveliest boy in Baghdad.

He blinked and reined himself in, and said, stammering a little, "I—I saw— The ships, my lord. Half the fleet is wrecked. There are ships' timbers and broken spars clear up the coast."

"And the cargoes?"

"Lost or ruined. The crews that survived are salvaging what they can. But, my lord, it's an ill sight to come to after a march like this."

"We'll have to come to it," Richard said, drawing himself up. "And now we have warning. I thank you for that. Are you hungry? Tired? Take a place on one of the wagons—say I sent you. See if one of the cooks can find you something to eat."

"I'm well, my lord," Mustafa said, though his stomach was a tight knot of hunger. He had water enough, melted from snow, and he had eaten yesterday. He would last for a while.

Richard eyed him narrowly but let him be. There was a council to call now, and decisions to make. He had already forgotten Mustafa.

That was as it should be. A king should rule. This king ruled well, mostly; even his failures had a certain splendor to them.

They were all forewarned, but the sight of Ascalon struck them dumb. They came to it near the end of a cold and windy day. Under a scud of clouds and a sinking sun, they looked out across a wasteland. Waste behind and waste before, and the heave and crash of the sea beyond. The very emptiness was a mockery, the sultan's backhanded gift after his defeat at Arsuf.

Richard held them together by sheer force of will. They burrowed into the ruins and dug out dens and caves, living like wild dogs in the wreck of the city. Some, when day came again, he sent to gather the flotsam from the shore, the broken bits of ships that could be cut and shaped into newer, smaller, handier craft for these uncertain seas. The rest began the by now familiar labor of rebuilding the fallen fortress, raising walls and building barracks. It was backbreaking labor, sometimes for a literal fact; but once the boats were built and sent to Cyprus for provisions, they had food to eat, and their dens and lairs were the best shelter they had had since Jaffa.

In the midst of this, Richard summoned Sioned. That was a rare enough occurrence, and she was busy enough with her doctoring, that she almost refused to go. But the squire was one of the adoring puppies who followed her about whenever they could. She would not have liked to expose him to the king's wrath.

Richard was at the wall, overseeing the raising of the stones and putting his hand to a few himself. It was warm work. Even in the winter chill, he had stripped to his shirt; the back and armpits were dark with sweat.

It was a while before he noticed Sioned. She occupied the time in reckoning how far the wall had come since yesterday and calculating how far it would go before tomorrow. It was an impressive calculation, for so few men, and so few of them masons or laborers. There were even knights among them, rank and arrogance laid aside, soiling their hands with common labor.

At length Richard turned from the setting of a stone as big as a destrier, to find her standing behind him, watching with interest. He started slightly, but then he grinned. "Little sister! What do you think? Are we great builders of cities?"

"As great as Alexander," she said. "What will you call this? Ricardia?"

He laughed and shook his head. "Ascalon will do. I'll leave the great vaunts to the Greeks and Romans."

"I'd never have taken you for a humble man," she said.

"Did I say I was humble? This is a fine and handsome city, and when it's done, it will be mine." He pulled out the tail of his shirt and mopped his brow with it. "I've a task for you, sister. Will you do it?"

"What is it?"

He grinned. "You're wary. That's good. It's not anything to endanger your immortal soul. I'm sending a deputation to Acre. I'd like you to go with it."

"What, are you sending me away after all?"

"Not in the way you mean," he said. "I'm making you an envoy. I've had a message from the French; I need someone trustworthy to bring back a reply."

She was not mollified at all. "Why are you asking me? There are a good half-hundred men in this army who can carry a confidential message."

"Because," he said, "I need you. Come to me after dinner. I'll explain then."

"Why not now?"

He snorted in exasperation. "After dinner. Be sure you come."

"Serve you right if I don't," she muttered.

Of course she went. She was curious, and she would wager that he was desperate. She gave him ample time to finish his dinner, and then a little more to dismiss the usual crowd that hung about until he went to bed.

His lair was larger than most. It had actual walls, and a roof that had been repaired with ship's timbers. Part was curtained off for a bedchamber; the rest held a table with a mended leg, an assortment of stools and chairs, and a rack of bronze lamps that must have come from some ancient Roman hoard. They were all lit, and a pair of braziers held back the cold.

Everyone on the Crusade had learned that winter why the infidels were in the habit of heaping carpets on their floors. Carpets were warm; the more of them there were, the farther one's feet were from the chill of stone or tile. Richard had amassed a fair treasure of carpets, and most of them had gone down on this floor. They made a handsome lair, brilliant with color, ornate with the intricate patterns of the east.

Richard was pacing that carpeted floor. He was not alone. A clerk attended him, and a squire waited on his guest.

She knew the young man who sat by one of the braziers, drinking mulled wine from a steaming cup. He was Richard's kinsman, his sister's son: the young lord Henry from Champagne. He was a little older than she was herself; he had acquitted himself well on the Crusade. He was a thoroughly sensible person, and seldom inclined toward the silliness of youth. He was also, and entirely incidentally, as pretty a young man as any in the kingdom of France.

He smiled at sight of her, then leaped up and bowed, brushing her hand with a kiss. She could not help but smile back. Henry was a charming creature, and very good company, when his duties left him time for it.

Richard beamed at them both. "Well, children? Do you think you can keep each other out of mischief on the way to Acre?"

Sioned's smile died. "You're sending him? Why do you need me?"

"Why, lady," Henry said with a face of tragic grief. "Am I so unbearable?"

"You know you are not," said Sioned. She fixed her glare on Richard. "Well?"

Richard shrugged, a roll of heavy shoulders. "You're not going to let me say I'm thinking of your pleasure on the road, are you? I didn't think so. I am, in point of fact, sister. Apart from the fact that I need something."

He was having a great deal of trouble coming round to it, which was not like him at all. She made no effort to come to his rescue, but let him flounder about until he stumbled into silence. With a hiss of frustration, he began again. "You're going to Acre with messages for my mother and the Duke of Burgundy—but yes, those could go with anyone. When they're delivered, you'll go on much more quietly to Tyre."

That caught her interest. She glanced at Henry. He knew already: there was no surprise in his face, although he listened closely.

"Milord of Tyre is up to something," Richard said. "We think he's treating secretly with Saladin. We also think he's going to make a bid for the throne of Jerusalem—which will require him to get rid of the man who currently claims it. There's a pretty little war brewing."

"Very pretty," she said. "That still doesn't explain why you need me."

"I need you," said Richard through gritted teeth, "because I'm told on all too good authority that milord Conrad is up to something more than simple treachery. He's made . . . alliances. The kind that you know how to recognize—and maybe how to break."

"Magic?" She spoke the word to see him flinch. "You don't think your mother has powers enough to flatten anything he can bring to bear?"

Richard was squirming beautifully. "Mother isn't here. You are."

"Your mother is in Acre, where you're sending me. Are you asking me to ally myself with her?"

"No!" Richard said too quickly.

"You don't trust her," said Sioned with slow relish.

"I trust her with my life," he snapped.

"That's not what I said," she said. "You think I'll do as I'm told, whereas she will do nothing of the sort. Have you forgotten everything you ever knew about me?"

"I remember that you can keep your mouth shut when it suits you, and that you clean up very nicely. Conrad has an eye for the ladies. Mother would put him completely on his guard. But a beautiful young sister, curious to see the sights of Tyre, might lull him into letting something slip."

"A beautiful young sister and a beautiful young cousin," she said. "Isn't it a little too obvious?"

"That's the beauty of it," Richard said. "It's so obvious as to be contemptible. While he's sneering at me, you can see whatever is there to see."

She had to nod at that, however reluctantly. "That's almost clever."

"Isn't it? And I thought of it all by myself."

She bared her teeth at him. "Don't expect me to take you for an idiot. Suppose I do this for you. What do I get out of it?"

"My favor."

"I already have that."

"Little minx," he said mildly. "I'll give you a manor, then. Do you want one in England or in Anjou?"

"Give me one here," she said, "when you take Jerusalem."

His eyes widened slightly. Good: she had surprised him. "You'd stay?"

"If I can."

"Done, then," he said. And to his clerk: "Brother Hubert, write it down."

"Also write," Sioned said as the monk bent to his parchment, "that I will hold said manor in vassalage to my brother, Richard, and no other Christian lord or king; but if this land should be conquered again, I may choose to whom I give my fealty."

The monk's pen scratched busily. She had been holding her breath; she let it out. Richard had voiced no word of objection. Henry was regarding her with an odd expression, as if he had never seen her before.

She was used to that. She regarded them both with a bland expression. When the king's decree was written and copied, signed and sealed, she took her copy of it and tucked it tidily away. "I'll do as you ask," she said then. "When do we go?"

"As soon as you can," Richard said. "When you come to Acre, ask Joanna to fit you out in proper gear. You'll go as a lady of substance and a king's favorite; and you'll look the part. I don't want you coming in front of Conrad in your usual old rag of a thing, or worse yet, Turkish trousers."

Trousers might intrigue the man, Sioned thought, but she held her tongue. In spite of herself, she was pleased with this embassy. She should be racked with guilt to abandon the sick and wounded, but it seemed she was as callow a soul as any other. To be behind real walls, in real warmth, maybe even with the prospect of a bath . . . it would be bliss.

She resisted the urge to scratch at the inevitable crop of winter vermin. Richard, having got what he wanted from her, had turned back to Henry. She should listen: there were things she needed to know, nuances of politics that would serve her. But she was lost in contemplation of hot water on skin too long deprived of it.

A name brought her abruptly back to the matter at hand. ". . . Saphadin," said Richard. "He may be there if Conrad really is plotting treachery with the sultan. He's a tricky one; don't try to out-wile him, you won't succeed. Be simple, be transparent. Be the pretty fool that you seem to be."

"I understand, uncle," Henry said.

So did Sioned. *He* would be there. He knew her—too well. He would know what she was doing and how. If he told Conrad—

She had better hope that he did not, or better yet, that he was not there at all. For she did want to go. She did want to see Tyre.

CHAPTER FIFTEEN

"Sweet saints!" said Henry. "You do clean up well."

Sioned laughed. She had done a great deal of that since she left Ascalon: he truly was delightful company. Now that they were in Acre, in the swirl and sparkle of a proper royal court, the war and its miseries seemed impossibly remote.

No one was hungry here, or wet, or cold. The ladies lived in perfumed comfort. Whatever her pretensions to asceticism, Eleanor had no use for wanton displays of self-sacrifice.

Joanna had taken on with relish the task of turning Sioned into a lady. The bath had been as wonderful as Sioned had imagined it would be: a proper eastern bath, and properly thorough. When she emerged from it, she was subjected to the basilisk scrutiny of Joanna's own personal maid. "A disaster," that worthy woman decreed, "but salvageable. Chin up, child! Don't slouch."

Sioned obeyed before she had time to think. She was pushed and pulled, primped and preened, plucked and curled and painted until she did not recognize herself at all. But Henry was delighted. So, to her dismay, were too many others. He protected her—and that delighted him, too. But she would have preferred to put on trousers again and retreat into Richard's army.

"Courage," Henry said. He had a quick eye and a soft heart. She resisted the urge to cling to his hand, but she was glad to let him stay at her side as she braved the court in her new guise.

This was war, in its way. She was fighting for her brother's cause. Her armor was Byzantine silk; her weapons were her eyes and her smile. She tempered them here, in the forge of Eleanor's court.

She still would have preferred sword and bow and a battle on a field. As splendid as they all insisted she looked, she was altogether unable to warble and simper like a proper court lady. She only knew how to speak plainly.

"Conrad won't care," Henry said when she had withdrawn from the fray, retreating to a quiet corner in the shadow of a pillar. "All you need do is be quiet and listen, and look beautiful. He'll never know the difference."

"I hadn't heard that Conrad was a fool," Sioned said with a touch of sharpness.

"Oh," said Henry, "he's not. But he does have an eye for a fine woman."

"He's a fool," Sioned said.

Henry grinned at her. "For you he will be—he and half the men in his court. They'll be in your brother's camp before they know it."

"That much I can hope for," she said. She smoothed the crimson silk of her gown and drew as deep a breath as she could in lacings so tight. "Back to the practice field, sir."

She held out her hand as she had seen one of the *pullani* ladies do, with an imperious flourish that made him laugh. He took it and kissed it and held it for a moment to his heart: light, no meaning in it, but still there was a fraction's pause. Then the world went on its way again, and the court with it.

This gilded warfare was exhausting. By evening Sioned was ready to collapse, but when she came to the room that she shared with three of Joanna's ladies, there was a page waiting for her. He wore the livery of Aquitaine.

Her heart stuttered in her breast. It was foolish; the queen would hardly do her harm while she was in Richard's service. Still, a summons from that lady was no trivial thing even for one of her own legitimate children. If one happened to be old Henry's by-blow, with secrets to keep, then there was good reason to walk softly.

At least she was dressed for a royal audience. She swallowed a sigh and followed the page to Eleanor's rooms.

The queen had left the court somewhat before Sioned had, and was now at ease, wrapped in a soft warm robe and seated by a brazier. One of her maids had been reading to her: Sioned heard a scrap of it. It was not what she would have called edifying, unless the romances of Provence could be said to instruct the listener in the arts of love.

Whether that remembrance of her own country had softened her mood, or whether she had set out to lay a trap, Eleanor was the soul of courtesy. "Lady Jeannette," she said, casting Sioned's name in her own tongue where evidently she found it more comfortable, "be welcome. Here, sit. Will you have wine?"

The wine was wine of Cyprus, rich and sweet, and mulled with spices. Sioned considered briefly that it might be poisoned, but Eleanor's weapons were of another sort. She drank with pleasure, if sparingly—she would need her wits about her.

Eleanor began softly. "My son thinks highly of you," she said.

"He trusts me," said Sioned.

The queen's brow arched. "I gather that trust is well placed."

Sioned shrugged slightly. "I do what I can. He's my brother and my king."

"In that order?"

"Would you prefer the opposite?"

"He is my son and my king," said Eleanor. She paused. "Indulge me now. Tell me what he sends you to Tyre to do."

Sioned chose her words carefully. She was being examined like a pupil in a school. What the penalty would be for failure, she did not precisely know, but she had no intention of discovering it. "There are two contenders for the throne of Jerusalem—which though it may be fallen is still a rich prize, particularly if Richard wins it back. Guy, who lost both it and the royal wife who gave him the right to the title, has been insisting that he is still the crowned and consecrated king. But Conrad, who rules in Tyre, has married the late queen's heir, the fair Isabella, and he contends that through that marriage he also took the right to call himself king.

"Guy is a fool," said Sioned, "and a waster of kingdoms, but he comes from Anjou and is sworn in fealty to its count, who happens in this generation to be Richard. Conrad owes Richard nothing. He took Tyre and held it after Guy lost the kingdom, and he won altogether too many knights of the kingdom to his service. And now the Duke of Burgundy has taken the knights of France to him. There may be a war brewing— one that has nothing to do with the war between Christian and infidel."

Eleanor nodded at the recital. "And your part is to seduce Conrad?"

That was bluntly spoken. Sioned resisted the temptation to be as blunt. "My part is to discover what he intends, and if I can, to dissuade him."

"To seduce him." Eleanor looked her up and down. "You do look the part. Can you play it as well?"

"Henry says I can, if I don't talk."

Eleanor's laughter was melodious still, a bright ripple of sound. It startled Sioned into speechlessness. "Men," said Eleanor, "are all alike. One glimmer of intelligence and they're paralytic with terror."

"Henry seems to control the horror well enough," Sioned said.

The queen's eyes sharpened. "You like my grandson?"

"I rather doubt he's for me," Sioned said dryly.

"Why not?"

"What can I bring him? A bag of medicines and a king's trust?"

"Neither is entirely worthless."

"Neither of them is a royal dowry."

"Do you want that?"

"Doesn't everyone?"

"Do *you*?"

"No," Sioned said. "Not for itself. For what it might buy me . . . maybe. If the prize is worth the price."

"You have a clear eye and a hard head. And," said Eleanor, "somewhat more than that. Is it true, what I hear? Have you been studying certain arts with certain of the infidels?"

Sioned went perfectly still. For all her pretensions to wariness, Eleanor had caught her off guard.

She must answer; silence would be more damning than a lie. But when she spoke, she chose to tell the truth. "You know I have, majesty."

"Why?"

"Because I must," Sioned answered.

Eleanor nodded as if in approval. "What irony," she said, "that of all my children, only Geoffrey had the power; and a simple fever carried him off. Yet you who are none of mine are everything that I would have wished for in a child of my body."

Sioned had her doubts of that, but she kept them to herself—even when the queen took her chin in those long fingers and tilted her face to the light.

"Beautiful," mused Eleanor, "and gifted in the powers. Yet I barely noticed you. You've been avoiding me, yes? Are you afraid of me?"

Sioned could not nod; the queen held her too tightly. She lowered her eyelids in assent.

"Good," said the queen, letting her go. "Fear is wise. Will you be continuing your studies?"

"If I can, majesty," Sioned said.

"Do it," said Eleanor. "Learn all that you can. Every weapon that they give you, you can turn to our purposes."

"Do you think they would give me weapons? Would they be as foolish as that?"

"Use your beauty," Eleanor said. "Use your gifts. Persuade them that you can be trusted."

"Do you trust me?" Sioned asked her.

"Richard trusts you," Eleanor said, "and I have means of assuring that his trust is not misplaced."

Sioned bent her head to both the assurance and the threat. She offered no promises, took no oaths. Nor did Eleanor ask them of her—whether out of arrogance or wisdom, Sioned could not tell.

"Jerusalem will be ours by the summer," Eleanor said. "Conrad may be part of it, or he may not. The choice is his."

"And if he sets himself against Richard?"

Eleanor shrugged minutely. "He's not a fool by any means, but he is ambitious. Ambition will be his downfall." She sighed as if in sudden weariness. "Go, child. Serve your brother well."

"Always," said Sioned.

The queen's expression hardened ever so slightly. "I do hope so. Go now. I must rest."

Sioned did not doubt it. The power that had been pressing on her with almost invisible subtlety had grown immeasurably stronger just after Eleanor professed exhaustion.

It did not penetrate her wards, though it cost her something in both strength and composure to sustain them against it. Only her outer thoughts impinged on it, harmless and rather vapid, and touched with fear of the great sorceress.

The fear at least was real, though Sioned might have preferred to call it hearty respect. The queen was drawing power from the earth below, taking in darkness with the light. If she had devoted all of it to the matter of enlisting her late husband's bastard in her magical army, Sioned would have had no hope of escape. But Sioned was a small concern among the many that engaged her.

Sioned staggered a little as she made her way to her room. The floor seemed unsteady underfoot. For a moment the world wavered and flowed. She was still in Acre, but there was no queen here; Eleanor was far away in England, and the Crusade, with all that it had hoped and fought for, was crumbling rapidly into nothing. A world of what-ifs, she thought; a world as it might have been. A world she neither wanted nor sought, nor ever wished to live in.

Then, between one step and the next, the earth was still. She walked through the web of the queen's wards in a country that the queen meant to conquer. Once she had conquered it, would she sail home? Or would she stay and rule? Did she herself know for certain which it would be?

Chapter Sixteen

Sioned walked abroad the morning after her interview with the queen—unwisely, any number of people would have told her, but she had a desperate need to be away from the court. She could feel the various currents of tension in the city, enmities as strong as any between Christian and Muslim: between parvenu and *pullani*, French and English, Pisan guard and Genoese garrison. They had been at each other's throats since Richard left there. A single spark could set any of them off; only by a miracle and by Eleanor's will did they keep such peace as there was.

The market was bustling on this fine chill morning, merchants doing a brisk trade among the many nations—though seldom, be it noted, the French. The bulk of them had gone to Tyre without pay from their own king and without the loan of pay from the English king. Those few who remained roamed about in packs, trading remnants of Saracen loot for bread and cheese and bad wine.

"So why aren't you in Tyre with the rest of the French king's dogs?" an English voice drawled from inside a tavern.

Sioned had paused to admire a bolt of silk in a cloth merchant's stall. The tavern was across the narrow street from it, crowded with soldiers who had been away from the battlefield too long. They were looking for fights with one another now, since the infidel declined to engage in warfare in the dead of winter.

The Englishman was sitting near the door. The Frenchman was farther in, but Sioned had no difficulty in hearing his voice: it was pitched to carry. "Better a king's dog than his catamite."

The snarl that rose at that was remarkably like a dog's, and came from more than one throat. The Englishman had friends. They were not all English, either: Sioned glimpsed livery of the Italies—Pisa, she supposed, if the men who wore it had risen up on Richard's behalf. The others, near the men from France, must be Genoese; one even carried the crossbow that was the famous weapon of his city. And what he was doing with that on a supposedly peaceable ramble through the taverns, Sioned would have dearly liked to know.

The snarl swelled to a growl. Words mattered little by now; all either side wanted was a fight. She heard the rumble and crash of tables overturned and pottery flung at walls and floor. Someone loosed a shout of glee, which broke in a dreadful gurgle.

She was completely mad to do what she did: not to turn and run like a sensible woman, but to kilt up her skirts and run toward the brawl. Trousers would have served her better, and her sword and bow better yet, but she had something that no one in the tavern had. She raised it as she ran, gathering it inside her, all the powers of the elements mingled in a net of magic.

When dogs fought in the king's camp, men flung water on them to cool their rage. Sioned flung magic. It struck like a gout of cold seawater, flinging combatants apart, swirling in a gust of sudden wind.

When the wind died, the tavern was quiet. The brawlers had fled. Bystanders picked themselves up, nursing bruises and murmuring in confusion. "An angel," one of them said. "An angel came and stopped the fight."

None of them spared a glance for Sioned in her plain gown and woolen mantle—save one. He was a *pullani*, maybe, or a Gascon, dark and slight; his coat of boiled leather was much worn and rather too large for him.

He seemed as harmless as an idle soldier could be. And yet something about him raised her hackles: a look about the eyes, a subtle tension in the body. He saw her; he knew her. He had marked her in memory.

A shiver ran down her spine. That was no Christian, and no soldier of the West, either. Even as she stirred, uncertain whether she would move toward him or run away, he melted into shadow and was gone. The last glimpse she had of him was strange: not dark but light, as if he were clothed in white.

Sioned started like a cat. The watcher had vanished. Someone else stood directly behind her—someone slight and dark and by no means a Frank. Her dagger was at his throat and a bead of blood welling scarlet from it before she recognized his face. "Mustafa!"

Richard's most loyal infidel stood utterly still. He wore tunic and hose like a Frank, and a hat instead of a turban, but he was most definitely not the man she had seen in the tavern. That one had raised her hackles on sight. This one made her feel safe. There was no other word for it. When he was there, she need have no fear of shadows.

Mustafa's face was unwontedly somber, his ready smile nowhere in evidence. His eyes were wary, scanning the street and the tavern. He shifted a fraction; she realized that her back was to a wall, and he stood between her and whatever might come.

"You saw him, too," she said.

He nodded. "You weren't wise to use magic here," he said. "The ones who watch, they notice. They'll remember."

"I may be safe," said Sioned. "The queen thinks she's bound me to her."

"No one is safe," Mustafa said, "where that one sends his hunting hounds."

"That one?"

"We don't name him here," Mustafa said. He laid a hand on her arm: for him, a rare liberty, and a sign of great disturbance of mind. "Come with me."

She was not minded to linger in that place where the Assassin had been. In her mind she would use that word. He could not be the first who had seen her in all her time in this country, but he was the first of the Master's servants that she had seen. And he knew that she had seen him. He had allowed it, most likely. To frighten her? To threaten? Even, perhaps, to warn?

Mustafa led her through ways of the city that she had not seen before, down dark and twisted alleys that reminded her that one of the towers of Acre was called Beelzebub. Part of her wondered, rather wildly, what she was doing following this Saracen through such places, but she trusted him—however irrational or even dangerous that trust might be. In that respect, maybe, she was like her brother. When she gave trust, she gave it excessively.

The ending was somewhat of an anticlimax: a postern of the citadel and a passage that, after a staircase or two and a door that yielded to his persuasion, she recognized as leading to the ladies' solar. She rounded on him in perfectly unreasonable anger. "I thought you were leading me somewhere interesting!"

"I was leading you somewhere safe." He seemed to remember that he was still gripping her arm: he let go.

She was not about to let him melt away as the Assassin had. She caught him and held on, stopping him where he stood. "You're supposed to be with Richard. What are you doing here?"

"Keeping you out of mischief," he said.

"Did my brother send you?"

He shrugged in the complex manner of the east, speaking volumes with a gesture. "He didn't prevent me. It seems I came just in time. I should have been quicker."

"But why—"

"Don't use magic again here," he said, "no matter how strong the temptation."

"Why?"

He tried very hard to slip away. She was too strong for him. "Tell me. Or I'll drag you into the ladies' bower and let them have their will of you."

He blanched. "I can't tell you here—the walls can hear."

"Whisper it," she said, relentless.

He sighed vastly, but he bent toward her ear. His whisper was barely to be heard. "Because of her. Because the more everyone underestimates you, the safer you will be."

"You think so?" She kept her voice down, but not to a whisper.

He set his lips together. "Please let me go, lady," he said.

"Why? Where will you go?"

"Not far," he said. "I promise."

She sensed the truth of that. He was greatly troubled for her. "You know something," she said.

He shook his head. He was not denying it, but neither would he speak. With a hiss of frustration, she let go his arm. He did not disappear as she had expected; he shifted instead, until he had established himself in her shadow.

It seemed she had herself a guardsman. She resented it less than she might have expected. Whether his unease gave birth to hers, or whether she also had had a burst of prescience, she was surprisingly glad of his presence.

He slept across her door that night. One of the ladies who shared the room squeaked with alarm when she saw a man on the floor, but the other two regarded him with lively interest. He was pleasing to the eye in his dark, slender way, and his eastern manners delighted them: he seemed to them a perfect image of a courtly nobleman.

Sioned did nothing to disabuse them of the notion that her brother had sent one of his squires to protect her. It was true, in its way; certainly Mustafa belonged to Richard, and he was at least as adept in the arts of war as a Frank of his age.

She heard him through the snoring of her bedmates, breathing softly and regularly. His sleep would be light, like a cat's: alert for the slightest hint of danger. She wove wards through that wariness, shaped to guard him even as they heightened his senses.

It was a quiet night, free of threats if not of fear. In the morning, a brow raised here and there at the sight of Sioned's new shadow, but it was hardly polite to remark on him. Even Henry, who recognized Richard's pet Saracen, simply nodded as if in satisfaction, and went about his business.

They would leave that day for Tyre, sailing on one of Richard's galleys. Sioned was horrified to discover how much baggage she was expected to bring with her. "A lady of fashion never travels light," Joanna said, laughing at her expression.

"But I don't have maids or a retinue or—"

"Now you do," said Joanna. She was enjoying this much too much.

She crooked a finger. A procession of ladies advanced into the solar, led by the redoubtable Blanche herself. There were only half a dozen when Sioned stopped to count them, but in that first moment of shock, they seemed an army.

"Joanna," said Sioned. "I can't—"

"You must," her sister said. "It's only practical. Or do you think that you can look after all your gowns and jewels by yourself?"

"One maid for that, surely," said Sioned, "but—"

"A single maid shames the rank and dignity of a princess. And," said Joanna, "she'd be sorely taxed to manage that princess' wealth."

"But I don't have—"

"No," Joanna conceded, "but you have the resources of a king at your disposal. Our brother asked that we give you all the pretensions to which your royal lineage entitles you. You needn't keep them afterwards—unless of course you want to."

"I would never want such a thing," Sioned said with heartfelt sincerity.

Joanna set her lips together and carefully refrained from comment. Instead she said, "Think of it as a battle. You're fighting for all of us, and for the Crusade."

That was one way of thinking about it—Sioned could grant her as much. "But, Joanna, I can't have this many women following me about!"

"You can and you must," Joanna said implacably. "Now, what is this thing you're wearing? Blanche! Did I not instruct you to see that she was properly attired?"

"I'm not in Tyre yet," Sioned began, but none of them was listening. They had her comfortable traveling clothes off her before she could mount any useful resistance, and restored her to the excruciating elegance of court fashion. There was no walking sensibly in those tiny and exquisite shoes, even if she would be allowed to soil her silken train in the common streets. She would be taken to the ship in a litter and carried aboard like an eastern lady, wrapped and bound as securely as a bale in a caravan.

It was war, as Joanna had reminded her, and this was a battlefield. She set herself to endure it, for her brother's sake if not for her own.

CHAPTER SEVENTEEN

Richard's ship sailed into Tyre with all its banners flying. Sioned, trammeled in royal estate, still managed to be on the galley's deck as they came to harbor in that ancient city. She had been aware of it from far out to sea. Even in a country so full of magic and so weighted with age, this place was old. Old as Nineveh, old as Tyre: poets had sung of such things even in Gwynedd where she was born.

Now she was here, on this island that the great Alexander had bound to the land with his causeway, looking up at towers that had stood since the dawn of the world. She had been afraid that the age of the city would crush her. Yet as she came to it, it welcomed her. It drew her in; it bade her rest in the warmth of its arms. And that, she had never expected—not in this city of enemies.

This was a city much less burdened with darkness than Acre or Jaffa or Caesarea. It was not a city of light—it was too old and world-weary for that—but evil had no power over these stones. Maybe it was that they were still so much a part of the sea. The cord that bound them to the land was narrow, and there were great wards on it: wards that Alexander himself had set, or Alexander's mages.

They were still making the purple here, the dye so rich and so rare that in older days it had been reserved for kings. She caught the stink of it on the wind as she was carried off the ship, a sharp reek of the crushed shellfish from which it was made.

"The stench of wealth," the captain said. He had taken a liking to her, perhaps out of sympathy for her trapped expression. "Here of all places, there's no mistaking where the money comes from."

"It's not evil," Sioned said. "Just strong."

"Strong it certainly is," said Henry. He seemed to be trying not to breathe too deeply. "Do you think Conrad is using it as a weapon?"

"They say he'll do anything that serves his purpose."

While they spoke, the ship had been settling along the quay. The captain excused himself; Henry had to withdraw among the men, to set them in order and to oversee the unloading of the horses that he and his two companion knights had brought. Sioned was left alone except for the flock of her maids, not one of whom had an intelligent word to say. They were chattering like starlings. Almost, vindictively, Sioned called up the spell that would have made reality of the semblance.

She caught herself before she succumbed to the temptation. For temptation it was, and not entirely born of her own heart, either. She raised the guard that she had let down on sight of Tyre, and wove the wards more tightly.

Mustafa was in her shadow again. She had not seen him come, but his presence reassured her considerably. He had squire's livery now, with the king's device, and so many weapons about him that the wards hummed in protest. They could stand fast against cold iron, but they did not like it.

The ship was moored, the men drawn up in ranks, as much as the deck would allow. Their eyes turned toward her.

Her rank was highest, her position most dignified. She must disembark first, with only a company of guards ahead of her.

She had been instructed in proper deportment: she allowed herself to be helped down off the deck, although she was perfectly capable of doing it unassisted, and let herself be bundled into a chair. Her maids would walk: fortunate women. She, the princess, must not set her delicate foot on the common earth.

Conrad had not met them or sent a delegation to greet them. He would have an excuse, she was sure, but it was a slight, an insult to the king whose envoys she and Henry were.

That would be dealt with. She, shut in the curtained chair, choking on the heavy perfume that had been favored by the last inhabitant, could only grit her teeth and endure. Her spirit at least was not bound; it was keenly aware of the streets of the city, how they ascended gradually and with many turns and doublings toward the citadel. She heard the hum and bustle of people in those streets, and the tramping of feet: her bearers' closest, her guards' farther away. Henry and his knights rode behind, a slow clopping of hooves, with now and then the clang of steel shoe on paving stone.

Her maids' chatter had barely paused with their advent on dry land. They had been babbling since Acre, so steadily and incessantly that it was, in its way, a protection.

Sioned was not yet so far gone as to listen to their nonsense. It was gossip again: follies and scandals, and a heated debate over the best way to arrange a wimple.

When at long last the chatter died, it heralded a halt in the procession. Sioned could feel the loom of the citadel, the heart of all that was here: ancient, rooted in the rock. The clash of spears, the challenge of guards, seemed somehow trivial before the power of that place.

Henry answered the challenge in his clear voice, pleasant but with an edge of steel. She half expected him to be turned away, but the guards let them all through.

They passed under the echoing arch of a gate and into a stone court. Sioned's chair lowered to the ground. It was all she could do not to leap out of it. She waited instead and impatiently for Mustafa's slim brown hand to part the curtain and for him to assist her to her feet. After so long in confinement, she needed the supporting hand: the light was dazzling, her body stiff from sitting.

When she could see again, and when her legs were steady under her, Henry had come to relieve Mustafa of his post. Mustafa retreated softly into his favored place in her shadow. Henry, at ease in the light, smiled at her and said, "Are you ready? The battle waits."

She drew a breath and nodded. The courtyard was ringed with armed men, all of them standing still, watching. Her own guard seemed terribly weak and small, her knights a pitiful number.

She had magic. She had Richard's strength behind her, the thousands of his army, and the threat of his wrath. She lifted her chin. They were all staring at her. The court in Acre had called her beautiful. Certainly her maids had done their best to make her so. She only had to think that she was—to know that when men looked at her, they were captivated.

It was alarmingly easy. If she had ever been baptized a Christian, she would have had to confess to the sin of pride. She contented herself with a resolution to end this game quickly and return to her wonted and unpretentious self.

Whether it was her beauty or his own curiosity that drew him out, Conrad came striding through the ranks of his guards. He was a dark man, not young, not tall, not particularly good to look on; what beauty he had was marred by the pocks and scars of an old sickness. And yet there was strength in him, and a steely determination that made him, if not beautiful, then certainly difficult to forget.

He bowed over Sioned's hand. Henry he barely acknowledged; the rest he left to his men. "Lady," he said. "Where has your brother been hiding such a jewel?"

She bit her tongue on the quick rejoinder, lowered her eyelids and watched him through the lashes. The corner of her mouth turned up just a fraction, because he would have been shocked to know what she was when she was not playing the demure princess.

He tucked her hand under his arm. "Come, lady," he said. "Be welcome in my city."

She dipped in a curtsey, but not too low: she was, after all, a king's daughter, and he but a marquis with pretensions. He seemed to take no umbrage. Maybe it was true, then, that a woman could do whatever she chose, if only she was beautiful.

What Conrad's court lacked in sparkle, it gained in martial spirit. The French were indeed here in force, with Hugh of Burgundy at their head. So too were too many of the knights of Outremer, and some of the Germans who still remained.

Hugh did not recognize Sioned. She had not expected such satisfaction as she felt when Conrad presented her to him, and at first he did not recall her name; then it dawned on him. His expression was most gratifying. Shock; astonishment. A flash of fear, as clear as if he had spoken the words. What knowledge had she brought with her? What secrets was she privy to? Did she belong to Richard, or to Eleanor?

So: he was afraid of the queen, too. Sioned began to wonder if Eleanor's terror, like her own beauty, was an artifact; if there honestly was nothing beneath it.

She brought her thoughts firmly to order and smiled at the duke. He could not manage a smile in return, although he had the wits to kiss her hand.

She was discovering the uses of silence. People had a compulsion to fill it. They raised whole edifices of conversation, while she had only to nod and occasionally smile, or frown if the occasion called for it. Hugh betrayed no secrets—yet—but several of his barons let her know that, as irked as they were with Richard, they had seen no more pay for their army from Conrad than they had from the English king; the King of France, safe in Paris, had sent nothing at all. "I do swear," said one, "that my men will take whatever they can get, and gladly enough, if only they get something."

She nodded; she smiled. She tempted them to new spates of words.

The ladies did not like her. That was a hazard of beauty; she had learned as much in Acre. When the men flocked about her, they ignored the ladies who belonged to them, or who had ambitions in that direction.

Sioned took note of them. Most were women of this country; chief of them was the royal lady of Jerusalem, the famous beauty, Isabella. She was everything that Sioned was not: tall, fair, with hair the color of beaten gold and skin as white as milk. The blood of the old Crusader kings ran strong in her. She was half a head taller than her husband, Conrad, and half again as broad.

Her sister Sybilla had been as much a fool as the man she had chosen to be consort and king, the beautiful idiot Guy de Lusignan. This younger sister hid behind beauty as Sioned happened to be doing, but when Sioned met those wide-set blue eyes, she saw there an intelligence quite as keen as her own.

Isabella was no fool, and no empty chatterer, either. She left that to her ladies. If she was jealous of the attention that Sioned had drawn, she did not show it. She studied it and Sioned; she kept her counsel.

This was a mind as keen as Conrad's. Sioned could not tell whether it was friendly or hostile. She thought it might be reserving judgment.

Henry had left her side to move among the court, scouting the battlefield. He crossed Isabella's path, engaged in conversation with a knight from France with whom he had struck up a friendship on the Crusade. The lady's eyes followed him as if drawn irresistibly.

He was as lovely as she, and in much the same mode, tall and fair. From where Sioned stood, seeing them briefly side by side, caught in a shaft of light, they were like images in a shrine.

Conrad moved in between them, intentionally or otherwise: a shadow, dark and stunted. Sioned shivered. For a moment he had no face, no living semblance, only the lightless dark.

Someone was babbling at her, heaping her with flattery, calling her a glory among women. She fixed her eyes on her feet and bit her tongue until she tasted blood.

*   *   *

At last she was allowed to retreat from the field. A servant was waiting, offering not only a room crowded with maids and baggage and a bed which she need not invite anyone to share, but a bath.

The maids declined, protesting that it was a sin to bathe in winter. Sioned leaped at the chance to be clean and briefly free of her entourage. They would have hovered and fretted and been conspicuously bored, but she sent them on ahead. She did not need to press them overly hard. They were as weary as she.

As she had hoped, the bath here was in the eastern style, and had been decently maintained—at Princess Isabella's insistence, one of the servants told her. "A blessing on the princess," she said, and meant it.

When she was clean, she went up to her room, attended by the servant and the silent, all but invisible Mustafa. She met one or two people on the way, but nearly everyone was in the hall. There were stretches of hall and stair, barely lit by lamps or torches, in which she and her tiny escort were the only signs of human life.

They were not the only things that moved there. Spirits she expected; the world was full of them. But this place quivered with shadows. Most were harmless, drifts of darkness passing through, ghosts or memories from long ago. A few raised her hackles. They watched as she went by, eyeless, faceless, but intensely aware of her.

She warded herself as best she could. The less of the truth they saw, the better. She turned her every outward thought to her body's comfort: how clean and sweet it was, and how beautiful, and how she would break even more hearts tomorrow, and make even more ladies jealous, and what a wicked pleasure that would be.

The shadows' intensity weakened. Their focus faded; they slid away. She wanted to stop, to prop herself against a wall before her knees gave way, but it was only a little farther to her room. She set her teeth and pressed on.

CHAPTER EIGHTEEN

Saphadin was not in Tyre. Sioned would have been surprised if he had been, but her heart persisted in being disappointed.

She made do as best she could with the court that had gathered in opposition to Richard. They were making no secret of that hostility, nor of their search for an excuse to provoke a fight. They had had hopes of one while Hugh was still in Acre, but Eleanor had driven him out of the city before he could seize it and hold it against her son.

Eleanor was no one's best-beloved queen here. *Bitch goddess* and *queen of harlots* were the kindest words that Sioned heard. Everyone undertook to remember that she had been Queen of France first, until she had run off with a young upstart a dozen years younger than she, who had battled and intrigued his way to the throne of England. It was conveniently forgotten that the King of France had annulled the marriage on grounds that his queen had given him only daughters—and therefore, in the reckoning of kings, no issue at all.

People did not hold their tongues where Sioned was. They

all knew that she was no child of Eleanor, and no friend to her, either. Some even went so far as to think that she had come to join them, to make common cause against the queen and her arrogant lout of a son. To them she had not existed before she appeared in the guise of a princess; they knew nothing of the nobody in Turkish trousers, the physician in Richard's army. Such a creature was as far beneath their notice as a mouse creeping across the floor.

It was better than she had hoped for, that people spoke freely; but she had come here to draw Conrad's fangs. He was a dour and secret spirit, who trusted no one.

Yet insofar as he could trust a living soul, he trusted his wife. Sioned sought her out on the third day, requesting an audience after morning Mass. Slightly to her surprise, the request was granted.

Isabella received her in the hushed chill of the chapel. A young monk was clearing the altar of its furnishings, but except for him, and for a maid who never looked up while Sioned was there, she was alone.

Sioned had eluded her maids but brought Mustafa. He was as demure as Isabella's companion, and more useful; the dagger he wore at his belt was only a fraction of his arsenal.

Sioned greeted Isabella with a bow, princess to princess. Isabella inclined her head in return. Sioned might be a king's daughter, that nod said, but Isabella was a queen.

Not yet, thought Sioned. "Lady," she said.

"Ah," said Isabella. "So you do have a voice. There are wagers in the court that you may be mute."

"I've become aware of the uses of silence," Sioned said.

"Yet now you see a use in speech."

"I would ask you something," Sioned said.

"Ask," said Isabella.

Sioned did not speak at once. She had had words marshaled and ready to ride, but under this level blue stare, they seemed feeble and overly transparent. Yet she could not think of any that would serve better. After a long moment she said, "It's being said that I came to swear allegiance to your husband. Do you believe this?"

Isabella was as careful with her words as Sioned. "I believe," she said, "that you will do whatever seems to you to be wisest."

"You credit me with wisdom?"

"I credit you with more intelligence than you might like." Isabella smiled faintly at Sioned's expression. "I asked questions of those who would know. You trained as a physician. You speak Greek and Arabic. We can use you, if you throw in your lot with us."

"And if I don't?"

"You travel under an envoy's banner. My husband is not above sending a messenger home with his head in a bag, but he has an eye for a beautiful woman. More likely he'll give you a noble escort and order them to kill you if you set foot again within his borders."

"That's sensible," Sioned said. "And you? Would you listen if I asked you to consider my brother's cause?"

"I am married to Conrad," Isabella said.

"You were married to Lord Humphrey," said Sioned. "Now you are not. You've been passed back and forth like a sack of wool. You'll be passed again if enough men in power decide there's need."

"To whom?" Isabella inquired. "Richard? Is his queen so easily disposed of?"

"No more or less than any other queen," Sioned said.

"Conrad would object," said Isabella. "He hates to let go of anything that he considers to be his."

"Are you his?"

"He considers me so," said Isabella.

Sioned shook her head slightly. "I asked if you were his—not if he laid claim to you."

"It would hardly be wise for me to deny it."

"What does he do," asked Sioned, "to men on whom you cast your eye? Will he maim or kill them?"

"I make sure that he never observes my eye on any man but his noble self."

"Wise," said Sioned, "but is it true?"

"I see now why you make a habit of silence," Isabella said

without perceptible rancor. "Did you come to court me for your brother?"

"That," said Sioned, "no. My brother is not looking for another queen. Nor—before you ask it—is his mother. They are both looking for an ally."

"Of course they would be," Isabella said. "Why do they think that I might throw in my lot with them? I do believe that my husband is a strong and capable ruler, whatever his faults."

"Do you believe in the Crusade?" Sioned asked her. "Do you believe that Jerusalem should be in Christian hands?"

"I believe that Jerusalem should be well and competently ruled by a man who takes his right to rule from me."

"If Conrad believed that," Sioned said, "he would be allying himself with Richard. Nothing that he does is aimed at taking Jerusalem—only at seizing what power he can for himself. He'll break the Crusade if it serves that cause, and sell Jerusalem to the highest bidder, provided that he wins and keeps the title of king."

"Is it your purpose to antagonize me?" Isabella asked.

Sioned met her stare. "You have eyes to see the truth."

"I see," said Isabella, "that all of you who come from the West, all of you brave warriors of the Crusade, will fight a battle or two, congratulate yourselves for having saved the world, and then sail away, leaving us to face the consequences. If I could be sure that any of you would stay, I would consider an alliance."

"Would you convince Conrad to do the same?"

"I make promises for no one but myself."

Sioned bowed to that.

"And you?" Isabella asked her. "What are you empowered to do? Can you speak with your brother's voice?"

"Within reason," Sioned said, "yes."

"If he will undertake to remain in Jerusalem for three years after he takes it," Isabella said, "and swear to it on holy relics, then I will consider what he has to say."

"Only consider it?"

"I will accept him as an ally," Isabella said. "Whether my husband will . . . that I can't promise."

"Can you keep him from interfering in the taking of Jerusalem?"

"I can try," said Isabella.

"Will you allow me to try as well?"

Isabella's brow lifted. "How far would you go to gain what you wish for?"

"Not as far as his bed," Sioned said bluntly.

Isabella bit her lip, perhaps to suppress a smile. "Try, then. But do nothing to harm him, or I will be forced to declare war on you all."

"If he is harmed," Sioned said, "it will be none of my doing."

Isabella accepted that. It seemed she heard no resonance beneath the words.

Sioned did not know why there should be. But this place affected her strangely. She took her leave without waiting for dismissal: a faux pas if there had been any courtier to see, but there was only Isabella and the silent maid, and Mustafa who cared for nothing but to keep his king's sister safe.

Sioned had won nothing tangible—only a promise of a promise. And, which was more immediately useful, the freedom to work such wiles as she had on Conrad.

She had not asked Isabella to keep secret what had passed between them. It was not her place to ask such a thing, and she had to trust Isabella to do what was wise. Alliances were built on trust. Mistrust only bred enmity.

Conrad was a notoriously mistrustful man. He slept not only with a dagger under his pillow but with a sword at his side. Wherever he went, he went surrounded by guardsmen. Rumor had it that they were sworn to him by blood oath. Certainly something bound them; Sioned could see it like a thread running from each man to his lord's hand.

He was not a sorcerer, nor did he keep one in his court. Like Richard, he was a practical man. He dealt in the things of the flesh, and left matters of magic to those who believed in it. In that he was very like Richard.

Sioned used none of her own magic to gain his attention. She relied on the arts of her maids with silks and paints, and on an art of her own that, although she had come to it late, was proving to be remarkably easy to practice. A glance, a smile, a tilt of the head—it was like a spell cast on any man she aimed at.

Conrad did not yield as easily as most, but yield he did. He who was mated to a golden beauty had a predilection for dark and round and small. They called his mistress the Damask Plum; not that Sioned ever saw her, for she was kept at a tactful distance in a house some distance from the citadel, but rumor had a great deal to say of her.

"You're more beautiful than she is," one of the French knights said. He was less given to flattery than some, and more given to gossip, which made him a useful companion. He was not flattering Sioned now, exactly; he was telling her about Conrad's mistress, how she was descended from the old kings of Tyre. "She has a face from the old carvings: rather more nose than fashion calls for these days, and a great deal of black hair. She's swarthy—not like you, your skin is cream—and her teeth are very white. She's witty and reckoned wise. They say she speaks seven languages. I know she sings like a bird."

"He likes a witty woman?" Sioned inquired. She was speaking a little these days in the low and dulcet tones that Blanche had enjoined on her—her natural voice, Blanche decreed, was much too crisp and practical to excite a man's desire.

"He likes *her* wit," Thierry said. "It's said she's a pagan—she still worships the old gods. Though I've seen her in church; not that I've ever seen her cross herself, but she does seem to worship the Lord God like the rest of us."

Sioned did not cross herself in church, either. She was more than slightly intrigued by this woman who did not show her face at court. It might be a diversion—she was well aware of that. And yet there were powers here that did not come from any Christian source, nor did they have a flavor of Islam. They were older than either.

Had Richard known of this woman when he sent Sioned

here? Sioned would wager that Eleanor had—and she would wager that Conrad suspected as much. Conrad saw webs within webs.

Suspicion could be its own worst enemy. She courted Conrad with her eyes and her smile, and with a little wit—not too much; she was saving it for a greater need.

He was waiting, the sixth morning after she had arrived, with horses and hounds and falcons. The page who had fetched her had bidden her to the hunt—and not in a way that offered her a choice. She might have attempted a refusal, to see what Conrad would do, but she was not ready yet to test his patience with contrariness. Today she would be obedient.

It was a small hunt. Isabella was not riding with it, nor was Henry. There were half a dozen knights of France and of Outremer, a company of guardsmen, and the falconers: perhaps two dozen all told. She was the only lady; the only woman at all, except for the redoubtable Blanche, who proved to have an excellent seat on a horse.

Between Blanche and Mustafa, Sioned felt rather well guarded. The riding clothes that had been inflicted upon her were somewhat more suited for looks than for use, but they would do. The same could be said of the mild-mannered little hawk which she was not even to carry on her own fist; a young falconer carried it for her.

She was not here for her own pleasure. This was Richard's hunt; she was only the hawk in his jesses. She rode beside Conrad, taking note that the horse he had given her, at least, was one she might have chosen for herself: a mare of desert breeding, fiery yet tractable, with silken paces and a feather touch to leg and rein.

There was significance in the choice of the horse. She suspected as she mounted in the courtyard of the citadel, but as she rode through the city, she knew: this was his mistress' mare. People took her for that lady, seeing her so mounted and accompanied. Many bowed; a few spat as she passed by.

She wondered if she was supposed to notice and be outraged. In fact she was amused. When they came through the gate onto the causeway, she found the road almost open, and room enough to let the mare run.

Cries of dismay rose up behind her. Idiots: they thought the horse was running away with her. But Conrad, close behind, loosed a bark of laughter. She glanced over her shoulder. He was grinning like a wolf.

She let the mare run beyond the causeway, reining her in at last where traffic thickened on the road, wagons and carts trundling to the market in Tyre. The mare danced and fretted, hating to plod earthbound after the exhilaration of speed.

The rest of the company caught her there, the guards and knights crimson with embarrassment, but Conrad was still grinning in delight—the first honest expression she had seen on that face. He offered no flattery, but simply said, "Marco. Let her fly the peregrine."

Marco, the chief of the falconers, had obvious doubts, but Conrad was master of his servants. He surrendered the princely bird, with a faint tightening of the nostrils as she took it on her fist. She held out her free hand; the falconer stared at it, until, with very slightly less reluctance, he surrendered the feather with which he had gentled the falcon.

She spoke to it softly in Arabic, because it seemed to her the language most suited for speaking to falcons. The grip of its talons was strong but not crushingly so. The wind ruffled the soft feathers of its breast. She smoothed them with the falconer's feather, and stroked it down the blue-grey back. The falcon eased into the pleasure of the touch.

She would never win Marco's respect, but he was less scornful than he had been. They rode up and away from the shore, departing from the road and its press of people and riding out through that rough and windswept country. Their falcons were eager, the game not too sparse—but it was not the hunt that Sioned had come for. Simply to be riding in the open air, feeling the wind on her face, with a good horse under her and a good falcon above her, was worth whatever it might cost.

Conrad had not come simply to hunt, either. When they

were out of sight of the city, they abandoned the pretext of hunting and took what appeared to be a goat track, but horses had traveled that way more than once since the last rain. It was steep and stony, and slippery in places. Sioned was glad of the surefooted mare.

The track led up to the summit of a hill, then down again to a circle of tumbled stones. It dawned on Sioned that these had been wrought by hands; it was a ruin, though what it had been, she could not tell. A village, maybe. A fortress long ago. It provided a little shelter from the wind, and a corner of a wall made a middling fair hearth.

The squires had brought charcoal to burn, and provisions that made a small feast. While it was being prepared, the horses threw up their heads; one of the stallions snorted explosively.

None of the men seemed alarmed. Sioned, who had been poised to leap up with dagger in hand, subsided with a faint sigh. Mustafa was as alert as the horses, but although his hand was resting on the hilt of his sword, he had not drawn it.

Horsemen rode down the hill from the east. They were dark men in turbans, all of them, and their number was precisely that of Conrad's company. That was meant, she thought, and it meant something.

Her hackles had risen, and not simply those of the body. Sparks crackled along the edges of her wards.

It was not the shudder of evil drawing near, but the tingle of magic at least as great as her own—trained magic, powerful magic, magic that she knew well. He rode in the midst of the infidels, distinguished from the rest by no mark of rank, but she would have known him if she had been blind.

Her own gust of anger startled her. So did the sudden, powerful urge to fling herself into his arms. She held herself still and kept her face expressionless, watching as Conrad welcomed his guests. They were not strangers to him; he knew most of them by name, the soldiers as well as the emirs, and of course the prince who led them.

They had brought bread and fruit and cheese and a freshly killed gazelle, which turned a small feast into a rather substantial one. The infidels set up a pavilion for it, with rugs to soften the stony ground, and braziers for warmth. In a very little while, this was a camp fit for a prince, or for a princely council.

Sioned did not move or speak through all of it. When the pavilion was up and the odor of roasting gazelle had set her mouth to watering, Conrad came and bowed in front of her. "Lady," he said, holding out his hand.

Her presence here was no accident. She let him draw her to her feet, though his touch made her shiver, and not pleasantly. As soon as she was upright, she slipped her fingers free of his. He seemed unperturbed; he led her to the pavilion, bowing at the entrance, inviting her to precede him within.

There was no fear inside that tent, and no danger but what stood at her back. Her heart was hammering even so. She paused to let her eyes adjust, opening the rest of her senses to the curtained and carpeted space.

He had been reclining against the far wall, but at her coming he rose. She meant to bow, but she found that she could not. She looked straight into his face.

He smiled at her, a smile so unaffected that she had returned it before she stopped to think. The nonexistent quarrel that had parted them, the grudge she bore him for considering that idiocy of marriage to Joanna, seemed ridiculous here and now, in his living presence. He had been her friend, though in war they must be enemies. He was still her friend; that, for him, had never changed.

The world faded but for the two of them: a moment out of time, where no other could hear or understand. It was a strong magic, and yet as simple as breathing—or as loving him.

"You still cherish a friendship," she said. "Yet you went away and never spoke a word."

"Would you have heard it?" he asked her.

"You should have said it," she said.

He looked down—he, the great prince, abashed. "So Safiyah said. But I thought I knew better."

"Men always do," said Sioned.

It was not an apology, or much of a peace offering, either,

but he accepted it as if it had been a much greater gift than it was. She did not know why that pricked her eyes to tears. Foolish heart; it knew no sense or reason. It only cared that he was there again, and the quarrel was gone, with only a faint reek of anger in its wake.

CHAPTER NINETEEN

Saphadin and Conrad talked of alliances, pacts of peace between Tyre and the House of Islam. Richard was not to be a part of them. Conrad wanted the title of king; if Saladin would help him win it, he would give Saladin Richard's head, and the heads of his whole army besides.

Sioned listened without surprise. The meal she had eaten lay in her belly like a stone. Her joy in Saphadin's presence was much darkened. She was here for a reason, and that was not to delight herself with the end of a quarrel. Conrad had brought her, knowing who she was, and knowing surely where her allegiances lay. He wanted Richard to learn of these negotiations.

But why? Richard was all too likely to muster a force of Franks and fall on Conrad with fire and sword. That would weaken and even break the Crusade, which would serve Saladin's cause admirably—but what was in it for Conrad?

Richard's death—supposing that that could be accomplished? Without Richard, Guy would have no hope of taking back the throne of Jerusalem. And if Richard's army was defeated, Conrad would own whatever wealth it had accumulated, which though depleted by the winter's miseries, must still be considerable. With that in addition to the treasure of Tyre, he could keep the French army with him for a substantial while.

It was complicated, but Conrad was a complicated man. So was Saphadin, but not in the same way at all. And Richard . . . Conrad might find that he had underestimated the Lionheart. Clever men often mistook Richard's warrior bluntness for stupidity.

Her head had begun to ache. She hated politics. The complexities of a text in an obscure language, the elaborate structure of a great spell, the mending of a broken body, all of those she could encompass. But this web of intrigue wearied her intolerably.

She forced herself to listen and remember, since it suited Richard's plan as well as Conrad's that she do just that. The words impressed themselves as if written on a page, bound into a book and laid away in her mind until she should have need to recover it.

To rest her eyes, and to relieve the ache somewhat, she watched Saphadin. Him she could not fault; he was only doing his duty to his sultan. He would negotiate with all sides and none, and win what concessions he could, then expect that his brother would take the rest by force. If he had done anything else, he would have betrayed his people.

Conrad spoke Arabic—not well enough for delicate negotiations, but he had no objection to using Saphadin's interpreter. If the man altered the sense of a phrase, Sioned saw how Conrad's eyelids flickered. That quick mind would be recording every slip and shift.

Sioned detected no deception. Conrad wanted Saladin's aid too badly, and Saphadin had too much of the advantage; they had no reason to lie to one another. Prevaricate, yes—conceal certain details, by all means. But nothing worse.

They ended amicably, if without reaching a firm conclusion. "There are things I must settle with my council," Conrad said.

"And I with my sultan," said Saphadin, bowing where he sat.

Conrad rose first, Saphadin an instant after him. They bowed to one another, gracious as almost-allies could be.

Sioned did not want him to go. The not-wanting was so strong that she gasped. Fortunately neither of them heard her—or so for a moment she thought. As Saphadin's servant assisted her to her feet, the man murmured, barely to be heard, "My lord says, tomorrow morning, go to the market in Tyre. Someone will find you."

There was no time for questions. Conrad had taken her arm in a light but unbreakable grip. She let him lead her out into the sun and the wind.

Conrad expected her to send word to Richard of what he had done. She would do that, but not yet. She did, when she came back to the city, send one of the maids to fetch Henry.

He took his time in coming. When at last he deigned to appear, it was nearly time for the daymeal; Blanche was busily undoing the damage that sun, wind, and freedom had wrought to the careful edifice of Sioned's beauty. Blanche, Sioned had already observed, was completely unflustered by that same windblown ride; her cheeks were as alabaster-pale as ever, her wimple still perfectly in place. Sioned did not even remember losing her wimple, though she had been aware of the moment when her hair escaped its pins and plaits and streamed loose in the wind.

It was nearly subdued again. Paint had done what it could to dim the flush of color in her cheeks. She sat perfectly still for Blanche to complete her handiwork, as her youngest maid brought Henry into the chamber.

"Princess Isabella sends her regards," Marguerite said innocently, "and will be pleased to see you in hall in a little while."

"So," Sioned said to Henry, "her highness is well?"

"Very well," Henry said. His voice was steady; he was not flushed as a man might be who had been caught doing something improper. "I do ask your pardon for not coming sooner.

She was insistent that we hear a singer who has just arrived from Paris, and I couldn't in politeness excuse myself until the song was over."

"It must have been a very long song," Sioned said.

"Endless," said Henry. "Did you have a pleasant hunt?"

"It was pleasant," said Sioned. "And illuminating. Has the court crowned me his new mistress yet?"

"Not . . . quite yet," Henry said. "Though some are close to it. They say the fair Elissa has shut herself in her house and will speak to no one."

"She has no cause for jealousy," Sioned said.

"Of course not," said Henry. "Nor does milord of Tyre, whatever anyone may be saying of me."

"That's rather a pity," Sioned said.

"You think so?"

"I think," she said, "that there is one who could be won over. The marquis is too deeply in love with himself. She looks for a man to love her as her beauty deserves."

"She is very beautiful," said Henry, "and well fit to be a queen."

"His queen?"

Henry shrugged. "He's competent. Men don't love him, but they serve him. He'd rule well enough, if he had Jerusalem."

"Better than my brother?"

"Lady," he said, "forgive me for honesty, but your brother is a general. He fights wars. He has no talent and no patience for the arts of peace."

She could hardly deny that; she knew Richard too well. "Can Conrad truly wage peace? Or will he simply feed his own power?"

"It will be to his advantage to hold what he wins," said Henry.

"And Conrad always serves that advantage." She sighed. "He's using me, you know. We weren't hunting birds. We hunted Saracens, and he stalked an alliance against my brother."

Henry nodded slowly. "He would do that. Did he win it?"

"Not quite," she said, "but close enough. He'll let the sultan keep Jerusalem, if he can be lord of the coast. Free access for pilgrims to the Holy Sepulcher, and no Muslim interference with the crossings of Jordan. Title of king to be given to Conrad, and a royal ransom in lieu of the keys to Jerusalem. It will be a rich and advantageous settlement, if the sultan agrees to it."

"It seems they didn't take our king into account at all," Henry observed.

"They didn't, did they?" she said. "I'm sure that was for my benefit."

"What do you think they'll do with him, then?"

"I think," she said, "that they'll wear him down with dissension and force him into battle with a broken army, then drive him out in defeat. They'll eat away at him, break his courage, belittle his strength, make his great gifts useless, until he has no choice but to run back to the West.

"That is," she said, "if they can. If he were alone, I think they'd have fair odds of doing it. With his mother here and his contentious kin under lock and key in Normandy, I'm not so certain."

Henry was silent for a moment. She had not thought that she would shock him, but maybe she had given him somewhat to ponder. After a while he asked, "Do you think my grandmother knows?"

"I wouldn't wager for or against it," Sioned said.

"She should know," said Henry. "So that she can think on it." Sioned was silent.

Henry took her hand suddenly and kissed it. "Brave and beautiful lady," he said. "If we win this war, will your brother know how much you had to do with it?"

"I rather hope not," she said. "I'm not a mover of worlds."

"No?" Henry pressed her hand briefly to his heart, then let it go. "Shall we go down to dinner? They're waiting for us."

She let him escort her, but her mind was not on the feast to which they were going. It was transfixed with the beginnings of a thought, one that she did not like to think—not least because she had been blind to it for so long. Henry did not care for Isabella because . . .

Because his eye had fallen on Sioned. She had not meant for it to happen. But there it was, as clear as a newly opened eye could see.

It need not matter. And yet, maddeningly, it did. She did not want this lovely man, except as a kinsman and a dear friend, nor was there any danger that she would be given to him in marriage. She had no lands or titles to offer him. He was safe from her.

She would have to see that he was aware of that. But not today. He could dream for yet a while.

It was not as easy to escape to the market the next morning as Sioned had hoped. Conrad was watching, and so, not surprisingly, was Isabella. They both wanted her attendance; then her maids pursued her, insisting that she must be made beautiful for the midmorning court.

She eluded them in the end by demanding a bath and, while they ran to prepare it, slipping into the plainest gown she had been allowed to bring with her, appropriating Blanche's dour black mantle, and disappearing among the servants. They barely noticed her; without her armor of silk, she was simply another pretty dark-haired maid sent on an errand for her mistress.

It was still morning, though barely so, when she came to the market. She knew better than to expect that Saphadin's messenger would have lingered, but she had to be certain.

She purchased a thing or two that she had been needing, and she listened to what people were saying. The French were not as hungry here as in Acre, but they felt the lack of their pay. Rumor was that Conrad would find means to recompense them at least in part; those who believed that were praising him and cursing their absent king.

"Have you heard?" one man asked another near the street of the dyers, where the reek of the purple dye was sharply distinct. "It's said the king tried to move on Normandy at the New Year,

but found the borders guarded by an army he had never expected to see."

"English?" his companion asked.

"You would suppose so, wouldn't you? But the man who
told me, who had it from a sailor off a ship from Marseille—he
swore that it was an army of the dead. Romans and Franks,
Vikings, Saxons—ghosts in ancient armor, with weapons that
bit deep. But the fear of them was greater."

"Do you believe it?"

"I believe that the English king has allies in unusual places.
Isn't he the Devil's get?"

"Ah," said the other, a gust of scorn. "They say the marquis
is the Devil himself. If that's so, then there's no love lost between him and his descendant."

Sioned was not the skeptic that this nameless Frenchman
was. Richard's lands were warded—how not? Eleanor would
have known from the moment Philip set sail for France that
once his own kingdom was secure, he would set his eye on
Richard's. It would strike him as wonderfully appropriate to relieve Richard of his western titles while Richard won a kingdom
in the east.

Clearly Philip had reckoned without the powers that
Richard's subjects could bring to bear. Philip was a right royal
and Christian monarch, but Richard was the son of a sorceress
and of the Devil's own.

She could not help but smile at the vision of Philip, surrounded by his monks and priests, confronting the armies of
the dead. Crosses and prayers could not vanquish them, and a
true Christian king regarded magic with holy horror.

She turned still smiling, aware of eyes upon her. Mustafa was
frowning formidably. "You led me a merry chase," he said.

"I'm sorry for that," she said, and for the most part she was.
"I had to elude you if I was to elude the rest. I knew you'd find
me."

"Of course I found you," he said with a hint of testiness. "I
found another, too. He's waiting, if you'll follow me."

She would have thrust ahead of him if she could, if she had

known where to go. He led her as quickly as the press of people would allow, from end to end of the market and into the quarter of the jewelers. Those streets were much quieter than the rest of the market: people moved softly here, and spoke in low voices, as if in awe of the wealth that surrounded them. Only the lesser beauties were on open display; the masterpieces were kept in locked chests, wrapped in silk and sealed with a spell. But even the bits of gaud and frippery were wonderful.

He was sitting in a goldsmith's stall, watching the artisan craft a flower in beads of gold. The light gleamed on the pure metal, dimming the rest of the world to a grey and featureless blur.

His face would have been clear to her in the dark behind the moon. He was dressed like a prosperous citizen, with nothing about him to mark him a warrior or a prince, still less an enemy of the Crusade.

He greeted her with a smile and a bow. The goldsmith kept his eyes on his work. He did not glance up even when Ahmad beckoned her into the depths of the shop.

It was a much larger place within than without. Behind a curtain was another, wider, dimmer room, and a stair that led to an upper gallery. There were windows there, looking out on a sunlit courtyard. Trees were heavy with oranges and golden lemons. Already a few had begun to bloom, waxy white blossoms amid the ripening fruit.

It was wonderful in the midst of winter. She breathed deep of the flowers' sweetness, and felt the tightness inside of her ease. "This country," she said. "It's full of wonders and sudden beauties."

"Great ugliness, too," he said. He bowed her to a chair in the carpeted room, and sat across from her. There was kaffé, and little cakes made with honey and almonds and spices. The taste of the kaffé and cakes reminded her poignantly of the summer and autumn in Jaffa, when she had walked between worlds to learn the arts of magic.

"Today I see the beauty," she said. And then: "I missed you."

He blinked. Had she actually managed to startle him? "You were walled and guarded like the fortress of Krak."

"I was angry," she said.

He widened his eyes. "Because of—"

"Because you agreed to marry Joanna."

"Joanna never agreed to marry me."

"But you did."

"I reckoned that I knew the lady; I knew what she would say. Meanwhile how could I insult her brother by refusing the prize that he was giving me?"

"You're a great diplomat. You would have found a way."

"Certainly. I let her do it for me."

"You never cared what I would think."

"Did you honestly believe that I would take your sister?"

"You didn't say you wouldn't."

"I . . . forgot how young you are."

She slapped him.

He sat still, with the mark of her hand blazing red on his cheek, and his gaze dark and steady above it.

It was she who could not keep her eyes from dropping. She flushed from brow to sole, mortified—with all her anger turned no longer against him but against herself.

She heard him rise. She tensed to turn and run, but her body would not obey her. He drew her to him, folded his arms about her, and tilted up her chin. She could not help but look at him. "Did you honestly believe," he asked her, "that I would take your sister instead of you?"

"Instead of—" She bit her tongue. "She's a queen. What am I?"

"Royal," he said, "and much loved by your brother. And," he said after a brief pause, "by me."

"You don't—"

"Lady," he said, "you gave me half the autumn and half the winter to pass from bafflement to anger and back to bafflement again—and then to know what was at the root of it. I asked the marquis to bring you to our meeting. It might have been insanity, but I had to know—I had to see—"

"How much I hated you?"

He nodded.

"I never hated you," she said. "Not even in the worst of it."

"Have you forgiven me?"

She lifted a shoulder in a shrug. "Maybe. Would you have? If she had been willing?"

"There was no danger of that."

"Would you?"

His breath hissed between his teeth. "I would have found ways to escape."

"I certainly hope so," she said. "She is beautiful. And desirable. And—"

"Never as much as you."

"Don't flatter me," she said crossly.

"I'm speaking the simple truth," he said.

"*She* is tall and fair. I—"

"Dark and sweet," he said. "Your eyes are wonderful, like the shadows at twilight—not quite blue, not quite purple. I never saw such eyes before."

"Violets," she said.

He frowned in puzzlement.

"They're flowers," she said. "They grow in the woods in the spring. They're shy—they hide in greenery. They're this same color."

"Beautiful," he said.

"I like the roses of Damascus better."

"I don't think," he said, "that I would be greatly taken by eyes the color of blood."

She snorted—inelegant and knowing it, but this man had no illusions about her. "They would be unusual."

"Too much so." He traced the curve of her cheek with his finger. "I shall go on preferring violets. Have they a fragrance?"

"A small one," she said, "though sweet. It's not glorious, like roses."

"Your cheeks are roses," he said. "Your neck is a white lily."

"My breasts are twin lambs?"

He gasped; then he laughed. "A pagan may quote Christian Scripture?"

"When it's apt," she said, "yes."

"And what would your own faith say?"

"That the Goddess is in all that is, and every woman is Her image."

"Certainly man is created in the image of God," he said.

"Man is the creature She made to please the woman, to serve her and make children with her."

"Man was made for woman?"

"We believe so."

"Fascinating," said that son of Islam.

If he had scoffed, or professed his own faith, she would have cast him off. But he granted her the dignity of her religion. In a warrior of God, in this God-ridden country, that was marvelous. She kissed him for it, meaning but to brush his lips with hers; but the heat of the touch bound them irresistibly.

After some little while they drew apart, but still in one another's arms. Sioned looked into those dark eyes. What she saw there both exhilarated and terrified her. "What shall we do now?" she asked him.

"What would you do?" he asked in return.

"Love you," she said. "Stay with you. But we can't do that. We're on opposite sides of a war."

"Not here," he said. "Not between us."

"If I send a message," she said, "will you come?"

"Always," he said. Then after a pause: "How long will you be in Tyre?"

"For as long as I'm needed," she said.

"For as long as that is," he said, "we can meet here. Send a message in the way that Safiyah taught you. As soon as I may, I'll come."

"Promise?"

"By my heart," he said.

She kissed him softly, with but a fraction of the heat that had bound them a moment before; but if she had let it, it would have burned them both to ash. "Soon," she said.

"Yes," he said. "Soon."

CHAPTER TWENTY

It was not as soon as Sioned would have liked, that she could see Ahmad again. Conrad watched her as closely as if she had been his wife—so closely that she wondered which of his spies had told him that she met a man in a shop in the city. She had succeeded after all, and too well: once he reckoned that her attention had wandered, he courted her as ardently as any knight in a song.

That was a strange time, that season of Lent in Tyre, between the winter and the spring. She saw Ahmad thrice, with more difficulty each time, but that only made the meeting sweeter. They spoke nothing of politics and nothing of parting. He taught her more of magic, but a different art now, an art of lovers: spells and enchantments that were best wrought by two who were bound in the spirit.

She was coming back from that third meeting, barely aware of where she walked, but remembering to keep her hood close about her face, when a man in servant's dress accosted her. She realized it when Mustafa's hand stopped her short. The point of his dagger rested against the man's throat. The servant's dark cheeks had gone grey.

There were protections on him, but Sioned caught no hint of ill magic. Her glance persuaded Mustafa to lower his dagger. The servant mopped his brow with his sleeve, and said as steadily as a man might who had a bead of blood welling from the great vein of the throat, "My lady asks your indulgence; she craves a moment's conversation."

"Indeed?" said Sioned. She followed the man's glance to the shadow of a colonnade. A dark shape stood there, swathed in a mantle. Sioned saw dark eyes lined with kohl, and a smooth ivory forehead; the rest was hidden in veil.

She inclined her head. The lady beckoned her into the shelter of the colonnade.

"Lady Elissa," Sioned said.

"Lady Sioned," said Conrad's mistress. Her voice was brisk and direct, like her glance. "I see why he fancies you."

"Yes," said Sioned. "I look like you."

The dark eyes glinted. "His tastes are consistent," she said. "Your eyes are more unusual than mine, and your skin is fairer. You're even more beautiful than rumor made you."

"Much of that is art," Sioned said.

"Beauty is always art," said Elissa. "At the risk of being thought a mere and jealous rival, I came to proffer a warning. My lord suffers no other man to touch the woman he chooses. That one you go to see—he is in danger."

"His spies are watching," said Sioned, "but we are watching them. My friend has taken steps to protect himself."

"That's well," Elissa said, "but have you done the same? He's death on betrayal, lady. Even a king's sister might not escape him."

"I know you are not merely jealous," Sioned said carefully, "and I know you mean to help, but I am aware of what kind of man he is."

"Are you?"

"Why?" asked Sioned. "Does he keep a secret chamber full of blood? Does he feast on the flesh of children?"

"Don't," said Elissa. "Don't make light of him. What he wants, he gets. He wants a throne, and he will have it. If he wants you, he will be sure to take you—whatever it may cost your friends or kin. Your brother was not wise to send you here, such an innocent as you are, with such a face. Or was he trying to get rid of you?"

Sioned's back stiffened, but she kept control of her expression. "I thank you for the warning," she said.

"One day you will," said Elissa. "I give you good day, and I truly wish you well."

With no more farewell than that, she was gone. Sioned stood in the colonnade, staring at the space where she had been. She felt odd, off balance, although Elissa had told her nothing she did not know already. It was as if the words had opened the way to understanding, to knowledge that she had been refusing to face.

What, that Conrad could be treacherous? She knew that. Then why did it suddenly matter so much more than it had before?

She returned to the citadel because she was expected, and because she was not minded to turn tail and run from a shadow. She redoubled her wards as she walked, although at that strength they dulled her magical perceptions. If an attack came, she would be guarded, but she might not be aware of it until it struck.

When it did strike, it came from no magical direction at all. There were armed men waiting for her in the citadel. Their faces were grim. The air had a reek to it that she knew too well: the stench of death.

She looked for Mustafa, but he was nowhere to be seen. He had been in her shadow until a moment before; now he had vanished. Anger gusted, passed. He must have his reasons; Mustafa always did.

Conrad advanced through the ranks of his guard and greeted her with cold courtesy. "There is something you must see," he said.

She had no choice but to follow him, but she did her best to make it seem that she went of her free will. She kept her head high, and shut her ears to whispers that ran in her wake.

The guards, and Conrad at her side, led her to a door she did not know, but from the size and richness of it, she could presume that it was Conrad's own. The scent of death was strongest here, with the iron tang that spoke to her of violence. Her feet were steady but her heart was cold as the guard in the lead flung open the door.

It was Blanche. She lay in a bed now stripped of its curtains, dressed in her wonted black. Her face and hands were starkly white.

Those hands were folded on her breast. There was a strip of ribbon wound in the still fingers, a ribbon that Sioned recognized: Conrad had given it to her, saying that it matched the color of her eyes.

"She was alive when we found her," Conrad said. "When we asked her who had done this, she spoke a word. That word was your name."

"She must have thought I was in danger," Sioned said with the clarity of shock. "Or—"

"You," said Conrad, but not to Sioned. The bark of his voice brought forth the youngest of Sioned's maids, the lovely Petronilla, much disheveled with terror and grief. She shrank from Sioned's stare, shuddering convulsively. She opened her mouth and began to wail.

Conrad gripped her arms and shook her into silence. "Stop that. Tell her what you told us."

Petronilla looked ready to burst out in howls again, but fear of Conrad stopped her. "I—I can't—I don't—"

"Tell her!"

Petronilla's eyes overflowed with tears, but her voice steadied enough to get the words out. "I—I saw—you were coming up from the hall. I saw you, and I was surprised, because you said you were going out. And I followed you because you might want me to wait on you. You found—you found her on the stair from the kitchens, bringing up the posset for Jeanne's winter rheum, and you told her you needed her. I hid because I didn't want to be sent with the posset—Jeanne snuffles and moans so abominably. Blanche found a servant to take the posset, and followed you up—up here. When she saw where it was, she said she wasn't abetting you in immorality—that's exactly how she said it—and you turned and I couldn't see, really, but I saw the knife and I saw Blanche go all white and surprised. Surely you remember, because you did it, and I saw the whole thing—and when you went away, I screamed and screamed, until somebody came."

"I'm sure you did," Sioned said acidly. "Do you happen to recall if I said anything?"

Petronilla swallowed hard. "I think—I think you said, 'Take this sacrifice in Satan's name.' "

One or two of the guards made signs against evil. Sioned ignored them, turning to face Conrad. "Do you believe this nonsense?"

"You were seen leaving the room," he said, "dressed just as you are now. Will you try to defend yourself?"

"I was not even here," she said. "I was in the city. Ask your spies who have been following me. Ask a certain lady with whom I spoke, just about when this good woman must have been dying."

"I shall ask," said Conrad. "But, lady, you were seen. There is no doubt that it was you; the witnesses are clear on that account."

"Has it occurred to you that whoever mounted this ruse was most careful to be seen? If I could ever have plotted such a thing—and believe me, my lord, that is as far against my character as anything can be—then I would have undertaken first and foremost to be invisible."

"That may be," said Conrad in the tone of one who makes no judgment. "Because of your rank and the dignity of your embassy, I will order you confined in your chamber and not in a prison. Whatever you wish to eat, drink, read, you may ask for."

"And then?" she asked.

"We will do our best to discover the truth of this."

"I do hope so," said Sioned.

The guards closed in, but she drove them back with the flash of a glance. She bent over Blanche. The face was still; if she had died in fear, it had not altered her expression from its wonted severity. Sioned laid her hand over the still fingers, meaning to offer respect and farewell. The touch dislodged a thing that had been clutched to the motionless breast: a small brown cake, fresh and still fragrant from the baking.

Behind her, someone gasped. The guards about Conrad drew in closer; those about her seized her and held her immobile. Their eyes on her were blind with horror.

She looked from face to face. It was not real yet, not in her heart, where fear should be blooming into terror. What that cake was, she knew too well. Anyone who lived in this country would know it. It was the Assassin's cake: Sinan's gift to his victims. But that these people should think—

It was convenient that they think it. Conrad was honestly horrified, she would have wagered on that, but beneath the horror was a gleam of satisfaction.

At his bidding, the guards searched her with hard hands. They found the little knife that she had had since she was a child in Gwynedd, which she used for cutting meat, and the larger, deadlier dagger that she kept for defense. That had been Richard's gift; he had taken it from a slain Turk. It had a chased silver hilt, and a verse from the Koran inscribed on the blade.

These men did not care to hear where it had come from. They wanted it to damn her, therefore it did. She saw no use in protest, but that served her ill: they took her silence for admission of guilt.

"Take her away," Conrad said. His voice was thick with disgust.

The maids had abandoned the room. They had left in great haste, from the look of the oddments tossed about, but everything that was of value, they had taken. Some of it was Sioned's;

the rest had been on loan from Joanna. There would be explanations to make when she came back to Acre.

If she came back to Acre.

She must not think that way. If Conrad had her put to death, he would bring down Richard's wrath—which he might be hoping for—but he might also lose the French. They were odd about women, those knights of France; even the horror of the Assassins might not prevent them from suffering an attack of chivalry.

She tried to persuade one of the guards to send for Henry, but the men who stood just inside the door, swords drawn, eyes fixed on her as if she could whip out a dagger and stab all four of them to death, were deaf to any words she might speak. Truly: she glimpsed a wad of cotton in the ear of the one nearest. They feared a spell, an enchantment of the voice.

She knew spells of that sort, but it had not occurred to her to use one. She had been sure that she was thinking clearly; now she began to suspect that it was the clarity of shock. She had never expected this, never planned for it, and certainly not foreseen it. Had Elissa known? Maybe she had. If so, her warning had been too late to be of any use.

Sioned knew what Eleanor had done in decades of captivity after she led one rebellion too many against her royal husband. Eleanor, locked away in the castle of Chinon, had studied the arts of sorcery. But Eleanor had not been taken for an Assassin.

She could die. She faced that fact, sitting on the bed in the lamplit room. Her mother's people claimed no fear of death; it was but a passing from world to world, and in time would come rebirth. But she had lived among Christians long enough to have learned their fear—even knowing that the dead could walk the world, and even speak to those with ears to hear.

There was no sense or reason in the shudders that racked her now. Death might not be terrible, but dying . . . that was another matter.

She pulled herself together. She must think. She was not powerless. Had Conrad done this? Had Eleanor contrived it to be rid of an inconvenience? Or was there another enemy whom she did not know? Was it Sinan himself? Did he know somehow, as a master of the black arts might know, that she had spied on his councils with Eleanor? Was this his revenge?

It was somewhat belated if so, and rather more blatant than he was known to be. She was hunting far afield. The answer, she had no doubt, was much closer to home.

She was alone but for four heavily armed guards. There were no wards on her, no magical protections: proof that no one here knew or suspected what she was. She must not let them suspect. She must seem as innocent and defenseless as she could.

It was all too easy to sink down weeping. The guards were not visibly moved, but she was not playing for them. She pretended to cry herself to sleep; then when she was still, she called in her arts and powers.

They were slow, reluctant. The aspects of air and fire were leaden, weighted with earth. She could not spread wings, could muster no strength to fly. She had wrought her wards too well, and woven them too tightly into the fabric of this place. It had made them stronger—so strong that they not only protected her against attacks from without; they bound her within, helpless to escape.

She gave way at last, exhausted, having gained nothing. She could not even sleep. She knew that if she tried, her dreams would be full of death and dying.

CHAPTER TWENTY-ONE

M ustafa's hackles had been up since he first passed
through the gate of Tyre. He did not like the air of
this place. Lady Sioned said that there was no evil
here, not in the earth or in the soul of the city, but she could
hardly deny that men's hearts were another matter altogether.

Marquis Conrad had a heart like a blighted tree. There was
good in him, surely, as there was in any son of Adam, and he
was a strong lord to his people. But the core of him was eaten
away with pride and rancor.

Even before his courtesan made her show of warning against
him, Mustafa had known that this venture would not end well.
Sioned was blind to foresight: her eyes were full of a certain
face, and her mind could think of nothing but that lord of
Islam. She fancied that she could balance Conrad and the lord
Saphadin, cozen one and love the other, and face no danger
from either.

But even Mustafa's premonition had not warned him that
the danger was so close, or that it would be so great. Whoever
had done this wanted Sioned dead—though whether it was

only Sioned he hated, or whether it was Sioned's royal brother, Mustafa could not have said.

It tore his heart to leave her in the hands of those cruel guards, but that same heart knew what he should do. She would find no help in Tyre. The lord Henry was not a prisoner, not precisely, but he was being kept from her; nor was he allowed to send messages to his uncle the king. He was still an honored guest, still treated with courtesy, but he no longer had the freedom that he had had before.

Mustafa made a devout and heartfelt prayer to Allah that Conrad would not execute Sioned before he could come back. She had magic, which Conrad did not appear to know, and she was clever and wise. She would defend herself as she could, for as long as she could. Allah willing, it would be long enough.

They had not yet sealed the stables when Mustafa came there, although he heard the captain of guards call out a company to see that no one left the citadel on horseback. His mare was weaving in her stall, little ears flat, cursing the existence of the gelding stabled next to her. He was just out of reach of her heels, which frustrated her to no end.

She would have been delighted to kick Mustafa's head from his shoulders, but he knew her too well. Her heel met the sting of the switch in his hand; before she could gather herself for a second assault, he was in with her, gripping her collar, and swinging her about until she left off trying to kill him.

Then, changeable creature that she was, she let him feed her a bit of sugar and saddle and bridle her, and lead her docilely out. The greater gates were already guarded, but the postern Mustafa knew of, which was not far from the stable, was deserted. He slipped out unnoticed, even as the stable door boomed shut, locking the horses within.

The marquis had not yet thought to close off the exits of the city. That would require a good part of his army and an excuse to go on a war footing, which he did not have. The danger, he would be thinking, was within the citadel. The malefactor was captured. He would be guarding his person most closely, but the city, for the moment, could fend for itself.

As desperate as Mustafa was to be galloping away from Tyre, he paused in the market for certain small necessities, and a larger one in the form of a bony mare with a wild amber eye like a cat's and a coat that, under the dirt and neglect, had a peculiar metallic sheen. He did not question the fate that had placed such a horse here when he needed it most; nor did he let the horse dealer see the eagerness in his heart. He would have struck an even harder bargain than he did, if he had not felt the pressing of time, but when he rode out of Tyre with his new purchase on a lead, lean ears flat at the indignity of a pack, he allowed himself the luxury of a smile.

Mustafa's Berber mare was as fleet as she was fickle. The mare from the market, whose blood had come from plains far away, ran neck and neck with her, with an easy, even contemptuous stride. The horses of the desert were fast, but the golden horses of the steppe could outrun the wind.

It took Mustafa three days to find the lord Saphadin. He had been within a day's ride of Tyre, but he had moved his forces the day Sioned's maid was killed. Mustafa found him camped in the hills near Jaffa, on a day of sudden spring.

The place that he had chosen was an oasis of blossoms and of greenery, fed by wells of clean water. It had belonged to the Romans once; there was still an old god watching over the chief of the wells, his bearded face much battered with age and human hostility. That he was still there at all was somewhat of a miracle. Someone had laid a wishing on him long ago, and though much eroded now, it protected him against the zeal of Christian and Muslim alike.

Between Tyre and this camp, Mustafa had put away the garments he wore in that Christian city and returned to the dress of Islam. It was a small thing, but he felt as if he had returned to himself. And yet as he observed the camp from the cover of an outcropping of rock, he did not see a return home.

These were Turks, he told himself, and Kurds, and a few Arabs. He was a Berber. Yet it was more than that. He had become, if not a Frank, then a dog of the Franks. He was no longer a warrior of Islam.

Inshallah, he thought: God's will be done. Or as the Franks would put it, *Deus lo volt*.

He went back to the hollow where he had left the horses. The two mares loathed each other and must be tethered well apart, but they declared a truce when he was riding one and leading the other. He made himself as presentable as he could, putting on the new coat he had bought in Tyre, and a clean turban; he tidied the horses, brushed and plaited their manes, and wove blue beads into their forelocks, to make them beautiful and to protect them from ill wishing.

Then he was ready. He mounted the mare from the east and led the Berber mare, driven by an impulse that he could not have explained. She was a slab-sided, snappish, opinionated beast, but her stride had proved surprisingly smooth and her responses unexpectedly light. She did not try to whirl and kick her companion more than twice, on principle, whereupon she settled to her business.

He rode openly down the track to the camp, hands held carefully away from weapons. The guards were alert; they barred his way, but offered no open threat unless he should demand one. "I come from Tyre," he said to them. "Tell your lord: from the lady in the citadel."

They looked hard at him. One, catching a glance from the man who must be their leader, trotted off into the camp. The others stood, watchful, saying nothing. Their curiosity was well reined in; but he had expected that. The lord Saphadin kept his men in good discipline.

The messenger came back fairly quickly. "He says come," the man said. He made as if to take the bridle of the mare whom Mustafa was riding, but the snap of her teeth warned him not to take liberties. He settled for walking somewhat ahead so that Mustafa could follow.

This was no great army. Mustafa reckoned maybe a hundred men: picked troops, the guard that rode with the lord Saphadin on his embassies to the Franks. He was going to Richard, then, as Mustafa had thought; and that was interesting so soon after he had been near Tyre striking bargains with Conrad.

Saphadin had been practicing his archery: they had set up targets on the edge of the camp, and his bow was strung, although there was no arrow set to the string.

His servant took the bow and unstrung it as Mustafa approached and dismounted and went down in obeisance. Saphadin drew him to his feet, eyeing the eastern mare with considerable interest. "Is that . . . ?"

"A horse of heaven," Mustafa said. "Yes, I do think so. She leaves the wind behind when she runs."

"God has favored you," said Saphadin.

He turned and began to walk. Mustafa followed, leading the two mares. Saphadin went not toward his tent but farther away from the camp. Guards trailed at a discreet distance.

When they were still in sight of the camp but out of earshot of it, Saphadin stopped in a circle of broken stones. Some were of a size and shape to sit on; he took one and with a glance invited Mustafa to do the same. Mustafa tied up the mares' reins and hobbled them and let them graze on the bits of new grass.

"I hope you will pardon me," said Saphadin, "for not immediately offering you guest courtesy. That will come, but for this I think perhaps you would prefer that no one hear us."

"You're wise, my lord," Mustafa said. "There's no telling who might listen, or to whom the words might go. Have you heard any rumors from Tyre?"

"None," said Saphadin. His face settled into a terrible stillness. "What is it? What has he done to her?"

Mustafa considered circling round to it, but that would only put off the pain. "She's imprisoned on suspicion of murder."

Saphadin's breath hissed between his teeth. "Who? Not Conrad, surely."

"Rather unfortunately," said Mustafa, "no." He told Saphadin what he knew: the woman slain, the slayer who had worn Sioned's face, the warning Sioned had received even as her maid was dying.

Saphadin heard him in silence, eyes fixed on the sky. Mustafa might have thought that his mind had drifted far away, but there was something profoundly intent in the way he contemplated the ramparts of clouds that built over the hills.

When Mustafa finished, the silence stretched. The mares were grazing side by side from the same patch of grass—improbable enough that Mustafa was almost alarmed.

He did not break the silence. Saphadin was thinking hard, from the way his brows had drawn together. After a long while he said, "To cast suspicion on her as an Assassin—that's outrageous, but also it's clever. People would actually believe it, because it's so improbable."

"They do believe it," Mustafa said. "There have been whispers, you see: that she's no Christian, that although she shows her face at Mass beside the marquis or the lord Henry, she goes only out of courtesy, and not out of faith. Where would such a whisper have come from, if not from an enemy?"

Saphadin nodded. "An enemy who has sown the seed of suspicion, so that people will believe that a woman from the far corner of the world could have sworn herself in fidelity to the Old Man of the Mountain."

"Whoever has done this knows too much," Mustafa said. "He knows what gods she worships, and he knew when she was out of the castle. If he knows what she was doing in the city—"

"I think not," Saphadin said. "That she went to visit a man, yes, but not who the man was. And that makes me think that it was Conrad who did this. Only he would care so much that she trysted with a man other than himself. It would suit him well to use the name and terror of the Assassins, and to cast that suspicion upon her."

"But he has no magic," said Mustafa, "and the witnesses swear that they saw the lady herself commit the murder."

"Did they? How bright was the light? She showed me how they had painted and prinked her for the court; her face was a mask, which any woman of like size and features could mimic."

"As closely as that?" Mustafa demanded.

"People see what they wish to see," said Saphadin, "and hear what they expect to hear. In the dim light of a castle, a clever woman with a gift for voices could be very convincing—and never need magic at all. I do almost pity her; she was evidence. Conrad would have been sure that she was destroyed."

"And so will our lady be," Mustafa said. "I pray God she's not dead already."

"She is not," said Saphadin with such certainty that Mustafa could not say a word. He closed his eyes for a moment and sighed. "No; she is not. I would know. She's still alive."

"But for how long?"

"He won't harm her," said Saphadin. He rose. "Now come. Be a guest for a little while. Put your heart at rest. Our lady will be safe—you have my word on it."

Nothing in this world was safe, Mustafa wanted to say, but he could not bring himself to gainsay this lord of Islam. This powerful sorcerer; this man who loved the lady Sioned. "If anyone can set her free, my lord," he said, "I know it will be you."

Saphadin's lips curved in a thin blade of a smile. It was the smile of a tiger, baring his teeth for battle. "In the name of the Merciful and Compassionate, it shall be so."

CHAPTER TWENTY-TWO

Ahmad entrusted the Berber to his own personal servants, who were instructed to treat him as if he were a
prince of the Faith. The boy was properly grateful,
which showed the excellence of his upbringing, but he could
not help but betray his deeper feelings. He wanted to be part of
what Ahmad did. He wanted to share in the saving of her.

"You've already done your share and more," Ahmad told
him. "Now let me do mine—and rest. We'll call on you later,
have no fear. Then you'll need your strength."

That reconciled him, somewhat. Ahmad drew him into a
quick embrace, as if they were brothers. "Be at ease," he said.
"I'll bring her out of that place."

Mustafa nodded. His eyes were rebellious still, and his back
was stiff, but his face was pale; he was swaying on his feet.
Rashid and Maimoun took him in hand before he fell over, and
carried him off into the inner regions of Ahmad's tent, to be
bathed and fed and put to bed.

Ahmad drew a long, steadying breath. Alone, without the
need to be strong, he could yield for a moment to the shock of

the news that Mustafa had brought. He had had no sign—no inkling. Not even a shiver in the spine. Which might prove that there was no magic in this plot, but it troubled him nevertheless.

She was not dead. If she had died, there would be a gaping wound where his heart had been, and a great span of emptiness at the core of his magic. She had become that much to him, nor had he known it until he heard that she might be put to death for a murder she was incapable, to the very soul, of committing.

That she could kill—he did believe that. But she would kill in battle or in defense of someone or something that she loved. Not at random, with calculated cruelty, to spite an enemy.

Mustafa was well taken care of. Ahmad called to him the captain of his personal troops and gave him instructions that he would follow to the letter. He did not like them; his face darkened as he listened. But he was obedient.

Then Ahmad could put on a plain coat in which was sewn a coat of mail, and fill a satchel with certain articles from a locked and hidden chest, and mount the horse that waited for him. She was not a horse of heaven, but she was hardy and she was wise, and most of all she was steadfast. She would stand firm and keep her rider on her back, even if the world went mad.

"My lord, will you go alone?"

He looked down from the saddle into his servant's face. "Allah is with me," he said.

"But, lord," said Hasan, "Allah loves best those who help Him to perform His will."

Ahmad smiled in honest affection. "Dear friend," he said, "the boy in my tent is much loved by one whom I love as my very self. Tend him for me; guard him and protect him. Keep him safe until I come back."

Hasan bowed to the ground. He was weeping, poor man, but Ahmad would not shame him by remarking on it. "Allah's blessing on you," he said, and touched his mare's side with a heel.

*   *   *

She went forward willingly, at ease, although the tilt of her ears told him that she knew there would be dangers ahead. He ran a hand down her neck—grimacing, then laughing briefly at the handful of red-brown hair that came away with it. Truly it was spring: the mare was letting go her winter coat.

For this journey he could not simply close the space between a place that was his—his house, his tent, his garden—and another on which he had set the seal of his magic. Even if he had not been traveling into the hands of enemies, he could not spare as much power as it would take to create and maintain the working. Instead he must travel by mages' roads, which Sioned called straight tracks. Her mother's country, she had said, was full of them. So too was this one, with its heritage of ancient magic.

He found the first road not far from his camp. It seemed a goat track, but it ran too straight for that, up over a long hill and out of the world that mortals knew. The seasons changed strangely there. Sometimes the land through which he rode was green with spring, and sometimes it was locked in winter. Sometimes there was no telling what season it was or what world he had entered; it was too strange to understand.

In all the worlds through which the road passed, he rode north and somewhat east. With each passage out of his own world, he traversed a whole day's journey in an hour's time. He paused for the hours of prayer, praying with all his heart, as Mustafa had done, that it was not too late.

As he drew nearer his destination, the passages became more difficult. The power that held this land was inimical, if not to all that he was, then to the particulars of his name and race and allegiance. But he must go on, if he was to do what he had set out to do.

At the gate of the last passage, which had the semblance of a stone arch opening into a valley of shimmering stones, Safiyah sat waiting for him. She seemed a stone herself, hunched and shapeless, clad in dusty black, but the power in her was like a cry of exultation.

He bowed to her as to the queen of mages that she was. The

hand that he raised to his lips was frail; the flesh was burning away from the spirit within. "Lady," he said. "You had no need."

"I had every need," she said. "What were you thinking, to come here all alone?"

He could not say to her what he had said to Hasan. It would be presumptuous. Her, he gave the truth. "I couldn't ask anyone else to run this risk."

"Could not?" she inquired. "Or would not?"

He flushed. She had always had the power to reduce him to a stumbling boy. But often, as now, she softened it with a smile. "It was noble of you, and wise in its way. Where you go, an army would never be enough, but a man alone might win the prize. Will you let me give you a gift?"

"Your gifts are beyond price," he said.

She inclined her head to the truth of it, then drew his head down to hers, touching brow to brow. "Have strength," she said. "Have courage. But in the moment of extremity, if all is lost—turn to mist and water. Become one with the air. Melt and vanish away."

The words were like a wash of cold fire. He shivered at the touch of them, and gasped as they came to rest in his heart. They were a spell of dissolution; yet also a blessing, and an escape if he would take it.

She kissed his eyelids and brushed her fingers across his cheek, soft as the touch of a spider's web. "God go with you," she said.

The way was open. She was gone from the gate. He knew a moment's profound loneliness, cold as a wind in the wasteland; then the warmth of her blessing washed over him. He was smiling as he passed through the portal and rode down through the valley of stones.

The gate out of the valley, like the gate into it, was occupied. But this was no friend to Ahmad or any of his kin. It was a shape in white, the color of mourning and of death. Its face was shrouded, its eyes hidden in whiteness. In its white-swathed hand was a dagger with a blade like a sliver of night.

Ahmad faced it without either stealth or fear. He made no move to draw weapon, but his hands knew where to find each one of them. "Take me to your master," he said.

The guardian spirit regarded him with unseen eyes. He had laid no compulsion on it, apart from the expectation that he would be obeyed. Spirits respected strength; they scorned bluster and empty show.

He waited in patience, sitting very still on the back of the most steadfast of his horses. The mare let one hip drop and let her head sink, seizing the opportunity for a nap.

Was that amusement in the tilt of the shrouded head? The spirit whipped about abruptly, dissolving into a whirlwind, and spun through the gate.

Where had been a vision of nothingness was a harsh and inhospitable landscape, a wilderness of stony crags. It was bleak and barren, but it was his own living earth, lit by a familiar sun and inhabited by a swirl of earthly spirits. They gathered always in places of power, even places of such terror as that which loomed on the crag above him.

Masyaf. Ahmad knew it well enough. When he was much younger, he had ridden with his brother to attack it; they had failed, and its Master had only grown stronger in the years since.

He could feel the great magic throbbing in his bones, drawn up from deep wells of the earth. Here was a center, a foregathering of powers. The crags were as thick with spirits as a hive with bees, swirling and swarming in the air and among the stones.

It had not been so twenty years ago. There had been spirits, yes, and Sinan had been a sorcerer of some repute, but all too obviously he had spent the years between increasing his power beyond anything that Ahmad could muster against him.

Ahmad's heart quailed. He called up the memory of her face and the thought of the world without her, and his strength flooded back. It was the strength of desperation, but it was all the greater for that.

His mare clambered patiently up the steep and narrow track. She did not care that arrows could fall from above, or a rain of boiling oil. That was a concern for men. She had hopes of a stable to rest in and cut fodder to eat, and a handful of grain if her hosts were generous.

Her equine practicality was a bulwark against fear. Focused on his own stomach, thinking of bread and meat, fruit and spices, sweet cakes and cups of steaming kaffé, Ahmad passed through the clouds of spirits as if he had been invisible. He was too purely of earth for them, his magic too thoroughly concealed.

They were simple spirits, most of them, but the higher he ascended, the more alarming they became. Their faces altered from fantastical to grotesque; they bristled with fangs and talons.

But worse were the battles among them. Spirits in their right minds, or such minds as they had, coexisted in an airy amity. These were as contentious as a pack of starving dogs. The more power they fed on, the greedier they became; they could never be sated. These in their turn fed the power in the castle atop the crag.

He fought his way through it as through a storm of wind— but this was no wind of earth. It buffeted his heart; it tore at his spirit. It tempted him almost beyond bearing, to fling himself into the cloud of living essences, to become a blind and mindless part of them. To surrender, to give way; to serve the Master on the rock and be served by him, feed and be fed, until there was nothing left of him, not even a whisper of fading breath.

He was no longer guiding the mare. She carried him of her own will, up and ever upward, with steadfast persistence. He clung to the saddle out of sheer bodily refusal to fall.

He must master himself; must win back the sight of eyes and mind. He must gather the tatters of his magic. He must be strong.

He found that strength in the stubbornness that was one of his less endearing faults; in the memory of her. Even her face was gone from his sight, so full was it with the swirl of warring spirits, but he remembered her scent and the softness of her hair, and the taste of her lips on his.

Her eyes. He could see her eyes. Violet, she called them, for the flower of her native country: a deep and dreaming color, like shadows in twilight. They were large and wide-set under a strong arch of brows; they met his stare directly, with a clear intelligence.

He felt her hands clasp his. She drew him up the track. With each step, the world became clearer. He saw the stones under the mare's hooves, and the steepness of the slope, and looking up, he saw the castle now unexpectedly close.

It seemed deserted. He saw and sensed no archers on the walls, arrow nocked to string, ready to shoot him down. The battlements were empty of guards. The gate was shut.

That was the last of the defenses: darkness and silence and the vision of emptiness. He rode up to the gate and stood with his head back, measuring the loom of it. Calmly then, with the power that had remained coiled in him through all the buffets of this journey, he smote the gate.

It rocked as if struck by a ram, and its iron hinges cracked. The mare shook her head at the sudden blast of sound. He sat quietly on her back and waited.

The sun had been low when he struck the gate. It nearly touched the horizon when at last the glamour faded from the castle. The gate was still cracked; with the passing of the enchantment, it groaned and sagged on its weakened hinges.

Slowly and somewhat gingerly, a smaller gate opened in the greater one. A man in white peered out. He was unquestionably mortal; he was old, if hale, and his face was deeply seamed with age.

Ahmad dismounted and led his mare toward the gatekeeper. The old man looked hard at him, as if he must remember Ahmad's face. He offered no gesture of respect. That was deliberate; he made sure Ahmad knew that. Ahmad smiled slightly and came on without pausing, so that the man had to draw back or be overrun.

*   *   *

There were lights within, lamps and torches, and men in white going about their varied business. One of them took the mare, after Ahmad had retrieved the light pack which she carried behind her saddle. Another took Ahmad in charge, leading him up a stone stair to a small but perfectly appointed bath, and rooms beyond it of remarkable warmth and luxury. Dainties of food and drink were waiting there, and a demure creature in a drift of veils that hinted at marvels beneath.

The bath was neither poisoned nor lined with knives. The cakes and kaffé were as innocent as if his own most trusted servant had made them. The elegant robe which the woman offered him was only a robe; no spells were woven in its fabric.

He declined her further services. She withdrew with grace that spoke of opportunities lost and delights forgone.

He could not bring himself to regret them. He ate one of the cakes. It bore little resemblance to the deadly gift that an Assassin left on his victim's breast. This was notably more pleasant: rich with sugar and almonds, laced with a tang of citron. The kaffé was hot and rich and just sweet enough to be satisfying.

It was expected that he rest; he did so, rather gratefully, and with care to keep a part of himself on guard. He was aware of watchers as he slept, eyes both mortal and otherwise, and voices murmuring words that he did not catch. They were surprised, he thought. They had not expected to see him in this place.

They should have, if their spies were as skilled as repute made them.

He woke as a warrior learned to do, all at once, ready for battle. The sky beyond the window was grey with dawn. Fresh kaffé was waiting, and a bowl of dates in honey, and a loaf of bread still warm from the baking.

He was hungry, but first he must pray. He performed the dawn prayers without haste, offering Allah his truest devotion. His prayers were all for her and none for himself. Today was a day of reckoning. Far away from here, in the city of Tyre, she was rousing from her own bed, preparing for her trial.

For a moment he wore that garment of flesh, knew the thoughts that ran within it, tasted the sweetness of her unmistakable self. Parting from it was a physical pain. He gasped as he straightened from the final prostration, and looked up at a man who stood looking down.

It was the man from the gate, the old man in white. He was taller than Ahmad remembered, and stronger; he stood erect, with a young man's carriage, although his face was as ancient as before.

Ahmad sat on his heels and laid his hands quietly on his thighs. "My lord of Masyaf," he said.

"My lord of many realms," said Sinan. "How unexpected to see you here."

"Your hospitality is beyond reproach," Ahmad said.

"Yet you have not availed yourself of all that was offered."

"I accepted everything that I could accept," said Ahmad.

"Ah," said Sinan. "A vow, then?"

"A binding of the heart," said Ahmad.

"Very touching," Sinan said. "Break your fast, my lord, and take your ease. When you are ready, I shall send a guide. Then we will talk."

Ahmad inclined his head. He would be calm; he would be his best-known and most noble self, the man the Franks called the great knight of Islam, the sultan's wise and sublimely politic brother. But the self that was inside, the eager boy who loved a woman, was desperate to settle it now, before another moment passed.

He quelled that part of his soul, and looked without surprise at the empty space where Sinan had been.

The bread was still warm, the kaffé steaming hot. He partook of them as a warrior does before battle, for the sustenance that they offered. They comforted him; the warmth in his belly somewhat assuaged the coldness in his heart.

Just as he set down half the loaf uneaten, a small spirit glimmered into being above his head. It was a faintly gleaming pale-blue thing like a corpse-light, bound by a cord of compulsion that drew it out and away from the room. Ahmad followed at the pace it set, which was not overly swift.

It led him through the castle, keeping to uncrowded passages but not avoiding places where men were, and even a few women: guardrooms, kitchens, gathering halls, places of prayer. It was a populous castle, with an air about it of high and holy purpose.

The holiness surprised him. The darkness that was in the earth and the air and all about this place was not plainly evident within these walls. They were shielded; protected. The men were bound as the spirit was, but it was a willing servitude. They were devout Muslims, true servants of Allah, confirmed in their faith and certain of their place in Paradise. They never knew what it truly was that they served.

The spirit brought him at last up a long and winding stair, not to the tower that he would have expected, but to a green and fragrant garden. Ahmad paused at the entrance of it, steadying his heart, gathering his forces. So: it was true. This was the Garden of the Assassins, that was said to be a corner of Paradise.

It was not the otherworldly Paradise in which dwelt the blessed of God. It was not the earth that men knew, either. Its flowers were too large, too luminous, too beautifully strange. Its grass was not exactly grass. The sky that arched overhead was the color of light under sea: shimmering blue and silver and green.

The Master of the Assassins sat in the midst of his garden. His chair grew out of the earth, a broad, gnarled stump of dark wood polished to the sheen of stone. His white garments glowed against it. His face had the same depth and quality as the chair, as if it too had grown out of this other-earth.

Ahmad looked into his eyes and saw the dark behind the stars. The thing to which he had given himself, the power he worshipped in return for power, was not Allah. Yet he gave it that name, and proclaimed it to the people who followed him. They believed it. Only he knew the truth.

Ahmad knew. Yet he had not come here to destroy it. He had come to invoke it.

He did not offer obeisance. The hate between them was too deep and the war too long. But for the life and love of a woman, he said, "I am not here in my brother's name or by his knowledge. He plays no part in what passes between us."

"I do know," said Sinan softly, "that you are your own man, my lord. If you speak for him, you do so out of the conviction of your heart."

"This is no matter of his," Ahmad said, "but it does concern you. Have you had word from Tyre?"

"Tyre?" said Sinan. His brow arched. "Why, no."

"Nor had I," said Ahmad, "until a messenger reached me yesterday morning. He brought news of a thing that I found to be altogether improbable. There was a killing, he said: a woman slain in the marquis' own bed, with a cake of a certain baking left on her body."

Sinan frowned. "A woman? In Tyre?"

"Indeed," said Ahmad. "The murderer was seen in the act. Witnesses swear that it was a guest of the marquis who committed the murder, a lady from the English king's following, his own sister."

"We do not count women among the martyrs of the Faith," Sinan said, "and certainly not women from the far ends of the world."

"That I know," said Ahmad, "as should anyone with any knowledge of your doctrine. But Franks care little for the finer points of our belief. They see the cake, they see the dagger, they cry Assassin—regardless of the truth of the matter."

"Indeed," said Sinan. "It is the easiest of accusations. This woman—tell me of her."

Ahmad's heart shaped her in the stanzas of a love poem. His wiser self said flatly enough, "She is the daughter of the late English king and a royal concubine. The king favors her; the queen of Sicily has had her in her train, although since they came to this country the king has kept her close by him. She has considerable gifts as a physician."

"He trusts her," Sinan observed.

"He does," said Ahmad. "He sent her with an embassy to Tyre to smooth matters with the marquis, if that could be done, and to win back the French to the king's cause. She succeeded in winning a good number of them, and in attracting the marquis' notice. That gained her nothing but sorrow. Now she is accused of murder, and there are witnesses to swear that they saw her commit the act. And yet that cannot possibly be."

"You have reason to know this," said Sinan.

Ahmad kept his gaze steady. "Excellent reason. She was, at the time, with me."

Sinan nodded blandly. "I can see that that might present a difficulty. Since you were known to be in the vicinity of Jaffa, and she was seen in the citadel of Tyre."

"She was seen wielding the knife. That condemns her irreparably."

"It is a pity," said Sinan, "and I see from your devotion and the reports of my own spies that she is a lady of remarkable attainments. Yet what would you have me do? It seems purely a Frankish plot."

"I believe," said Ahmad, "and the messenger who brought this word to me believes, that it was conceived by the marquis himself out of jealousy and hatred. It serves a manifold purpose: it destroys her, spites the English king, and casts the blame on you."

"And you? What is the loss to you?"

"I lose her," said Ahmad.

"Surely," said Sinan, "a man of your accomplishments should find it simple enough to free her."

"Surely," Ahmad said. "Have you no care for the insult to you and your following?"

The dark eyes hooded. "Should we be insulted?" Sinan inquired.

"Perhaps not," said Ahmad. "I have some curiosity, myself, as to how the lord of Tyre eluded our spies, contrived a deception, and laid the blame at your door, all without perceptible evidence of magic."

"He is a very clever man," Sinan said.

"Exceedingly clever," said Ahmad.

There was a silence. Ahmad made no effort to break it. He had sown the seeds. It was Sinan's choice whether they should lie fallow or burst into bloom.

CHAPTER TWENTY-THREE

The silence stretched. The sky shifted and flowed, shimmering with myriad lights and colors. Somewhere nearby, water fell softly, drop by drop.

Ahmad's eyes followed the sound of it. A spring welled up from the not-quite-grass, trickled down a slight slope, and gathered in a basin. The basin was silver, reflecting the too-strong green of the grass.

Ahmad approached the basin. It was half-full of water, and should have mirrored the colors of the sky. Instead he looked down into a hall of stone. The arches, the tiles, the high peaked windows, were of the east, but the court that stood in it was unmistakably Frankish. Priests were thick there, hung with crosses, and knights of Temple and Hospital, and smooth-shaven courtiers in the latest fashions from France.

She stood in the midst of them in a plain linen shift, with her black hair tumbling loose and wild down her back. Her wrists were manacled; chains bound her ankles. She was thinner than he remembered, and paler; her eyes were enormous in the delicate oval of her face. Yet she did not seem frail at all.

Her shoulders were square, her back erect. She looked straight into the face of the marquis as he sat enthroned on the dais.

It was indeed a throne, that high carved chair, although he did not yet affect the crown that should go with it. His mantle was the true deep purple of Tyre, and his collar was of heavy and gleaming gold. He did not have the stature or the beauty to carry it off, not as Guy his rival did, but his bearing almost made up for the lack.

It was not given to Ahmad to hear the words of that trial, but he could see the faces of those who were there. They made him think of hungry wolves. She was no meek lamb, but she was prey; they would devour her.

"She'll be condemned to death," Ahmad said.

"Most likely," said Sinan directly behind him.

He neither started nor turned. "There will of course be consequences, and likely a war. That would suit the marquis very well."

"She is in no honest danger," said Sinan, "nor do you need my help to spirit her away. What is it you want of me, then? Revenge?"

Ahmad set his lips together.

"There is a price," said Sinan.

Still Ahmad said nothing.

Sinan was smiling, and not pleasantly: Ahmad heard it in his voice. "I will do as you are so subtly refraining from asking. When the price is paid, you will know."

"You will not touch her," Ahmad said. "She is not yours, not now, not ever."

"I lay no claim on her," said the Master of Assassins. "Not now, not ever."

Ahmad kept his back erect, though he wanted to fall bonelessly to his knees. "So be it," he said.

He had no recollection of closing his eyes or letting down his guard, and no memory of leaving that garden. Yet between one moment and the next, he passed from standing on a greensward to sitting in his too-familiar saddle. The road down which the mare plodded was nowhere near Masyaf, and yet he recognized it. The sea heaved and sighed alongside it. Some distance ahead, he saw the loom of a rock, and the battlements of the citadel of Tyre.

He felt for a moment the brush of wings, dark and soft, and a ripple of cold laughter. He was a mage and not a weak one, but the Master of Assassins was considerably more than that.

He had sold his soul for a woman. Somehow, even setting it in words could not make him regret it. Even knowing that Sinan had seen clearly. If Ahmad had only wanted to free her, he would have done it. He would have had no need for the journey to Masyaf, or for that conversation in the garden.

There had been need. Conrad had trespassed where he had no right or authority to go—both in laying hand on Ahmad's beloved, and in laying the blame on the Master of the Assassins. For that he would pay.

The mare halted with her face toward Tyre. Sinan had a nasty turn of humor: he had sent Ahmad where he meant eventually to go, but not until he had made certain preparations elsewhere. If he turned back, time would be wasting. She was safe for this night, perhaps, or as safe as a condemned murderer could be, but the dawn would see her death.

Strict wisdom would have led him to turn back, to carry out the plan he had conceived on the journey to Masyaf. But there was Tyre, and she was in it, with the shadow of death hanging over her.

This was a temptation, and more of Sinan's mockery. Even knowing that, Ahmad could not choose the course of wisdom. Maybe this was the price: to become a fool for love, as if he had been a headstrong boy and not a man of full and seasoned years.

If that was so, then he would pay it. He stripped the mare of saddle and bridle and set a wishing on her, and turned her loose. She meandered off in search of grass. Much sooner than the road's curve warranted, she turned a corner and disappeared.

Ahmad stood alone between the sea and the sky. At that thought, he laughed. He was all alone—but for the myriad spirits that, sensing his power, had come flocking to stare and marvel. They swirled as thick as about the walls of Masyaf, but there was no darkness here.

As he looked up at them, he knew that God had sent them, and laid them like a weapon in his hand. His heart sent thanks to the Merciful and Compassionate, even as he called upon these armies of the air. He laid no compulsion on them, but spoke to them as if they had been men of his own nation. "If you are so minded," he said, "you can help me greatly."

Most of them did not respond, but a few swirled in closer. They were jinn and afarit, spirits of wit and grace, who could choose good and evil as men could. He bowed in respect. They bowed in return.

"Do you compel us?" asked the foremost of them, a great shining shape of wings and claws and horns, with a voice like the roar of waves beneath the sea. "Do you invoke us by the seal of the one who bound us and enslaved us to mortal will?"

"I do not," said Ahmad. "I ask it of your free will, to prevent a great injustice, and to protect an innocent."

"No child of Adam is altogether innocent," said the great jinni.

"This is a pure soul," Ahmad said. "Do you doubt me? Come and see."

"Are you tempting me? Or challenging me?"

"Why, both," said Ahmad.

"If your claim is false," said the jinni, "then you are ours for a year and a day, to do with as we will."

Ahmad's teeth clicked together. This venture was threatening to cost him a great deal. "And if my claim is true?"

"We will bow at her feet and offer her our devoted service."

"For a year and a day?"

"For as long as it pleases her to command us."

"That could be a lifetime," said Ahmad.

"Your people live but a moment. We live thousands of years. To look on one of you who is the pure essence of divine fire—

that would be worth a score or two of years. Because we choose it, you see. Because no compulsion lies on us, except our own will."

"That is a great gift," said Ahmad.

"So it is," said the jinni, "if she is that most unlikely of creatures: both human and pure."

His companions murmured assent, a mingling of unearthly voices. There were not so few of them after all; others had come as they spoke, until Ahmad stood at the center of an army of spirits. Sioned would be a mighty general if Ahmad won this wager.

They were waiting with the patience of beings who did not age or die. He scraped his wits together and surveyed his forces. The sun was sinking, staining them all as if with blood. So much the better: night would increase the power and terror of this army of air.

He gave them their orders. They had discipline—better than men, because they were wiser. Some took wing in the air, others plunged into the sea. The great jinni lifted him up and sprang aloft on wings as vast as the sky.

He was safe within the curve of those talons, and comfortable enough once he had recovered from the shock of the sudden leap. The sea below was awash with light. The rock of Tyre was a loom of black at the end of its causeway. Lights flickered there: torches along the walls, and late passers within, making their way toward their houses. They would not be aware of what passed above them, unless they had magic.

The army of the jinn drifted lazily on the wind, waiting for the fall of dark. The sky above Ahmad's head was obscured by the jinni's wings, but he could see far out over land and sea. He watched the sunset fade and the stars come out.

When the night was fully fallen, the jinni began to spiral up and up. Just when Ahmad was certain that the great creature meant to dash him on the rocks below, it folded its wings and stooped like a falcon, straight upon the darkened city.

Ahmad's heart was in his throat as the battlements rushed toward him. The jinni's laughter boomed in his ear. In the very instant when they would have struck the stones, its wings shot out, braking its fall. Softly, lightly, with the delicacy of a butterfly's landing, the jinni set Ahmad on the roof of the citadel.

He was dizzy, reeling with speed and shock, but the warrior's instincts rose quickly. The air was full of wings and eyes. The army of the air had fallen on Tyre.

He could not stop to gape at it. Time was short; the guards would be distracted, but not forever. He ran toward the tower that rose on the seaward side. There was a door in it, and a guardroom—blessedly deserted—and a stair leading downward.

At the top of the stair he paused. It sounded as if the city had been attacked with grapples and siege-engines. Voices cried out, weapons clashed. There was even, far away, the boom of a ram.

For an instant he wondered wildly if Richard had come after all, or if another army had invaded Tyre. But the land about the city had been utterly silent as he flew over it, and there had been no hint or intimation of mortal assault. These were the jinn carrying out his orders, and their uproar was most convincing.

The castle boiled like an anthill—but all downward toward the army of shadows. Never upward, where the true invasion was.

He waited at the base of the tower, wrapped in darkness, while the citadel emptied of fighting men. It seemed an endless while, but he kept a tight grip on his patience. He could sense her not far away—not in a dungeon, then, or imprisoned in the city. She was awake, alert, but she had raised no powers. There was no taste of fear about her.

There were guards. Two of them—there had been more, but those had gone to fend off the apparent invasion. He gathered certain forces and called to him the words of a particular spell. When he had come down through deserted corridors to the one over which they stood guard, he sent the enchantment of sleep ahead of him.

The guards rocked, swayed, and slid down the wall in a grating of mail. He laid a hand on the brow of each as he passed, and filled their sleep with dreams of sated desire.

The door was bolted from without, but there was no lock and no need for a key. He slid the bolt as softly as he might.

The room within was soft-lit, but there was no lamp burning. It was her own light, a gentle moonlit glow. She sat up clasping her knees, still in the shift that he had seen reflected in Sinan's scrying-basin, with her hair loose about her shoulders, black as the night beyond the walls. Her eyes in that light were dark and deep, meeting his with a soft intensity.

He gasped as if she had struck him. His heart had leaped and begun to pound.

He needed his wits about him, and he must master his magic if they were to escape this place before the Franks understood that their sudden enemy was a thing of air and darkness. He summoned every scrap of discipline that he had learned, and calmed the beating of his heart, then focused his mind on what he was about to do.

He reached to draw her to her feet. She did not rise to meet him. Her arms remained clasped about her knees. Her brows had drawn together. "So the diversion is yours," she said. "Are you mad?"

"Are you so eager to die?"

She shrugged off his flash of temper. "I'm not going to die."

"You haven't been condemned to death?"

"Of course I have," she said. "What, you don't think I have enough magic to escape?"

He opened his mouth, then closed it. "I know you have enough magic. It's only—"

"You came galloping to rescue me. How did you find out? Did you come to meet me, and find rumor instead? The city's been buzzing with it."

"The Berber came to me," said Ahmad: "Mustafa."

Her brows rose. "To you? Not to my brother?"

Ahmad nodded.

"But why—" She broke off. "Of course. Magic. Richard doesn't have it and won't use it, and Conrad would make sure I was dead—or he would try to make sure—before my brother could come with force of arms. Conrad wants a war with my brother. Couldn't you have credited me with the wits to prevent it?"

"You are very welcome," said Ahmad. "Your gratitude moves me deeply. Your—"

She launched herself from the bed into his arms, bearing him backward bruisingly into the wall. She pinned him there with her weight and glared into his eyes. "You didn't need to do this!"

"I could do no other," he said.

"You *are* mad."

"They do say love is madness," he said. "Time is flying, lady. Will you waste a perfectly good diversion and a rather costly bargain, or will you rein in your pride and come with me?"

"Are you accusing *me* of pride?"

She had drawn back a bit when she bridled at him. He got a grip on her and heaved her over his shoulder, and let the force of the movement carry him through and out the door.

She amazed him by not putting up a struggle, though she cursed him steadily in her mother's language. The sound of it made him think of water running over sharp and jagged stones. It was a grand language for curses, she had told him once: better even than Arabic.

As long as none of her curses came bound to a spell, he cared little. He could not run under her not insubstantial weight, but he could walk swiftly back the way he had come.

The stair was more than he could face at speed and under such a burden. He set her on her feet, not particularly gently, and cut across her stream of invective. "Will you walk, or shall I drag you?"

Her teeth snapped together. "Don't tell me we're flying out of here."

For answer he gripped her wrist and began to climb. She had to follow or be dragged.

At least she did follow, and she left off her cursing. She needed all her breath for climbing. He set a punishing pace, though his legs ached and his lungs burned.

Part of it was pique, but part was honest urgency. The sounds of ghostly battle were dying down. The jinn were growing bored, or reckoned that they had amused themselves enough. They were not like men, to take pleasure in looting and killing, though it was a great entertainment to watch mortals shriek and run from monstrous apparitions.

The stair was far longer than he had remembered, but at last it came to an end. The night air was a great relief after the closeness of the tower.

Somewhere on the climb, his grip on her wrist had shifted until their fingers were intertwined. She stood shoulder to shoulder with him, looking up, as the great jinni came down from the sky. Her expression was as fearless as ever; she was grinning in unalloyed delight.

The jinni touched the stone of the roof with taloned feet. Its wings spread from end to end of the citadel. They drew in and mantled as it went down, bowing on its face at Sioned's feet.

"Pure spirit," it said. "Child of fire."

The laughter that welled in Ahmad had an edge of hysteria. He bit it back.

Others had come behind the great jinni to bow likewise, making deep reverence before a mortal whose spirit was pure. Their lord rose upright, towering to the stars, and said, "We are yours, lady of light. We offer ourselves to your will."

She was clearly baffled, but equally clearly she could see the need of the moment. "Can you take us away from here?" she asked.

The jinni bowed its great horned head. "Your wish is our command."

"You have my gratitude," she said with a pointed glance at Ahmad.

The jinni laughed, a soft rumble. It took them up together, cradling them like a pair of birds, and carried them away from her captivity.

Chapter Twenty-four

Sioned did not know whether to kiss the man or kill him. It was a grand and knightly thing he had done, marshaling an army of the jinn to rescue her, but there was nothing wise about it. And Mustafa . . . she would wring his neck when she saw him, for inciting Ahmad to this madness.

The jinni, for whatever incalculable reason, would not do as Ahmad commanded, which was to carry them to his house in Damascus. "The lady commands," it said.

She sat in the protection of its hands, looking down at the darkened world, and tried to set her thoughts in order. When Ahmad burst in on her, she had been calling to mind every spell she knew, and gathering powers to free herself before the dawn. For all her haughty words, she had been losing hope. She did not have the knowledge. She could turn the executioner's axe to a plowshare and transform her chains into garlands of flowers, but she could not spirit herself away. She did not have the art of the mageroads, or of binding place to place with a cord of strong magic. She could not even comfort Henry.

"Henry!" She sat bolt upright. "Gods help him, he's still in Tyre. They'll blame him. They—"

"Shall we fetch him?" the jinni inquired.

She shook her head. "No. No, he should stay—my brother needs him there. But if you could keep him safe—if you could protect him—"

"As you command," said the jinni. "And you, lady: where does it please you to go?"

She frowned. "I don't want war among the Franks. Let Conrad know that I was freed by the armies of the air. Let him think I'm an Assassin if it suits him—but don't let him blame my brother."

"It shall be done, lady," the jinni said.

"As for me," she said, "I'll vanish for a while, until the marquis has found another obsession. Damascus will do as well as anywhere. On one condition."

The jinni waited, but it was not the spirit of fire to whom she spoke. "You will explain everything that you have done. And you will teach me all that I should have known, that would have kept me out of this predicament."

"Gladly," said Ahmad.

"Damascus, then, of your courtesy," she said to the jinni, "where this lord of men directs you."

The jinni bowed its enormous head and banked on a wing, wheeling away from the sea, toward the pit of darkness that was the land.

It was the strangest journey she had ever taken, and yet also the most sublimely comfortable. She lay at ease in the loose clasp of fingers as long as her whole body. The wind blew chill through the vast curve of talons, but the jinni's substance was fire; she breathed clean cold air but was enfolded in warmth.

Ahmad sat on his heels just out of easy reach, hands on thighs, head bowed. Having told the jinni where to go, he was resting; she thought he might be praying. He was not working magic.

The light of moon and stars shone softly on him, limning the lines of his profile. Even on this wild venture, there was a calm and self-contained look to him. He always knew exactly who he was and what he was about.

It was preposterous that he should have raised an army of the jinn and come roaring to her rescue. Preposterous, and yet not inconceivable. If she could believe what it meant. If she could accept the truth. That he loved her—enough to risk everything that he was or had done, to save her from the threat of death.

She said nothing while they sailed through the air in the jinni's talons. Dawn was just beginning to glimmer in the eastern sky when it circled above a city of domes and minarets, covered markets and a burgeoning extravagance of gardens. Even from high above and even through the stench of closely crowded humanity, she smelled the heady sweetness of flowers. Roses and jasmine—sweetest of all flowers that grew.

The jinni deposited them on a roof that she knew well, set amid a circle of gardens: the house in which she had learned so much of magic, and come to love the master of the house. Its roof was a garden. Roses bloomed in profusion, and jasmine tumbled out of pots and grew headlong down the walls. The great creature trod with care lest it trample them, bowing again before her. "We are yours," it said. "If you have need of us, invoke us in the name of Allah, and in the name of His Prophet, and by the seal of Suleiman—which although it never bound us, is still a great power among our people."

"I thank you," she said, bowing in return, "and wish you and your kin well, wherever you may go."

"Some of us will always be near you," said the jinni. It bent the great golden orbs of its eyes upon her. "Pure spirit. Blessed of Allah. May He protect and keep you—as we shall do, for the wonder of your existence."

"What—" she began. "I am not—" But the jinni was gone, leaving behind a swirl of wind and a faint scent of heated bronze.

She rounded on Ahmad, only to find that he was almost gone himself—downward into the house, with a glance that bade her follow. She could be contrary and refuse, or she could be sensible and let herself be led.

*   *   *

The house was precisely as she remembered it: a place of beauty and grace, order and peace. Servants were waiting as if they had been expecting her; they greeted her gladly, as a familiar and much loved guest. They took her away to be bathed, pampered, fed—the ritual without which no hospitality was complete. She could hardly object to it. The bath alone was a blessing beyond price; she had dreamed for days of being clean and properly clothed.

They offered her a choice: garments of the east or Frankish gown and chemise. She chose light trousers and long soft shirt and brocaded coat, but not the veil that lay folded on top of them. She did let a shy and tongue-tied eunuch plait her hair and suspend a jewel between her brows, an amethyst almost exactly the same color as her eyes.

They would have preferred that she sleep once she had eaten, but Ahmad was awake; her bones could feel it. "Take me to him," she said, and kept saying it until they obeyed.

He reclined on a divan in a room of green and golden tiles. His robe was of amber silk embroidered with creatures remarkably like the jinni that had brought them here. He too had bathed; his hair was still damp, his eyes soft as if he had slept while his servants tended him.

She planted her feet, ignoring the servant who tried to coax her into a chair, and stood with fists on hips, glaring at Ahmad. He blinked like a cat, deceptively lazy, and smiled in return.

"Tell me what you did," she said. "Why are the greater spirits worshipping me? What did you tell them? Why did you—"

"They wagered with me," he said, "that a human could not be a pure spirit. I assured them that one human could. It appears they agreed. Now you have the fealty of the armies of air. It's a great gift, and may prove useful."

"It was a *wager*?" She could have hit him. "What would you have had to pay if you'd lost?"

He shrugged. "Nothing unduly terrible. A year and a day in their service."

"A year and a day," she said, "in the middle of a war. Love's a sickness, they say, and I believe it. I am not worth that much."

"You will pardon me, lady," he said silkily, "but you may not be the best judge of that. In any event I won the wager. I gained you powers that you will be glad to have."

"Powers that I could use against you and yours, to win victory for my brother. That wasn't simply foolish, my lord. It was stupid."

He stiffened. She rather hoped that he would lash out, but he was too much in control of himself—now that he had no compelling need to be. "Time will prove either the wisdom or the stupidity of my choices," he said.

"I hope for your sake that they were wise."

"As do I," he said with the flicker of a smile. "Lady, will you sit? Be comfortable? Forgive me a little?"

She did not want to do any of those, but a belated sense of courtesy convinced her at least to take the chair the servant had left before bowing himself out of the room. "We can't be doing this," she said. "We're on opposite sides of a war."

"So we are," he said. "Does it matter?"

"It should!"

"Ah," he said. Just that.

"I don't know," she said through clenched teeth, "how I can love a person so much, and want so very badly to throttle him."

He grinned, so sudden and so startling that she could only sit and gape. "Why, that's passion, beloved."

"It's my father's thrice-bedamned temper," she snarled: "the black heart of Anjou. Aren't you glad I come by it honestly?"

"I am glad you are in the world, however you came there," he said.

"And I," she said, "cannot help—"

Words were feeble; words were useless. She abandoned her chair to kneel beside him. He did not resist, at all, as she drew him close. He tasted of cloves and honey.

It was a tearing pain to draw back, to separate herself from him. "Your wives," she said. "Your children. Where—"

"In Egypt," he said. "All but Safiyah. She is here. A handful of my sons are with my brother. Would you meet them?"

"Would they meet me?"

"They would be honored beyond measure," he said.

"Because you order it?"

"Because you are yourself." He took her hand and kissed it, a brush of lips so light and yet so potent that it shivered in her bones. "The Christians' humility—it's a contagion. You should shake it off; see yourself as you are. Glorious. Splendid. Beautiful and beloved."

He was making her dizzy. "Beautiful," she echoed. "Beloved."

"Wonderful," he said.

"I can't," she said. "I can't resist. I can't be sane or sensible. I can only love you."

"Why should you want to resist? This is the will of God."

"Is that what it is? It's like a wind from heaven. I'm blown like a leaf."

"Yes," he said, loosing the word in a sigh.

"We do believe in fate," she said. "But also that we can choose. I—choose—"

He silenced the rest. He was gentle, but he was not either tentative or shy. This was an art he knew well.

She knew only what she had heard and seen. She had never properly understood it. It was a clumsy and rather ridiculous thing to look at, but to be in the midst of it . . .

She had lived in this body for twenty-odd years. She thought she had known all its quirks and foibles, and all the things that pleasured and pained it. She had never known the full round of its senses. Brush of lips and tongue across bared breast; flutter of fingers down her belly. Murmur of words that were both prayer and love song, gusting breath across skin that felt eerily transparent.

She knew then that she was beautiful, because he knew it. *With my body I thee worship* . . . words that had intrigued her in the Christians' wedding rite, because they were so utterly pagan. Now she understood them. They were truth.

If she had stayed in Gwynedd, this would have come to her years since, in a holy rite, at the hands of a priest of the old gods. She was glad that she had been kept from that; glad that she had waited, to have this gift to give him, whose soul had been part of hers from before time.

From that memory of life upon life, she drew a memory of art and skill, mingling instinct with remembrance and finding the steps in the dance. She was all bare; he was still in shirt and trousers: Muslim modesty. She found laces and fastenings. The fine muslin slipped free.

Men's bodies she knew; she had healed a myriad of them. But this was his, all his own, and therefore hers. His skin was fair where the sun never touched it. He was not a massive man, but he was well made, supple and strong: a rider, a swordsman, born and bred to war. She traced the lines of scars, memories of old wounds, and a knot in his arm that spoke of the bone broken and knit somewhat awry.

If he had come to her for mending, the bone would have set straight. He saw the thought: his eyes glinted. She bit him, but lightly; he barely flinched.

Wildness rose up in her. She grappled, rolling him onto his back, holding him still with her weight. He was still laughing inside. The heat of his body warmed the length of hers. She was suddenly aware of her breasts pressed to his breast, and her hips to his hips, and—

She shifted. He moved to match her. Her breath caught at sudden pain, but she did not recoil for more than an instant. Her body began the slow rocking rhythm that she had seen . . . often enough. Now she knew why people did it so. The body knew.

His breathing came quicker now, but he kept the same slow rhythm, letting her settle to it. He was guiding her, oh so subtly, just as he taught her magic. There was magic in it, a magic of body matched to body and heart to heart.

It was she who quickened the pace, with an urgency that seized and mastered her. Her whole mind and being were centered on the joining of bodies, on the throb of the flesh, on the manifold incarnations of pleasure, each more intense than the last, until with a cry of astonishment and triumph, it came to a crescendo.

She clung to it, craving it, but flesh was not strong enough to bear it. She dropped down gasping, racked with spasms that died away into the very center of her.

She blinked away completely unexpected and unwarranted tears. He had raised himself on his elbow, regarding her gravely, but with the faintest hint of a smile in the corner of his mouth. She had no strength to kiss it, but she could raise her hand to brush it with a fingertip. "Mine," she said. "You are mine. I'll share you, because there was so much of you before you knew me, so many duties, so many obligations—but you belong to me."

He arched a brow. "Indeed? Do I have a say in it?"

"No," she said.

He laughed. She loved his laughter: it was pure gladness. "Then I am bound. I belong to you. And you," he said, "to me."

"That goes without saying," she said.

CHAPTER TWENTY-FIVE

S ioned had studied magic before. Now she learned the full extent of it: all that was given to one who had bound her soul to that of another. Two had become one, and that one was greater than either.

How long she spent there, she never knew precisely. There were days, nights, but they did not match the sense in her bones of time's passing in the world beyond the garden. It seemed a wondrous while, yet never long enough to learn all that was to be learned—or to love in all the ways that she could love.

Safiyah was there, as he had said, but when she was not teaching the way of arts and powers, she kept to herself. It was deliberate; when Sioned, struck with guilt, ventured to call on her outside of lessons, her door would not open. "This is your time," said the eunuch who stood guard: "yours and his. Accept it as a gift, and savor it to the full. It will not come to you again."

That was Safiyah's voice speaking through the eunuch's tongue and lips. Sioned bowed to it and to the will behind it, and, low and low, to the grace and generosity of the lady who given the gift.

*   *   *

"She was my first lover," Ahmad said, "and my teacher in all things. I owe her more than I can ever repay. Never pay it back, she tells me; give it in turn, and pass the knowledge to one who is worthy."

"As you both have done for me."

He kissed her, which distracted them both admirably, but she was too stubborn to let go of a thought once she had got hold of it. A good bit later, as she lay in his arms and he was sliding slowly into sleep, she said, "You have been beyond generous."

"On the contrary," he said, "I have been thoroughly selfish. You're the half of me, you see. How could I not give you all my heart and all my knowledge, and everything else that I can give?"

"But I've not given—"

"Remember what our teacher said to me," he said. "Don't give back. Give in return. That's the price and recompense of what we are."

He said the last of it from the edge of sleep. She lay watching him, loving the play of lamplight across his face, and thinking of what he had said. He was beyond hearing it, but she said it regardless: "Glory and splendor. That is what you are. I pray the gods I can be worthy of you both."

Sioned started awake. It was hours or days after she had spoken to Ahmad of gifts and giving—years, maybe; who knew? She was cold: she had risen from her bed some time since to read from the book of spells that Safiyah had given her, but somewhere between a charm against boils and an invocation of the hosts of heaven, she had fallen asleep.

She raised her head from the page and flexed her shoulders, wincing at the pain of cramped muscles. It was very late, though not quite dawn. A wan moon cast a lattice of light across the floor, shining in through the high window.

Had there been a moon before?

Something was standing in it. At first it was so insubstantial she thought it a trick of the moonlight, but little by little it grew more solid. It was no larger than a large man, and the shape it wore was that of a man, but horns grew from its brow; the hands it folded to its breast as it bowed low were fierce with ivory talons.

She met its eyes that were as yellow as a cat's, and knew which of the jinn it was. "My friend," she said in honest gladness. "Well met again. Are you well? Is all well in the world?"

The jinni smiled: an alarming sight to see such an array of fangs in a face that, for the most part, was human. "You are gracious, lady," he said—it was a he; she had not been certain before, but she was different now. She knew things that had been hidden, and understood much that had been obscure. "Your gladness makes me glad, though you may not be so happy when you hear the news I bring."

Her heart stopped. "Richard. My brother. Is he—"

"Safe," said the jinni, "as ever he was."

"Henry? Joanna?"

"Safe," the jinni said again, "and no war to put them in danger; not yet. The truce still holds, though not for much longer. The sultan will be needing his brother, for promises to make and break."

The words were like a gust of cold wind, a lash of reality amid the golden forgetfulness. "I've kept him too long. When morning comes, I'll tell him. I'll make him go."

"Not yet," said the jinni, "and not him. You."

"I? But—"

"The world changes," said the jinni. "Forces move. Look in my eyes and see."

She was not afraid to see the truth, she told herself as she met that golden stare. At first she saw only the yellow orbs and the fire of the spirit that inhabited them. Then the gold washed away before a flicker of images. Richard's face grinning out of a coif of mail, and a caravan of easterners under guard, and all their wealth heaped at his feet. Eleanor in a sunlit bower, listening to a player on a lute, but in her eyes was darkness visible. Conrad in his council chamber, alone but for his most trusted servant.

That servant was a man of Conrad's age, his milkbrother; they had nursed at the same teat and grown in the same hall, and knew each other as well as any two men in the world. Yet as she watched through the jinni's eyes, she saw how the man was when Conrad's attention was not on him. The same darkness that was in Eleanor was in him.

She followed the track of it through the eyes into the spirit, and thence to a place of eerie and otherworldly beauty. The Garden of the Assassins: Ahmad had shown it to her so that she could know of it and be warned. He had shown her its master, too, the man who had surrendered his soul for the sweet kiss of power.

He was, to the first and most shallow glance, simply a strong old man dressed all in white. But there were depths upon depths to him. The fanatical warrior of Allah: he had been that, long ago, until he found another power that would serve him better: the sorcerer, the master of dark magic, crouched like a spider in its web, ruling a world of shadows and secrets. He served the power that lived in the earth, the old dark one, shadow and serpent, tempter and betrayer, enemy of all that walked in the light.

He had found the fount of Paradise, and sworn fealty to the Serpent. Iblis; Sathanas. Set of Egypt, doomed and destroyer. There was dark joy in his service, and a black splendor in the freedom that he granted: freedom from guilt, from shame, from fear of doing harm.

Oh, it was tempting. Eleanor had offered Sioned a taste of it, but this was the full draught of the fountain. She had power; she was a mage, and growing stronger, the more she honed her skill. Yet there were restraints and strictures, paths that were forbidden, powers that she was not to invoke. There were no strictures on this. She could do whatever she pleased, with all the power that she could ever wish for.

All the kingdoms of earth, she thought. This land had been a battleground for powers of light and dark since the world began. Everything was stronger here. Hate, love. Evil, good. Death and life.

It was no great virtue that turned her away from that temptation. It was the memory of Ahmad's touch, the way he had of brushing his fingers over her skin, so light it was barely to be felt, but that delicacy of sensation was a subtle and exquisite pleasure.

Christians made a sin of the body's delight. Islam knew better. Love of the body was every man's duty, and the obligation of every woman. God had wrought it as His most wonderful creation.

She found her way back to her body. It was still sitting in the moonlit chamber, with the book of spells open before it and the jinni regarding her with wide yellow eyes.

"Conrad," she said. "He's in danger. And I'm supposed to care? He was about to put me to death."

"The world changes," the jinni said as he had before.

Spirits did not think as humans thought. "Were you not supposed to serve me?" she asked this one.

The jinni bowed low. "We serve you, I and mine."

"It serves me to keep Conrad out of danger?"

The jinni bowed again.

She could not be angry. As well be angry at the wind. "I must speak with my lord," she said.

The jinni made no objection. He melted into the moonlight, just as the moon set. He would return, but not for a little while.

That day she was much occupied in the conjuring of spirits, but not of the jinn; Safiyah expected that she master the lesser elementals and the small powers of earth and water and air. At night Ahmad was unusually ardent; he took her out of all memory, into a world that was only the two of them. In what brief moments of clarity she had, she wondered if he knew that this time of peace was ending; but she turned away from the thought.

She let herself forget the jinni's words. A small niggle in her center, a minute pang of guilt, impinged on her now and then, but stronger than that was the determination that she would not leave this place out of time. Not until she absolutely must.

Most nights there was no moon in this world beyond the world, but there were always stars. They wheeled in patterns that seemed subject to Safiyah's will, or occasionally to Ahmad's.

Tonight there was a moon, almost but not quite full. It was waxing: there was a quality to its light, a sense of rising to culmination, which was clear to her newly opened eyes. Its light spread in a pool at her feet.

She had been asleep beside Ahmad. Somewhere, she still was. But her awareness was alone in the room full of moonlight. She stepped into the pool. Light swelled up over her and drowned her.

It was night in Tyre as it was here: a night of moonlight and frustration. The lady of Tyre was in her bath—endlessly. Her lord, waiting to dine with her, began to grow faint with hunger. He left her to her pursuit of cleanliness and scented beauty—with some hope of recompense later—and went on his own pursuit of dinner.

The daymeal in the citadel was long over. The lady's dinner was not ready, because she had not yet called for it. "Although, my lord," said the maid who brought the message, "if you'll wait a while, I'm sure we can—"

"Never mind," said Conrad in a fit of sudden pique. "If you can't feed me now, I'll find someone who will."

"My lord," his servant said. "I'm thinking I know who'll feed you before you starve. Your friend the Bishop of Beauvais—you know how his cook is; sometimes they dine halfway to midnight."

Conrad clapped loyal Giacomo on the shoulder. "Good man! Come, we'll see if milord bishop has a place left at his table."

"He does set a good one," Giacomo said with a sigh of

remembrance. "That way his cook has with lamb, garlic, a bit of thyme . . . ah!"

"Ah indeed," said Conrad. "Quick, fetch my cloak and a torch. We're going calling on his grace."

Giacomo nodded and smiled and bowed, but his eyes were veiled.

Conrad took no more escort than the one man. It was quite unlike his wariness, but it was late, the city was quiet, and once his temper had calmed, he was in a remarkably cheerful mood.

"The messenger today," he said as they left the citadel behind, walking down by torchlight through the moonlit streets: "the one who purported to come from Acre, who insisted on talking to me alone—he actually came from the English king. The rumor we've heard is true, he said. Richard has offered to make Guy king of Cyprus—if Guy will give up his claim to Jerusalem. He asked me if I would be willing to consider the title, if Guy surrenders it."

"Wonderful news, my lord," said Giacomo, "if it's true."

"I believe it is," Conrad said. "Didn't you think the messenger had a remarkably exotic look to him, even for a man of Provence? He's not a Frenchman at all. In fact, when I pressed him, he confessed himself a Saracen—Richard's dog, the boy from Africa."

"My lord!" said Giacomo with evident surprise. "Why, his French is perfect."

"His Italian, too," said Conrad, "and his Latin, and I'm sure his Greek and Arabic as well. He has the gift of tongues. He assured me that this is no trick. Richard means what he says. He's taken thought on it, and he sees, finally, what we've seen for years—that Guy is an idiot. He can't have a fool bumbling about and getting in his way if he's going to take Jerusalem."

"So he means to do it at last," Giacomo said.

"By Pentecost," said Conrad. "With me beside him—if I'll go. If he gives me the crown and the kingdom and enough of the loot from the caravans he's been capturing lately, I'll be his dearest ally."

"I should like to see you crowned king in Jerusalem, my lord," Giacomo said.

"Most likely I'll be crowned in Acre," said Conrad, "but who's to stop us from doing it again when we have Jerusalem?"

He was frankly lighthearted. Even when he came to the bishop's house and found the bishop gone to bed and the tables being cleared away, and not a scrap or a morsel to spare for a poor starving lord, he only laughed. "No, don't drag his grace out of bed," he said to the servants, "nor the cook, either. Maybe when I get home, my lady will finally be out of the bath."

They pressed a cup of wine on him, which he drank down for courtesy; much warmed and rather tipsy, he forayed again into the night.

The moon was higher, but the dark seemed deeper. It coiled in the streets, with a dank scent about it, like sea fog. Tendrils of it crawled in Conrad's wake, dimming the light of the servant's torch. The walls of houses and shops closed in; the streets seemed ever narrower, winding and twisting and knotting upon one another.

Very occasionally they met other passersby, shadowed figures hastening toward light and safety. None of them offered a threat, or likely recognized the lord of the city wandering alone but for a single servant.

He came round a corner not far from the citadel, walking quickly now for his stomach was in open revolt, and ran headlong into a pair of men in monks' cowls. They recoiled; Conrad cursed under his breath, favoring a foot that had been trampled.

One of them peered at him in the torchlight and mimed broad delight. "My lord! What good fortune. We were just looking for you. A letter's come, it's very urgent, see—Brother Iohannes here, he has it, safe in his breast."

Conrad frowned. Giacomo was close at his back with the torch, which had begun to gutter and smoke. A gust of that smoke blew suddenly into his eyes; he coughed, gagging a little, but when he tried to retreat from the smoke, Giacomo stumbled against him. The monks drew in closer, the silent one fumbling in his robes.

Inadvertently, as it seemed, the three of them had trapped

him. His hand groped for his dagger, but Giacomo was in his way, catching at him, tangling him in his own mantle.

He never saw the blade that killed him. It stabbed up from beneath, under the breastbone and into the heart. His last sight in the world was of Giacomo's face; his last word a question: "Why?"

"Power," said Giacomo, "and glory."

Conrad was dead before Giacomo had said the last of it. Giacomo let him fall sprawling in the street, and spat on him. "That for love," he said. "That for a lifetime of groveling. I sold your soul for Paradise."

"And you shall have it," said the monk who had not spoken before.

Giacomo could not answer: the point of a dagger just touched the membrane of his heart. With a small grunt, the monk thrust it home.

CHAPTER TWENTY-SIX

Sioned fell headlong into her cold and barely breathing body. Someone was shaking it, slapping it, and shouting at it, which was a tremendous annoyance. She fended him off with a buffet of wind and a gust of temper.

The temper was stronger than she had meant. He flew backward and struck the wall with sickening force.

She scrambled out of the knotted bedclothes, heart in throat. He was conscious but badly winded; his face was greenish pale. She breathed strength into him and soothed his bruises as she could, reassuring herself that there was nothing broken.

She opened her mouth to speak, brimful of apologies, but he forestalled her. "Don't," he said. "Don't be sorry. I lost my wits; I of all people, who should know better. You were as near dead as made no difference. I should have known what it was, and been wiser than to startle you out of it."

"I had already come back," she said. "It was over—what I was taken to see." Even as she said it, the memory flooded and nearly drowned her. "I have to go. I can't stay. I have to—"

"Tell me," he said.

She did not know if she could, but once she got the first words out, the rest came in a rush. Every moment was as vivid as if she lived it anew. She saw more this time, sensed more: more darkness, more foreboding. Part of that was simply that she knew how it ended, but some was greater clarity of understanding. She knew who had done this. She could guess why.

Ahmad's face stilled as he listened, emptying of all expression. When she had told him all she knew, she left the rest to him: to speak or to be silent.

Dawn grew grey in the silence. The light of the nightlamp dimmed and paled.

The hour of prayer had come and gone, and he had done nothing about it. That shocked her a little. He was a good Muslim always, in all his observances.

The sun was nearly up when at last he spoke. "This is a terrible thing. It changes too much; sets too many forces at odds. And it is my fault."

"How can it be your fault?" she asked him.

"I . . . made a bargain," he said.

"With the jinn?"

"Before that," he said. "With the Old Man of the Mountain."

Her breath hissed between her teeth. "You, too? What did you sell him? Your soul?"

"I hope not," Ahmad said. "There is a price, but he has yet to name it. When the time came for him to take it, he said to me, I would know."

Sioned's head was aching. She forced herself to think clearly, to see everything that there was to see—and not to indulge in a fit of anger that he had kept this from her for so long.

When she could trust her voice and her powers of reason, she said, "I'm sure he wants you to think you had something to do with it—but I don't believe this is the price. It's too convenient for too many people, and it serves your cause too well. Whatever he wants of you, it's not your ease or benefit."

"This isn't the price," Ahmad said. "This is the thing I paid for. I told him the name of the one I hated, and the reason for the hatred. The rest I left to him. This guilt is on my head; this debt of the spirit is mine to pay."

"I don't think so," she said stubbornly. "I have guilt—somehow I was supposed to prevent it, or change it, and I turned my back. You did little to alter anything, except maybe to make it happen faster. Even that is my fault, since you did it for me."

He glared at her, but suddenly his face lightened; he laughed, if painfully. "We are clever, aren't we? We take the woes of the world on our shoulders."

"This is true," she said. "I caused this: your guilt; the marquis' death, though my bones tell me he was marked for it long before I set foot in Tyre."

"We are all at fault," said Ahmad. "We can't stay any longer. My brother is going to be wanting me beside him as the Franks tumble in disorder."

"My brother would probably prefer that I lose myself at the ends of the world," Sioned said, "but he'll have to suffer my presence regardless. After I go to Tyre."

That took him aback. "Tyre! Are you mad?"

"Probably," she said. "But Henry is there, unprotected."

"They'll kill you. They already believe that you committed murder; then you vanished in the midst of a phantom battle. Now their lord is dead, and you can wager that he was found with an Assassin's cake in his hand. If you show your face, they'll rend you limb from limb."

He spoke sense—altogether too much of it. But she thought now that she understood the jinni's message. It had not been about Conrad; it had been about Henry. "I have to go," she said.

She waited for him to thunder, "I forbid it!" But he knew her too well for that. He went quiet instead, lifted himself up with a soft groan, and greeted the servant who had come in with kaffé and new bread and a bowl of fruit stewed in honey with cloves and cinnamon.

The man's eyes were fixed on the toes of his slippers. Sioned realized that her only garment was her hair. She reached for the first thing that came to hand: one of the coverlets from the bed.

She was hungry—starving. Gods knew when she would eat again. Hakim was still refusing to look at her. She wheedled him into a smile, though not into raising his eyes; he was pleased to fetch the things she asked for.

Ahmad still had not said anything. His bath was ready; usually she shared it, and a grand sharing it was, but today she let him go to it alone. She could have left then, and maybe should have, but she wanted to bathe, too: a ritual cleansing, as it were, before she faced what she must face.

He was gone a long time. She began to suspect that he had seized the opportunity to escape without an open quarrel, but also without farewell. Her temper had risen to a fair pitch when he reappeared, clean, tidy, and dressed to travel.

She was still naked under the wrapped coverlet, with her hair in a tangle and a last bite of bread on its way to her mouth. He would have been well within his rights to regard her with disgust, but there was no such thing in his eyes. "I couldn't go," he said. "Not without a word."

"Good," she said, biting it off.

"Will you not consider coming with me? I'll deliver you safe to your brother, and together we can find a way to save your cousin in Tyre."

She shook her head. "It will take too long. Just let me go. I've got an army of the jinn; what harm can an army of men do to me?"

"Too much," he said grimly. "Sioned—beloved—"

"Don't you have a war to fight?"

"Not with you!"

They both stood astonished at his vehemence. For lack of anything better to do, she pulled him to her and kissed him, then thrust him away—truly away, through walls of worlds, into his camp that waited for him somewhere in the hills of Syria.

She had caught him off guard, or she could not have done it. It left her weak but not incapacitated: testimony to the training that she had had and the strength that she had gained—and her sheer outrageous luck, that she could have done this without disaster the first time she ever attempted it. Even sending him from warded place to warded place was dangerous. She could have destroyed them both.

But she had not. He was safe in his camp. He did not come roaring back as she had half dreaded. It seemed that he saw the sense in what she had done, once she had done it—or else he was too stark with rage to muster a counterattack.

There was a bath waiting, and clothes that were suited to a lady of the Franks. She must summon the jinn to protect her. Then she must go—but not before she had done one further thing.

Safiyah was in the room where they most often studied magic, the library with its trove of treasures. She had her small black servant with her; he was writing down words as she instructed, learning the language of magic as Sioned also had done. She finished the lesson before she acknowledged Sioned's presence: a courtesy to the pupil, and one that Sioned had known to expect. Fortunately for her sense of urgency, the lesson had been nearly done.

Then at last, having praised the child for his diligence and dismissed him to do as he pleased, Safiyah turned her attention toward Sioned.

Sioned had nothing to be ashamed of and nothing to hide, but she still felt like a child brought to account for a transgression.

Safiyah did not flay Sioned alive for her many sins. She simply said, "If you die, my lord will not be able to live."

"Your lord is a strong man. He has kin, wives, children, to all of whom he is devoted. He'll survive; he'll go on. He won't die."

"Nor will he live," Safiyah said. "Life will be a burden, dragging itself out from day to day, until death is a blessing."

"Time heals grief," Sioned said.

"Not when souls are torn apart," said Safiyah.

"What shall I do, then?" Sioned demanded. "Shut myself in a cave and never come out?"

"Be careful," Safiyah said. "Be as sensible as you can. Remember that men are not as strong as we are, for all their loud protestations to the contrary, and that while you could carry on, he could not. He loves you with all his heart, child, and without you he would have no heart left."

"Whereas I had none to begin with," Sioned muttered.

Safiyah's lips twitched. "We are colder than they, and harder. We're fiercer, too, and stronger in defense of what we love. You love your kin, and that is right and proper. Of course you must protect them. But protect yourself, too—for his sake."

"I can promise to try," said Sioned.

"That will do," Safiyah said. "Come back to us, child, when the world changes again. You have kin here, and people who love you. Remember that."

Sioned's throat was tight. She had come expecting a reprimand, and received only understanding. It was almost too much to bear.

She had no words to say. She took the thin hands and kissed them, and embraced the frail body—so strong within, so fragile without—and left before she lost her composure altogether.

CHAPTER TWENTY-SEVEN

Mustafa should have left Tyre as soon as he had delivered Richard's message, but it was late and he was tired, and whatever the marquis' faults, he treated royal messengers well. There was food that a Muslim could eat, and a sleeping place in the hall—though before he could claim that, a page tugged at his sleeve.

The lord Henry had a room to himself, and servants who were his own, and guards to keep him there. But he could bring a guest in, offer him such hospitality as a man could accept whose religion did not allow him to drink wine, and give him sleeping room if he would take it.

"Do you know where she is?" Henry asked when it was polite to speak of anything but trivialities.

"I know that she escaped from here," said Mustafa, "and that someone—or something—provided a diversion while she did it."

"It's said the Assassins came for her," said Henry, "or the Assassins' demons. But I would never believe that of her."

"It wasn't the King of the English," Mustafa said.

"She was meeting a man in the city," Henry said. His tone made Mustafa's eyes sharpen. "They said it was an Assassin— that she was performing foul rites with him, and plotting destruction. I think . . . it was someone she knew, and someone she maybe . . ."

Mustafa was not one to betray secrets, but he was moved to tell this man the truth. "It was the lord Saphadin. I went to him when she was captured; I told him what I had seen. He would have come for her, and taken her where she would be safe."

"Saphadin?" Henry looked as if Mustafa had struck the wind out of him. "The lord Al-Adil? The sultan's brother? God's bones!"

"You never suspected?"

"I didn't—" Henry raked fingers through his close-cropped hair. "She ran off with *him*?"

"Would you rather she had stayed and been executed?"

"No!" Henry snapped in an unwonted fit of temper.

"Then you can be glad that she's safe. I'm sure she is that— wherever she is."

"He could save her," Henry said, sinking down onto the bed, weighted with gloom. "He could sweep in with armies of God knows what, and carry her off like a knight in a song. And what could I do? I sat here, not even chained. I would have let her die!"

Mustafa had no comfort to offer, except to remind Henry of the truth. "She didn't die. You would have if you'd tried to stand between the marquis and his prey."

Henry was little comforted, but at least he was quiet. He did not move or speak as Mustafa retreated to a corner for his evening prayer, then spread a blanket and lay on it, determined to get what sleep he could.

He was uneasy. It was nothing he could put a name to, nor did it have anything to do with the city itself. This was something different. Something was stirring. Maybe Conrad had awakened it when he cast blame on the Assassins.

Conrad had not been at dinner. He was waiting to dine with his lady, people said. But Isabella was in a strange mood this evening. Mustafa had seen her before she went up to her rooms, seen how odd her expression was, as if she walked in a dream. He had paid no attention to it then; he had been preoccupied with finding Henry.

As he lay in the corner of Henry's room, the memory began to haunt him. Dark had fallen beyond the walls; the night was deep and preternaturally quiet. The revelry in the hall had died early. He tossed on his blanket.

Henry had gone to bed; he was motionless behind the curtains. His breathing was deep and regular. If he was not asleep, he feigned it well.

The door was barred, the window too small for even Mustafa's narrow body. He was imprisoned here until the guards without chose to let Henry go.

It had been terribly foolish of him to trap himself here when he could have been in the hall, free to come and go. He could only wait and try to pray, and hope that whatever was in the air, it would not harm him or the man in the bed, who had begun, very softly, to snore.

A sudden tumult brought Mustafa staggering to his feet. He had slept a little after all; his mind was thick with fog. People were shouting, screaming, crying. He strained to catch words amid the babble. When he succeeded, at first he did not believe what he heard. "Conrad! Conrad is dead!"

Henry lurched through the curtains of his bed, as bleared and astonished as Mustafa. He had slightly more presence of mind: he hammered on the door until the bolt shot back and a wild-eyed guard peered in. "We're going out," Henry said to him.

There was a breathless pause. Mustafa would not have been surprised if the guard had gutted Henry with his pike, or if he had slammed the door shut and refused to open it again. But the man either had the habit of obedience, or was wise enough to be afraid of Henry's hot blue glare. He scrambled back out of the way before Henry ran him down.

*   *   *

The hall was in an uproar. Henry cut through the crowd with his bulk and the power of his rank; Mustafa clung as close as he could. They mounted the dais, man and shadow; Henry raised his voice in a bellow that overwhelmed the lot of them.

His gimlet eye fixed on one man who seemed most distraught, but who had found his way to a sort of calm. "Tell us," Henry said.

Word by word, Henry got it out of him. The marquis had gone to dine with his friend the bishop, but that was long hours ago. His squire at last had gone looking for him, and had stumbled over him, sprawled in the middle of a street. There was a black dagger in his heart and a cake clutched in his hand, still warm—though that was impossible; the corpse was stone-cold.

The squire had paused for a fit of hysterics, which had brought out the watch. Where they had been while their lord was stabbed to death, God knew—or Satan; for this was surely the handiwork of his servants. They were making up for lost time now, having sent a man to the castle with the news while they brought the lord's body back more slowly.

Half the city seemed to have followed them. It sounded like a storm coming, a long low rolling sound shot through with shrieks and wailing. The hall was silent, listening. Eyes rolled white; faces were stiff with fear.

"*She* did it," someone muttered. "She came back—she and her allies. She finished what she started."

One instant Henry was on the dais, listening as intently as the rest. The next, he was down among the throng, fingers clamped about the man's throat. "No woman's hand was in this," Henry said in a low growl that managed to reach the farthest edges of the hall. "Least of all hers. She was an innocent, condemned by one man's jealousy. You can thank the Lord God that some good angel came to her rescue."

The man gasped for breath. His face had gone an ugly shade of crimson. Henry raked his glare across the hall. "There will be no more lies spoken in this place. I take command here until the succession shall be settled; I bid you therefore withdraw and wait, all but the marquis' personal guard and the members of his council. When morning comes, there will be orders and dispositions. For now, take what rest you can. You will be needing it."

Henry was an affable young man, with an easy manner and a light touch with the servants. But when he took command, men obeyed before they could think to resist. The hall cleared with remarkable swiftness and not a word of grumbling—though Mustafa was sure there would be plenty of that once men were out of Henry's sight.

He did not consider himself dismissed. He was invisible in Henry's shadow. Someone would have to get word to Richard, but he was not offering himself for the task.

Nor did Henry ask him. He called for a courier, and when one came, wide awake and dressed to ride, he had prepared a letter by his own hand, brief and to the point:

> To my lord Richard, King of the English, Duke of Normandy, Count of Anjou, and all the rest of it: Conrad is dead. We suspect Assassins. I've taken command here. Come if you can, or send someone with power to speak for you. But whatever you do, do it quickly.

He signed it with a flourish and sealed it with the ring that he wore, which he had taken from a Saracen emir. It was not a Muslim thing, nor yet a Christian. Mustafa thought it must be of old Rome: a tiny and perfect carving of a running stag.

The courier took the letter, bowed over it, and tucked it securely in his satchel. He did not wait to be dismissed.

Henry had already turned away from him. The marquis' body had come home at last, borne on a hastily cobbled bier—it proved, beneath the silken coverlet that must have been torn from some wealthy citizen's bed, to be a wooden door, taken no doubt from that same citizen's house.

Conrad was most certainly dead. The cake in his hand had finally gone cold, and the dagger was still in his heart, thrust up from beneath the breastbone.

Somewhere, women were wailing, loudly mourning the dead. But not here. Not his lady, who came to stand over him.

She had taken time to dress and to paint her face, so that she was the image of a royal lady, as flawless as if carved in ivory. She looked long at the body of her husband, but did not touch it. Her face wore no expression.

No one ventured to speak while she stood there. They were all eyeing this lady who carried in her the right to the throne of Jerusalem. Already eyes were sharpening, glances darting, as men weighed one another, reckoning their chances.

When she looked up at last, her gaze came to rest on Henry. He was watching her quietly, but Mustafa did not see any such heat in him as radiated from her. He must know that she wanted him: she had been as open about it as she dared in front of so jealous a husband. Did he know how strong that wanting was?

Most likely he did not. He bowed over her hand, courteous as always, but there was no passion in his glance. "Lady," he said, "please accept my condolences. If there is anything you wish, any command—"

"Find the ones who did this," she said. "See that they pay."

"Certainly we shall do that, lady," Henry said.

She looked hard at him, as if searching for more; he met her gaze with cool politeness. Her shoulders sagged visibly. She raised her hand to her brow; she swayed.

He caught her before she fell, and assisted her to a chair. Servants brought wine and cool cloths and wafts of perfume.

It was artfully done, but it did not touch Henry's heart. She gave it up soon enough and let the council settle to business. There was a funeral to arrange—quickly in this climate—and policy to decide, beginning with the securing of the city against attack.

Mustafa had come round to a decision of his own. He was not needed here, nor were they saying anything that he needed to hear. He would be more interested to know what people were saying outside of this hall and in the city. Conrad's death altered the balance in this precarious country—though in which of several directions, he could not be certain.

Just as he began to slip away, a new commotion brought all eyes to the door.

Wherever she had been, it seemed to have agreed with her. She had a bloom on her, and a light in her eyes that made Mustafa blink, dazzled—and he was not a man for women. She was dressed in Frankish fashion in cream-pale linen and violet silk; her veil was a drift of mist over her elegantly coiled and plaited hair. There was just a hint of paint on her face, of kohl about her eyes.

She did not come alone. Her guards wore Frankish mail and white surcoats without device. They were tall and broad as Franks could often be, with pale stern faces within the coifs of mail. But their eyes were not Frankish eyes, nor indeed were they mortal at all. They were the precise and burning blue that lives in the heart of a flame.

Mustafa resisted a powerful urge to fall down on his face. These were great lords of the jinn, or he had no eye for magic. And she . . . she had grown. She had been a fair apprentice of the art when last he saw her. She was considerably more than that now.

None of the Franks could see what Mustafa saw. They believed the illusion: that she came escorted by men of their own kind. It both reassured them and deterred them from seizing her and executing the late marquis' sentence.

Henry leaped up from his seat with a complete lack of self-consciousness and ran to pull her into his embrace. There was passion; there was the fire of the heart.

She returned the embrace with every evidence of gladness and deep relief, but it was the gladness of kin restored to kin. She was the first to free herself, to hold him at arm's length and smile. "I'm glad beyond words to see you well," she said.

"And I," he said. "Saints and angels! Lady, your loss was sorely felt."

"Not as sorely as if I'd left my head on the executioner's block," she said dryly.

His face darkened. "You're in no danger here. You have my word on that."

"So I can see," she said, looking about at guards and council, who were staring as if they could not help themselves. As her glance passed Mustafa, she granted him the briefest flicker of a smile.

She spared no one else more than a moment's glance. She approached the bier on which Conrad lay and stood gazing down at him as his wife had, with almost the same lack of expression; but hers had a distinct scent of brimstone beneath. "He learned a hard lesson," she said.

"The hardest of all," said Henry. "It will be a long while before another man uses the name of Masyaf to conceal his own transgressions."

She nodded. Her eyes lifted to Isabella then. "Lady. Insofar as you suffer grief, I offer you condolences."

Isabella inclined her head with icy graciousness. "Have you come to help us, then?" she inquired.

"If I can," said Sioned, "yes. And if you will permit."

"Can I prevent you?"

"You can send me away," Sioned said. "Now that I know my cousin is safe, I'll go, and offer no objection."

That tempted Isabella: her eyes yearned for it. But she was too wise and practical a princess. "Stay," she said. "Be pardoned for any sins against the realm or its late master. Help us if you can. When Islam gets word of this, it may find us ripe for the taking."

"Islam knows," Sioned said. One of the guards set a chair beside Henry; she sat in it, leaning toward the rest of them. "Richard is coming. If I'm to be listened to, I counsel that you guard your walls and wait until he comes. My lord of Burgundy, will you—can you—put aside your differences in this extremity?"

The duke flushed. "We are all Christians," he said stiffly, "sworn to the Crusade."

"It's good of you to remember it," she said.

"So should we all," said one of the lords of Tyre. He had been one of Conrad's traveling companions from the Italies; his name, Mustafa recalled, was Marco. He had the look of a pirate and the mind of a thief, but he was clever, as all of Conrad's intimates were. The late marquis had not been inclined to surround himself with stupid men.

Marco turned his shoulder to her, subtly cutting her off from his consideration, and faced Isabella. "Lady, however long it takes the English king to fight his way here, he should find a united city when he comes, under strong command. As much as it pains me to suggest it in the first flush of grief, it would be best if there were no gap in the succession. The power resides in you. Will you make use of it?"

Isabella arched a brow. "You offer me a choice? How unusual. Is that wise?"

"We trust that you will choose wisely," Marco said.

"What if I should elect to return to my first husband?"

Marco smiled. Others blanched slightly, but one or two tittered: the light, false laughter of courtiers. "I'm sure that peerless gentleman and scholar would be pleased to take you, although he has been heard to observe that in his worst nightmares he finds himself crowned and set on a throne."

"We all know Humphrey has no desire to be king," Henry said, "which makes him unique among the men of this Crusade. I rather admire him for it, myself."

"And you?" asked Isabella. "Would you take a throne if it were offered?"

"That would depend," said Henry, "on whether the throne was worth taking."

"You don't think Jerusalem is worth the cost?"

"Lady," he said, "you ask difficult questions. But then Jerusalem is a difficult kingdom. Would I be King of Jerusalem? That does tempt me. Will you give me time to think about it?"

"You may have a little time," she said. "But not too long. I believe this murder is meant to cast us into disarray. If we draw together instead under even stronger leadership than before, and pursue the war without wavering until the end, we win far more than a city or a tomb. We win the respect of our enemies, and teach them never again to take us lightly."

Henry bowed to her as deeply as a knight should to a queen.

"By tomorrow I shall know my decision. If you choose another man meanwhile, and that man will make a strong king, I will give my service to him in all good heart."

"I won't choose another," she said, too soft almost to be heard.

Maybe he heard her; maybe he did not. He bowed again and turned back to the council, which focused now on the matter of defending the city against the possibility of attack.

Mustafa slipped out soon after that. So, as he discovered, did Sioned.

Her jinn had not accompanied her, which was a greater relief than he could have expressed. He was interested to notice that her silken mantle was lined with plain dark wool, and that with its hood over her head and its drab folds wrapped about her, she made a convincing serving maid.

She caught him in a quiet corridor and pulled him into a tight embrace, then kissed him on both cheeks.

"Lady!" he protested. "What was that for?"

"For fetching the last man I thought I wanted to see," she said, "and indirectly for saving me from the axe. That was enormously insubordinate of you."

"I'm not *your* dog," Mustafa said. "I was looking out for my skin. Your brother would flay it off me if I let you come to harm."

"Obviously he didn't," she observed, "or you wouldn't be here. It even seems he trusts you."

Mustafa shrugged uncomfortably. "I told him what I'd done. Once he'd thrown me across his tent and bellowed at me until I couldn't hear properly for a week, he granted that I hadn't done too hopelessly mad a thing."

"Then he got you out of his sight by sending you here," she said.

"Not immediately," said Mustafa. "I ran errands to the sultan for a while, then he had me scouting raiding parties between Jaffa and Ascalon until he called me back for this. I was offering the marquis the crown of Jerusalem."

"Her ladyship has offered it to my cousin," Sioned observed. "My friend, will you do a thing for me? You're free to refuse. Will you go to Acre and tell the Queen of the English everything that has happened here, exactly as you've heard and seen it?"

Mustafa felt the blood drain from his face. "You'd send me to *her*? You *are* angry with me!"

"Only a very little," she said. "You don't have to go. I'll send one of my guards in any case—he'll be proof that I have authority to speak to her. But the message will be more convincing if it comes from you. You're Richard's man; she knows that. You carry his trust as well as mine."

"You mean that she won't eat my soul if she knows her son will object."

Sioned bit her lip. She was trying not to laugh, he could see. "The queen is a great and formidable power in the world, but she is not an eater of souls."

"Would you stake your own on that?"

That killed the laughter, though it did not dismay her as much as he had hoped. "She could seduce me to darker powers than I ever want to know, but she'll let me make the choice. She won't touch you. You're far more useful as you are."

Mustafa was dubious, but he could not refuse her. Nor could he yield to cowardice, however prudent it might be. "I'll go," he said, "and pray you tell the truth, or I'll haunt you ever after."

She grinned at that. "You would be good company," she said. "Go with your God, dear friend. Come back as quickly as you can."

CHAPTER TWENTY-EIGHT

Richard and Eleanor arrived together, having met on the road half a day's journey from the city. Both had made great speed; it was only the third day since Conrad was found dead.

The marquis had been buried the day before, laid in a tomb in the cathedral of the city. The mourning for him had had an air of ritual; he was not a man whom people loved. Still there were many who regretted his passing, because he was a strong lord and he would have been a competent king.

Isabella received Henry the evening before the king and the queen came to Tyre. She awaited him in the solar of the castle, in perfect propriety, attended by a pair of maids and a watchful guard. Henry came alone, still in the somber robes he had worn to the funeral and to the feast that followed it.

She was in white, the color of eastern mourning. It paled her gold-and-ivory beauty, and aged her, so that he could see clearly the shape of the bones beneath the skin. She was even more beautiful for that, and even more queenly.

She was very desirable. And yet he had to say, "Lady, I came to beg your pardon. This is a greater decision than I can make alone. Will you wait a little longer, until I've spoken with my cousin the king?"

She was disappointed, that was clear. But he had not refused her. He hoped that comforted her. She inclined her head, granting both pardon and petition. When she spoke, it was of other things: the weather, which was growing hot; the gardens of the castle, which were blooming; the funeral, which had been properly grave and dignified.

It was not easy conversation. She had the art of pleasant speech, but there were stiff moments and awkward pauses. They were strangers, amiable enough but he felt no spark between them. He was rather shamefully relieved when she dismissed him.

"Need that matter?" Sioned asked.

He had not sought her out, not exactly, but one way and another he had found himself in the room where she was. It was a stillroom; she was brewing something pungent, and grinding something even more pungent in a mortar. It was remarkable, he thought, how quickly she had made herself at home here; and how, without the need to pretend to the marquis that she was a lady, she had fallen back into her old self. People had learned quickly to come to her for doctoring, although there were half a dozen noble physicians in the castle. None of them, as one of her patients averred in his hearing, knew half as much plain and useful medicine as she did.

One of the guards who had arrived with her was always nearby, looming and silent. Henry had not heard a word out of either of them in two days. They had something to do with her safety here; exactly what, he was afraid to ask.

Instead he found himself telling her of his conversation with Isabella. He had always been able to talk to her easily, fluently, never at a loss for words. Their silences were companionable.

"Need it matter?" she asked him now. "Marriage is a union of great houses, a binding of wealth to wealth. It makes no difference if you can't carry on a conversation, if you can share a realm and make heirs together."

"She didn't love the marquis," Henry said. "She loved the lord Humphrey, I think, in her way, but he never wanted to be king, and was never suited to it."

"Some priests will tell you love is a sin," she said with a slant of the eyes that made him smile in spite of himself. "Marriage is for getting children, there's no more to it than that. She's beautiful; she must be pleasant to the touch. You can do your duty by her, surely?"

"I can be a stud bull if that's what's required of me." He did not know why he should be so cross. He was being offered a beautiful lady, and with her a crown and a kingdom. He should be beside himself with joy. Instead he was in this small and odorous stillroom, telling his troubles to the woman who—

The woman who—

She did not know. Nor did she share it. Her heart was given to the knight of the Saracens. When she looked at him, she saw a dear friend, but never what he wanted her to see. Never a lover.

She had no lands or property to bring him. She was no blood relation, but the Church in its convolutions of logic would call her kin because her father had married his grandmother. Consanguinity: so convenient when a man wanted to be rid of an inconvenient wife, and so simple when he needed a reason not to marry a particular woman. But how could he find reason not to love her?

"I told her highness that I'll talk to Richard," he said after that slight but significant pause. "It's a coward's way, I suppose, but I couldn't think of anything better to say. I should take what she offers. It's splendid—royal. Troublesome, too, but when did I ever shrink from a challenge?"

"You would make a good king," she said. "Better than Conrad. You're younger; prettier. People love you. You know how to lead them, and how to command them."

"Are you telling me I should do this?"

She shrugged. "How many men are given a kingdom and a

bride all at once? It's an ungodly short widowhood for her, but this is a war; the wise act quickly or not at all."

"I don't think I'm wise," Henry said. He sat on the bench where the sick or wounded sat to wait for her, head in hands.

"What do you want to do?" she asked him. "If you had free choice, what would you choose?"

"You don't want to know," he said.

"Don't you want to be a king?"

"I would be glad to be a king."

"But not with that queen?"

He was silent.

"I think you would learn to love her," she said, "and certainly to respect her. She'll be a strong queen to your strong king."

"If we have a kingdom to rule."

"You can bring the Crusade together, you and Richard. Enlist the French again, gather them all, raise the army and take Jerusalem."

He lifted his head. "If Richard delivers as rousing a speech as that, I'll be taking the cross of Crusade all over again."

"You should all take the cross again," she said, "before you fritter away the rest of this Crusade."

"God's feet," he said, but mildly. "You have a hard heart."

"I'm old Henry's daughter. I come by it honestly."

A bark of laughter escaped him. "I came here for comfort and you gave me a call to arms. Is this how you heal the sick?"

"I give them the medicine they need," she said. She finished grinding her powders and poured them into the pot, stirring carefully so as not to spill a drop. The pungency rose to an eye-watering stench, then with startling suddenness, transmuted to a clear green fragrance, like new grass with a hint of wood violets.

"Magic," he said. He caught her hand quickly and kissed it, and left her to her various enchantments.

They came in the morning, the king and the queen together. They well knew the uses of royal pomp; because they came to a place of mourning, they muted the brightness of their banners and hung their shields and lances and the caparisons of the horses with black. Yet they were still splendid in the bright sun of spring, crowned with gold, Richard on his golden charger and his mother on a snow-white mare.

Eleanor chose that day to put aside all pretense of weakness and ride as she had ridden fifty years ago, when she was young and sworn to another Crusade. For once she even outshone her son. There was no other queen in her train, not this time. She had left her daughter and her daughter-in-law behind.

She swept into the hall with the rest of her train borne head-long in her wake. So swiftly had she come, and with so little pause for ceremony, that Isabella—never the most punctual of women—was just coming down from her solar, intending to meet the royal guests at the gate.

She stopped short on the stair. Eleanor stood at the foot, haughtily erect, in deep blue to Isabella's stark white. "Madam," said the Queen of the English, "you would be late for the Last Trump."

Isabella bridled, but she was far too well-bred to reply in kind. She said with tight-drawn civility, "Majesties. Be welcome to my city."

"Yours indeed," said Eleanor, "and you've done well with it, under the circumstances. Now, if you please, call your council. We have matters to settle that will not wait."

Isabella had no power to stand against that force of nature which was Eleanor. She did as she was bidden, as did everyone when it was Eleanor doing the bidding.

The council met as swiftly as it could. One man was still in rid-ing clothes, another properly dressed but with his hair and beard in disarray. Yet once they had gathered, they had to wait upon the queen's pleasure. Richard came in soon enough, in hearty good humor and prepared to entertain all of them with tales of the new campaigns: Saracen raiders caught and killed, caravans captured and their riches taken into his treasury. But he did not begin the council.

Eleanor was not taking her ease. As soon as she had reached the suite of rooms that was judged fit for a lady of her rank, she sent one of the servants to fetch Henry. He was on his way to the hall; he allowed himself to be diverted, half in curiosity and half in fear. A summons from Eleanor was never to be taken lightly.

She had put off her traveling clothes and was being dressed for the council. Henry had been her page in his day; he fell all too easily into the role again, holding the mirror that traveled with her wherever she went, that was of pure polished silver. Her reflection in it had gained beauty in the dozen years since he last performed the service. "Freedom suits you," he said.

She smiled. He had forgotten how bright that smile could be; she was such a terrible force in the world, but when she was young, said those who could remember, she had been the most vivacious of women. "Freedom delights me," she said. "There's not a man alive now who can lock me away."

"None would dare," Henry said.

"Indeed," said Eleanor. "Now, sir. I've been fetched here by a most interesting message, delivered by a rather interesting messenger. I gather the council of Tyre has been kingmaking while the marquis is barely cold in his tomb?"

"They say," said Henry, "that time is of the essence; that the infidel will move soon, and there must be a strong Crusade to stand against him. No one is suggesting seriously that Guy be brought back from Cyprus. This kingdom needs another king."

"They say rightly," she said, "and they say that you have been offered both the crown and the hand of the lady who bears it."

"So I have," he said. "It's a tempting offer."

"Of course it is," said Eleanor. "Why haven't you accepted it?"

He fought a powerful urge to fidget like the child he no longer was. "I . . . reckoned that you would want a say in it."

"You reckoned rightly," she said, "but that would not have stopped you if your heart had been in it. Did you hope I would forbid it?"

"Would you, majesty?"

"If I did—would you turn against me?"

"No," he said. "No, lady. It's no small thing to be offered a crown, but I think I'm man enough to live without one."

"There is a way," she said, "to escape the difficulty. If the crown goes to another by right of war rather than marriage—if it goes to the great general, to the conqueror of Jerusalem—then his beloved nephew, the young and valiant knight, well might find himself next in succession."

Henry widened his eyes. He was not about to pretend that he did not understand her. "How will you—he—do that? Won't the fact that he already has a queen be an impediment?"

"Not if it's done as I foresee: by acclamation, by the will of the whole Crusade. Then Isabella will be bypassed altogether."

"But if there's no blood-right—"

"He is the liege lord of the last king," Eleanor said, "which gives him a certain right to claim whatever belongs to his vassal. And he has another, stronger right: the right of conquest. If he takes Jerusalem, what man will dare contest his taking of the title?"

"Does he want it?"

Eleanor smiled slowly. "He will."

"But, Grandmother," said Henry, knowing full well that he could be going too far, "does he even want to stay once he's won the city? Won't he go back home to Anjou and then to England? What if—"

"He will stay," said Eleanor, "if he must. If the price of victory is that he take the title and the duties that accompany it for a certain span, greater or lesser—he will do it. Then when the span is over and he sails home, some worthy successor will take the crown and the throne. That successor could be you."

"Would the successor be required to take the bride who bears the blood-right?"

"It would be politic," she said, "and practical as well. Her dowry is rich. But if that revolts you, there are convents in plenty that would be glad to count a queen among their number—and all the property that she can bring as her dower to God."

"That would be a waste," he mused not entirely reluctantly, "of lands and riches. Of beauty and wit, and I think a little wisdom."

"She's wise enough," Eleanor said with a wave of dismissal. "Do you want her, then? Would you be willing to take her on condition that you leave the crown to Richard for as long as he stays in this country?"

"That could rouse dissension," Henry said, "and rally people to what they fancy is my cause."

"So it could," said Eleanor. "She's best disposed of, then, in a suitably cloistered order, until the time is ripe to bring her out and attach her blood-right to your claim."

"She won't consent," Henry said. "I believe she has no calling to religion."

"Consent can be won," Eleanor said with dangerous gentleness. "A vocation can be found even in the most barren heart. If later it proves that both consent and calling were false, why then, what gratitude might she offer the knight who rides to her rescue?"

"You do think of everything, lady," Henry said.

"Of course I do," said Eleanor. "I've learned the hard way to leave nothing to chance—and if I must gamble, I always leave an escape. I've served my last day in prison, in this life or any other."

Yet you would imprison her, Henry thought, but he did not dare to say it.

It was well he held his tongue. Eleanor said, "We have a bargain, then. Richard takes Jerusalem and gains the crown by acclamation. You stand heir to him until he goes back into the west. Then the kingdom is yours."

"And in the meantime?"

"In the meantime," said Eleanor, "the lady of Jerusalem will retire to a convent to repent her sins and to mourn the untimely death of her husband, in which her sin of sloth played a part. The kingdom will be held in the hands of its High Court, such of it as is still left, with the aid and assistance of the lords of the Crusade. Of course the King of the English will speak strongly there, and his words will be heard, and better yet, heeded. There will be no question, once Jerusalem is taken, as to who is best fit to bear the crown and the title."

Henry bowed to her will. "Go," she said. "Shine in council. The king should be seen, and the king's heir. I'll come when the two of you have charmed them sufficiently."

He left her sitting still while her maid settled her wimple and veil at the perfect angle. She was the living image of a queen. The Crusade would bow before her as Henry had. How could it not? Where Eleanor was, no lesser will could prevail.

PART THREE

JERUSALEM
June–July 1192

CHAPTER TWENTY-NINE

The army of the Franks spread over the stony hills beyond Beit Nuba, a day's march from Jerusalem. Heat shimmered over them, even so close to sunrise; a pall of dust sat above them, buzzing with flies.

And yet they were in high good humor; they laughed and sang in the shade of their tents, sharing out a ration of wine that the king had ordered for them. Their numbers were about to double, rumor had it: the young lord Henry was coming from Tyre by way of Acre, with all of the French forces and a company of knights newly come from England and Normandy—fresh strength, fresh steel, fresh horses to strengthen the Crusade.

That was Eleanor's doing. Duke Hugh, it was said, had contemplated seizing Tyre and holding it against Richard, but in Eleanor's presence he had never gone beyond the thought. He had taken the cross anew at the feast of the Ascension, side by side with Henry of Champagne.

"Ah, Mother," said Richard when he heard. "What would I have done without you?"

He was in even greater good humor than his men. He still would not look on Jerusalem—but he would see it soon. Today he was to receive a familiar guest: the lord Saphadin had come one last time from the sultan with offers of settlement and peace.

Sioned had been up a little earlier than usual; she who was never ill had been drastically indisposed, although it passed within an hour of waking. She found herself ravenous then, and went looking for whatever the cooks might have saved for her.

She knew that Ahmad was coming to the camp today. She had not seen him in the flesh since she went to Tyre, though she had seen him often in dreams. They were on opposite sides of the war again. She found it did not grieve her as much as it would have once. She feared for his life each time he rode on a raid, but she would have done that if he had been a Christian knight. The love between them was unshakable. One day, if they both lived, they would be together. That day would be soon, the gods willing.

There was a peculiar pleasure in being more or less anonymous in trousers and headdress, watching him ride in as she had the first time, the greater part of a year before. She loved the way he sat on a horse, the way he carried his head high in its turbaned helmet, the way he acknowledged greetings with a princely bow and now and then a swift smile. They loved him here, enemy though he was; he was a man after their own heart, a knight and a warrior, a worthy friend and adversary to the Lionheart.

He had come with a handful of his sons, young men all stamped with the familiar lines of his face. She had not seen so many of them together before. Had he brought them for her benefit? They were a fine pride of young lions, clear-eyed and light on their feet, with a watchful look as befit soldiers on guard about their lord, but no shrinking of fear.

Richard plucked the father from the midst of them and pulled him into an exuberant embrace. "Saphadin! My good friend! It's splendid to see you again."

Ahmad returned the embrace with somewhat less exuberance but no less cordiality. "Malik Ric. You look well." He said it in Norman French, and fluently enough, too, which made Richard roar with delight.

"You've been studying! We'll make a Frank of you yet."

"Not in this lifetime," said Ahmad, but with a smile.

Richard carried him off to the council. Sioned meant to be there, but she lingered for a little while to take the measure of his sons. Most of them were mortal, but two—the oldest and the youngest—shimmered with magic. She thought she saw in them a memory of Safiyah as well as of their father.

The thought made her smile. Her morning's indisposition was gone, but there was an odd warmth in her belly. Her hand came to rest over it.

She started. It could not be. She could not—

And why not? She knew how children were made. She had done a great deal of it in that place out of time. It would have been more astonishing if nothing had come of it, than that something evidently had.

She had been taking pleasure in seeing him without his knowing it, but she had had every intention of stealing a moment to speak with him when he was done with Richard. Now she wondered if she should approach him at all. They shared the secret of their time together, a secret she had told to no one but Henry. To everyone else she had said only that she was safe in the care of a friend. Most, Richard among them, had concluded that Henry had made some arrangement to spirit her out of Tyre; it was then supposed that she had been kept in a house of religion until Conrad was safely dead.

It was certainly a more credible story than the truth. Henry, bless him, had seen the sense in keeping silence. That silence now was habit, a habit she had been inclined to break, at least in Ahmad's presence. But this new secret changed things.

She wanted it to herself for a while. Not too long—even the voluminous garments she could hide in would not conceal it forever—but long enough to understand what she felt. Whether it was joy or apprehension; delight or dread; or a mingling of all of them.

She had meant to slip into the council under the canopy by Richard's tent. Instead she went back to the surgeons' tents, where there was occupation enough, preparing medicines and bandages for the battle that was coming.

It was harder than she had expected. To know that he was in the camp and to turn willfully away from him was a wrenching in her middle. But that same middle had roiled with morning sickness a bare hour before, and the memory bolstered her determination to be alone. He should know; he deserved to know. But not for a while.

The lord Saphadin had been studying the *langue d'oc*, but he was not yet sure enough of his knowledge to trust himself in negotiations. He trusted Mustafa for that, as Richard did, in an easy colloquy that rambled all around the doings of every common acquaintance, the weather, the hunting, the state of the roads, until it came at long last to the point.

"I've had enough of dallying about," Richard said. "It's time to do what I came for. I'm taking the Holy Sepulcher."

"It is time," Saphadin agreed, "though maybe we can settle it even now without bloodshed."

"That would be a pleasant outcome," Richard said. "What is your brother offering?"

"That you come in peace," Saphadin said, "and take charge of the Holy Sepulcher. We keep the Dome of the Rock and the east of Jerusalem. From here to the sea, you keep, and from Tyre to Jaffa. We keep Ascalon and all lands north of Tyre and west of Jerusalem. Pilgrims have free passage through all the lands, and caravans pass unmolested."

"Tempting," said Richard, actually managing to sound as if he meant it. "Fair, in its way. How would we seal it? Meet in the Holy City and pray at one another's shrines?"

"That would do," said Saphadin. "We might also, in time, consider such an alliance as you proposed before. The Queen of Sicily objected too strongly to an infidel marriage, but perhaps another lady of your people would be amenable to a match."

"That's always a possibility," Richard said. "Do you have any particular lady in mind?"

Saphadin lifted a shoulder in a shrug. "I might. When all else is settled, we'll speak of it. Yes?"

"Yes," said Richard without evident suspicion. Mustafa had not realized he was holding his breath until he suddenly remembered to breathe.

That was all, in the end, that they had come to say. They took their time in parting, letting their conversation wind down as leisurely as it had arrived at its purpose. Maybe they were a little reluctant to part. The next time they met would be across a battlefield.

They both knew that. Saphadin declared that he would bring Richard's agreement to his brother, but Richard would not keep the peace for much longer than it took Saphadin to reach Jerusalem. As soon as Henry arrived with his reinforcements, the attack would begin.

At length Saphadin drained his cup of sherbet, rose, and took his graceful leave. His escort was waiting. He did not dally—not precisely—but he took his time, carefully not looking about for someone whom he had been expecting. That person did not appear. Mustafa could not tell if he was disappointed. Certainly he was in no haste to ride away; when he did, he did it slowly, as if he had all the time in the world.

Mustafa was somewhat surprised himself. He had seen Sioned earlier, but not since the council began.

Whatever her reasons, they must have been sufficient to keep her away. He did not doubt that he would discover them in time. Like Saphadin, he was in no hurry. He had more than enough to preoccupy him elsewhere.

Richard yawned hugely and stretched, and peered at the sky beyond his canopy. There was not quite enough time for a hunt—whether he hunted gazelle or Turks. He could hold audience before dinner, he supposed, and then dine with his war council, and tell them what the sultan's brother had said. It would be good for a little amusement, and some speculation as to how matters would be settled later, after he had won Jerusalem.

But first he would take the cup of wine a servant was offering from the shelter of his tent. He did not drink wine when he entertained Muslims; it was a courtesy, and one they were grateful for. Sherbet was pleasant enough, but today he had a noble thirst. Wine lightly watered would quench it admirably.

He had not seen this servant before. It was an old man, grey-bearded, in the long soft shirt and loose trousers of this country. He served the wine with quiet grace, and a bow calculated to remind Richard of their respective stations.

Richard noticed servants. Most noblemen did not; servants were hands to fetch, that was all, and bodies to use as they saw fit. Richard had a spark of curiosity in him, to know their names and their kin and where they came from. He knew all the men who waited on him, both his squires and pages and the native servants who had come, some as captives, others of their free will.

This one did not look like a captive. He performed his service with the air of one who grants a favor, and waited with visible patience for Richard to drain the cup. It was good wine, not too heavily watered, and cold—cooled with snow as the sherbet had been. Richard drank it down and smacked his lips. "Good! Do I know you, sirrah? Are you newly come to the camp?"

"Very newly, majesty," the man said. His French had a strange resonance to it, as if another voice rang beneath it, in another tongue. "Will you come within, majesty? We have fresh linen waiting, and a clean cotte."

Richard was never averse to a change of clothes, especially in this heat. His guards were standing about, unconcerned. Mustafa had made himself scarce. There was no one else nearby to trouble him. "A bath? I don't suppose that would be forthcoming as well?"

"Not immediately, majesty," said the servant, "but if you would wait . . ."

"Never mind," Richard said. "I'll take the clean clothes and welcome."

The servant bowed again, not quite low enough for mockery, and stood back to let him enter the tent.

The clothes were new indeed, and beautiful: fine white linen and crimson silk. Richard thought he recognized the silk from the last caravan he had taken.

As the old man dressed him, he said, "I don't believe I've heard your name."

The servant was kneeling in front of him, fastening the laces of his hose. Richard thought he saw the faint curve of a smile on the bearded lips. "You have heard it, majesty," the old man said, "but not perhaps in this place."

That was an easterner: forever mysterious. Richard had learned not to bellow in frustration; it only made these people more determined to be cryptic. Richard peered into the old man's face. "I never forget a face," he said. "I've never seen yours before."

"You will see it again," said the old man. His smile had widened. He dressed Richard in the cotte, deftly, while Richard stood scowling at him.

"You're not a servant," Richard said suddenly. "Tell me what—"

"Not this time, I think," said the old man. He laid a golden collar about Richard's shoulders, and held the coronet that he wore to feasts and councils. Richard, well trained by decades of servants, bent his head.

The old man crowned him as servants had done for time out of mind. But this was not the same. The weight of the coronet seemed unwontedly heavy, its clasp unusually cold. He met the old man's eyes as once, on a day of purported ill omen in England, he had met the gaze of the archbishop who crowned him king.

That good man had meant him no harm; he had proved unshakably loyal, the best of servants. This man was neither good nor harmless. He fixed Richard with a basilisk stare, cold and unblinking. "Go, majesty," he said. "Be king. Your people are waiting for you."

"I'm not king because of you," Richard said. The words burst out before he could stop them.

"Not in England, majesty," the old man said. He bowed low, even to the carpets that softened the stony ground: and that was mockery but also, in its way, a promise.

Richard reached to grasp him, to shake at least a name out of him, but he was gone. The only evidence of his presence was the kingly finery in which he had dressed Richard, and the coronet still cold on Richard's brow.

He began to suspect who had come here—not that he wanted to believe it, but he had heard all the stories. None of them had said that the Old Man himself came to his victims; but then none of the Old Man's victims had been an anointed king.

The chill that ran down Richard's spine was not exactly fear. It was excitement, and a flash of anger. Whoever had let this interloper in would pay for it, and dearly.

But not immediately. Richard had thinking to do. He would see Sinan again; that, the Old Man had promised. Meanwhile he would strengthen his guard and take measures against such powers as the Old Man wielded. He should have done so long ago, and at least since Conrad was killed. But he hated to live in fear, whether it was his own or that of his guards.

He settled the coronet more firmly on his head, against the instinct that would have ripped it away and flung it as far as it would go, and stiffened his spine, and went out to be king to his people.

CHAPTER THIRTY

Sioned was awake when Richard's page came to fetch her.
It was not quite midnight; most of the camp was asleep.
But lamps burned in Richard's tent, and he was pacing in
it, measuring its confines over and over.

She knew how that felt. She had been upbraiding herself viciously for letting Ahmad go without so much as a word of greeting. He could die before she saw him again, and she would have
refused to see him because she had been too cowardly to face him.

She sat in a corner and waited for Richard to pace himself
out. He did that eventually, stopping short, spinning on his
heel, glaring down at her. She stared calmly up.

"Something's got you in a fair fret," she observed. "Why
don't you tell me what it is, and give yourself a little peace?"

"I don't know if I'll have peace again," Richard muttered.
"Not as long as that one is alive."

"And who of many would that be? Your brother? Has he escaped from Rouen?"

"Not while my mother is alive," Richard said. "And no, it's
not dear Cousin Philip, either, or anyone else beyond the sea."

"Saladin?" she asked.

"Ah," said Richard. "He's a fair and honorable enemy. It's a privilege to fight him."

"Then you had better tell me who it is," she said, "and why you need me."

"Who wears white and carries a black dagger, and toys with the lives of kings?"

The skin tightened between her shoulder blades. "*He* came here?"

"Into this very tent," Richard said. "He played the servant and tormented me with riddles; then he vanished."

"He didn't threaten you? Harm you?"

"No more than veiled hints and coy half-promises," said Richard.

"I can protect you," she said, "if you'll allow. There are arts, expedients—I can—"

"I don't need those mummeries," he said. "He wants me alive and fighting fit, or I'm no judge of men or devils."

"Then what—"

"You're clever," said Richard, "and you've studied arts that I prefer not to think about. You know more languages than the whole pack of my interpreters. I want you to find a way to destroy him."

She opened her mouth. No words came out. Richard, always direct to the point, had leaped past every possible preliminary. Even she who knew him had not expected this. "You want me to—"

"Why are you so shocked?" he demanded. "I'm not blind, little sister, or deaf, either. I know what you've been up to when you haven't been mixing potions for Master Judah. Your mother is a famous sorceress. You're her daughter in all respects."

"But how did you—you know you never—"

"Against that son of the Devil," Richard said grimly, "I'll use any weapon that comes to hand. *Any* weapon. Do you understand?"

Sioned nodded, speechless.

"Everyone's in horror of him," said Richard. "He's devoted

his life to cultivating it, between the rumors and mystery of his cult and the occasional judicious murder. Not one person has ever dared to think of the natural solution."

"A man can be killed," she said. "But that one—I'm not sure he's a man at all."

"Whatever he is," said Richard, "he's cursed well guarded. That's why I need you, sister. You're the only one of your kind that I trust. Find a way to destroy him, any way in this world, and I'll find someone to do it."

"Why, so I won't sully my lily-white hands?"

Richard snorted. "Considering some of the stains I've seen on them, that's the least of my worries. I don't want you killed. Master Judah would kill *me*."

"So I'm to hunt down a devil, and then stand back while someone else takes the kill."

"If that's the way you want to put it," Richard said, "yes. Will you do it?"

"Even if it involves magic?"

"Even then," said Richard, though he grimaced. "God knows I've no use for wand-waving and spellcasting, but if that's the weapon I need, that's the weapon I'll take. I want this country clean of him."

"And if it's not possible?"

"Try," he said.

Richard never did ask for easy things. "I may need to ask for help," she said. "If and when I do, you are not to question the source of it. That's my condition. Will you abide by it?"

"What will you do? Go to the Devil himself?"

"If I have to," she said.

He rolled his shoulders as if he stood in armor that galled him. "Do it," he said. "Whatever you have to do. Give me that son of the Pit."

"Certainly I will try," she said.

When Sioned left Richard, she was in a rather remarkable state of mind. It was by no means unlike him to order the death of an enemy, but for that of all men to be willing to resort to magic . . . Sinan must have shaken him badly.

Richard, shaken, was a dangerous beast. Sinan would have done far better to keep his distance, cultivate his alliance with Eleanor, and let Richard be.

Could it be, she thought, that the great sorcerer had made the mistake of underestimating his adversary? Had he had some falling-out with the queen? Or had he thought to play them both, one against the other, for some as yet unfathomed purpose of his own?

She would be running short on sleep for a good many nights after this. What to do, how to do it, how to ward herself against discovery, where even to begin—she shut herself in her tent and lit her lamp and sat in the soft dim glow.

The tent was tiny, but spirits paid little heed to the limitations of earthly space. The great jinni fit himself to the confines of those narrow walls, and yet she still saw him as a vast and puissant spirit; even hardly taller than a mortal child, he kept the fullness of his power.

He bowed before her as he always had, insisting that she was a pure spirit, and that he must serve her for the sheer astonishment of the fact. Sometimes his brother came with him, but tonight he was alone—insofar as a spirit, born of fire, could separate itself from the essence of his kin. "My brother has set me a task," she said. "The sorcerer on the mountain—can he be destroyed?"

The jinni mantled like a falcon. His face had grown more human the longer he called himself her protector, but just now there was nothing human or comprehensible about it. "That one is beloved of Iblis," he said. "He has paid a great price to be warded against all the perils of the earth."

Sioned's heart did not sink, exactly. She would have expected nothing else of so wily a sorcerer. But she had let herself hope that he was a more or less mortal enemy, who could be defeated by more or less mortal means.

"He is no longer mortal," the jinni said.

"Is he invulnerable?" Sioned asked. "Really? Completely?"

The jinni did not answer directly. "He keeps the Seal of Suleiman. It not only binds the will of any living thing, it imbues its wielder with strength and protection."

"Then if we can take it away from him—"

"No one, man or jinni, has succeeded in finding it," the jinni said, "still less in stealing it."

"Yet it can be found," Sioned said. "It can be stolen. It can even be destroyed."

"Maybe," said the jinni.

"I need books," she said. "I need to know all I can about him, the bargains he struck, the spells that guard him—everything. Can you bring me such books?"

The jinni bowed. "I will bring you books," he said.

Already his substance was thinning and fading. She should let him go; the sooner he came back, the sooner she could begin. But she held him with her will. "Be careful," she said.

Was that a smile on the barely substantial face? "I am always careful," said the jinni, just as she released him. He winked out like a flame.

Sioned sat alone in the lamplight and acknowledged, not at all easily, that she had sent the jinni on a useful but hardly conclusive errand. She should have sent him not for books but for certain persons who had read and remembered all of those books.

She would perform that task herself. Now. Tonight.

The spell was simple. It needed no more than the clear light of the lamp, a word of blessing in the language of the Prophet, and a focusing and directing of the mind into the heart of the flame.

Safiyah seldom slept. It was an aspect of age, she had told Sioned once, that she almost welcomed; in its way it lengthened the time left to her. She was awake tonight in a brighter light than lamps alone could muster, absorbed in contemplation of a great and luminous crystal. The power of the stone washed over Sioned. It made her bones throb and her skin tingle; the small hairs on her body quivered and stood upright. It was not unpleasant; it was the crackle of strong magic, unmistakable and by now familiar.

She waited courteously on the other side of the flame for Safiyah to finish her divination and acknowledge the watcher's presence. In the way of magic, the time passed both quickly and slowly: quickly as the stars wheeled, slowly as she waited in the thrum of the crystal's power. It refreshed her as if she had slept the night through: wonderful and unexpected, and profoundly welcome.

Safiyah raised her eyes at last and smiled. The warmth of her welcome outshone the lamp's flame. "Well met again, dear friend," she said.

Sioned found herself blushing. "Maybe not so well," she said, "as sorely as I've neglected you."

"I've felt the brush of your thought," Safiyah said, "and the love that warms it, too. It's more than enough."

That made Sioned blush all the more hotly. "I'm still remiss. I only come to you when I can use you. Maybe, when the war is over—"

"It will be soon," Safiyah said. "Then we may be to one another what God and fate have decreed. Until then, what do you need of me?"

"Help," Sioned said baldly. She told Safiyah the whole of it—Richard's command, Eleanor's bargain, all that concerned the Old Man of the Mountain. She did not mention the thing that concerned Ahmad.

Safiyah heard her in silence, asking no questions. Sioned suspected that she knew most or all of what she heard; that the crystal had shown her everything. Its glow had held steady while Sioned spoke, but when she finished, it swelled to the brightness of the moon.

Safiyah gazed into it unflinching, though it filled her eyes with light. She spoke slowly, softly, weighing each word. "There are tales of sorcerers who hid their hearts away, and so made themselves invulnerable. The hiding place is always a mountain of glass or a tower of adamant—a great gaudy place where none but a fool would think to hide a treasure. I would expect that one to be more clever."

"It's not a heart he keeps," Sioned said, "but a Seal. He must keep it about his person; he'd be mad to hide it anywhere else."

"Maybe so," said Safiyah. "There are spells of finding, which you may try; but some of them are dangerous, and may end in his finding you."

"What else can I do?" Sioned asked her.

It was an honest question, and Safiyah answered it as such. "My husband has made a long study of this enemy. If anyone can help you find a way to destroy that one, he can."

Sioned bit her lip. The taste of blood was sudden and iron-sweet. "This helps him," she said mostly to herself: "it frees him from the pact he made. It helps his brother, who has been that one's enemy from his youth. It frees us from terror; it removes temptation, and the lure of his devil's bargains. It helps all of us."

Safiyah inclined her head.

"Lady," said Sioned, "for all our sake, then—would you ask him? Would you discover what he knows?"

"It would be better if you asked," said Safiyah.

Of course it would. Sioned cursed her for seeing the obvious, and herself for being a fool.

Safiyah's gaze on her was gentle, but it saw much that Sioned would have preferred to keep hidden. "Speak to him," she said. "Trust him. Always trust him, even when the war comes between you."

"I do trust him," said Sioned.

"With your life? With your spirit?"

Sioned could not find words to answer that.

"Let him help you," said Safiyah. "For your sake he will do it."

And when he did it, Sioned thought, he would see what she was hiding. Everything would change.

Chapter Thirty-One

Sioned came back from the heart of the flame to find her
tent heaped with books and scrolls: a mage's trove of
them, some in languages that she had never seen or imagined. There was a small jinni sitting on the heap of those, looking rather like a tasseled and turbaned frog; yet its voice when
it spoke was as rich and orotund as a bishop's. "I serve you," it
said, bowing low.

She bowed in return, less deeply. "You are welcome in my
tent," she said. "May I offer you—"

"Peace," said the jinni, "and ink and pens and parchment. If
you will, bright lady."

She sent one of Richard's pages to fetch what the jinni had
asked for. She could give it peace easily enough: she needed sleep,
however little of it she might manage. The jinni was deep in
scrolls by the time the ink and pens arrived; it reached blindly for
them and went on reading, its big round eyes barely blinking.

She should be reading those books which she could understand. But first, sleep. She scaled a mountain of books to find
her bed on the other side, open and welcoming.

*   *   *

It was three days before Sioned mustered the courage to face Ahmad. Henry still had not come. He was close, the scouts kept insisting, but the Saracens knew it and were harrying him. Richard sent out a company to find and help him, then after half a day of pacing, snarling, and trying everyone's patience, he gathered another troop of knights and set out himself.

The camp without him was no quieter. He had left the Archbishop of Canterbury in command; Hubert Walter, though a quiet and clerkly-looking man, had a will of iron, and he was determined that the army be well ready to rise and march as soon as Richard came back. If Saladin took it into his head to leave off fortifying Jerusalem and fall on the Franks in their king's absence, he would find no easy enemy.

Sioned waited until after nightfall to begin the spell. The scholar-jinni was deeply engrossed in a book of many strange leaves, tall and narrow and written in a tongue that was spoken, it said, on the roof of the world. Its presence was more a comfort than a distraction.

Sioned hardly needed to speak the word of power or to kindle the flame. He was present in her heart, rousing as if from sleep, smiling as he grew aware of her. She could see a little of where he was: a room of stone, warm with hangings, soft-lit with lamplight. One of his sons was asleep at the foot of the bed on which he was sitting. He had a scroll open on his knees, but something in the way he sat told her that he had not been reading it even before she intruded on his solitude.

He was in Jerusalem. She could feel the power of the place even through the veil of the flame. It was not the power she had expected, even camped so close to it. She had thought to find more light and less darkness; more peace and less throbbing discord. It was so old, this city, and so heavily imbued with sanctity, that it could scarcely sustain the weight of itself.

He seemed undismayed by the paradoxes of the city, and glad almost beyond bearing to sense her presence. "Beloved," he said.

She almost wept at the word; her tongue had echoed it before her mind was aware. She would have fallen through the flame if she could, into his arms, but that power was not given her—and well for them both. They were in the places in which they were most needed.

Time was short. Something hunted them—something that she feared she knew, a power that rode on the winds of magic as a vulture circled the mortal sky. "I need to know," she said. "To destroy our common enemy. Your lady said—"

"She told me," Ahmad said. "I've searched through all I know, and everything that I can call to memory. I found the same old tales, the same legends, but nothing of use."

"She said that it's something you know," said Sioned. "Something maybe you found when you helped your brother to besiege the castle, or something you discovered when you went to him again."

"Or anything I could have read or thought or seen in the years between," he said with a wry twist. "No, don't frown; I trust your instinct and hers. Will you walk in memory with me? It may be this needs another eye, a fresher mind."

"Gladly," she said, "but how—"

"Swiftly," he said. "Come."

The thing that stalked the edges of awareness was drawing closer, but he seemed unaware of it. He caught her and drew her in, spinning through a whirl of darkness and flame.

His eyes were at the heart of them. They opened on his house outside of Damascus, a place she had come to love better than anywhere in the world. Its gardens were rich with summer, the light in them golden, but the rooms within shifted from sunlight to moonlight and back again, through all the phases of night and day.

They were rooms of memory, places he had been and seen. They passed in rapid succession, dizzying in their multitudes, until one caught, wavered, paused.

An army besieged a fortress on a high crag. The force was strong, its engines powerful, but the fortress stood unmarred. It mocked them with its changelessness.

Sioned recognized the man who commanded the army, although she had never seen him face to face. He looked like Ahmad, but somewhat smaller, somewhat thinner, and somewhat finer drawn. He had no magic, but his spirit shone with a white light, such purity as the jinn would have bowed down and worshipped.

He was, in that moment of memory, on the raw edge of frustration. He had given the command to retreat; the engines were being taken down, the camp disbanded. It was a wise decision, but he was not at all happy to have made it. "Allah! Why can't I be the end of him?"

"It's not his time," Ahmad said. They were standing side by side on an outcropping of stone, not far from the dismantling of the siege-engines. He was still quite a young man, and his magic was just beginning to know itself, yet he was still beyond question the man she knew. He had the same cool composure; the same air of quiet self-restraint.

"If it's not his time now," Saladin demanded, "then when will it be?"

Ahmad lifted a shoulder in a shrug. "God knows," he said.

"God keeps His counsel," Saladin muttered. "I need a source that is more forthcoming."

"All men are mortal," Ahmad said. "Even sorcerers like that one can be destroyed."

"How?"

"I don't know," said Ahmad.

"Find a way," Saladin said.

Ahmad bowed. The memory melted into a blur of speeding days.

Some Sioned almost caught—almost remembered. The rest passed far too quickly to grasp. Only one slowed enough to be understood.

An old man sat in an eerie and beautiful garden. Its flowers were too strange, its greenery too bright for earth. The man was human enough, or so it seemed. She knew his face all too well, though he was younger here and stronger than he had been in his passages of magic with the queen.

He did not speak. The chair in which he sat was peculiar, like the stump of an ancient and twisted tree. It grew out of the otherworldly soil, writhing its stunted branches, grappling the dirt with its roots.

It was, in its way, the image of the man who sat in it. She sensed no stronger magic in it than anywhere else in the garden, no evidence that Sinan had set the heart of his power there. And yet as the memory faded, she held on to that tormented shape.

And something more. Something very close by it; a glimmer, half-seen, barely remembered, and yet . . .

Darkness roared upon her. The stalker had found her. She had been on guard, or so she thought; she had had wards. They crumpled like parchment.

Ahmad was nowhere within reach. She could not go hunting him—that would bring the stalker down on him. She turned as best she could and fled.

She was bleeding magic. Her wards were in tatters. The flame of her conjuring was lost in the swirl of darkness.

It did not know her name, in which was the greatest power and the strongest binding. It groped, clawing at her unprotected self, seeking the word that would grant it power over her. She guarded it with all the strength that she had left, and as she guarded it, she ran.

A clear voice rang across the starless sky. It brought the hunter wheeling about, jaws opening wide, fangs dripping pallid light. Safiyah stood in a gleaming gate, wrapped in white. She spoke again in a tongue of which Sioned knew only a little, words of summoning and of irresistible temptation. *Come to me. Conquer me. Make me your slave.*

The hunter knew her name and the measure of her power. It abandoned Sioned to fall on that great queen of mages.

Sioned gasped in protest and tried to catch it, but she was too weak, her movement too slow.

"Now!" cried Safiyah as the hunter fell upon her. "Run!"

The gate was open. Safiyah had sprung aside from it, leaping to meet the hunter. Sioned veered, but a buffet of power flung her aside. The gate caught her and spun her down and down, out of darkness into light, and into shadowed dimness—the dimness of a tent heaped high with books, lit by a single lamp.

Sioned's body was cold, but never as cold as her heart. The door of the spirit was closed to her. Safiyah was trapped on the other side of it, sundered from all help both mortal and otherwise, doing battle with the hunter.

The armies of the jinn could not come to her, not through those walls of power; Sioned's little bit of magic was helpless to defend her. The hunter would kill her, and there was nothing Sioned could do. Not one thing—except lie in her chill bed and remember: every word, every image. Over and over. Seeking the thing, the one thing, that would give her the answer. If there was an answer at all.

CHAPTER THIRTY-TWO

In a lifetime of raiding caravans, Mustafa had never seen one larger than the great riding that wound up through the stony hills from Bilbais in Egypt to the sultan in Jerusalem. Heat-shimmer made the line seem endless. Hundreds, thousands of camels rocked and swayed under massive burdens. The stink of them rose with the dust, and the sound of their passing was unmistakable: the rumbling of bellies and the chorus of moaning and squealing that proclaimed their opinion of this labor that had been forced upon them. Horses and mules crowded all through the line of them, so many as to be beyond counting. Together they were as vast as an army.

If the size of the caravan had not been proof enough of its value, the size of its defending force left no doubt whatever. Mustafa counted three thousand men both armed and afoot, Turks and Bedouin for the most part, intermixed with the small brown men of Egypt. They bristled with weapons; companies of them rode up and down the line on their fast little horses.

A riper or more tempting fruit had never begged to be plucked. Mustafa followed the caravan for the better part of a

day, counting its beasts of burden as best he could, and reckoning the quality of its defenders. They never knew he spied on
them. When he came close enough to see the face of the
guards' commander, his brows rose to his turban.

"Falak al-Din," he said to Richard: "the lord Saphadin's
brother. He has none of his brother's wit or charm. He's a
plodder; he does as he's told. Now there's no one to tell him
what to do, and a caravan the like of which I've never seen."

Richard's grin was as wide and white as a wolf's. Mustafa
had ridden nightlong to find him, and had caught him just at
dawn on a raid not far from the castle of Blanchegarde. There
were a score of Turkish heads on pikes around the perimeter of
his camp, trophies of his latest skirmish, but this news that
Mustafa brought paled his raid to insignificance.

"How close is it?" he asked Mustafa.

"If you muster and ride today," Mustafa said, "you can ambush it in the hills of Judea, well before it reaches Jerusalem."

Richard's eyes narrowed as he calculated. He no longer
needed a map, though his sleepy clerk had one at hand if he
asked for it. He knew this country as well as many who were
born in it. "Three thousand men to guard it, you say?"

"Maybe a little fewer than that, my lord," Mustafa said.

"Close enough," said Richard. "Are you up for another ride?
I'd not ask it of you, but I need someone I can trust."

"Give me a fresh horse," Mustafa said, "and I'll ride to the
world's end."

Richard laughed and pulled him close, and kissed him on
both cheeks. "Good man! Stop for a bite and a sip, then take
your pick of the horses. You'll find the Duke of Burgundy in
Blanchegarde, snugged up with as many buxom ladies as he can
get his hands on. Wake him up and haul him out—but nicely.
Tell him he can have a third share of the loot if he'll lend his
forces to this venture."

Mustafa bowed to the floor of the king's tent. When he
straightened, Richard caught him and kissed him again, on the

lips this time, laughing at the prospect of a battle, and loving Mustafa for bringing him the news of it.

There was no time to stop, or even to pause. Mustafa slipped free of the king's hands and ran to find the food and drink that he had been promised, and then to choose himself a horse.

He was exhausted but intensely alert. He saw the figure in the shadows outside the tent, the pale gleam of dawn on hair so fair it was nearly white. Blondel was watching, and he was not smiling.

Mustafa put him out of mind. There was a battle coming—a splendid one, for glorious spoils. The French would join it; how could they not? They were grumbling again, threatening yet again to abandon this tedious war, but the promise of gold would bring them running.

Even as swiftly as Richard moved, Saladin's spies were swifter. Half a thousand men rode in haste from Jerusalem to warn the caravan. They had been wary before, but now they were at the height of alertness, sending scouts out on all sides. The new forces allowed them to double the active guard on the caravan, without sacrificing overmuch sleep.

Richard heard the news without dismay. He had close to a thousand knights, a thousand Turcopoles, and a thousand infantry; he could match the enemy closely enough in numbers, and every man under his command was whipped to a froth of eagerness. He had promised each one of them a fair share of whatever they won, which if the caravan was as rich as they all suspected, would make them wealthy men.

He laid his ambush carefully. The enemy expected it in a broad dry riverbed that came down from the spine of the mountains: they sent a strong company of scouts through it to overturn every stone. Mustafa watched them from above, sharing an outcropping of stones with a handful of Richard's tame Bedouin. They were brothers, and apostate to Islam. Mustafa did not trust them, but they were as dazzled by the prospect of riches as any of the Franks. They would be loyal until it came time to divide the spoils.

The caravan's scouts took a long time to be sure the wadi was clear of enemies. When at last they rode back to their commanders, Mustafa sent one of the brothers to Richard to tell him the way was clear. It was a fine place for an ambush: broad enough and clear enough to grant passage to the caravan, but walled steeply on either side, and narrowing as it rose up toward the mountains.

The sun had reached its zenith while Mustafa waited for the enemy's scouts to finish their explorations. The heat was like a living thing. He was glad of the desert robes he had put on for this venture; they made a rather acceptable tent, propped up with a camel goad. He sipped water sparingly as he waited, ears sharpened, watching for signs of the caravan's coming.

It advanced like a dust storm, coming on slowly, held to the pace of the mules and the camels. It would have to stop either within the wadi or just outside of it; it would go no farther than that before nightfall.

Unless, Mustafa thought, it went on in the dark. It might; it could hope to outstrip Richard and escape toward Hebron, where Saladin's forces were much stronger and Richard's far weaker.

If he could spy on the commanders . . .

For that he would have to penetrate the wall of guards and spy close in. In a smaller caravan he could not have dared it: there, all the guards knew one another. But in this one, thousands strong, he might pass unnoticed, with his Berber face and his nondescript robes.

Two of the brothers went with him. He would have preferred to go alone, but they were insistent. "Are we not as skilled as you? Have we not spied in worse places than this? Will you not need someone to take the message to Malik Ric, if there's need of swift action?"

That last was all too convincing. He left the rest of the brothers to do as they saw fit, and took the two young rakehells with him, slipping from shadow to shadow, making themselves one with the dust that shrouded everything in the caravan's wake.

Mustafa tracked Falak al-Din by feel more than by sight. The emir had been traveling in the rear, but as the day wore on, he moved up toward the van, peering ahead as if he could see the army of the Franks waiting in the hills at the wadi's end. The slopes were empty even of birds.

Saladin's commander had ridden ahead with a handful of his men, but came back as Falak al-Din reached the head of the caravan. They greeted one another curtly. Mustafa would have liked to know the root of that, but he could hardly abandon his posture of camel driver to ask questions. Maybe it was only that Falak al-Din was a Kurd and the other was a Turk. There was no love between those two nations.

"No Franks ahead," said the commander, whose name was Aslam. "The road's clear. If we stay on it into the night, we may give them the slip."

"What, try to march in the dark?" Falak al-Din said. "It's easy to see you haven't done much traveling with caravans. These aren't soldiers. If they're not herded like their own camels, they'll wander off Allah knows where. We need the daylight to keep them all on the road."

"If you stop," said Aslam, "the Franks will catch you."

"I don't believe that," Falak al-Din said. "If he were that close, he'd be in the wadi, and there's nothing there. He's a day behind us at least, I'll lay wagers on it."

"You'll wager, sure enough," said Aslam. "The stakes will be your life."

Falak al-Din's beard jutted with the stubborn set of his jaw. "We're camping as soon as we reach the mountain—there's water there, at the Round Cistern. We'll march immediately after the dawn prayer. Will that at least begin to content you?"

"No," said Aslam, biting off the word.

"Then live with it," said Falak al-Din, turning his shoulder to the emir.

Aslam looked as if he would have dearly loved to sink a dagger into the idiot's back, but he was too civilized a man—and perhaps too well aware that, fool or no, this was the sultan's kinsman. He swallowed his temper and spurred his horse back to the body of his troops, who were riding somewhat ahead, bristling with weapons.

Mustafa thought Aslam might ride on at nightfall, but when the caravan camped by the great stone water basin that gave the place its name, Aslam camped also, high on the hill above the rest. From there at least he would see any enemy that came—if that enemy came with lights in the dark.

When the sun had set but there was still a little light left in the sky, Mustafa left the camels he had been driving to the care of those whose proper task it was. There were sentries all along the rim of the camp, and troops of guards roving as far afield as the terrain allowed. Mustafa, wrapped in his dusty djellaba, with the two Bedouin soft-footed behind, crept out as he had crept in.

They almost eluded the guards. Young Ali's misstep betrayed them: he slipped in the last of the light and sent a fall of rock down the slope onto a guard's head. Daoud bolted like a rabbit, full on a waiting spear. Ali had better luck; he disappeared into the dark. Mustafa tried, but there was a guard at every turn.

He circled, a dagger in each hand. One of the guards had ripped the djellaba from him; another had lit a torch, the better to see the fight. They were treating it as sport, laughing and mocking him in one of the more guttural Turkish dialects. The sight of his face made them whistle and whoop. *Flower of steel,* they called him, and *Beauty in the night.*

It was unlikely that they knew he was a spy for the Franks. A caravaneer might be fool enough to go wandering about after dark, and these men were not above a little casual rape.

Wrath howled out of the night, a whirlwind of deadly steel. Blood sprayed black-crimson in the torchlight. Turks shrieked and died. An iron hand heaved Mustafa up and flung him over a saddlebow. He clung blindly as the horse reared and spun.

When the world went still again, the camp was out of sight. Mustafa's captor let his horse fall from a flat gallop to a jarring trot, then a walk and a hard-breathing halt. Others came up around him, maybe a dozen from the sound of them.

"Well, men," said Richard in a voice meant to carry no farther than the circle, "we've got what we came for. First one back to camp wins his pick of the loaded camels."

Grins flashed in starlight. Richard's was as wide as any. Mustafa clutched the saddle before he could be flung off into space.

They did not go far. A little distance down the wadi, which the caravan's scouts had been sure was free of enemies, Richard's army was making its stealthy way toward the caravan. He stopped in the midst of it and set Mustafa dizzily on his feet, stripping off the djellaba that had concealed him. He was dressed in mail beneath.

There was water for Mustafa, and bread that must have been baked the morning before. He had eaten in the caravan and drunk water from the cistern, but he had learned never to refuse a meal: Allah knew when he would find another.

Richard would have sent him back to Blanchegarde. That was ridiculous; he pretended not to hear. He persuaded the master of horse to give him a mount and the master of arms to equip him with a Turcopole's weapons, and joined the march, back the way he had come.

CHAPTER THIRTY-THREE

The caravan woke before dawn, secure in the conviction that the terrible Malik Ric was at least a day's journey away. No one had found the slain guards: Richard's men had hidden their bodies too well. As far as anyone in the caravan knew, they were safe from him.

After the first prayer of the day, as the last of the camels was loaded and driven protesting into the line, he attacked.

His forces boiled up out of the wadi and scattered the caravan like a flock of geese. The guards were caught completely by surprise. Some were not yet mounted, some not even armed. The scouts who should have warned them were lying in the wadi with their heads hacked from their shoulders.

Aslam on the mountain was better prepared, but even he had not expected so sudden or so devastating an attack. He scrambled his men together and sent them charging down from the heights, howling the praises of Allah.

Richard's Franks laughed at them. They had no help; no reinforcements. Every one of the caravan's guards had fled. Falak al-Din did not even try to stop them. He was leading the rout, bolting back toward Egypt.

Mustafa clung to Richard's shadow. He was everywhere on the field, rounding up horses and mules and camels, cutting down guards who were too slow to escape and gleefully overseeing the taking of the spoils. They were rich beyond conceiving. Gold and silver, silk of Byzantium and of Ch'in, jewels in glowing profusion; sugar, spices, wheat and barley, tents and cured leather and weapons innumerable. There was enough here for a long siege in Jerusalem, with every comfort for the besieged; and Richard had won it with hardly a drop of Frankish blood spilled.

He kept a tight rein on the looting. Men who fought over spoils found themselves staring down the length of a sword into the king's cold eyes. Those who stood guard would have their share. They were needed: Aslam, though vastly outnumbered, would not give up. His Turks harried the line with sudden charges and showers of arrows from their short strong bows.

Mustafa had taken all he needed: a bag of rubies and sapphires that fit tidily in his purse, a beautifully balanced sword of Indian steel, and a coat of crimson silk that caught his eye irresistibly. He folded it and laid it in his saddlebag, and went to try the sword on Turkish necks.

Aslam had divided his forces in three. Two ran along the edges of the Frankish line. The third kept the advantage of the high ground. They had their eye on Richard, with growing frustration as he refused to stop in any one place. He was too wily to make himself a stationary target.

The caravan was so large, the spoils so rich, that after the first spate of exuberance the Franks simply rounded up the beasts of burden and began to drive them back toward Blanchegarde. They did not trouble to open the packs and bales; they would do that when they were safe in guarded walls.

Aslam's men harried them, but the Turcopole archers shot them down one by one. Mustafa accounted for three that he knew of, before a prickle in his spine sent him back toward Richard.

The king was herding Frenchmen. They were not as well in

control of their greed as the English and the Syrians; they kept wanting to stop and crow over their conquests.

Duke Hugh was not there to restrain them. He had neatly cut off his third of the caravan, counting beasts of burden while his clerks reckoned the tally of their burdens. They were already on their way to the castle.

These were stragglers and heedless looters, as likely to seize a prize from one of their own as from a hapless caravaneer. Richard drove them like cattle, laying about him with the flat of his sword. Those that fled, his personal guard disposed of as if they had been the enemy.

Mustafa knew better than to risk killing a Frank, even one who was stealing from his own countrymen. He drifted back toward the edges of the now diminished line, keeping a wary eye on the Turks above. They would have to charge soon, if they were going to charge at all.

Richard appeared beside him, as sudden as one of Sioned's jinn. His helm was at his saddlebow, his eyes narrowed as he took the measure of the men on the mountain. He said nothing, but his glance brought in a score of his knights, fully armed on their heavy destriers. With them came thrice that number of crossbowmen, heavy weapons up and cocked, ready to loose the bolts on any Turk mad enough to venture the charge.

Aslam's sword swept up, then down. *"Allah!"* he shrilled. *"Allah-il-allah!"*

"Deus lo volt!" Richard thundered back, with his men behind him in a rolling echo.

The Franks were the rock, the Turks the tide: dashing upon them, swirling and recoiling, coming back again and again in desperate search for an opening anywhere in the line. It was a wall of steel, spitting crossbow bolts, rolling inexorably over the faster, more agile, but far lighter and less well-armed Turks—and even at that, the Turcopoles could match them speed for speed and twist for twist.

Aslam had done his best, but his mode of fighting was not suited to a severely outnumbered force, even with the dubious advantage of higher ground. His drums beat the retreat.

But Richard was in no mood to let this enemy escape. He unleashed everything at once: crossbowmen, light horsemen, and the devastating charge of the knights. They rolled over Aslam's men and crushed them.

Richard was at the head of the charge, his golden stallion making nothing of the steep stony ground. Aslam's mare was faster and less heavily burdened, but she caught her foot on a stone and went to her knees. Richard was on her before she could rise again. Aslam blocked the sweep of the heavy broadsword, but his blade cracked and shattered. Richard's second blow hacked through his neck, cleaving it in a single and well-practiced stroke.

Richard caught the head as it fell, eluding the fountain of blood, and hung it by the long plaits from his saddlebow. The eyes were still alive; Mustafa, still in Richard's shadow, was transfixed. That instant of shock nearly cost him his life. Only his mount's sudden veer and shy and his reflexive parry kept him from sharing Aslam's fate.

The Turk who would have killed him joined Aslam in death, but his head stayed where it fell. Richard was not collecting heads today, now that he had Aslam's.

Mustafa, shaken into full alertness, accounted for two more Turks. Then there was none. The hillside was littered with the corpses of men and horses; the caravan was a cloud of dust rolling toward Blanchegarde. There was no Turk left alive. All of Aslam's men were dead, killed in the battle. They would dine in Paradise—quite unlike the caravan guards, who if they were lucky would come back alive to Egypt, and who if they were not, would find themselves in the hell of cowards.

Richard paused on the summit where Aslam's camp had been. A fire or two still smoldered there, and oddments were scattered about, bits of belongings that the Franks had not seen fit to take away. He swung from the saddle and stooped, stiff in his mail, and took up a tassel cut from a horse's bridle. It was a particularly beautiful shade of blue, with an amulet woven in it, a charm against the evil eye.

On a whim he tried to braid it into his stallion's forelock.

His fingers were swollen with heat and exertion; they were not as deft as they usually were. Mustafa took the tassel from him before he could cast it off in frustration, and plaited it neatly between the stallion's eyes. Fauvel was sweet-natured, for a stallion; he rested his broad forehead against Mustafa's breast and sighed. He knew he was protected, as any wise horse would.

Mustafa smoothed the pale mane on the golden neck and smiled at Richard. "A fine victory," he said.

Richard's temper melted away before a broad and exuberant grin. "Isn't it? Isn't it glorious? Have you ever seen such a caravan?"

"Not in all my days," Mustafa said.

"Ah," said Richard, cuffing him lightly. "What are you, eighteen, nineteen? You're a child. I'm twice your age, and *I've* never seen the like."

Mustafa did not remember how old he was. He supposed he was nineteen. Maybe twenty. It did not matter. Richard had won, and so had he.

"It's thanks to you we did it," Richard said. "You'll be rewarded—no, don't shake your head! Of course you deserve anything you can ask for. But don't ask now. Wait, and think about it. Later you can tell me."

That suited Mustafa, for whom *later* could stretch into *never*. He found himself holding Fauvel's rein while Richard strode through the remnants of the camp, rounding up his men and sending them toward Blanchegarde.

Mustafa took both his own horse and Richard's down the hill to the cistern and let them drink. In a little while Richard came down. He was alone but for a squire; the rest of his men were on the road.

"Mustafa," he said in a tone that made Mustafa's brow arch. "I've another great favor to ask you. You can refuse—I won't force you. Will you take word of this to my mother, and tell her everything? This is a victory she should share. Tell her that when she comes to me in Jerusalem, I'll heap her with jewels and gold and wrap her in silk."

Mustafa bowed. He was no more enamored of the dread

queen than he had ever been, but he could not refuse Richard anything. This time, he thought, she would actually be glad to see him—once she heard the news he brought.

"Take this with you," Richard said, pulling a ring from his finger. It was a signet, a ruby carved with the leopards of his line. Mustafa took it and kissed it and laid it away in his purse, safe beside the little bag of jewels. Richard embraced him and kissed him on both cheeks. "Bless you," he said, "and ride quickly. Take remounts from Blanchegarde—whatever you need."

Mustafa bowed again and murmured thanks. His mare was waiting, fresh enough for the journey to the castle, and even a little impatient. She did not like to stand about when there was a race to be run. He sprang into the saddle, saluted Richard, and gave the mare her head.

Queen Eleanor was indeed pleased to hear of her son's victory—so much so that she gave Mustafa a bed to sleep in and a page to wait on him, and a gift of gold that he could not in courtesy refuse. He kept a little of that, enough for such needs as he had, and gave the rest to beggars on the road as he made his way back to his king. They all praised him lavishly and showered blessings on his head, wishing him a life of good fortune.

He was feeling very fortunate as he came back to the camp at Beit Nuba. Henry had come at last, and the camp had more than doubled in size; Mustafa had to pause at the edge of it to get his bearings.

He was wearing the desert robes that he most often wore when he went out spying, both because they were practical and because they attracted no suspicion among the people of this country. They were a small difficulty in meeting Frankish sentries, but he had Richard's ring, which had won him through to the queen and brought him back intact to the king's camp. He expected no trouble once the guards had seen that; at worst they would drag him off to Richard, or to one of Richard's generals, all of whom knew him perfectly well.

These guards were French, and not friendly. They examined Richard's ring from every angle, and called in their captain to aver that yes, its carving did look like the Plantagenet leopards. They found his little hoard of gold, too, and his jewels in their silken bag. "Thief of a Turk," one of them muttered, not caring that Mustafa could understand.

Mustafa kept a steady grip on his patience. "Take me to the king," he said. "I've come from the queen in Tyre; he'll be wanting to see me."

"Oh, he'll want to see you," said the captain with a little too much relish. He nodded to the guards who held Mustafa between them. They pulled his arms behind him, not gently, and bound them with cords that cut even through the sleeves of his robe.

He gritted his teeth and endured. This was not the first time he had been brought in like a felon. He had learned not to protest, and never to struggle. The quieter he was, the fewer bruises he would earn before he saw the king.

They quick-marched him through a part of the camp that had been bare hillside and thorny scrub when last he saw it. Richard's tent was down below in the shelter of the valley, with his leopard banner flying from it, silken image of the ring that resided now, with Mustafa's bit of wealth, in the captain's purse. Richard was in residence, then, and not out on one of his raids.

Mustafa's captors took him not to the king's tent but to one pitched on a hill that looked toward another, higher hill. That one was called Montjoie, because from it one could see Jerusalem.

This was a great lord's tent, larger and richer than the king's. It had come from the caravan; Mustafa recognized it. Falak al-Din had settled into it the night before he lost everything.

Now the Duke of Burgundy had taken it and filled it with spoils. He was entertaining several of his countrymen, among them a bishop who crossed himself at sight of Mustafa.

Mustafa could not bow; he was bound too tightly. But they had not gagged him. "Messire," he said in his best and most lucid French, "the king is waiting for the messages I bring. If you would send me to him—"

"Yes," said the duke. "The king waits." He inclined his head to his guests. "If you will pardon me, my lords . . ."

They could hardly do otherwise under his grim stare. The bishop seemed vastly gratified, although for what reason Mustafa could not tell. He was beginning to wonder if he should worry. Something was odd. The air had a sharp tinge to it, like brimstone. But it had nothing to do with magic. This was pure human malice.

There were men waiting in a tent near the duke's, with instruments that made Mustafa forget his determination not to struggle.

"You have been accused," the duke said, "of treason against the king and the army of the Crusade."

Mustafa's heart was hammering so hard that he was dizzy. His breath came in gasps. And yet he could not help but laugh. "Treason? For being the king's messenger?"

"You have spied on us on the enemy's behalf. Some say you serve the sultan. I wonder," said the duke, "whether it may not be another whom you serve. You were in Tyre, were you not, when the marquis was murdered?"

"I do not serve that one," Mustafa said through clenched teeth. "I serve the king, and only the king. I was in Tyre on his business and that of his mother—as you well know, my lord. Who accuses me? Does the king know?"

"The king knows," said the duke.

"Then take me to him," Mustafa said.

"In time," said the duke.

"Take me to him," Mustafa persisted. "He knows me. I have his trust. I—"

"Do you?" the duke asked. "Do you really? He may be enamored of your fine brown body, but he is not a complete fool. Under sufficient persuasion, even he can see the truth."

"There is no truth in these accusations," Mustafa said. "Tell me who makes them."

"I make them." The voice was trained for sweetness, but

venom made it harsh. Blondel was not smiling. Was that disappointment which soured his glance? Maybe he had expected to take more pleasure in the moment.

Mustafa understood a great deal just then. The fear in him turned cold and clear. "What do you accuse me of?" he asked.

"Of spying for the infidels," said Blondel. "Of serving the Old Man of the Mountain. Of murdering or helping to murder the marquis in Tyre. Of plotting to murder the king."

"Can you prove any of this?" Mustafa demanded.

"I have witnesses," Blondel said. "You were seen in conversation with men in Tyre who are believed to have been in the Old Man's service. You attempted to implicate the king's sister in your plot, and succeeded so far that the marquis himself accused her of a murder she never committed. She nearly died for that. Then when she escaped, you had perforce to execute the plot—and the target—yourself."

"You can't prove that," said Mustafa. "It never happened."

"Witnesses aver that it did," said the duke. "Two of them are men whom I trust. They saw you, infidel. You were seen plotting sedition with agents of the Old Man."

"Whoever these witnesses saw," said Mustafa, "it was not I."

"They will swear on holy relics," the duke said. "On what will you swear, infidel?"

"On the king's hand," Mustafa said. "I will swear on that, for my hope of Paradise."

Blondel laughed, modulated like a scale on his lute. "Well played, Saracen! Do you think we'd let you within dagger stroke of the king?"

"You can bind me," Mustafa said, "but bring me before him. I will swear to him that I am his man and only his, and have been since the moment I saw him. I never conspired against him, nor have I betrayed him."

"We will test that," said the duke. To his credit, he did not seem as eager to put Mustafa to the test as some of the others, and Blondel most of all.

Mustafa looked that one in the face. "I have done nothing," he said.

"You lie beautifully," said Blondel.

Mustafa set his lips together. There was no justice; no regard for truth. This was revenge for things he had never done.

When the pain began, he screamed. He did not have that kind of pride, and it made the pain a little less. If he had been Blondel he would have screamed in scales, but he had no such gift.

They did not want plain noise. They wanted words; a confession. But he had none to make. He had not done anything that they accused him of. He had told them so. It did no good to tell them again. It would have done him good to lie, but that much pride he had. He would not confess a falsehood.

CHAPTER THIRTY-FOUR

When the new army came to swell the forces of Crusade, Sioned was too deeply buried in books to notice. The only emotion she had been letting herself feel was grief for Safiyah and guilt for her loss—and even more determination to keep her distance from Ahmad. The books were an escape as well as a compelling duty.

She had found hints and suggestions and elusive trails that led nowhere useful; and time ran on. The jinni with the frog's face exhausted its store of books, but lingered, perhaps for lack of a better place to go.

Neither of them had come across anything of use. Sioned had found a cure for boils and a spell for summoning the winds. There were many for destroying demons, but none for destroying a man who had made himself invulnerable.

She learned of the army's coming when the commander of it presented himself in front of her. She blinked at him. He looked about at the books, the inks and pens and parchments, the lamps that burned unceasingly, and said, "God's teeth! This is a cave."

Sioned had not known that the front of the tent unlaced from the sides and could roll up like a canopy. The sun dazzled eyes too long unaccustomed to it. The jinni dived into the shelter of his heap of books. Sioned would have liked to, but she was transfixed, ensorcelled by the light.

Henry grinned at her. It seemed he could not see the jinni, or he would have been more baffled and less lighthearted. "Ah! that's better. You look as if you've been in there for days."

"I have," Sioned said. "When did you come back?"

"Days ago," he said. "I'd have come sooner, but there's a war—a nuisance, but there you are."

"A terrible nuisance," she said. "You'll be marching soon, then."

He nodded. "It's almost time."

"Time for Jerusalem." She shivered lightly. It was not her holy city, but she could not deny the power of the place, or the strength of the call that had brought this army across the sea. It would end soon, in victory or defeat; and the world would change, whichever way the battle went.

Henry had brought wine in a jar, and cups, and a napkinful of sweets. Sioned could not remember when she had last eaten.

The sweetness of wine filled her mouth. It was well watered and laced with honey. Henry's eyes were on her. She was suddenly and rather uncomfortably aware of him: his youth, his strength, the beauty of his face.

Rescue came from a quite unexpected source. One of the jinn swooped down like a hawk on its prey. She had seen it now and then, taking its turn on guard. It was a more human-seeming creature than most, like a winged and bat-eared man. It took no notice of the human with her, bowing low at her feet and saying in a voice like a great organ played softly, "Lady of light, you must come."

Sioned stared at the creature. Its errand must truly be urgent if it would come now, in daylight, in front of a human man. Henry was gaping like a fish. "Is that—am I—"

"Lord of afarit," she said, "prince of the powers of the air, your presence is welcome. Your errand—if I might know—"

The ifrit lowered the lids over its great lantern eyes and said, "You must come."

It would never ask such a thing lightly. She brushed it with a small spell, a charm of truth-seeing. It was as it seemed to be, a spirit of fire. No darkness tainted it.

"I will go," she said. "Lead and I will follow."

It led; Henry followed her. Only the little frog-scholar remained with the books and the wine and the scarcely touched sweets.

Sioned had no expectations of where she would be led, except that it might be to Jerusalem. But it was not so far at all. The ifrit had folded its wings and composed its appearance so that it seemed to be a tall guardsman in cloak and helmet, conducting the king's sister and his nephew on an errand of importance.

Henry was enthralled. "Is that really a creature of the fey?"

"It's an ifrit," Sioned said, "a spirit of air."

"And it serves you?"

She nodded a little sharply. She did not want to talk about it.

Henry regarded her less in awe than in delight. "Why, that is wonderful! That's how you escaped from Tyre, isn't it? They took you. Did you fly? Did they carry you through the air?"

"All the way to Damascus," she said.

"Wonderful," he said, beaming at her. "Simply wonderful."

Sometimes he reminded her that he was Eleanor's grandchild. Not often: he was an honest creature, and honorable, as Eleanor never had been. But this easy acceptance of magic, this sheer delight in it, had a flavor of the queen as she must have been before she embraced the darkness.

Sioned was glad that he could be delighted; for as the ifrit led them through the camp to the quarter which had been taken by the French, the skin between her shoulder blades began to prickle. Something ill was waiting, some trouble great enough to draw the attention of the jinn.

It seemed they walked at a measured pace, but no man

impeded them, and the way that should have been convoluted was clear and straight. In a very little time they stood near the Duke of Burgundy's tent, where an armorer had his forge. From deep within the forge, she heard sounds that made her leap into a run.

They were torturing Mustafa. Later, in Master Judah's tent, she would reckon the count of his wounds and mark the causes of them. Here she saw only the blood and the fire, and the slim brown body stretched on the rack. She did not think at all. The ifrit was like an extension of her own hand, leaping ahead of her, breaking the bonds, lifting the limp form in its strong arms.

"Hold!" cried the Duke of Burgundy. "That man is a traitor to the Crusade."

"*This* man?" Sioned made no effort to hide her incredulity. "This is Richard's dog. He could no more betray his king than the Devil could turn Christian."

"Then the Devil is a holy friar," said Blondel from behind the duke, "because there has been treason committed."

"Oh yes," Sioned said, looking him up and down. "There has been. What did he do to you, to deserve this?"

"He betrayed the king," Blondel said.

She met his pale stare and held it fast, though it tried its best to slide away. "You think the king betrayed you," she said. "And because you could no more harm the king than he could, you did your best to destroy him. I understand that, but I will never forgive it."

"I don't need your forgiveness," said Blondel with a curl of the lip. "The king believes me. He loves me, not that infidel."

"That may be so," she said, "but if it is, then this is even more inexcusable. If this man dies, it will be on your head. And if he lives, and you ever threaten him again, even with so much as a glance, before the powers of heaven and earth, I will see what you pay. Would you sing again? Throw yourself at the king's feet and on his mercy, and tell him the truth. Tell him that you lied. Or that vaunted voice of yours will wither and die."

Blondel's hand flew to his throat. His face had gone slack. He tried to speak; no sound came. He gasped.

"You may speak," she said, "to retract your lies. Speak here, and speak well. Then speak before the king. Then your voice is your own again. Defy me and I keep it forever after."

A croak escaped him. That horrified him far more than simple silence. He clutched his throat; his fingers clawed. His mouth opened and closed.

"Remember," she said.

Mustafa's body would heal. The ifrit had brought Sioned in time; nothing was broken, and nothing was damaged that would not mend. A few days' rest, a few bandages, a posset or two—he would be as hale as he had ever been.

His spirit was another matter. Jealousy and malice did not trouble him unduly, and he was no weakling when it came to pain, but his accusers agreed that Richard had believed the accusations. And Richard was nowhere in evidence. Sioned had sent a man to fetch him, but the man had not come back. She should have sent a jinni; the spirits of earth and air were unaccountably fond of Mustafa, and would have seen to it that Richard came at the summons.

Just as she was about to ask that favor of the ifrit who had brought her to Mustafa, who was still standing guard in the surgeons' tent, a commotion heralded the king's coming. Henry had fetched him. She had known when Henry left; he had an army to command, and he had already given her far more time than he could spare.

Yet there he was in the light of the long summer evening, bowing like a squire as Richard strode into the tent. The king had been in council: he had the ruffled look that Sioned recognized, like a hawk too long in the mews.

He brought the light with him, and the heat of summer in the hills of Jerusalem, gusting like a wind across Sioned's face. Mustafa, who only this morning would have bloomed in it, turned his back and hid in coverlets.

Whether he intended it or not, the movement laid bare the weals that were not severe enough for bandages. They were ugly, livid and swollen, glistening with salve. Richard's breath hissed between his teeth. "God damn them to hell! They were supposed to hold you until I could question you. By the saints, I'll see they pay for this."

Mustafa did not respond. His fists were clenched. The angle of his shoulders was tight with rejection.

Richard lowered himself to one knee. He stretched out a hand, but thought better of it. There was no scrap of skin within reach that would not hurt if he touched it. "See here, boy," he said with rough gentleness. "I don't have to believe what they tell me, but I do have to lend an ear when men of influence swear on holy relics that one of my servants is a traitor. Especially when they're French, and I need them to help me win this war."

Still Mustafa was silent.

Richard rounded on Sioned. "Good God! Did they take his tongue?"

She shook her head. "He's not badly hurt, considering. There's no permanent damage."

"Well, good," said Richard a little too heartily. "Good! I'll damage the ones who did it, you have my word on that. But I do need to ask—"

"You will ask him nothing," said Sioned. "Not now, not later. You've done enough."

"No," said Mustafa. His voice was hoarse, as if he had forgotten how to use it. "No, don't hate him. He had to do it. Let him ask. I'll give him the answers I can give, though he may not like them."

Richard had not won as many battles as he had by giving way to confusion. "Are you going to tell me the charges are true?"

"No," said Mustafa. "They're all lies. I serve no one but you."

"Why?"

Mustafa raised his head. His face was set and still. His eyes were clear. "Because every dog must have its master."

"Some dogs will follow any man who feeds them."

"Some dogs can only follow one man."

Richard nodded. "I believe you," he said.

Mustafa sank down with a sigh.

"You do understand," Richard said, "that the people who did this to you will pay. But first I need them to help me take Jerusalem."

"I understand," Mustafa said.

CHAPTER THIRTY-FIVE

Word of the caravan's fall reached Jerusalem near evening of the day that it was lost. A bruised and dusty servant came riding on a stumbling mule, perched atop an empty packsaddle. His tale ran to the citadel ahead of him and reached the sultan in a tumult of confusion. But the essential fact was clear: the caravan was gone. The Franks had taken it.

Ahmad was with his brother when the news came. They had been talking of small things, the doings of wives and children, the training of horses, the flight of falcons. But their thoughts were of the war, measured in fits and starts and sudden silences. Richard would move soon. The second army of Franks had joined the first. The king would have to use them both and quickly, or lose his hope of taking Jerusalem.

The caravan had been the sultan's hope. He needed its gold and silver to pay his troops, and its silks and jewels to give as gifts to his emirs and his allies and to the caliph whom ultimately he served. Its horses and camels had been meant for his cavalry, its mules for the baggage train of any army that he might bring to the field. The provisions it had carried would have supplied Jerusalem through a Frankish siege.

It was all gone. The messenger swore to that, once he was brought to the sultan—lying on his face, shaking so hard that his tale came in gusts. "They took it all. All of it. The men you sent—dead. All killed. The rest ran. Some died. They weren't taking heads—they had too much else to take."

"Everything?" said the sultan—the first word he had spoken since the news had come to him. "Everything is gone?"

"Down to the last dirham," said the messenger. He was remarkably fearless for a man who brought such news. It was not courage, Ahmad thought; it was shock. He could not believe in the reality of what he had seen, even as he told the tale of it.

The sultan had lived a lifetime of war; it had taken its toll, heavier with each year that passed. But in this hour he had aged years. His eyes were bleak, his face worn and old. His hands trembled on the hilt that the messenger had laid in his lap. The blade of the sword was broken off, but enough was left to read the beginning of a verse from Holy Koran: *On the day of Resurrection shalt thou be paid what thou hast fairly earned.*

It had been Aslam's sword. The sultan had given it to him.

"He broke it," said the messenger. "Malik Ric. He broke it and slew the emir."

"Of course he did," the sultan said as if to himself. His finger traced the chasing of the silver hilt, the pattern of leaves and flowers that unfurled along the guards.

People were crowding into the room. It had been a chapel when the Franks held the city; there was still the shadow of a cross on the eastern wall. Some of those who came spat at it with ritual disgust.

The sultan seemed not to see or hear them. He stroked and stroked the hilt of the broken sword. Aslam had not been a particular friend or a kinsman, but what his death meant . . .

"We are lost," he said. He looked up from the hilt into Ahmad's face. "That caravan was my sole hope of paying my troops through this season. Now, even if enough of them will stay for long enough to drive the Franks back from the walls, they'll abandon me soon after. Then the Franks will overwhelm us. Jerusalem will fall."

"My lord!" cried one of the emirs. "Will you surrender so soon? We hold this city; its walls are fortified, its cisterns deep. We have provisions enough for a siege—not as many as we had hoped, but enough. We can break the cisterns between here and Beit Nuba, and foul the wells. That will give the Franks pause, particularly those who remember Hattin: they'll think long before trying to march in summer through waterless country. We hold the advantage. This is a setback, not a disaster."

"It is a disaster," said the sultan. "Not only can the Franks take Jerusalem. Now they can turn and take Egypt. They have the wherewithal: money to pay their men, and beasts of burden enough to carry their baggage. They're no longer bound to their ships and the sea, or forced to use their own infantry as pack camels."

"And if they take Egypt," sighed someone well back among the crowd, "they'll cleave our hip and thigh, and leave us gasping in the sand."

The emir who had spoken of advantage was drowned out in the flood of doom. The caravan was lost—hope was lost—the war was lost. Even Ahmad was buffeted with hopelessness. It swept over him and drowned him, until he was close to wailing and beating his breast as some of them already were, while the sultan sat cradling the broken sword, tears streaming down his face.

Ahmad tore himself away. Jerusalem was a dangerous place. It was like a burning glass; emotions, caught in the eye of it, flashed into flame. Wards and spells could not defend a man for long. The power of the place twisted and broke them.

The whole city was caught up in grief and dawning panic. Soon enough the recriminations would begin. The war was crumbling about them, defeat on defeat and no clear victory to rejoice in. "Allah has abandoned us!" they cried in the streets and in the halls of the citadel.

Ahmad's own men were housed in the quarter nearest the Tower of David. He sent out the call to bring them in, and spent the time before they came in determining that nothing had changed in the heart of the city's magic. This despair was as honest as it could be under the influence of the place. The strength of the Crusade, the force of its victories, sapped the will of Islam and robbed the jihad of its power.

Armies were made of men, and like men, they grew old. The man who led the Franks was twenty years younger than the sultan—twenty years' worth of strength and warrior zeal. He had his fair share of troubles, but the sultan's were worse. Turks and Kurds were if anything more contentious than Richard and the French.

Ahmad's men were not their usual eager selves, but they were calmer than most. He appreciated the irony: the weakness of soldiers from Egypt had lost the caravan, but these Egyptian troops were the best in Jerusalem. He sent them to guard the city's walls, and bade them keep watch for anything strange or out of place. His searches had yielded nothing, but there was still a niggle of suspicion. Something was amiss.

It would come when it came. He could only lay his snares and wait.

The sultan called a council of all his commanders who could come to Jerusalem within the week, and a great number of elders and leaders of cities and tribes, to consider the fate of the jihad. He sent armed men to break the cisterns that remained between Jerusalem and Beit Nuba, so that there was no water to drink anywhere in those hills. He made dispositions among his troops and in the city. Then he locked himself away to pray.

Four days after the loss of the caravan, Ahmad came back to his lodgings after a long day in the storehouses, determining just how brief the siege of Jerusalem was going to be. His mind was on food and sleep—no great amount of either, if they were going to go on siege rations soon. He was lightly aware of the currents of magic through the city, marking where they shifted and eddied.

One such eddy was waiting in the shadow of the door, seeming a shadow himself, until he unfolded into a slender young man in the garb of the desert. He had a bruised look to him; he moved stiffly, as if he had been beaten, but the worst of it had nothing to do with bodily pain.

"Mustafa," said Ahmad in surprise, but in welcome, too. "What brings you here? Is she—"

"She's well, my lord," Mustafa said. Even as stiff as he was, he moved with grace, bowing at Ahmad's feet.

Ahmad raised him and drew him into the house. The servants had dinner waiting; they calmly added a second portion to their lord's, ignoring Mustafa's protest. "I'm not worthy to dine with a prince. If the servants will make a place for me at their table—"

"You are a guest," Ahmad said, lifting the lid from a steaming pot. "Ah! Cook has made a tagine. How did he know we would be entertaining a man from your country? Here, try it; it smells wonderful."

For all his protestations, Mustafa's manners were princely enough. Faced with Ahmad's refusal to treat him like a servant, he sighed faintly and allowed himself to be a gracious guest.

They ate the fowl stewed in dates and fruits and spices and resting on mounds of couscous, speaking of small things, none of which Ahmad remembered once the words were spoken. Mustafa was hungry, although he tried to hide it; he did not refuse a second portion, or a third.

When he had had his fill, and had belched to show his appreciation, Ahmad called a servant to escort him to a room and a bed and rest. The man would also, in response to a glance from his master, determine whether a physician should come to tend the boy's wounds. Mustafa had said nothing of them, allowed no sign of pain to touch his face, but Ahmad was a hard man to deceive.

Khalid the servant came to his master much later that evening. Ahmad had found that sleep eluded him. He was reading by lamplight, tracing out the words of old spells. Safiyah had taught them to him when he was much younger; they were full of the memory of her. It was a warm memory, with no sadness in it, even when he reflected that none of these spells would have served the war—unless there was some martial purpose in transforming sow's udders into silk.

Cowhides, now . . . enough of those might almost make up for the loss of the silk from the caravan.

He was growing silly in his exhaustion. Khalid's coming was a welcome reprieve. The man had training as a physician, although he had found a stronger calling in attending a lord's needs. "Nothing broken, my lord," he said, "and nothing irreparably harmed. Whoever did it was a fair journeyman of the trade."

"Has he said anything?" Ahmad asked.

Khalid shook his head. "He's gone inside himself. Some men will do that when put to the question."

"Was it one of ours?"

"I think not," said Khalid. "He did say a word or two—he came from Beit Nuba. How he passed the patrols and the city guard, Allah knows."

"My thanks," Ahmad said.

It was a dismissal. Khalid bowed his head and withdrew.

Ahmad sat with the book in his lap, but his eyes were not on the crabbed and ancient script. His visitor intended no harm, or he would never have passed the wards on the door. And yet, like the air of this place in this inauspicious season, his presence, his coming here just now, was oddly and indefinably askew.

It was not in Ahmad to cast him out, even knowing that he might have brought ill fortune. He was a guest, and a guest was sacred.

CHAPTER THIRTY-SIX

M ustafa was gone. Master Judah's assistant, with a tent-
ful of sick and wounded to tend through the night,
had taken little notice of the infidel in the corner.
Mustafa had feigned sleep until the lights were lowered, then
when no one was watching, he had slipped away. He was long
gone by dawn, when someone finally noticed the empty bed.

No one honestly seemed to care, except Master Judah, for
whom losing a patient—to death or escape—was a personal af-
front, and Sioned, who reckoned herself Mustafa's friend. She
should have taken him into her tent, and not abandoned him
among strangers.

They all expected her to tell Richard that his dog had fled.
She would rather not, just as she would have preferred not to
know where he had gone. If she had been Mustafa, and had
been wounded in the heart as he had been, she would have
gone back to Islam and left all of Christendom behind.

She turned toward the mountain of books, but it was not the
refuge she had hoped for. The camp was rumbling softly, like a
lion growling in its sleep. The union of nations was tenuous.

They were already quarrelling: resurrecting old battles, beginning new ones.

Richard would have to march within the next handful of days, or his army would disintegrate where it stood. Even the spoils of the caravan could not erase the differences between English and French, Angevin and Burgundian, Pisan and Genoese, or between all of these and the knights of fallen Jerusalem.

She did not delude herself that her brother delayed for her sake, but her failure to find an answer had done nothing to speed him on his way. If the answer was in books, it had not seen fit to present itself. The jinn had found nothing that they saw fit to tell her.

She sat amid the tottering piles and propped her chin on her fists, glaring at the unresponsive air. Something was eluding her. Something perhaps small, but vitally important. A word, a vision, a memory . . .

Ahmad had walked with her in remembrance, recalling his encounters with the Old Man of the Mountain. The first slipped away unnoticed, but the second, the otherworldly garden, teased her with a sense of rightness. The answer was there, somewhere.

Bards in Gwynedd learned to remember every detail of any place they visited. Her training was incomplete and might betray her, but she could test the strength of it.

She settled more comfortably in her nest of books and cleared her mind of distraction. The sounds of the camp dropped away. Her awareness shrank to the compass of her single self.

She walked through worlds within worlds, elaborate edifices of thought and memory. She sought one among the many, a place of elegant arches and airy domes, which might have been a summerhouse in Damascus. That was the memory of Ahmad within her, beautiful and intricate, with its many rooms and gardens.

One garden in particular called to her. A paradise—was that not what the Persians called a garden? This was an eerie and otherworldly beauty, but a serpent coiled in its heart.

Sinan was not there in this memory, but his strange throne grew out of earth in the midst of the garden. In her vision or dream or foreseeing, that stump of broken tree drew her toward it. She could see as she came closer how it was rooted deep. It was not dead, although it had seemed so; at her coming it stirred and unfurled and put forth shoots that became branches. The branches, opening to their fullest extent, grew and thickened and sprouted leaves. The green of those leaves glowed like emerald, and the blossoms that budded and bloomed among them were shimmering pearl, swelling into fruit: blood-red, dusk-purple, sun-gold.

With the tree grew the serpent. It was a jeweled thing, supple and beautiful, with a bright sardonic eye.

"Sardonyx," Sioned said. "Chalcedony."

The words startled her back to herself. The garden, the tree, the serpent—she understood at last what and who they were. And one more thing, one last memory, stayed with her as she left the vision behind. The serpent had been coiled about the tree's heart. It was a stone, a dull thing, nondescript, seeming of no account save that the serpent so subtly protected it.

There was the thing she had been seeking, in the place where, after all, she would have expected it to be. It was the heart of Sinan's realm, guarded at every point. What hope had she of piercing those manifold walls?

Who else could even try? She yearned for Ahmad, for his power and protection. But he was in Jerusalem, on the other side of the war.

This venture was meant for her. She had found it by Sight and not by art; by instinct rather than by knowledge. Her fault for taking so long to understand; to see that the Sight of her own people was as potent in its way as the eastern books and spells and words of power.

She closed her eyes. The garden was burned in the dark behind the lids. She could see every leaf, every stone, and the one amid them all, brown and lumpen and ordinary. On its face were written words that, as she comprehended them, limned themselves in fire.

The Seal of Solomon was embedded in the trunk of the tree of Paradise. Sinan had taken the garden and a part of the power of the Seal—but not all of it. As to the how and why . . .

She sent out a call without compulsion—her courtesy to the jinn, which set them free to choose their obedience. The one she called came quickly, dancing in the lamp's flame, wreathing his wings with fire.

"A fair day to you," she said to the great jinni.

He bowed within the flame. She could never read his face, it was too alien, but she thought his expression was more somber than usual. "Lady of light," he said. "What would you ask of me?"

"That you carry me," she said, "if you will, to a certain place. I'll not ask you to stay there, but only to bring me to it."

The jinni's wings spread to their full extent, which caused the flame to stretch most strangely. "You must not go there."

"I must," she said.

"It is death."

"Still I must," said Sioned.

"None of us can protect you there," the jinni said. "Those walls—they hold the spell at bay. Once within them, any of us would be bound, compelled to obey the one who rules the stone."

"I know that," she said. "Didn't I ask you simply to bring me to the walls? I'll find my own way past them. But if you can't take me that far, I won't compel you. I won't ever compel."

"And so we love you," the jinni said. "Will you do this?"

"In any way I can," she said.

The jinni sighed vastly. He sounded like the sighing of waves in a sea cave, faint and far away yet all the more potent for that. "It will kill you."

"I hope not," she said.

"Then I will take you," said the jinni. "If you must, and if you will not be turned away, I will go. I will keep you as safe as I can."

"If you do that," she said, "I'll free you from your service."

"You cannot free me," said the jinni. "What I give you, I give of my free will. Only promise to live as long as you may."

"I can always promise that," she said a little shakily.

The jinni bowed to the ground of whatever otherworldly place he inhabited, then straightened and stepped through the flame. She met him midway, for if she hesitated, or allowed herself to think, she would lose her courage.

For this journey the jinni was no larger than a large horse. She rode on his shoulders ahead of the great beating wings, clinging to the tendrils of his hair. It was like a horse's mane, strong and thick; the wind whipped it over her wrists and arms. When she looked down, she saw the earth far below: the mountains of Syria, and on the world's rim the blue gleam of the sea.

She had come without weapons, without even a book of spells, dressed for a day's labor in a tent. She dared not conjure herself a cloak or a grimoire, still less a bow and quiver or a dagger. If she was to reach the garden undetected, she could not blazon her magic across the firmament.

The jinni, being made of essential fire, was warm enough and to spare. The chill of the upper air was almost pleasant after the heat of summer below. She determined to take pleasure in the sensation, and so hold fear at bay.

All too soon the sky changed. Its lucent blue darkened to Tyrian purple and thence to black, but there was no light of stars. They were in the world and out of it, both at once, flying between the real and the unreal, the mortal and the magical. The jinni was warm under her, and alive, though not as humans were. She fought the urge to cling tighter.

Here in the between-place, the wards of the garden had little strength. Yet as they drew closer to that place of power, there was enough to shudder in her skin. The jinni began to labor in his flight, buffeted by currents in the air. Often he rocked and swayed; once he dropped with sickening speed, plummeting like a stone, and just as abruptly swooped upward again. She clamped her eyes shut, though it did no good in the dark, and hid her face in the jinni's mane.

The air's tumult grew worse as the jinni struggled onward.

In the mortal world the wards would have been deadly. Here they could not kill, but they could make it brutally difficult for anything to pass the walls.

She fed the jinni what strength she could, seeping through her hands into his shoulders, until he hissed and snapped at her. "Don't! You waste magic."

"But—" she began.

"Silence," he said.

Her teeth clicked together. The jinni was wiser than she, much as she hated to admit it, and he knew this between-world as she did not. He needed every grain of strength he had for this struggle. Even her brief distraction had sent him reeling back, losing time and speed, so that his flight was more labored than before.

She must not despair. She must trust her mount and guide, and nurture her magic, gathering it inside her, feeding it in whatever way she could: with the strength of her spirit and the knowledge she had drunk since she came across the sea. The life in her womb, as young and small as it still was, nonetheless succeeded in making her stronger. She who had been one, now was two. Even in guarding the second, she fed her power.

It would be a mage, this child. She was deeply glad, even as she wondered whether its father would share her joy.

At length the jinni hung motionless in the dark, straining every sinew simply to keep from tumbling backward. Sioned drew a breath, prepared to unleash her magic—but before she could betray them both, there was a sound like the cracking of a stone. The jinni fell out of the dark into the fierce dazzle of sunlight.

Once more he plummeted, but this time she forced her eyes open. He was making no effort to brake his fall; his wings were tightly furled, his body slack.

She must not doubt. Doubt slew magic. She must believe, and trust, that the jinni would not let either of them be destroyed.

With a ripping crack, the great wings snapped to their fullest extent. The air keened as the jinni's descent slowed. At last Sioned dared look down.

The garden lay below, a jewel amid a wilderness of jagged stones. The stones were mountains; the garden lay in the heart of them. Without magic there was no coming to it: the sides of its walls were sheer, the waste beyond unmarred by any track.

Sioned looked for the angel with the flaming sword, but it seemed that was a myth or a memory. There was a wall of fire—magical fire—but no living being stood in the midst of it.

The jinni came to earth outside the wall. His body shuddered, buffeted by the power of the garden and its protections. That he could speak at all amazed her; she was awed that he could speak clearly, even serenely. "I cannot pass the wall or the gate. The Seal within—it would bind me. I do not wish to be bound."

"Nor should you be," she said. "Will you wait for me? Can you?"

The wide shoulders hunched; the wings drew in tight. "I will wait as close as I can bear to be."

"Don't stay so close that you're caught," she said.

The jinni's lips drew back from a formidable array of teeth. "Such care you have, bright lady, for my poor self."

"How will I escape," she asked, "unless you help me?"

"Your soul has wings," the jinni said. He bowed before her as he so often insisted on doing, but as he rose again, he did not retreat at once. He lingered, hovering. Insofar as a creature so fierce and so inhuman could be said to fret, he was fretting. "I do not like to leave you here."

She did not like to be left here, but she had made her choice. "Wait for me," she said to the jinni.

She paused briefly, gathering the last scraps of her courage. Without the jinni there was no escape: the slope of the mountain dropped away sheer. The garden glowed before her, illumining on a low and ominous sky.

To pass the wall and the wards, she must seem perfectly harmless: a waft of wind, a ray of light, a dust mote drifting innocuously into the garden. Her mind emptied of thought.

She felt nothing, knew nothing, was nothing but softly shifting air.

It was dangerous, that working. A spirit could lose its knowledge of self and become in truth what it seemed to be. Yet she could not cling to any part of her awareness, lest the wards find it and destroy her.

CHAPTER THIRTY-SEVEN

Sioned drifted through the walls of air. They were like ice-cold fire. If she had had a self to know pain, she would have cried out in agony. But she was nothing, no one, no more than a breath wafting over the undying grass.

She fell to ground that, however supernal in its origins, was mortally hard. The walls rippled and shimmered behind her. She seemed as much herself as ever. The child was safe within wards and the womb. If some part of her had lost itself to the wall, she was not aware of it.

Slowly she rose. The garden was not precisely as Ahmad had recalled it. The unnatural green, the strange flowers, the dizzy-ing sweetness, yes—he had remembered those rightly. But something was different. There had been no spirits in his mem-ory, no powers but Sinan and the garden itself. Now, as she looked about, every leaf, every flower shimmered with the pas-sage of beings who were not of earth nor yet of heaven.

They were thickest about the tree, which stood as in her vision, laden with leaves and flowers and fruit. Sweeter than roses, sweeter than jasmine, the scent was stunning, intoxicating, glorious.

She did not see the serpent until she was almost close enough to touch it. All the spirits leaped and swirled and spun, bound by the power of the thing that the serpent guarded, yet singing in their captivity. They made her think of Christian angels before their god, though no Christian would have approved of the thought.

The serpent was asleep, as far as she could tell. Its lidless eyes were open perpetually, but its head rested on the lumpen plainness of the Seal, its long body draped over bole and branches, its tail hanging down, limp and still. It was even more beautiful than in her vision: body of ebony, bands of ruby and citrine and pearl, and eyes like ruddy amber. Between those eyes shone a moonstone as large as a pullet's egg, which glowed like the moon, the light of it waxing and waning as the serpent breathed.

Before she passed through the wall, without even thinking of what she did, she had picked up a stone the same size and color and shape as the Seal. It was still clutched in her hand, heavy as iron, and cold. Her warmth had not touched it. Yet as she held it up, near despair, for the serpent would know that this chill thing was not the Seal, warmth seeped through it. The power of the garden worked even on so mortal a thing.

The serpent's eyes seemed to stare into hers, seeking the inner places of her soul. It was asleep, she told herself. She began a soft, winding song, a song of sleep, serpent-sleep: darkness shimmering with light, and dreams of small struggling prey.

The spirits slowed their dance about the tree, captured by the spell. The moonstone's pulsing took the rhythm of waves in the sea, a long surge and sigh. Sioned reached up among the branches. The luminous fruit swayed, brushing against her lips, tempting her to bite into it, to discover if its taste was as sweet as its fragrance.

It was not wisdom that kept her from succumbing to temptation. She was so far gone in terror that she was perfectly calm. She could not think of anything but the serpent and the stone. If her singing faltered, if her spell failed, the serpent would wake with her hand among its coils.

The Seal was cold—as cold as the stone had been. Was she to be betrayed after all?

No doubts. No fears. The Seal was nested in a notch in the trunk. Wood had grown about it. She worked her fingers down as far as they would go, taking no notice of pain. The Seal was caught fast.

She drew the dagger she wore at her belt. It was Ahmad's gift, lovely with its ivory hilt, and wickedly sharp. Its shimmering Indian steel sank easily into the wood of the tree and pried loose the Seal.

The serpent stirred, flexing its coils. She froze. The forked tongue flicked once, twice, thrice. The third time it did not withdraw; it lay as slack as the serpent's tail.

Swiftly but not hastily—never hastily, lest she fail—she slipped the mortal stone into the gap where the Seal had been. It fit well enough. The Seal had a cord of plaited silver, black with age but still supple. It seemed perfectly natural to slip the cord about her neck and let the Seal slide down beneath her chemise to rest between her breasts.

It was only briefly cold. Its magic did not touch her—strange, but a great relief. She sheathed the dagger and drew back from the tree. The spell of sleep was still coiling through her. She turned toward the edge of the garden, where the walls rose, shimmering like the dance of spirit-lights in the northland sky.

Her singing had paused as she contemplated her escape from those walls. A hiss was her only warning. She dropped and rolled through pure instinct.

The serpent's strike arched above her head. A drop of venom splashed her hand. The pain of it was beyond agony. It seared through her body.

The serpent snapped back into its coils. She could not stand; the poison had robbed her legs of strength. She crawled, hand over hand.

The serpent struck again. She had not known what strength she still had in her, until she found herself coiled in a ball out of the serpent's reach.

Spirits swirled like water about her. The Seal—they were bound to it.

The Seal . . .

Somehow she managed to stand. How her knees held her, she did not know. Her hand clasped the Seal beneath coat and chemise. She looked into the serpent's eyes and said, "Be still."

The serpent stilled. Its eyes glittered, but its mind and volition were hers. "Guard the stone," she said. "Protect it from all who come. Forget my face, my presence, but remember my voice. Remember my command. Guard the stone."

Slowly the serpent's head lowered to the stone, coming to rest on it. The moonstone's light flared as if in a great sigh, then dimmed almost to nothing.

Sioned could not collapse, not yet, even with the serpent's venom closing her throat and dimming her eyes. There was one last spell which she must raise, which would take everything she had. But she must do it.

She wrought an illusion. It was a simple thing, and shallow, but its surface gleamed convincingly. It declared to any who sought this place that the Seal was still there and its power still lay on the garden. It would, gods willing, persuade Sinan that the heart of his power was safe. Only if he came to the garden in his own flesh and person would the illusion fail. She had to pray that he would not do such a thing; that the affairs of the world so preoccupied him that he would not be moved to take a moment's rest.

For one who wore the Seal, the walls of air were no barrier. She walked through them on feet that had gone numb, stumbling but keeping grimly erect.

The jinni was waiting just without. He caught her as she fell, and leaped into the air, clasping her close, not speaking a word.

Much too late and on the edge of nothingness, she understood. She had the Seal, that thing which the jinni loathed and feared above all else. She had the power to compel him and all his kind. The jinni, knowing it, hating the very thought of it, nevertheless kept his word. He had come back for her. He was taking her away to safety.

*   *   *

Master Judah barely blinked at the personage who brought the king's sister to him for tending. It was wearing as human a form as it could bear, enough like a very large and very ruddy Frank to pass casual muster, but the master's eye was never casual.

At the moment however he was far more concerned with Sioned than with her unearthly guard. "She's burning alive," he said. "What—"

"Poison," said the jinni in its great organ chord of a voice. "Venom of the serpent that lives in the garden."

The master started slightly, then shook his head. "I thought I heard—"

"You heard rightly," the jinni said. "Be quick, mortal man. Heal her."

"As you say," the master said, "I am a mortal man. If this is what you say it is—"

"You know," said the jinni. "Heal her."

The master was never one to argue with the inarguable. He called for assistants, but the jinni would not let Sioned go. He shrugged and said, "Come."

When there was no battle to fill the surgeons' tents, or when the army was healthy enough not to overwhelm the physicians with a plethora of diseases, the most direly ill had the luxury of a separate and smaller tent. It was as airy as anything could be at Beit Nuba in the summer, and scrupulously clean: even as the master brought his new patient in, one of the apprentices finished spreading the beds with fresh linen.

There were soldiers in the beds, one just past the crisis for dysentery, the other wounded in a raid and uncertain yet as to whether he wanted to live or die. The master bade the jinni lay Sioned at some distance from these.

She was shuddering with the onslaught of the fever, but she had clawed her way to consciousness. As Judah bent over her, she clutched his hand. "My brother," she said. "Fetch—"

The rest was lost in gagging and coughing, but Judah did not need to hear it. The assistant who was nearest did not need to be told; he turned and ran.

To the next nearest, Judah said, "See if the cooks have any snow left. Tell them sherbet can wait; this lady cannot. If they have none, we'll sink her in the cistern. But—"

"Snow," said the jinni, "we can fetch. The cooks should send strong broths and lees of wine."

Judah's brow went up. "So; you have some skill in healing."

"I watch mortals," said the jinni. "Heal her."

"When I have the snow," Judah said, "we can begin—"

The jinni did not stir, but Judah's mouth had fallen open. What had been the corner of a tent in the hills of Judea, well along toward noon of a day in midsummer, was now the summit of a mountain, white and gleaming with snow.

Judah wasted no time in gawping. He got a grip on both of the assistants who stood as stunned as he had been, and flung them toward the patient. They at least had training enough to know what he wanted, and sense enough not to flinch for modesty's sake. They stripped her to her chemise and packed her in snow, then fed her such medicines as there could be for such a poison: herbs to strengthen her heart, and a potion for the restoration of her humours, and leeches and a lancet for the hand that had taken the brunt of the poison. The leeches shriveled and died; the lancet released a gush of foulness. It was little enough, but even a little might make the difference between life and death.

Richard wasted very little time in coming at the master's call. There was a flock of courtiers in his wake, which the assistants held back, by force if need be. Richard ignored them. He dropped down by Sioned's side. "God's bones! What have you done to her?"

"She's poisoned," Judah said. "We're bringing the fever down. We've given her medicines, such as we have. The rest is for her to do."

"Poisoned? Who—what—"

"She walked in the garden," the jinni said, "and the serpent struck at her. She is fortunate: its venom merely touched her hand. If its fangs had sunk in her, she would have died where she stood."

"What—" said Richard.

Sioned's hand gripped his arm. Even Judah had thought her sunk in coma, but she had clung to the shreds of awareness. "I brought it back," she said through chattering teeth. "I—brought—take it. It's under my chemise. Take it!"

Richard frowned. Judah, suddenly emptied of patience, found the blackened silver chain about her neck. Her eyes were clouded, blind, but she smiled in his direction. He drew forth the thing that she had come near to killing herself to win.

It looked like a clay seal such as merchants might use to mark a jar of wine. There was no elegance or grace in it, nor any beauty of design, only letters in Hebrew of an ancient style.

He did not want to read them. If he did so, his world would change beyond retrieving. Yet as he held the seal by its chain, the letters burned through the mirror of his sight, deep into his mind.

This was not a Christian thing. It was not Muslim, either. It was of his people, from the days of Solomon the wise king, about whom so many legends were woven.

This one, it seemed, was true. He held the Seal of Solomon in his hand, the seal with which the great king bound the powers of earth and heaven. He looked from it to the face of the Christian king, and with no thought at all, gave it into Richard's hand.

"Put it on," Sioned gasped. "Promise you won't take it off. Promise!"

"I promise," said Richard. "Is this—"

"Yes," she said.

His body sagged briefly. "Thank God!"

"Put it on," she said with the last breath she had.

He slipped the chain over his head and let the Seal fall into hiding beneath his shirt. "How do I—" he began.

She had no answer to give him. She breathed too shallowly; despite the magical snow that did not melt as its mortal kind did, her skin was still dangerously hot. The passing of the Seal had neither helped nor harmed her—to Judah's relief; he had been in dread that once it left her body, so would what life was left in her. But she clung to it, if tenuously.

"You may go now," Judah said to the king. "If there is any news, I will send a messenger."

Richard knew a dismissal when he was firmly presented with one, but he dug in his heels. "Is she going to die?"

"Not if I can help it," Judah said grimly.

"Keep her alive," Richard said.

That was precisely what Judah intended to do. He turned his back on the king and set about assuring himself that while she was no better, neither was she notably worse.

Richard lingered for a while, but Judah ignored him. At length he left Judah in such peace as he could have until Sioned either recovered or died.

CHAPTER THIRTY-EIGHT

A week and a day after the sultan sent out his summons, all the commanders of Islam who were within reach had come to Jerusalem. The last arrived before the evening prayer, and gave himself up gratefully to bath and food and rest.

That evening after the prayer, the sultan called his council. Tomorrow was Friday, the holy day of Islam. The day after that was the remembrance day of Hattin, five years past: the battle in which the Kingdom of Jerusalem had fallen to the sultan's armies.

The sultan was determined that the council recall that mighty victory. "I'll remind them," he said to Ahmad and to his eldest son Al-Afdal as they prepared to go into the hall. "I'll bid them remember not only what we were then, but what the Franks were and are and always shall be."

"Led by an idiot?" his son asked. "Not this time, Father. Everyone says that. This time, the Franks could win."

"Malik Ric could win," the sultan said. "Without Malik Ric, they're led by factionaries and fools."

"But how do we—"

The boy broke off. He was young and he had a temper, but he was not slow-witted. "Father! You wouldn't call on *that* one. You hate him."

"The hatred is mutual," the sultan said. "No, I would not do such a thing, even to serve my dearest convenience. I'll look for other and less vile ways to separate the Franks from their king."

"You are a saint," Ahmad said. "Pray Allah your rectitude doesn't destroy you."

The sultan shook his head. "I'm no saint. I'm a coward. I'm scared to death of losing my soul."

"Do you know," said Ahmad to himself, "I don't think I am. How very strange."

Neither the sultan nor his son seemed to hear. Ahmad fell in behind them as they walked down from the sultan's rooms to the hall.

The knights of Jerusalem had held their court here in this grandiose place, with its heavy pillars and its arches that were all dignity and little grace. The lords of Islam had pulled down the crosses and covered the figured mosaics with carpets, but it was still an elusively Christian place.

The council had been seated when the sultan came, sipping sherbet and nibbling bits of sweets. They rose and bowed together, even those so elderly or so obese that they moved with difficulty. It was a great tribute; it brought tears to the sultan's eyes, which he made no effort to conceal.

One of them stepped forward: a scholar more than a warrior, but well born and well spoken and above all loyal to the sultan. He was hardly a young man, but his eyes shone with a young man's zeal. "Sire," he said, "if you will forgive the liberty, we have spoken among ourselves, and we agree: let us gather by the Rock from which the Prophet, on whose name be blessing and peace, was taken up to heaven. Let us stand there and fight until the last of us is dead. Then Allah will take us as He took His Prophet, and we will feast in Paradise."

They all murmured agreement. The sultan was silent. After a long while he lifted his head and sighed. "You are good men," he said: "good Muslims. All of Islam looks to you for courage and strength."

"We are with you to the death," said one of the Kurdish emirs. Even the Turks nodded; first one and then another leaped up and prostrated himself and swore his life to the sultan.

Their loyalty, their love and devotion, acted on him like rain in a desert. The lines of care and pain receded from his face. He stood straighter, held himself more firmly. He almost smiled.

The smile did not linger past the door of the hall. He was still heartened, still strong, but as he settled once more in his private chamber with his brother and his son, he turned his hand palm up. A bit of paper rested in it, written in a crabbed hand.

Al-Afdal plucked it from his father's palm and read aloud: " *'The battalions of the mamluks are against a siege—they fear another disaster such as cost us Acre. They advise battle, as swift and devastating as may be. Then if we have the victory, we gain the lands from here to the sea; if we fail, we have some hope of escape. If you insist upon a siege, sire, the mamluks declare that some one of your kin must remain in the city, or all your forces will break apart—Kurd with Kurd, Turk with Turk, and God forbid that either take orders from the other.'* " Al-Afdal looked up from the paper. "Father, are our straits that dire? Who wrote this?"

"It doesn't matter who wrote it," the sultan said. "He speaks the truth. But I had hoped to avoid a battle."

"It would be better if we forced one," Al-Afdal said. "There's no water for the Franks, but we have whole cisterns full. If we can lure them out of their lair and keep them in the dry land, we'll destroy them as we have so many times before."

"We do keep the advantage of water, don't we?" said the sultan with the flicker of a smile, which swiftly died. "Still, a siege would wear them down without costing us overmuch blood. They can't starve us out before they give way to thirst. Who knows—their own constant sickness of dissension may conquer them even more quickly than lack of water."

"I can stay," Ahmad said.

They both looked at him as if they had forgotten he was there. He had been unusually quiet, but then he had had nothing to say.

"I'll stay in Jerusalem," he said, "if you judge it wiser to go. The mamluks will follow me in your name—there are so many from Egypt; we get on well together."

"So you do," said the sultan. He sighed. "Ah, God; despair's a tenacious thing. I'm sick of fighting. I'm old; I want to rest. Do you think I ever will, except when I'm dead?"

Al-Afdal's hand flicked in a warding gesture. "Avert! Father, don't speak of such things. It's bad luck."

"Everything is written," said the sultan. "There is no luck; only fate."

"If it's written that you die," said Ahmad, "you die. But a man should live his life to its fullest, or it's all been for nothing. Remember joy, brother. Remember victories. You'll have them both again."

"Will I?"

A prickle ran down Ahmad's spine. He was the only one of his brothers whom God had given the gift of magic. Yusuf was wise, and he was a leader of men—incontestably. But he was neither mage nor seer.

Even the least magical of men could sometimes be touched by the hand of God. The sultan was in a strange mood tonight, sunk in despair and yet, in an odd way, exalted. "It ends here," he said. "One way or another, tomorrow or a month from tomorrow, this war is over."

"Maybe so," said Al-Afdal, "but it's not lost. We'll win this, Father. We're sworn to it."

"You are good and loyal men," the sultan said. "Will you stay with me? You can sleep if you like. I'm minded to pray."

His son nodded. Ahmad reckoned that he could stay for a while; there were things that needed doing, but they could wait an hour or two. A little peace would soothe his soul.

*   *   *

In the end it was nearly dawn before he went back to his lodgings. He had joined his brother and his nephew in prayer; then
he had slept a little. He was thinking of an hour in his own bed,
then a bath, breakfast, fresh linen, as he passed the mamluk on
guard at his door. The man was wide awake, quiet but alert:
doing his duty as a good servant should.

The wards of the house were untouched. His young guest
had not gone out since Ahmad left that morning; he had not
even left the room in which he had lain for the past several days.
If the sultan was sunk in despair, Mustafa was buried in the
deepest reaches of it.

He was not asleep, although he tried to pretend that he was.
Ahmad stood looking down at him. There was little to see but
a tight knot under a sheet. After careful consideration, Ahmad
plucked the sheet from him.

He was fully clothed, all but the shoes and the turban.
"Leaving so soon?" Ahmad asked him.

Mustafa's body unknotted, creaking as he stretched; he hissed
at the pain of healing scars. His eyes were calmer than Ahmad had
expected, and clearer. "I should never have come here," he said.
"I was angry; I despaired. God will judge me for it."

"God judges us all," said Ahmad.

Mustafa shook his head. He had the humorlessness and the
perfect self-absorption of the very young. "He betrayed me, but
who's to say my betrayal hasn't been worse? I knew what he
was, what he would do—how he is a king first and always—and
still I gave way to jealousy and spite. I knew better!"

"How have you betrayed him?" Ahmad asked. "You've said
nothing to anyone here."

"I came here," Mustafa said. "I could have chosen any
refuge, anywhere. I chose one among his enemies."

"You were wounded in the heart," Ahmad said. "You didn't
choose as unwisely as that; you've told us no secrets, and you
know we won't ask. We may be enemies, but we are honorable."

"You are more honorable than the Franks," Mustafa said

with a twist of the lip. "Please forgive me if I've offended. I'll leave as soon as the gates open."

"Today is the day of prayer," said Ahmad. "Stay with us; worship Allah in this holy city, and ask for His forgiveness. Then you may go."

"Won't you ask me where I'll go?" Mustafa demanded.

Ahmad shook his head. "Some things it were best I not know. Will you bathe? Eat with me? It will be dawn soon; we can say the morning prayer together."

Mustafa bowed. Good, thought Ahmad: he was acting and thinking. He must have made good use of his days in seclusion.

He still had a bruised look to him. It would be a long while before that went away. Perhaps it never would, though Ahmad dared to hope that he was a stronger spirit than that.

The sultan led the midday prayer in Al-Aqsa, the Father Mosque, that sat beneath its silver dome in the vast court of the Dome of the Rock. Far more splendid prayers rose up to heaven from that glorious golden dome, but he was in a mood for quieter devotions.

He had come exalted from his night of prayer, but on the ride across the city from the Tower of David to the Dome of the Rock, all his fears and exhaustion and the weight of despair had come crashing down upon him. He wept as he rode. As he took his place in the foremost ranks of the faithful, tears streamed down his face.

Ahmad caught Al-Afdal's eye. The boy was scowling. Ahmad was in better control of his face, but he was in no cheerful mood, either. To win a war or to withstand a siege, men needed strength; they needed a certain brightness of spirit. Even the sultan's most loyal followers could see how beaten down he was. How long could they hold fast, if their lord did not?

He glanced to his right, where Mustafa stood and bowed and knelt with the rest of the long line of men. He was dressed as a mamluk from one of the Egyptian companies, with Ahmad's device embroidered on the sleeve.

It was courageous of him to join in these prayers. Ahmad noticed which of them he did not share; how he refrained with considerable care from invoking Allah's blessing on the sultan's cause.

That was honor, though it had fixed itself on a Christian king. Ahmad could admire it, even understand it. He found himself smiling faintly as he performed one of the many prostrations.

His mind was not on God. Nor, except peripherally, was it on his brother. This place was suffused with sanctity. He focused on small things, mortal things, to keep his mind from losing itself in light.

His wards had no strength here. He was reduced to ordinary means of maintaining vigilance: his eyes, his hands, the force of mamluks whom he had placed discreetly all about the sultan.

There was no warning, no ripple in the pool of holiness. They believed that they were doing God's work, those mamluks who turned on either side of the sultan. Their eyes were soft as if with sleep; their expressions were rapt. They struck for the glory of God: one for the throat, one for the heart.

The sultan sank slowly down. Ahmad leaped, not caring if he fell on a blade. But the loyal mamluks were faster than he. A scarce heartbeat after they rose up against their lord, the traitors were dead.

The sultan sagged in Ahmad's arms, dragging him down to the floor. He was still breathing. Certainly he was wounded, but maybe—maybe—

He gripped Ahmad's hand with all his strength. The bones ground together; the pain made his breath catch. But he did not try to free himself.

"Brother," said the sultan. "Brother, try—a siege—you must—"

"Hush," said Ahmad. He felt strange, remote, as if walled in glass. The ripple of shock was still advancing through the mosque: men leaping up, craning, staring, crying out.

The sultan's mamluks closed in, standing on guard—now that it was too late to protect him. None of them belonged to

Sinan. Ahmad made sure of that with a swift and deceptively simple spell. If he had not been a fool—if he had not fallen into complacence—

His brother stirred in his arms. Life was draining out of him. Ahmad called in all the powers he had, all the arts and skills, to stop the blood, to heal the wounds. But the cavity of Yusuf's chest was filling with blood, seeping from the pierced muscle of the heart. He was drowning inside his own body. Maybe a great master of healers could save him. But not Ahmad, whose gifts lay elsewhere.

People were shouting, struggling. There was fighting: men screaming invective, cursing one another, doing battle over whether the sultan was alive or dead.

That was the sound of an empire crumbling. "Brother," said Yusuf, barely to be heard. "Whatever you must do, do."

"You won't die," Ahmad said.

"I am dead," said Yusuf. He drew in a breath; it broke in a spate of coughing. Somehow, through it, he spoke the words of Faith: "There is no god but God, and Muhammad is the Prophet of God."

"No," said Ahmad, but it was an empty sound, without sense or meaning.

No emptier than the body in his arms. With the last of those most sacred words, Yusuf's soul slipped free. Ahmad could not catch it or stop it. Its face was turned toward Paradise. Already it had forgotten the world of labor and pain.

That world had erupted in tumult. Ahmad should stop it. The emirs, Al-Afdal the heir—none of them had the presence of mind. They were all either gaping in mindless shock or running wild through the mosque and out into the court of the ancient Temple.

But if Ahmad rose and took the reins, he would have to let his brother go. He could not do that. The body was cooling even in the day's heat. In time it would stiffen, but for the moment it still had the suppleness of life.

He looked down into his brother's face. The lines of care and fear had smoothed away. Yusuf did not look as if he was asleep; no sleeper was ever so pale or so still. But he had died in peace.

He had left a house of war. Ahmad laid him down as gently as if he could still feel the jarring of movement on his wounds, and said to the mamluks, "Let no one touch him but the servants of the dead."

They bowed. One, even as he straightened, whipped about and flattened a shrieking, dancing madman.

Matters were grievously out of hand. The emirs were scattered; Al-Afdal had vanished. One man in mamluk's dress stood motionless in all that chaos, surrounded by a strange stillness.

Ahmad met Mustafa's gaze. Mustafa looked down at the sultan, then up again at Ahmad. Ahmad watched the choice take shape. It did not sadden him particularly. A man did what a man must. Had not the sultan bidden Ahmad do precisely that?

Mustafa bowed to them both, the living and the dead. An eddy of confusion passed between. When it cleared, Mustafa was gone.

CHAPTER THIRTY-NINE

The King of the English sat in the shade of a canopy, sipping sherbet cooled with snow from Mount Hermon. He had suffered a bout of fever, the latest of all too many in this pestilential country; it had flattened him for two days. He was mending now, and none too soon, either, but he was still shaky on his feet.

"Your medicines are good," he said to his physician, "but my sister's are better. How long are you going to let her lie like a dead thing?"

"It's not a matter of letting," Master Judah said. His tone was cool but his lips were tight. "She is alive; the fever is gone. But she doesn't wake."

"Will she?" Richard asked. "Can she?"

"I don't know," said Master Judah.

Richard scowled. When he had bidden her find the key to the Old Man's destruction, he had also bidden her leave the fetching to someone else. He should have known that she would ignore the second half of his command. She was as much a Plantagenet as he was; she did as she pleased, with little enough regard for anyone else's wishes.

The Seal hung heavy about his neck. It had not left him since she insisted that he take it. Whatever it did, it obviously did not protect him from the ills of the flesh. More than once he had considered shutting it away in his treasury, but he never quite brought himself to do it. She had been so insistent, and she had paid so high—it was a tribute of sorts, and a superstitious hope that as long as he wore the Seal, she would cling to life.

He drained his cup of sherbet. The hand that filled it anew did not belong to his squire. Blondel had been walking very softly since he confessed to accusing Mustafa of treason. Richard had not seen fit to punish him, but with that one, silence was more cruel than blows.

Richard was not ready yet to speak to Blondel. He turned his attention instead to the entertainment that several of his knights had arranged for him, to speed his recovery, they said—and, they did not say, to while away the time until he decided whether to attack Jerusalem. That decision should have been made days ago, but the fever had intervened. If he did not make it soon, he would lose his army. The French were growing fractious again; the English pined for their wet and misty country.

But today he would not think of that. He would watch what promised to be a very good fight: the settling of a dispute between a knight from Burgundy and a knight from Poitou. The exact details of the disagreement were not particularly clear, but they hardly mattered.

So far the Burgundian was getting the worst of it. He was not as young or by any means as thin as his adversary, and the heat, even this early in the morning, was taking its toll.

Richard watched with professional interest, because the Poitevin was a jouster of some renown; but when he laid a wager, he laid it on the Burgundian. The lesser fighter had the better horse, lighter and quicker and, though it sweated copiously, less visibly wilted by the heat. The Poitevin's coal-black charger was enormous even by the standard of the great horses of Flanders, and although it lumbered and strained through the turns and charges of the joust, no sweat darkened its heavy neck.

Having handed his gold bezant to the clerk who was keeping track of the wagers, Richard let his mind wander even as his eye took in the strokes of the fight. He liked to do that: it helped him think.

He would not camp in sight of Jerusalem. If it happened he must ride where he could see the city, he had a squire hold up a shield in front of his eyes. He had sworn an oath: he would not look on those walls and towers or the golden blaze of the Dome of the Rock until he had come to take it for God and the armies of Christendom. But scouts who kept the city in sight said that it had been boiling like an anthill since the evening before.

None of his spies had come in with reliable news. He missed his dog of a Saracen, and God help Blondel if the boy had either died or turned traitor in fact as well as in name. Mustafa would have known the cause of the turmoil in Jerusalem. These idiots had only been able to report that all the infidel raiding parties had begun to swarm back toward the city, and messengers—all of whom, damn them, had escaped pursuit—had ridden out at a flat gallop on the roads to the north and east and south.

God knew, there were rumors enough on the roads and in the villages. The sultan was preparing a killing stroke against the Franks; Islam was under siege from some hitherto unforeseen enemy; Jerusalem had been invaded in the night as Tyre had been, by an army of jinn and spirits of the air. There was even a rumor that no one credited: that Saladin himself was ill or wounded or dead.

Richard had prayed for that. He was not fool enough to expect that it was true. God only answered prayers when it suited His convenience.

The fever was still in him, making him giddy at odd moments. He focused once more on the fight.

The Poitevin was winning, curse him—the Burgundian was

near done for. The knights who had wagered on the champion were reckoning their winnings already.

The Poitevin's horse collapsed abruptly. In the same instant the Burgundian flailed desperately at the Poitevin's head. The heavy broadsword struck the helm with a thunderous clang. The Poitevin dropped like a stone.

The horse was dead—boiled in its own skin without the relief of sweat to cool it. The knight was alive but unconscious. The unexpected victor sat motionless astride his heaving and sweat-streaming destrier, until his squire came running to get him out of the stifling confinement of the helm and lead him dazedly off the field. His face in its frame of mail was a royal shade of purple.

As men from the cooks' tents hauled the fallen horse off to the stewpots, a different disturbance caught Richard's attention. "See what it is," he said at random, waving off the clerk and the winnings of his wager. Several of the knights and squires nearby sprang up to obey, but Blondel was quickest on his feet.

Richard's eyes followed him as he ran. Whatever his sins of jealousy and spite, he had the grace of a gazelle.

He came back so swiftly that he seemed to fly, and with such an expression on his face that Richard rose in alarm, half-drawing his sword. "Sire," he said. "My lord, come. Please come."

Richard only paused to order his attendants to stay where they were. They did not like the order, but they obeyed it. With Blondel for guide and escort, Richard strode toward the camp's edge.

One of his scouting parties had come in with a captive: a slender man in the robes of the desert, with the headcloth drawn over his face. He seemed not to care where he was or who had caught him. He sat on the rocky ground, cross-legged in the infidel fashion; his head was bent, his shoulders bowed.

"He was headed here, sire," the sergeant said. "He didn't resist at all, except to stick a knife in Bernard when he tried to pull off the face veil."

Bernard nursed a bandaged hand, but Richard could see that he would live. Of the infidel, Richard was not so sure. He reached out; his men tensed, on the alert, but the infidel made no move to attack.

He drew the veil aside from a face he knew very well indeed. He heard the hiss of Blondel's breath, but the singer knew better than to say a word.

"Mustafa," Richard said. His heart overflowed with joy and deep relief. "Thank God—Mustafa."

At the sound of his name, Mustafa stiffened slightly. His skin had the waxy look of a man who has taxed his strength to the utmost. His eyes were blank, blind. He was not truly conscious; all that held him up was the warrior's training that let him sleep upright wherever he happened to find himself.

Richard called for his men to fetch a litter. While they did that, he sent Blondel to fetch Master Judah. "Tell him to attend me in my tent. And tell him why."

Blondel flinched as if Richard had struck him. For a moment Richard wondered if he would offer defiance, but instead he bowed and spun and ran.

This time Richard did not pause to watch him. The litter was taking too cursed long. Richard lifted Mustafa in his arms and carried him back through the camp. People stared, but Richard paid them no attention. Let them gape and wonder. It would keep them occupied.

Master Judah was waiting in Richard's tent. Even as quickly as Richard had come there, the master already had a bed made and a bath waiting and all made ready for the care of a wounded man.

That at least was not Mustafa's trouble—not more recently than his encounter with the Duke of Burgundy. Those hurts were healing well, with fewer scars than Richard might have expected.

As Master Judah examined him, Mustafa began to struggle, as if swimming upward through deep water. This time when his eyes opened, they saw Richard. They saw precious little else, but they fixed on his face with feverish clarity. "Malik Ric," he said. "My lord king. *My* . . . lord king. It was a choice, you see. I made it. It may kill me, but I couldn't make any other. In the end. When—"

"There," said Richard, gentling him as if he had been a panicked horse. "There. You're safe here. You have my word. No one under my command will lay a hand on you again."

Mustafa did not hear him. "Sire," he said. "The sultan is dead."

How peculiar, Richard thought with the cool remoteness of shock. It never occurred to him to doubt the truth of it, if Mustafa said it. Mustafa never lied.

The one rumor everyone had discounted, and it was true. "Assassins?"

Mustafa nodded.

Richard drew a breath, then let it out. The Seal was heavy and cold against his breast. He sat beside the bed, leaning toward Mustafa.

The boy groped for his hand and clutched it with strength enough to bruise. With that for a lifeline, he said, "Sire, I need your forgiveness."

"*You* need *my*—" Richard broke off. "What on earth for?"

"I left you," Mustafa said. "I was angry. I was hurt; I wanted to hurt in return. I went to Jerusalem. The lord Saphadin took me in as a guest. I thought I could serve him; he's an honorable man, and he was kind to me. But when my anger went away, I couldn't do it. My loyalty is given, and can't be taken away." He sucked in a breath, shuddering. "I saw it," he said. "I saw the sultan die. I was going to leave sooner, but the lord Saphadin asked me to stay through the day of prayer. He took me with him to the Father Mosque, where his brother was leading the prayer. In the midst of it, as we all performed the prostrations toward Mecca, two of the sultan's mamluks, the most trusted of his servants, whom he had loved like sons, rose up and killed him.

"I was there beside him, my lord," Mustafa said. "I killed one of the Assassins. Another mamluk killed the other."

That did not surprise Richard. Mustafa never boasted of his prowess in war, but he was as sublime a predator as any cat. He killed fast and clean, and altogether without compunction.

"So you avenged the sultan," Richard said. "You weren't paid well for the service, from the look of you."

Mustafa shook his head. "I didn't give anyone time to be grateful. The city was in terrible disorder. The lord Saphadin was doing what he could, but it was like a madness. People were running wild, shrieking and striking at one another—crying out that every man was an Assassin. They set fire to a street of houses near the Wailing Wall, and tried to loot the storehouses, but the garrisons were able to stop that. I escaped when the messengers went out to summon the sultan's emirs and his brothers and his sons—all but the eldest, who was there already. I came to you as fast as I could. I would have been faster, but my horse was shot from under me, and it took a while to steal another."

Mustafa fell silent, as if he had run out of strength. Master Judah's glare promised dire things if Richard pressed him much harder.

Richard rubbed an old scar that ran along his jaw under his beard, letting that narrow dark face fill his vision while the tale filled his mind.

Blondel had crept into the tent while Mustafa spoke—not excessively wise of him, but he never had been able to keep his curiosity in check. His round blue eyes were narrow, his full mouth tight, as they always were when he saw Richard with Mustafa. It was a pity, Richard thought, that two of the people he trusted most in the world were so confirmed in enmity.

"Blondel," he said in a tone that he knew would catch and hold the singer's attention. "Go to Hubert Walter. Tell him what you've heard here. Have him call the war council, and quickly. There's no time to waste."

Now that errand Blondel was by no means unwilling to run.

He nodded, bowed just a little too low, and ran once again to do his king's bidding.

The Archbishop of Canterbury had called the council in the pavilion that they used for such things. It had housed a prince's harem once; the scent of perfume clung to it, almost overwhelming the homely stink of men in a war camp.

They knew the cause of the council as soon as they saw Richard's face. "So it's true," Henry said. "Saladin is dead."

"Dead as Moses," Richard said. Grins flashed around the circle; even the most self-consciously dignified could not suppress the surge of joy. He turned his eye on the Duke of Burgundy. "So, my lord: what will you do? If you turn your back on this and take your loot and march to the sea, I won't stop you. As for me, I'm marching to Jerusalem."

Duke Hugh loathed the ground Richard stood on, but two things could supersede that loathing: a sufficient quantity of gold, and his oath of Crusade. "I'm marching to Jerusalem," he said. "I swore my life to defend the Holy Sepulcher. By God and Saint Denis, I'll keep that vow."

"Amen!" It was ragged, but it was a chorus. All the French were with him. The English and Normans and Angevins . . .

Richard willed them not to shame him. Hubert Walter, that good and loyal man, raked them with a glare more suited to a sergeant than an archbishop, and said firmly, "We'll follow you, sire, to the gates of hell—and beyond, if that's your command."

Not all of them agreed, but it was more than any man's pride was worth to say so. Richard took note of who frowned and who would not meet his eye, and considered which of them he could put in the front of the fight. They would earn their right to the cross of Crusade.

"Sire," said, of all people, the Grand Master of the Temple. "Not to deter or dissuade you, but have you recollected that there's no water between here and the city? The sultan broke all the cisterns and poisoned the wells. It's the driest of dry land—

and my knights remember Hattin, where a king insisted on a march without water, and lost his kingdom for it."

"Oh, indeed," purred a baron whose fief had been great once, but who owned nothing now but his armor, his destrier, and an abiding thirst for revenge on the infidels who had robbed him of his domains. "And who incited the king to make that march instead of staying where there was water and a chance of fighting off the infidels? I seem to recall a circle of long wagging beards and blood-red crosses."

The Grand Master's cheeks were flushed above his uncut beard. He traced the sign of the cross over the red cross on his breast, and opened his mouth, no doubt to thunder denunciations.

"My lords," Richard said, cutting him off. "Will you quarrel among yourselves when Jerusalem is ripe for the taking? We'll move toward evening, my lords, and take with us as much water as our camels can carry. We'll march by night—in the cool and the dark, we won't need to drink as much. With luck and God's goodwill, we'll break down the gates of Jerusalem before dawn."

"Jerusalem," sighed Hubert Walter. "Is it true? Will we see it at last?"

"God willing, when next any of us sleeps in a bed, he'll sleep in Jerusalem," Richard said.

"It's real," Henry said in wonder. "It's happening. After all, and after so long."

Richard watched the wonder touch the rest of them, even the most jaded—even the Duke of Burgundy. Hugh might loathe Richard, but he had a certain liking for Henry. As he swayed, so did they all, even the most determined of the naysayers.

"Jerusalem," the archbishop said again. "Holy, high Jerusalem." He swept his glance across them all. "Well, my lords? Shall we capture ourselves a city?"

The roar of assent was not confined to the pavilion. The servants, the squires, the men hanging about and craning to hear, joined in it, a long rolling wave that swept through the camp and rang to the sky. God help the infidels who heard it, for surely their blood ran cold.

Richard's own blood was up. At last—the battle he had been waiting for since first he heard of this Crusade. At last, he would look on Jerusalem.

CHAPTER FORTY

In the heat of the afternoon, when everything was ready but the mounting and riding, Richard retreated to his tent. He would not linger there for long; it was hot and close, and the air was slightly sweeter outside under his canopy. But if he would rest—and truly he should, for God and Saint Morpheus knew when he would sleep again—then he must do it out of sight of his army.

A page wielded a fan, which helped somewhat with the heat. Richard stripped and lay naked on his cot. The breeze from the fan cooled the sweat on his skin. A curtain of gauze kept out the myriad stinging flies and some of the dust. It was almost pleasant, and surprisingly restful.

As he lay there with his arm over his eyes, he heard a soft footstep and an even softer shuffle, then a swift scamper as the page took advantage of the reprieve. Richard lay motionless, barely breathing. He had recognized the step; now he caught a hint of musk, which Blondel the singer was girlishly fond of.

Blondel plied the fan for a little while, nearly long enough for

Richard to fall asleep. Then, softly, he began to stroke Richard's hair.

Richard sighed and lowered his arm, turning to fix the singer with a hard stare. "Trying to worm your way back into favor, then?" he said.

Blondel flushed, then paled. "Will you ever forgive me?"

"If you ever honestly repent," Richard said, "I might."

"I do repent," said Blondel. "Before God, sire, that is the truth."

"Ah," Richard said, "but what is it that you're sorry for? You'd as soon cut my Saracen's throat as look at him. Jealousy is flattering, boy, but a little of it goes a very long way."

Blondel's face was a tumult of emotions: anger, grief, guilt, fear. "I can't help it, my lord," he said. "I love you too much."

"Yes," said Richard. "You do."

Blondel gasped. Richard felt no pity for him. It was only just. Jealousy had nearly cost him a loyal and useful servant. Blondel would not indulge in it again, if he hoped to remain in Richard's favor.

Slowly Blondel drew back. Just as he would have moved out of reach, Richard caught his hand. He froze. Richard drew him in.

Then Richard also froze. Something had changed: a dimming of the sunlight that slanted through the open tent flap, a shift in the currents of the air. Blondel's musk was strong in his nostrils, but another scent crept through it, a scent as familiar as his own skin. Attar of roses.

Wherever his mother went, that fragrance followed her. A priest had told him once when he was very young, that the odor of sanctity was the scent of roses. He had asked, not entirely innocently, "Does that mean my mother is a saint?" The priest had sputtered and gobbled most satisfactorily.

A shadow came in with the scent, drifting through the flap and the veil. It was a shape of darkness, barely substantial, perhaps not really there at all; but his mother's presence imbued it with a certain shiver of terror.

The shadow halted just out of reach. It had no face, only darkness, but the tilt of its head was unmistakably Eleanor's. So too the voice, although it seemed dim and faint, as if it came from very far away. "Tell your boy to leave," it said. "This is between the two of us."

Richard bent his head toward Blondel, who crouched staring like a rabbit in a noose. The singer needed no further encouragement. He dropped the fan and fled.

The queen's shadow sat on the stool that he had vacated. It was eerie to watch it move as she moved: her gestures, her peculiarities of gait and posture. Richard kept it in the corner of his eye: it was less disconcerting. "I suppose you're here to help me conquer Jerusalem," he said.

"I have helped you," his mother said. "The sultan is dead. Now I would thank you to give me the thing you wear about your neck."

"No," said Richard. "It was given to me on condition that I keep it and give it to no one."

The shadow stiffened. "You have no faintest conception of what it is or how to wield it."

That was true, but he was not about to admit it. "I know enough to understand that it should stay where it was given. The former owner might come calling for it."

"Yes," said his mother, "and he'll blast you where you stand. I have the means to resist him."

"Do you? You're that strong, are you? Or have you had help? Have you made another of your bargains with the Devil, Mother?"

The shadow did not stir, not even a fraction, but Richard fought an almost uncontrollable impulse to dive for shelter. Much was bruited about of the black temper of Anjou, but the white-hot passion of Aquitaine was no less potent.

It could not sway him to her will—not now, not with the Seal of Solomon about his neck. Nor did her words, though they were cruel enough to cut. "You stubborn child! You'll destroy us all with your foolishness."

"I come by it honestly," he said.

"Give me the Seal," said Eleanor.

"No," said Richard.

Her shadow contorted with frustration, twisting and deforming like a column of smoke in a sudden wind. Richard watched, fascinated. He knew little of magic and would have been glad to know less, but this much he knew: things of power came with strictures, rules that could not be violated except at great cost. If she had been able simply to take this thing, she would have.

It was an unusual sensation, to hold power over his mother. He found that he enjoyed it a great deal. "I'll make you a promise," he said. "When I'm done with this thing, when I'm free to give it as a gift, you'll have it. It won't be long now. We're on our way to Jerusalem."

"You'll lose the Seal," she said. "You'll lose everything."

"Maybe," said Richard. "Maybe not. However that may be, I'm not giving the Seal to you until the war is over." He rose. "Now if you don't mind, I have a battle to fight."

He discovered that he was holding his breath. It was never the wisest choice to defy his mother, and yet it griped his belly to think of giving the Seal to her. Maybe he could not use its power, but some deep part of him did not want his mother to wield it, either. Even to take Jerusalem. Even to destroy the Old Man of the Mountain.

In her own person she might have been able to overwhelm him. In that form, her only power over him was in his memory of old fear. He was a man now, a warrior and a king. He faced his fear; he fell upon it and conquered it.

She gave way. This was not the end of it, he knew very well. But if she let him be until he took Jerusalem, he would be reasonably content.

For a long while after her shadow faded into the hot and dusty air, he sat on his bed and tried not to shake. For all his bold pretenses, he was still to a degree the small and headstrong boy who had looked on his mother in absolute adoration. She was all that was wonderful and powerful and terrible, and his place in the world was to bow at her feet.

He thrust himself up, banishing the memory with a hawk and a spit and, for good measure, a quick sign of the cross. Then he bellowed for his servants. "God's arse! Have you all gone to sleep? We have a war to win!"

CHAPTER FORTY-ONE

Sioned was not dead. She was not alive, either; she was rather well aware of that. Her body lay in the physicians' tent. Sometimes she hovered above it, watching one of the assistants bathe it or feed it or dose it with potions. The fire of fever died slowly. The child within . . .

She was still alive. Sioned could see her enfolded in the womb, and something wrapped about her, something that shimmered with a subtle radiance. It was some little while before Sioned realized that it was her own magic. So strong was a mother's instinct, and so staunch in defense of her child.

The body guarded its burden. The spirit wandered among the spirits of air, bound to its source by the thinnest of threads. It had a purpose, a reason for wandering, as the body had a reason for clinging to life. The spirit likewise guarded something—a secret, a deception, a sleight and an illusion. In a garden outside of the world, a serpent kept watch over a common stone. The one who claimed the stolen Seal, who had entrusted the great part of his power to it, did not yet know that the Seal was gone. Her spirit, airy thing that it was, sustained the spell that clouded his mind and concealed the loss.

It could not hold forever. The edges of it frayed continually. The longer she was away from her body, the more difficult it was to knit them up again. If Richard did not take the Seal soon and wield it against the Assassin, both her protections and her deceptions would fail. Then Richard would have no defense against the Old Man's wrath but his determinedly unmagical self.

Spirits did not count days. Suns rose and set; time blurred into a single shining present. But events recorded themselves in her awareness. She saw the war winding to its conclusion. She saw the sultan die.

The sultan was a great and shining creature in this world, a man of power, beloved of his God. The Assassins' daggers set him gloriously, blindingly free. He never even looked back, but sped on bright wings toward the light of Paradise.

It was a powerful temptation to follow him, but another, greater power held her to earth. The sultan was glorious, but his brother was pure and gleaming beauty, an edifice of magic so wondrous and so complex that she could only hover above it, rapt.

He was not aware of her. All his mind and strength were focused on his grief, and on the struggle to make order of chaos. She drifted away, grieving because he grieved, into the wild rejoicing of the Frankish camp.

Time had folded upon itself. The sun had shifted; the light was different. She heard the king's council, and saw where each man went thereafter, and what he said to those about him— both those he trusted and those he did not. She would remember each of those later, if she could.

The spell was fraying badly now, endangering the thread that bound her to her body. Sinan, having disposed of the sultan and so fulfilled his bargain with Eleanor, had begun to suspect that something was amiss. All too soon he would go seeking the source of the wrongness, and find it in the garden.

If only Richard could take Jerusalem, the city's power would guard him. Then she could let go. It was incumbent on her, then, to make sure that he did conquer the city—that the Seal was safe and the spell of protection and concealment intact, and the battle free to proceed without interference from Masyaf.

A small and slightly saner part of her observed that she had taken on far more than her strength could manage. She could not listen to it. She must hold on and be strong, and pray that it was over quickly.

She had, while she drifted in the aether, been frequently attended by tribes of the jinn. They did not address her or distract her, but their presence held other forces at bay. The great jinni she did not see. He had his own preoccupations, she supposed.

Sioned was there, riding a dust mote in the shaft of sun through the tent flap, when Richard banished his mother—a bit of boldness for which he would pay dearly later. Much later, she hoped, for his sake.

She lingered while he dressed and ate and prepared to march. As she hovered near him, one by one the jinn appeared, circling about her, flocking like birds. The great jinni himself came; he said nothing, but settled behind her as if he had been a guard.

She was not apprehensive. Not exactly. The force of Richard's determination drew her in its wake, strengthened by the power of the Seal. He did not know how to wield it, no, but it was rousing; it sensed the power in him, the magic that slept deep. Too deep ever to wake, she would have said, but the Seal was no ordinary amulet.

Her body was not so far in earthly distance, but impossibly remote in the ways of magic. If she returned to it, she would be subject to its laws—and those, at the moment, were the laws of the deathly ill. Yet she had a sudden, powerful need for earthly substance: to walk in flesh, to ride with the king toward Jerusalem.

The great jinni stirred, reaching toward her. *Come*, he willed her. *See.*

She went where he led. At first she thought he was leading her to her own body, but he paused just short of it, in her little tent. Mustafa was sitting there, a little wan but upright and conscious. He had just finished dressing himself in the gear of a Frankish sergeant, all but the helmet, which dangled by the strap from his hand. He was in pain, but not terribly so; his wounds of the body were healing.

Quite without thought, she poured herself into him like water into a cup. He was open and welcoming. Despair had left him; he was at peace with his choices, but in that peace was a singing emptiness. It begged her to fill it.

So, she thought: this was how demons entered into men.

It was one way, the jinni observed from his vantage above her. Mustafa had been protected. But she was a pure spirit; she was welcome in his heart.

He knew that she was there. He was not afraid, or even particularly surprised. If anything, he was glad to know that she lived, although he fretted a little for the safety of her body. She soothed him with the warmth of her surety. She would be well. Would he take her with him into Jerusalem?

It was strange to feel his nod; to be inside of him, looking out through his eyes, slowly growing aware of the body that he wore: the aches and small persistent pains, the slight gnawing of hunger, the itch between his shoulder blades. Her magic flowed through and over him. The itch, the pains faded. He stared at his arms, which were clean of bruises and burns, and flexed his fingers, even the several that had been broken.

It was all gone. She was a little dizzy, but his own strength had fed the working; he was tired, somewhat, but food and drink and the prospect of a battle would mend that. He turned in the small crowded space, stretching as high as the roof of the tent would allow, swooping, spinning, whipping out his dagger and plunging it into the heart of a lurking shadow.

The shadow gibbered and fled from the bite of cold steel. Mustafa retrieved his dignity with his helmet, and stepped out of the tent into the breathless heat of late afternoon.

The army was forming in ranks, moving slowly, taking its time. Men were filling waterskins from the wells and loading them on camels, burdening them until they groaned in protest.

The men and horses would carry a full day's ration of food and fodder, but no more. Water was the most vital provision, and of that they had as much as their beasts could bear.

Richard was risking everything in this one stroke. He left the baggage in the camp under guard, and most of the food and supplies. "Jerusalem will provide," he said as Mustafa rode up behind him on a commandeered horse. He was in his battle mood, brilliant and a little mad; it was a brave man who would cross him now.

Mustafa's appearance in his sight might have roused his uncertain temper—since Mustafa was supposedly still prostrate from wounds and exhaustion—but aside from a single hard, measuring glance, Richard ignored him. There was still a great deal to do: orders to give, troops to muster, affairs to settle in the camp and with the court.

Sioned, enfolded in Mustafa's mind, watched Richard narrowly. The Seal was hidden beneath his armor, its presence veiled by a sort of glamour. She could, if she tried, feel a distant shadow of its power, a subtle drawing of heart and mind toward the man who wore it. Even a powerful mage might think it no more than the magic of his kingship.

It was easy from so close to maintain the spells, but difficult, too: the Seal's power tempted her, whispering at her, luring her toward it. Mustafa, bless the gods, was unmoved by it. His magic was different, a thing more of seeing than of doing. He knew that the Seal was there, he saw the shimmer of it on the king, but he was deaf to its blandishments.

The army began the march just before sundown. The air was still blazingly hot, but the edge was off it. By full dark it had cooled noticeably. The stars were clear overhead, barely blurred by the dust of the army's passage.

Richard had disposed the army in much the same order as at Arsuf, with his English and Normans and Angevins in the center, the French in the van, and Henry with the warrior monks and the knights of Outremer in the rear. He rode up and down the lines. Mustafa held a place close behind him, which none of his knights or squires saw fit to challenge.

Blondel might have ventured it, but he was still in fear of Richard's wrath. Richard marked him among the men of Anjou, riding with a company of mounted archers. He would have been just another anonymous shape in the dark, but as Richard glanced in his direction, he took off his helmet for a moment and raked fingers through the pale glimmer of his hair in a gesture that was achingly familiar. Richard had to admire him for riding to the battle when he could have stayed safe and at ease in camp. The singer did not lack for courage, whatever his faults.

The hills around Jerusalem were deserted, empty of scouts and patrols. They met only one troop of defenders, a party of Turks who had been late in receiving word of the sultan's death. They were riding headlong to the city, apparently unaware that the Franks were on the march across their track.

Richard loosed the Templars on them. The warrior monks cut them apart with holy glee.

The Turks died on the slopes of the hill called Montjoie, from which the first Crusaders had had their first sight of Jerusalem. Richard was with the rear guard then—as if to thrust himself to the van would turn all this to mist and dream: he would wake and find himself prostrate with another fever, and Saladin still alive, and no hope of winning the prize he had dreamed of for so long. But even as slowly as he rode, in the end he rode past the hacked and bloodied bodies of the Turks, up the stony ascent to the summit.

There he paused. The Holy City spread itself before him, sprawling over barren hills and valleys so holy that they could barely support the weight of living green. On this night full of stars, it was a darkness on darkness, shot with streaks of fire.

When he looked down, he found his army more by feel than sight. There was no moon; the stars were far and faint through a haze of dust. His skin was gritty with it under the weight of padding and mail.

The horse Fauvel snorted softly, pawing with impatience. His steel-shod hoof sent up a shower of sparks.

In almost the same moment, a comet of fire arched up over Jerusalem. Then at last Richard saw the outline of walls and towers and the golden flame of the Dome of the Rock. He also, with astonishment, saw David's Gate open below the loom of its tower. There were no lights visible in the tower, no sign of guards on the wall or in the gate. Torchlight gleamed within, casting a golden glow across the meeting of roads that led up to the gate.

It could be a trap. Richard had meant his attack to focus on the gate, though the rams would not be needed after all. In their place he sent a company of crossbowmen. They took their positions out of ordinary bowshot, and sent a barrage of bolts into the open gate.

Nothing moved inside it. No hidden troops fell screaming from the towers. The gate was empty, open and inviting.

Richard turned on Mustafa. "Is this your doing?" he demanded.

The boy shook his head. "Not mine, sire," he said. "There's no ambush—I can feel it. It's empty."

"Someone is giving us the city on a salver," Richard muttered. He rubbed the scar under his beard, frowning. Whoever had given him this gift must expect a payment—and the price would not be cheap.

His army was growing restless, waiting for him to make up his mind. The Templars, hotheads always, were all too eager to slip the leash.

Abruptly Richard shut off doubts and fears. War was a gamble. Let him cast the dice, then. With his eyes fixed on the open and beckoning gate, he said to the chief of his heralds, "Now."

The man leaped to obey. His clear voice echoed through the hills and resounded from the walls. With a cry of trumpets and a thunder of drums, the first wave of the attack swarmed out of the hills and fell upon Jerusalem.

CHAPTER FORTY-TWO

Richard had intended to go in with the rear guard, but as the vanguard surged toward the gate, he could not bear to hang back so long. He clapped spurs to Fauvel's sides. It hardly mattered if anyone went with him; his eyes and soul were fixed on the flicker of torchlight within the open gate.

He was neither the first to pass beneath that echoing gate, nor by far the last. Although he had never been in the city, he had committed its ways to heart against just such a day, praying every night and every morning that it would come to pass.

This was David's Gate, the gate of the north and west, guarded by the Tower of David in which the kings of Jerusalem had lived and ruled and fought. The Tower seemed deserted, empty of troops and even of noncombatants. The Street of David that ran inward from it, nearly straight through the middle of the city until it reached the Beautiful Gate of the Temple on the other side, was as empty as the Tower, but for crumpled shapes that proved to be bits of abandoned baggage: an empty sack, a heap of broken pots, a chest with its lid wrenched off and nothing within but a scent of sandalwood.

Richard was deeply, almost painfully aware of the holiness of this place, the sanctity of every stone. The thing he wore about his neck, which he tried not to think of too often, had grown inexplicably heavy, as if its worn and friable stone had transmuted into the cold heaviness of lead.

He shook off the creeping distraction—it was not quite ghastly enough to be horror—and focused on the city about him. He was neither priest nor magician but a fighting man, and there was a fight ahead—that, he was sure of. But where? Not, he hoped, in every street and alley of this ancient and convoluted place.

There were signs of struggle along the street as he advanced, remnants of rioting, but as yet no bodies. He ordered his men to be on guard against ambush, sending a troop of them up to the roofs and walls and dispersing another through the alleys that converged on this broader thoroughfare. He had begun to suspect where the infidels had gone.

The Dome of the Rock was a great holy place of Islam. It stood where the Temple of Solomon had once stood, and protected the stone from which the Prophet Muhammad had been lifted up to heaven. It was not the heart and soul of their faith— that was in Mecca—but it, and the city in which it stood, were most holy and most revered in their religion.

It was also a great fortress and storehouse, built as a mosque and then transformed into the stronghold of the Knights Templar: the Templum Domini, the Temple of the Lord. Saladin had died within the confines of its wall. It could withstand a lengthy siege, even if the rest of Jerusalem fell—and then, surely, the defenders would look for hordes of reinforcements from the sultan's kin in Damascus and in Egypt.

It had to fall quickly. Richard could not afford a siege.

He sent his vanguard ahead, with the second wave behind it, his own men from his own domains. The third rank, Henry's troops and the knights of Outremer, would go in after a pause and sweep the city behind the rest, taking it street by street if need be.

They all had their orders, their plan of battle. It was in their hands now, and in God's.

*   *   *

A quarter of the way between David's Tower and the Temple, at last they met opposition: a barricade across the broad street and turbaned Saracens manning it. The Norman destriers ran over them. It cost a horse, gut-slit by an infidel who died under the battering hooves of the beast he slew, but none of Richard's men fell, even when archers began to shoot from the rooftops. They were ready for that: shields up, interlocked as they pressed forward. Somewhat belatedly, the archers began to drop: the men Richard had sent to the roofs had finally come this far.

There were two more barricades between David's Tower and the Latin Exchange, where half a dozen skeins of streets met and mingled. One barricade they broke as they had the first, but at higher cost: there were more men here, and more archers. They lost a man-at-arms there, arrow-shot in the eye.

The third barricade was broken when they came to it, all of its defenders dead. Either there was dissension within the late sultan's army, or the citizenry had made their choice as to whom they wished to lead them. Past the fallen barrier, as they marched warily around the looming bulk of the Khan al-Sultan, they found the way clear, with only dead men to bar it. Walls on either side rose high and blank, windows shuttered, gates locked and bolted.

Richard was preternaturally aware of the force he led, as if it had been a part of his own body. He felt as much as heard the troop of Germans who ventured to creep off and begin the sack before the city was won. An English voice called a halt to them, and English troops barred their way. They snarled like a pack of dogs, but they were quelled, for the moment.

Morning was coming. The sky was growing lighter. He could see the Dome of the Rock floating above the walls and roofs of the city, seeming no part of earth at all.

No time for awe. Not yet. The Beautiful Gate was heavily manned. There were turbaned helmets all along the wall, archers with bows bent and aimed downward at Richard's army.

He rolled the dice one last time. He sent for the rams, but while his messenger sped off toward the rear, he brought up the heaviest of his heavy cavalry, the German and Flemish knights on their massive chargers. The beasts were as fresh as they could be on this side of the sea, with the cool of the dawn and the cautious slowness of their progress through the city.

Richard addressed them in a voice that was low but pitched to carry. "I've heard that a charge of armored knights could break down the walls of Babylon, and those are three lance-lengths thick. This gate's not near as thick as that. There's not much room to get going, but we'll give you all we can, and cover you with crossbow fire. Just break that gate for me."

They eyed that great slab of wood and iron, sheathed in gold. Some smiled; some even laughed. Some simply and eloquently donned their great helms and couched their lances.

The rest of the army drew back as much as it could. It must have looked like a retreat: Richard heard whooping and jeering on the wall. The charge prepared itself behind a shield of English and Norman knights.

When it was ready, the crossbowmen in place, Richard raised his sword. As it swept down, the knights lumbered into motion. Their shield of knights melted away, then came together behind them.

Crossbow bolts picked off the Saracen archers with neat precision. The knights were moving faster now, building speed from walk to an earth-shaking trot. Lances that had been in rest now lowered. The few arrows that fell among them did no damage, sliding off the knights' armor or the horses' caparisons, to be trampled under the heavy hooves.

The Saracens above the gate hung on, though more and more of their number fell dead or wounded. The charge struck the gate with force like a mountain falling. Lances splintered. The destriers in the lead, close pressed behind, reared and smote the gate with their hooves. The knights' maces and morningstars whirled and struck, whirled and struck.

They broke down that gate of gold and iron as if it had been made of willow withies, trampled over it and plunged through.

The second, less massive but still powerful charge thundered behind them, Richard's English and his Normans chanting in unison: "*Deus lo volt! Deus lo volt!*"

A battle waited for them in the court of the Temple, mounted and afoot: the dead sultan's gathered forces under the command of a prince in a golden helmet. That helmet had been Saladin's, and the armor had been his, too; but he had never ridden that tall bay stallion, Richard's gift to the great knight and prince of the infidels, the lord Saphadin. The first light of the sun caught the peak of his helmet and crowned him with flame.

Richard's knights plunged deep into the waiting army of infidels. His lighter cavalry, his archers, and his foot soldiers were close behind them. The court could not hold them all. Over half waited in reserve outside, or had gone up on the walls to deal with the archers whom the crossbowmen had not disposed of.

It was a hot fight. The enemy had been herded and trapped here, but they had not been robbed of either their courage or their fighting skill. They contested every inch of that ancient paving, right up to the gate of the golden mosque.

Richard faced Saphadin there. The prince had lost his horse some while since. He set his back to the barred door; Richard left Fauvel behind to face him on foot, man to man and sword to sword.

In the months that they had known one another, this was the first time they had met face to face in battle. Richard was taller, broader, stronger; his reach was longer, his sword heavier. But Saphadin was quicker, and he had more to lose. He drove Richard back with a flashing attack. He was smiling, a soft, almost drowsy smile, deep with contentment.

It was the smile of a man who had decided to die, and had chosen the manner of his death. He was wearing himself into swift exhaustion. It was a grand and foolish gesture, showing off all his swordsmanship; he would know, none better, that Richard could simply wait him out.

Richard waited, keeping sword and shield raised to defend

against the whirling steel. He was aware while he waited of the battle raging around him. His men were gaining the upper hand, but they were paying for it. There were too many of them in too small a space, and their heavier horses, their weightier armor and weapons, were beginning to tell on them as the sun climbed the sky.

It had to end quickly. Richard did two things almost at once: he firmed his grip on his sword as Saphadin's swirl of steel began to flag, found the opening he had been waiting for, and clipped the prince neatly above the ear; then, not even waiting for the man to fall, he spun and bellowed, "*Now!*"

Richard's forces had been waiting for that word. Well before the echoes of it had died away, they struck. His archers and crossbowmen had won the wall, and began a withering rain of fire. In the same moment, his reserves charged in through the Beautiful Gate, swarming over the enemy, surrounding them and bringing them down.

CHAPTER FORTY-THREE

When Mustafa and Sioned together saw how David's Gate was open and the Tower deserted, they saw in it the darkness that was the Master of Masyaf. If he was not in the city, then his power was. And the spells on the garden were weakening rapidly.

As Richard pressed the assault on the city and the Temple, Mustafa slipped away into the darkness of the deserted streets. Sioned within him was dizzy and dazzled with the power that slept in these ancient stones. It was all she could do to keep her focus, to ride in his heart and not spin away into nothingness.

The spell of the city overwhelmed the faint song of the Seal, and that was well—but here where the Seal had been made and where the great king of the Jews had wielded it, it was waking. She could feel the strain in her wards, the bonds slipping free.

He was here—the Old Man himself. He had concluded his bargain with Eleanor: he had lured and tricked the infidels into the trap of the Temple, and opened the city to the Franks. There would be a price for that, and he would not be slow in demanding it.

Mustafa was a gifted tracker, but there was too much magic here. Just as it concealed the Seal, so did it conceal the Master's whereabouts. He followed a trail through the Street of the Bad Cooks, holding his breath against the cloying reek of a hundred cooks' and bakers' stalls, but it ended in a blank wall and a barren door. There were only mortals cowering behind it, dwellers in the city who waited and hid and prayed that the sack, if and when it came, would not fall upon them.

Richard's coming had been no surprise. The city was ready for him: the barricades up, the Temple fortified. Mustafa caught a rat in the shadow of a baker's stall, a thief looking to steal the invaders' leavings. He squeaked abominably, but amid the gibbering were a few words of sense. "One came before the sun set, and persuaded the emirs to take a stand in the Temple. He was most convincing. They were in despair; they grieved terribly for the sultan. They were driven like sheep."

Dawn had come without Sioned's even realizing it: his face was clear to read. He was telling the truth as far as he knew it. Nor was he an Assassin. The city was full of them, but this was an honest rat.

Mustafa let him go. He vanished into an alley.

Sioned had already forgotten him. A monstrous blow nearly smote her into the aether. The thread that bound her to her body stretched almost to breaking.

The serpent in the garden had roused from its long sleep. It lifted its head drowsily to assure itself that the stone it guarded was still safe. In the moment of her inattention, when she focused on the thief, the spell shriveled into mist. The serpent saw what it had been protecting, and rose up in hissing rage.

For a searing instant, Sioned knew the whereabouts of every Assassin in Jerusalem. They burned like embers in her consciousness.

Indeed he was here—the master of them all. He was terribly, perilously close to Richard and to the Seal. And, she saw as her magic stretched to take in the circle of men about Richard, to Ahmad.

Mustafa's mount, in keeping with his sergeant's guise, was a

Frankish cob, and speed was not its greatest strength. But it was sturdy and imperturbable, and for these streets, it was fast enough. It managed a quite acceptable pace, even a gallop as it came to the Street of David. It hurtled over and around barriers, flotsam, the all too frequent sprawl of a body.

They were riding into the battle now, a steadily rising clash and clangor, battle cries and shrieks of the wounded. Mustafa in Frankish dress, on a Frankish horse, met no opposition. No doubt the king's army took him for a messenger.

The Beautiful Gate was down and broken. Men struggled in the ruins, packed so close together that they could barely move. Franks thrust inward; Saracens thrust them out again.

Mustafa left the cob with a pang of regret that quivered in Sioned's consciousness—it was a loyal beast, and it would be lucky to survive the day—and took to the walls. He went up them with breathtaking speed and skill, finding handholds where Sioned saw only smooth stone.

She had never been more helpless than she was then, borne within Mustafa's body, with her magic all scattered and her wits in scarcely better straits. She could focus on one thing: on finding the Old Man wherever he was hiding.

Daylight was well broken now, the morning advancing, and the heat rising. Mustafa heaved himself up over the rampart, found that stretch of it empty of defenders, and paused for breath.

From here he had a clear vantage over the court of the Temple. It was a mass of struggling men, tossing banners, swords and knives and spearheads now flashing brightly, now dark with blood.

Sioned found the king with the eyes of the heart, even before the eyes of Mustafa's body could follow. He was up against the gate of the great mosque, locked in combat with a man in a golden helmet wound with a snow-white turban.

She would have known that one if it had been blind dark and if he had been in sackcloth. He was wearing the sultan's armor and the sultan's famous helmet—no doubt to hearten his troops, and to remind them of what they fought for.

She could not take time to watch the duel, however deadly

and beautiful it was. She slipped free of Mustafa's body, rising on currents of power that swirled and eddied all through this place. The Dome was thick with spirits, the sky swarming with jinn and afarit, watching rapt as mortal men paid tribute in blood to the ancient powers.

The darker spirits and the shades of the dead were feeding on that outpouring of blood, and fattening on slaughter. She searched for one that was both dark and secret, rooted deep in earth and sending tendrils through the heart of the city.

It was hidden, but not well enough. She found it a scant man-length from the combatants, crouching against the wall of the mosque. It wore the semblance of a soldier of Islam and the face of a boy, young and feckless, clutching a bloody sword.

It was strangely dissonant to see that smooth face worn like a mask over old darkness. Sinan watched the duel with taut intensity. His spells were woven about Ahmad, a black and writhing tangle, breeding and nurturing despair.

They groped constantly toward Richard, but slipped past without touching, as if he were globed in glass. It would be expected that his mother would protect him whether he willed it or no, but as Sinan hurled stronger and ever stronger spells at him and he fought on untouched, Sioned watched suspicion dawn in those cold dark eyes.

Sioned struggled against the tides of the spirit, currents that tugged at her, urging her up and away from the dim and bloody earth. She could have the peace that the sultan had found; she could depart from all these cares and troubles.

It was not her time. She fought her way back down the spirals of air, gathering jinn as she went, until she hovered in a cloud of them, directly above Sinan's head.

He looked up. The jinn were not afraid of him now that he no longer had the power of the Seal. His eyes widened. The sight above him was terrible: swirling wrath, edged with fangs.

The spell-web about Ahmad frayed and melted into air—too late: Richard's sword was already in motion, smiting him down. Sioned lashed out with a wishing, to turn the blade, but Richard did not mean to kill, only to stun.

When she looked again, Sinan was gone. He had left nothing in his wake but a spell that, before she could guard herself, had caught her and snapped about her like a noose.

This was her death—of the soul as well as the body that she had abandoned. She did not greet it peacefully, although a moment before she had been ready and willing to slip away into oblivion. She struggled wildly, blindly, without knowledge or sense, only the pure will.

The jinn could not touch her. Sinan's binding was set to trap any who tried—and they, pure spirit without flesh to anchor them, however tenuously, were even more subject to dissolution than she.

The battle below was ending. The warriors of Islam were dead or taken; the sack had begun. Faint and far away, Sioned heard the bellow of Richard's voice, calling for men to take the lord Saphadin, to secure the Temple and the city, and to put a stop to the looting and pillaging. "Not here," he declared. "Not this city. This is holy ground. Any man who rapes or sacks or burns within it will lose his head."

He was not aware of her at all, even through the Seal. No one was. The one who might have sensed her was unconscious, borne away to captivity in the arms of strong English yeomen.

Unconscious was not dead. His magic was still there, freed of the bonds that Sinan had tried to lay on it. She was desperate; else she would never have ventured it. With the last shreds of her will and strength, she flung herself toward him.

Sinan's binding strained. Her spirit frayed. If she judged this wrongly, with what little of her was left to judge, she would kill Ahmad with herself. The distance between them was a breath's span, or a gulf between worlds.

There was little left of her but the will to reach him. Sinan's working rent her, gnawing and devouring. Ahmad receded with all his bright magic, his knowledge and power. He was lost in darkness and dream.

Somewhere in the depths of it, awareness sparked. The light in Ahmad brightened; the power, the beauty of it, grew stronger.

Sinan's spell caught hold of it. Too late to stop it, too late to protect her beloved—she could not even save herself.

Darkness swept over Ahmad. She sank down into it.

Lightnings cracked. The full force of Ahmad's power smote the Old Man's spell and shattered it—nearly taking Sioned with it. She would not have cared if it had. There was nothing left of her to care. But in the last instant, Ahmad caught her, enfolded her, and kept her safe.

She drifted in enormous quiet. It could have been death, but there was still a thin thread winding out of the light, and her body at the end of it, alive. She could not see Ahmad, or Sinan, or the army of the jinn. Yet she felt Ahmad like the warmth of arms about her, guarding her, slowly feeding her power and strength until she could sustain herself.

Her body was waiting. She was not ready to go back to it. She must not—Richard—

You must, Ahmad's will said, *or you die.*

"Sinan will come for the Seal," she said, shaping each word so that it was distinct. "My brother doesn't know—"

He would not help her to hold back. He thrust her toward her body, so sudden and so strong that she could not resist him. She was locked in it, confined in flesh, before her will found itself again.

He had bound her there with a spell remarkably similar to Sinan's, save that its chains were of light rather than darkness. There was less pain in it, and less fear, but no more freedom. She was trapped until he saw fit to let her go. No amount of struggle or protest would budge the working.

He left her there with a touch as soft as sleep, and a whisper of a promise. "Be at ease. All will be well."

Ease was the farthest thing from her mind, but she had no choice. She was helpless to stir from this rampart of flesh, and all but emptied of magic. Richard would have to fight alone, unless Ahmad could help him—Ahmad, whose body was as unconscious as hers.

Trust, he said. *Have faith.*

Faith was a thing for people of the Book—for Christians and

Muslims and Jews. She was a wild pagan. She had only herself
and the gods to rely on, and the gods were notoriously capri-
cious.

Not mine, he said as he slipped away. *Rest. Sleep. Be strong.*

Easy for him to say, she thought sourly; but her heart was no
longer quite so heavy. He had done that to her—that headstrong, arrogant man. "May your God protect you," she said to
the memory of his presence, "and bring you back to me."

CHAPTER FORTY-FOUR

By noon of that endless day, it was done. The Temple of the Lord was taken. The defenders paid the price that the knights of the Kingdom of Jerusalem had paid at the slaughter of Hattin: the high ones died or were held for ransom; the ordinary troops were bound and led away to be sold into slavery.

Saphadin was alive and reasonably well. Master Judah had taken charge of him, under heavy guard. Richard had no intention of letting him go; he was far too valuable a hostage.

For the moment he was safe. Richard's men admired him greatly, as the great knight and prince that he was. The Old Man of the Mountain was another matter. Richard could not be certain that Saphadin was not the Assassins' next target.

Richard would have to trust the vigilance of his guards to keep the sultan's brother safe. For now he had a conquest to secure.

His army was under control. There were a few Frankish heads on pikes among the heads of Turks and Kurds, and more than a few would-be pillagers who had discovered the fear of God.

Then at last he could go to the place that he had dreamed of for so long. He did not want to make a spectacle of it, but as he mounted Fauvel and rode back through the city, he found himself at the head of a swiftly growing procession. All of his men who were not preoccupied with the aftermath of battle, and a good number of the people of Jerusalem, had fallen in behind him. They were singing—raggedly at first, then a lone determined voice lured them into a chorus.

It was Blondel's voice, a little ragged with exhaustion, but clear and strong. He offered none of his secular songs now, no love songs or even songs of war, but the great anthem of Mother Church: *Vexilla regis prodeunt*.

Indeed the king's banners advanced in processional, claiming the victory and claiming Jerusalem. He entered the Church of the Holy Sepulcher, and found it dim and hushed and redolent of old stone. The infidels had not defiled it, except to take down every cross and crucifix. The vigil lamp above the Sepulcher was burning—miraculously, men would say later, but Richard saw the monk who lit it.

His heart was full. Some of those behind him advanced on their knees, weeping and beating their breasts in an extravagance of devotion. He was not so saintly. He walked toward the tomb that had inspired so much passion, that he had won back for Christendom.

It was a low, dark, unprepossessing place, seeming small to hold so much sanctity. Its emptiness was its holiness: the absence of the body, the memory of the one who had risen from it. He could think of no words to say to it or the God who had lain in it. He laid his sword on it, wordlessly; knelt for a while in contemplation; then rose.

The crowds in the shrine drew back. He barely noticed. He walked out as he had walked in, alone within himself.

*   *   *

It was near dark when he emerged. That surprised him. He could not have been in the shrine for as long as that—but the sun was gone, set in blood, and the stars were coming out.

A flock of people waited for him. He only took notice of the squire who knew where he could find a bath, dinner, and a bed for an hour or two before he went back to securing the city.

Those were in the Tower of David, in what must have been the royal lodgings before the fall of the kingdom: rooms wide and airy for a castle, fastidiously clean, and about them still a hint of eastern perfumes. Maybe Saladin's ghost would walk those halls tonight. And maybe not. Richard cared only that the basin for the bath was full and the water hot, and dinner was waiting, and the bed was ready, clean and fresh with herbs.

The bath was bliss on his aching bones, his bruises and the few small wounds. The servants were deft and quiet; one of them was adept at soothing away aches and the raw strain of exhaustion. He sighed and closed his eyes.

"So, king of Franks," said a soft voice in his ear, speaking Latin with an eastern accent, "are you satisfied with your victory?"

Richard was abruptly and completely awake. The Seal on its chain, which he had all but forgotten, weighed leaden heavy. He knew who knelt behind him—knew as if the man had come before him in the hall of audience, with heralds announcing his name. The Old Man of the Mountain had wielded his magic yet again, passing walls and guards as if they had been shadows.

Richard kept his eyes shut, his body slack. He was thoroughly vulnerable here, naked in the bronze tub, and no weapon in the room, not even a knife for cutting meat.

Sinan went on bathing him with a servant's skill. He shuddered in his skin, but he would never, for his life's sake, let the man see him flinch.

"Did I not do well?" the Old Man asked, still in quite good Latin. "Have you complaints of the gift I gave you?"

"I have no complaints," Richard said, deep and slow, as if half in a dream.

"Now you will do your part," the Old Man said.

"My . . ." It was hard not to open his eyes and glare. "Surely you mean my mother's?"

"Yours," said the Old Man, "as she promised me."

Richard kept his hands at his sides, although they had clenched into fists. He would not, as he yearned to do, clutch at the Seal on his breast.

The Old Man did not touch or attempt to take it, though his hands had been wielding the sponge within a hair's breadth of it. Could it be that he could not see it?

He must know that it was there. It had been his until Sioned stole it, and even Richard in his willful ignorance knew that magic called to its master.

The natural outgrowth of that thought, that the one who wore the Seal was its master, was more than he could face. Yet it might save his life.

He felt a cold soft kiss at his throat, and the faintest, barely perceptible sting of the dagger's edge. "Remember," Sinan said. "I can follow you wherever you go, find you wherever you hide. Keep the bargain and your life is sacred to me. Break it, and you die."

"I made no bargain with you," Richard said.

"It was made for you."

"What—who—"

Sinan's voice had a smile in it, a flicker of cold amusement. "What! You never knew? Or did you choose not to know?"

"Your words are wind," Richard said. "Wind and emptiness."

"So that is how you do it," said Sinan. "Your mother treats with Iblis. You preserve your Christian purity by blinding yourself to her machinations—even as you profit from them. She pays the price. You reap the rewards. How fortunate for you—and how convenient."

Wind, thought Richard with every scrap of control that he could muster. Emptiness. He would not be provoked into rage, not now, not by this of all his enemies. He must be strong; he must be cold. He must—yes, he must turn away yet again from the truth of what his mother was, for her sake as much as for his. When the time came he would face it. But not now. Not in the midst of so deadly a battle.

His skin prickled with more than the cooling water of the bath, or even the touch of the knife. Something had changed. Someone—there was a new presence in the room. He opened his eyes at last, but there was nothing to see. The newcomer was behind them both.

"My dear young spy," Sinan said. "Come round where we can see you. But slowly, and no daggers, please. I should not like to be startled and cause my blade to slip."

Mustafa did as he was bidden, although his demeanor was hardly obedient. Blessed fool: he had been trying to creep up on the Master of Assassins.

It was brave of him, and could be deadly—and it distracted Sinan. Richard felt the momentary waver, the slightest slackening of the pressure at his throat. He surged up and round, in a whirl of water.

The dagger flew wide. The Old Man smiled up at Richard. His eyes were dark, full of dreams. Maybe Richard wore the heart of his fabled power, but he was still a sorcerer of great strength and guile.

Richard dared not take his eyes off the man, even to warn Mustafa against taking rash action. He had to trust the boy's good sense.

Sinan's eyes were a sky full of stars. They beckoned him, beguiled him. They tempted him to fall into them, mind and will, heart and soul.

This must be how he ensorcelled his Assassins. Was that what he would make of Richard? An Assassin king—a royal slave. What beauty; what irony.

What insanity. Richard wrenched his eyes away, keeping Sinan on the edge of vision, on guard against further treachery.

Sinan's breath hissed. "You," he said. "You . . ."

The Seal flared into sudden, searing heat. Richard cursed and clapped his hand to it. It was cold under his palm, white-hot on his breast—weird dissonance, yet it helped him focus. He felt Sinan's will like a blast of wind outside of a tent: buffeting the walls, teasing him with fits and gusts, but he was spared the worst of it. The Seal was his protection.

Sinan mastered himself with an effort that contorted his face for a moment into a demon's mask. "You have something of mine," he said. "It was stolen from me: a thing of little value, but very dear to me."

"I know what it is," Richard said bluntly.

The Old Man's eyes narrowed and began to glitter. "Indeed, king of Franks? But do you know how to master it?"

"Odd," mused Richard. "My mother asked the same question. She wanted it, too. What can you give me that she can't?"

"Your life," Sinan said.

Richard laughed. "Why, messire! She gave me that life—which gives her a prior claim. Try harder."

"I gave you Jerusalem," Sinan said. "I opened its gates. I lured its defenders into the Temple, ripe for the slaughter. Surely that is worth the seal of a king who died two thousand years ago? If it is a seal you wish for, I can give you one far newer and more beautiful, and well endowed with power and glory."

"Well then," said Richard, "why not make yourself one, if it's as easy as that?"

"Because," said Sinan, "it has certain capabilities of which I can well and thoroughly avail myself, but which are of little use to you."

"Ah," Richard said. "You need it to hold your realm together. It's your key to the garden, isn't it? And it's much easier to keep all your slaves in thrall, if you have help. Still, messire, you are a powerful sorcerer, even I can see that. Surely you can make do."

"I can do that," Sinan said, "but I would prefer not. What price would you like from me? Another conquest? Damascus, perhaps? Cairo?"

"That is tempting," Richard said. "Can you give me the whole house of Saladin, with all his kin and kind?"

"It can be done," said Sinan.

Richard nodded, rubbing his beard as if in reflection. He kept his eyes on Sinan. Mustafa, apparently forgotten, was easing slowly round, out of the Old Man's sight. His hand was empty, but it hovered near where, Richard happened to know, he concealed one of several sharp and deadly knives.

Richard hated haggling, and he had little love for diplomacy—it was only haggling for princes. But if it would engage Sinan until Mustafa could sink a dagger in his back, Richard would do it and gladly.

"I still cannot be killed," Sinan said with his serpent's smile. "That much power I have, and keep."

Mustafa paused, but only briefly. He would test that assertion, his expression said. This after all was a master of lies.

"That is truth," said Sinan.

"What is truth?" Richard asked: a very old question, which had been asked in this very city, by the one who had lain in the Sepulcher.

Mustafa was still in motion. The Old Man whipped about. Richard saw the flash of metal, and a darker, stranger thing, a blood-red gleam.

Sorcery. The Seal stirred on Richard's breast. He started violently, perilously close to casting it off—God, he hated magic! But when his hand tightened on it, he found himself clutching it closer than ever. All the hairs of his body stood on end. The deep part of him, the part he would not acknowledge, quivered and began to wake.

Mustafa twisted away from the Old Man's blade, but the bolt of sorcery caught him a glancing blow. His gasp was more eloquent of agony than any shriek.

Richard did a blind thing, a mad thing, a thing completely without thought: he ripped the Seal from about his neck and flung it at Mustafa.

Dagger and sorcery dropped alike. Sinan leaped up as lithely as a boy, reaching to pluck the Seal from the air.

The Seal twisted—curving away from him, settling like a tamed bird into Mustafa's outstretched hand. Mustafa hissed and recoiled, but the chain caught in his fingers. Sinan fell on him with a hawk's cry.

Mustafa struck him with the Seal. The blow was ill aimed, with little force; it should barely have stung.

Sinan made no sound at all. He shrank in upon himself, withering and shriveling, dwindling to the image of utmost age. All the power, all the life and youth and strength, drained out of him, until he crumpled mewling to the floor.

Mustafa's face twisted. He dropped to his knees beside the drooling thing, set hands to the raddled neck, and snapped it as if it had been a dry stick. Then he cut the head from that broken neck, working with great concentration, all the while with the Seal dangling from his hand.

There was no blood. It was all gone, all shrunk to dust.

When Mustafa began blindly to hack at the headless body, Richard caught his hand. Somewhat surprisingly, he stopped; he looked up. His eyes were perfectly clear. "You should cut out his heart," he said, "and bury him in holy ground. Or he'll come back."

"I think you've killed him dead enough," Richard said.

Gingerly he set hand to the chain from which hung the Seal. Mustafa's fingers tightened briefly, but when Richard tugged, he let go.

Richard had been thinking that he would grind that monstrous thing under his heel, and so the world would be shut of it. But once he had it, he could not bring himself to destroy it. It had shielded him; it had destroyed the enemy of Christendom and Islam alike. In a way, he owed it something.

The chain found its way about his neck. The Seal settled in its accustomed place beside his heart. He pulled Mustafa to his feet.

The boy rolled his eyes at the Seal, but he was a wise child— he did not speak of it. Richard brushed a finger across his chin where the beard was beginning to thicken, and said, "You did it, boy. You destroyed the Old Man of the Mountain."

Mustafa shook his head. "It wasn't I. I didn't—"

"Don't lie," Richard said. "If I thought you'd take a kingdom, I'd give you one. It's the least I can do, after what you've done."

"I don't want anything," Mustafa said, "Just let me stay near you. Let me serve you. It's all I ever wanted."

"Gold, then," said Richard. "A place of your own. Good weapons. Horses—you must have horses."

Mustafa shook his head, as stubborn in his way as Richard. "I only need enough to keep me fed and clothed, and a mount and a remount, and a place at your back. I don't want any more."

Richard glowered at him. "Damn it, boy. Can't you make it easy to be in your debt?"

Mustafa lowered his eyes. "No, my lord," he said. "I'm sorry, my lord."

"You are not," said Richard, but without anger. "Take what you will take, then, and be sure I'll give as much again and again—for without you I would be that man's thrall, and God help the Crusade."

Mustafa looked up. "There is one thing, sire." And when Richard raised his brows: "The Old Man's heart. Give me that."

"If he has one," Richard said, "you're welcome to it. Though what you want with it—"

He broke off. Better not to ask. He was in the world of spirits and sorcery: that was all too obvious. Mustafa was comfortable there. Richard, by God, was not.

He would keep the Seal. It was too dangerous to give away. But he was damned if he was going to let it rule him. He was a king of men, a commander of armies. Sorcery was no part of what he was.

"God's feet," he said. "I need another bath. Fetch someone to get rid of this."

He jabbed his chin at the body beside the tub. Even as he opened his mouth to say more, it fell in upon itself, collapsing into dust. Mustafa sprang too late, snatching at the heart; but even as his fingers closed about it, it puffed into nothingness. Not even a smudge remained.

The Old Man of the Mountain was destroyed. Richard was victorious in Jerusalem. There was still a great deal to do and settle, and Richard had best be getting to it. He called for his servants, for a new bath for himself and another for his savior, and never mind Mustafa's objections to such royal pampering. Mustafa had done a glorious, a heroic thing. He would simply have to live with the consequences.

CHAPTER FORTY-FIVE

The High Court and the council of the kingdom elected Richard King of Jerusalem, but the truest acclamation and the most sincere election was that of the army and the people of the city. The barons and the bishops did what was politic. The people followed their hearts.

Richard did not pretend to be surprised. Nor—and on that, there had been numerous wagers—did he refuse the crown when it was offered. The one likely contender for it, the young lord Henry, was the first to propose that Richard be given the kingship, and the first to offer him fealty.

No one spoke of the lady in whom supposedly resided the right to the throne. She had not been seen since Conrad was laid in his tomb in Tyre. She was alive—there was no rumor of her death—but immured in a convent.

That queen was out of play. But Eleanor was very much in evidence. She arrived in Jerusalem on the day after Richard was named king, entering in full and royal state, escorted by the Queen of England and the Queen of Sicily, amid a flock of noble ladies and daughters of high houses in Outremer and in the west. They were adorned with the spoils of the East, glorious in gold and silk.

Richard met his mother at David's Gate and rode with her to the Holy Sepulcher, where, as he had done before her, she lingered a long while in silent prayer. The shrine was more nearly itself again, the crosses restored and all the lamps and candles lit. There had been a great rite of reconsecration after the city was taken, in which the Patriarch of Jerusalem and the Archbishop of Canterbury and a phalanx of lesser clerics scoured out the dust of Islam and restored the blessing of Christian sanctity.

Sioned had come to Jerusalem two days after it was taken. Master Judah made no secret of his disapproval—she had lain near death for days and was still weak from it—but she could not lie useless at Beit Nuba. Once she was up and about and in the sunlight, strength poured into her with miraculous speed.

Unlike the queens, she entered without fanfare, coming in with some of the baggage from the now mostly dismantled camp. Master Judah had established himself in one of the old hospitals near the Tower of David, and settled quickly to the task of tending the wounded and looking after the sick. He maintained an air of studious calm, but there was a luster on him that had not been there before. He was in the greatest of all holy cities, the city of his own people. He had, in a way that was very real and very immediate, come home.

Sioned astonished herself with the same sense of having come where she belonged. This was not the city of her belief, but as she walked those streets that had borne so much worship and so much contention for so long, she felt herself settling into it as into a well-worn garment. It was right that she was here.

Some of the Muslim captives were kept in Master Judah's hospital: the wounded, and those who had some skill in the arts of medicine and surgery, whom the master could put to use while their kin negotiated their ransom. Sioned was put to work among them, because she spoke Arabic and because she harbored no hostility toward them. From them she learned of the royal prisoners in the Tower of David: several of the sultan's sons including his heir, and a handful of his brothers, the chief of whom was the lord Saphadin. Richard had set no ransom on him or on the prince Al-Adil; he was debating what he should do, people said, and considering that it might be wise to keep those two as bargaining counters.

She did not go to see Ahmad. He was safe, she heard; his wounds had been slight, and the blow to the head was healing well. Richard was treating him with every courtesy, as a friend who happened to have been on the opposite side of a war.

By the time the queens came to Jerusalem, Sioned had settled into a life that she could live, she thought, indefinitely: days in the hospital, nights in a pleasant room that opened on a stair, and that stair led to a garden on the roof. She slept on the roof more often than in the room, lulled by the scents of rose and jasmine. There was a nightingale in a larger garden nearby, which sang her to sleep.

Sometimes during the day she had leisure to walk through the city, to visit the markets that had come alive with the conquest and were full of wonderful things, or to look on the many shrines and watch the pilgrims come and go. She had not been to Gethsemane yet, or Golgotha, but she had spent a long afternoon in the court of the Temple, now cleansed of the wrack of battle, and gone down to the old wall, the wall of the Temple of the Jews, so heavy with grief and old anger that she could not bear it.

Preparations for Richard's crowning were proceeding with frantic speed. He had taken Jerusalem on the remembrance day of Hattin. He announced his desire to be crowned on the feast of Mary Magdalene: the day on which the first King of Jerusalem was given his crown and his title—eighteen days to cleanse the city, settle the armies, convene the High Council, and prepare a magnificent feast and festival. The king's chamberlain was beside himself, and the servants were in a frenzy.

Sioned would have happily remained anonymous among the crowds at the coronation, but Richard had time amid all the rest of his duties to remember that he had a sister other than Joanna. She came in from the market, the week before the crowning, to find a company of Joanna's ladies waiting with bolts of silk and chests of jewels. The king's sister, they said, was to appear in her proper rank and station, and they were entrusted with the achieving of it.

This would not be as desperate a case as her expedition to Tyre. They went so far as to agree to less extremely fashionable attire; the wimple and veil were almost plain and the cotte cut less than strangling-tight. They did not remark on the soft curve of her belly—it was barely visible yet.

When they were done, even she could confess herself satisfied. Wimple, veil, and chemise were of fine muslin the color of cream. The cotte was of silk the same luminous blue-violet as her eyes, subtly brocaded, laced with silver cords. Joanna's ladies had sewn strings of sapphires round the bodice and down the sleeves, interwoven with pearls. She hardly needed the heavy collar of silver and sapphire, or the girdle that matched it, weighing her down with royal wealth. Even the shoes were of violet silk embroidered with pearls.

She looked well in it. Very well, for a fact. It was almost enough to make her vain.

The day of Richard's coronation dawned bright and preternaturally clear, with a promise of blistering heat. He would be feeling it: he rode in procession from the Templum Domini to the Church of the Holy Sepulcher in the hour of terce, halfway between sunrise and noon. He rode under a golden canopy, which at least kept the sun off his head, but the crowds along the thoroughfare and the bulk of the procession suffered the brunt of the light and heat.

The ladies, like the king, had the blessing of a canopy. Berengaria elected to ride in a litter, but Eleanor and Joanna scorned such a thing. Fine horses carried them, and fine mules their ladies.

Eleanor was not at all perturbed by the demise of her most

useful ally. It had been a service—and a reprieve. Sinan had held to his part of the bargain; his death removed the need for payment.

Richard still had the Seal. It was quiescent, biding its time. Eleanor had chosen not to ask for it—not yet. Not until the crown was safe on his head and Jerusalem was safe in his hand. Then she would demand that he keep his promise.

The procession was lengthy and moved slowly. Richard was at the end of it, with his ladies just ahead. The front of it was an army of priests and monks led by the Knights Templar and the Knights of the Hospital, escorting the Patriarch and all the bishops and archbishops of Syria and the Crusade. Behind them rode the barons of the High Court, then the lords and knights from the west, then at last the royal ladies and the king and a rear guard of chosen knights in gold-washed mail and surcoats of cream-white silk.

As they marched, they crushed sweetness: flowers and garlands flung from the rooftops, and drifts of rose petals scattered thickly underfoot. Women called out to them and dropped veils and sleeves on them, while their husbands and brothers and sons brandished banners blazoned with the golden crosses of Jerusalem.

There were no infidels in the procession. This was a day for Christians, for the victors of the Crusade. Some of the more illustrious captives would be at the feast after, but as guests, not prisoners. Richard could be both gracious and generous in victory.

Sioned let herself be glad for him. Tomorrow the world would come back with all its wars and quarrels. This difficult realm, this house of war, would need a great deal of ruling, even with the House of Islam thrown into disarray by the death of its sultan and the captivity of his kin. Richard would have to decide whether to march on Damascus or drive toward Egypt— while keeping his own army intact, which was an undertaking in its own right. Far too many of them, of all nations, were firmly convinced that now the Holy Sepulcher was won, they were free to go home. It mattered little to them that the tomb could not stay won if men were not there to protect it. That was for others to do, they said. Their duty was done.

But today there was only joy, and the glory of victory. The procession ended at last in the cool dimness of the Holy Sepulcher, where the Patriarch waited in front of the tomb. Richard's sword still lay there, its golden hilt gleaming.

On entering the shrine, Richard was divested of his massive golden mantle and his golden mail. In a simple linen shirt like a penitent, he advanced on his knees down the length of the church and prostrated himself before the Sepulcher. All the while the choir sang the *Te Deum*, he lay there, abject in humility.

As the great *Amen* died away, the Patriarch raised him to his knees, anointed and blessed him, and held the crown above his head. It was a simple thing, wrought of iron, with little adornment: more helmet than royal coronet. The Patriarch said, "On this day nigh a hundred years ago, the good knight Godfrey was persuaded to take this crown. He was greatly unwilling; his electors resorted to force, until at last he gave way. He was a humble man, a great warrior of God, who lived for nothing but to serve his faith and to defend the Holy Sepulcher. Even after he had accepted the crown, he begged not to be called king. He was a guardian, he said, a protector: the Defender of the Holy Sepulcher.

"These are lesser days and we are lesser men, but God has seen fit to restore to us the tomb in which His son was laid before his Resurrection. Once again we are given the charge of protecting His own. Once more we have chosen a king to command our armies, to oversee our court and kingdom, and to defend the Holy Sepulcher."

The Patriarch paused for breath. The crown was heavy: even with his acolyte supporting them, his arms trembled. Yet he would not shorten the rite for mere fleshly frailty. He gathered himself and began again. "Richard, King of the English, Duke of Normandy, Count of Anjou, manifold lord of the realms of the west, do you accept this crown and this kingdom, and all that attends it?"

Richard knelt motionless. The light of lamps and candles turned his hair to copper. His eyes were on the crown, but only the Patriarch could read what was in them.

After a long pause he said, slowly at first and then with greater clarity, "I accept it. I accept it all."

That was truth, Sioned thought. He did accept it. For all his faults and for all his failings, Richard did not shrink from either duty or obligation, if they came attached to the things that he truly wanted. And he did want this. With all his heart he wanted it.

The crown settled on his head. He, accustomed to the weight of kingship, barely bowed beneath it. Acolytes laid on his shoulders a massive mantle of Tyrian purple. He rose in it, as true an image of a king as had ever stood in this place.

The roar of acclamation was deafening. It went on and on, strong enough to rock the pillars, until it rose to a crescendo and slowly died.

CHAPTER FORTY-SIX

Richard carried his exaltation back to the Tower of David and the feast of his coronation. Sioned had caught a little of it, a singing gladness that made her laugh at the feeblest jests—and that before she had taken a sip of wine.

She was at the high table with the rest of her kin, and Henry had managed to have himself seated beside her. It was not exactly his proper place—that should have been at Richard's right hand—but he had argued persuasively that Queen Eleanor should hold that place of honor. Then there was the Patriarch, and the Archbishop of Canterbury, and Hugh of Burgundy who must at all costs be placated while he led a substantial portion of the army, not to mention the queens Berengaria and Joanna. Henry's place, as he pointed out, was well down the table, and he was glad to take it.

"Someday," Sioned said, "your tongue is going to talk you out of your rank and station."

"Not likely," Henry said. "I'm going to marry Isabella, did you know? Now the crown's safe on my uncle's head, dear Grandmother has decided that it's time to trundle out the royal bride."

"You don't sound unduly cast down after all," Sioned observed.

He shrugged. "I've had time to think, and to stop being a silly child. I don't like her much. I certainly don't love her. But that's a noble's lot."

Certainly it was, Sioned thought, and very likely Eleanor had exerted something more than earthly persuasion—though Henry did not seem spellbound. He was the same bright presence as always, and still yearning after her, too. He kept sliding eyes at her as if he could not help himself.

It made her a little sad. If she had been as legitimate as Joanna, with a crown and a royal title, Isabella might not have been preparing for her wedding.

Foolishness. Of course she would have. She was the heiress of Jerusalem; Richard's interception of the crown did not change that. Any heir that he might sire, supposing he could be brought to do such a thing, would be intended for England and Normandy and Anjou. Jerusalem belonged to Isabella's children, whoever their father might be.

In the meantime Henry was highly amusing, and Sioned was in a mood to be amused. She almost let herself forget the other side of the table, down toward the end, where a few men in turbans ate food prepared for them by cooks versed in the laws of their faith.

She could feel Ahmad's presence like sunlight on her skin. He seemed oblivious to her, carrying on a conversation with a youth who resembled him closely, who must be the sultan's heir, and exchanging occasional banter with one or another of the lords who sat nearest. His French had improved greatly; he had a strong accent still, but he was quite decently fluent.

He mourned his brother—of that there was no question. But he did not hold Richard to account for that. He was gracious in defeat as Richard was in victory; he conducted himself like a guest and not a sullen prisoner. His young nephew, Sioned was interested to note, was following his uncle's example. He was young enough to sulk mightily if given occasion, but he had his pride. He would let these Franks see how little their conquest troubled him.

He was very like his uncle. He even—her eyes sharpened. Yes, he had magic. It was young and raw and still discovering itself, but there could be no doubt of it.

That could be interesting. What if—

"Sioned?"

She blinked. She had forgotten where she was, or that Henry was speaking to her. He smiled at her, but his eyes were just a little sharp. "You should go to him," he said. "Truly, you should."

She shook her head. "That's past," she said. "It's done."

He arched a brow. "Oh? Is it? Come now, cousin. You can't lie to me."

"Am I lying? What use can there be in pining after him?"

"Maybe a great deal," Henry said. He took her hand. "You should stop and think, cousin. You're not usually this dense."

"What—"

"Think," said Henry.

Sioned did not see what there was to think about. There was Ahmad, Richard's prisoner until Richard saw fit to let him go. There was she, Richard's bastard-born sister, deeply and richly content in Master Judah's hospital.

And there was their child, waxing in her womb, and she still had not told anyone of it—though Master Judah must know; he had tended her for days in her sickness. That could not continue. Even if she could hide her swelling middle until the child was born, she had no intention of spiriting it away to be raised by strangers. This was her child—her daughter. She would raise it as her mother had raised her: with no need of a father, unless the child herself chose.

She left the feast early. She was tired; that was not a pretense. She had lost her taste for wine, and she was not, after all, in the mood for carousal. Henry insisted that one of his guardsmen escort her back to the hospital, but he stopped that when she reminded him that she had her own troop of protective spirits. The great jinni himself took the form of a squire in mail, looming formidably at her back as she made her way out of the hall.

Ahmad was waiting near the gate. She had not seen him leave the feast; indeed she could have sworn that when she left, he was deep in conversation with Richard.

At the sight of him her heart stopped. He was leaning against the wall, arms folded, conspicuously at ease.

"You look very comfortable," she said, "for a captive."

The corner of his mouth curved upward. "And you look very uncomfortable, for a conqueror," he said.

She glowered at him. "You know I had nothing to do with—"

"Beloved," he said. "Are you forgetting? I was there. I know what you did. That was a great theft, as great as any in a story."

The flush began in her middle, quite near the child, and flowed rapidly upward. "I only did what was necessary."

"Of course you did," he said. "I'm to ask if you will come. Your brother wishes to see you."

"He does?" Sioned made no secret of her disbelief. "With you as his messenger?"

He bowed slightly, regally, but with that same beguiling flicker of a smile. "I am your servant, lady."

She snorted inelegantly, but her curiosity had roused. A wise woman would have thrust firmly past him and gone back to the hospital to take refuge in her solitary bed. Sioned, who was only intermittently wise, said, "Take me to him."

Ahmad said nothing as they walked back through the passages of the castle. Sioned's guard was silent, treading like a cat behind them. She did not venture to guess what Richard wanted. Conversation, probably; she had seen as little of him as of Ahmad, although she had not been avoiding him.

Richard must have slipped out of the hall shortly after Ahmad had. He was in the solar behind it, flushed with wine but clear enough of mind. A page was with him, and Eleanor.

At sight of the queen, Sioned nearly turned on her heel and ran, but she had come too far to turn back now. This was more than a brother desiring a moment of his sister's company. There was an air of seriousness in them, but there was nothing particularly dark about it.

"Sister!" Richard cried as she hovered in the doorway, leaping up from his chair and pulling her into the room. He insisted that she sit where he had been sitting, and plied her with sherbet made with sugar and citron. She was glad of that, although there was hardly time to savor it.

Richard had welcomed Ahmad, too, although with somewhat less enthusiasm. When they were both seated, Richard stood grinning at them. "Sister," he said, "this lord of Islam has presented a rather remarkable solution to a dilemma or two of mine: what to do with him, and how to manage relations with the infidels. Mind you I proposed it once, but the lady was anything but willing. It seems I offered the wrong lady."

Sioned was not quite a hopeless idiot. She knew what Richard was getting at. "He asked to marry me," she said. Her voice was flat.

Richard's grin vanished. "Don't tell me the prospect revolts you, too."

She ignored him. She fixed Ahmad with her most merciless glare. "Why?"

"It is rather logical," he said. "Our realm is in massive disarray. Jerusalem is a Frankish kingdom again, under a king who might actually have the wit and the capability to rule it. It's a time for forging alliances—and for drawing claws, too, if truth be told."

"Indeed," said Eleanor, dry as dust on Golgotha. But for her and her spells, Ahmad could have flown out of this place, free as a falcon. He was captive in more than the body, a fact that appeared to dismay him little, but it was inescapable.

He smiled sweetly at his jailer. "Ah yes, my claws are most assuredly drawn. Yet still I am a danger to this fledgling kingship—unless I can be sealed to it with bonds that I have no desire to break."

"So I'm to be your shackles," Sioned said. "How long will it take you to resent me?"

"Rather a long time," he said. "I would say never, but what is certain in this world?"

"Suppose I do this," she said. "What do I gain from it? I have no dowry, unless you'd count a box of medicines, a gown or two, and an army of the jinn."

"A rather significant dowry, that last," he said with a glint of laughter.

"Don't be ridiculous," Richard said. "I'm giving you more than enough riches to take to a noble husband. Lands, titles, gold, shares in trading ventures—"

"A house," she said, "in Jerusalem. And a demesne outside of it, with income, and the wherewithal to pay the knight's fee."

"Well," said Richard, "that, too. Hubert Walter's seeing to it, now he's found the charters of the old kingdom—God bless the sultan's clerks, they didn't touch the archive, though damn the French for trying to burn it before my Normans stopped them."

"So I'm rich?" she demanded. "I have titles? I can make this choice for myself?"

"Provided you choose him," Richard said, "yes."

"And if I don't, I go back to being Master Judah's burden? Wasn't there a promise of payment for a certain service? Did I not perform it?"

"You did perform it," Richard said. "You'll get your house. But if you marry this man, it will be a much handsomer one."

"Did he tell you why he thinks I would marry him? Or even why he wants me?"

Richard scowled. "You're my sister, aren't you? You're a beauty—more than Joanna, if you want the truth. You're not a queen, but he says he doesn't want one. He declares that he doesn't mind that you're as overeducated as a woman can get, and he thinks your medical skills will be useful. He's an infidel, but you were never baptized—didn't think I knew that, did you? He doesn't object to a pagan, he says, as long as she's reasonable about the children. I should think you'd be glad to get him. He insists that he'll be glad of you."

"Reasonable," she said, "about the children. There will be children? And they're to be Muslims?"

"Would you rather they were pagans?" Richard snapped. "It's not as if you were half a nun, the way Joanna sometimes seems to be."

"I would be a wretched nun," Sioned said. "Now if you were to make me an abbess . . ."

"Don't tempt me," said Richard, "or I'll up and do it."

"I'd have to be baptized first," she said, "and all things considered, I think I would rather marry an infidel."

It took Richard a moment to understand what she had said. Even then, he eyed her narrowly, mistrusting her. "You're agreeing to it?"

"I think I am," she said, "provided that he agrees to certain conditions. I will live in Jerusalem; if he wishes to live elsewhere, then I must be free to choose whether to go or to stay. I will not give up my work in the hospital. If he takes another wife after me, he will do it with my consent, and only with my consent. And when it comes to the children, the sons are his to convert to Islam, but the daughters are mine, to raise as I will."

Richard looked ready to burst out in wrath, but Ahmad's hearty laughter stopped him short. "Lady! Oh, lady! What glorious conditions. I'm glad to accept them. Delighted. Have you more? I'll take them all."

"There is one more," she said. She stood. They all watched her, even Eleanor, as if she were a force to reckon with. That was a novel sensation; she was not sure if she liked it. But she would have to grow used to it. She had given up her happy anonymity; she was about to become a power, a lady of rank and standing.

She took Ahmad's hands and pressed them to her belly. "Your daughter," she said, "will be born at the winter solstice." She was aware out of the corner of her eye of Eleanor reckoning times and spans, and Richard gaping with beautiful astonishment. "Remember: if you agree to this marriage, she is mine, just as she would be if I had never told you of her at all."

Ahmad sat unmoving. He was a mage, however trammeled his power. He could well see what drifted and dreamed inside her. "*Ya Allah!*" he breathed. "What a wonder she is." His eyes flashed up into Sioned's face. "But no more so than her mother."

Sioned wanted desperately not to blush, but she had never had that power in his presence.

"God's ballocks!" Richard burst out. "You two have been at it since—"

"I was not in a convent when I was rapt out of Tyre," Sioned said as gently as she could bear to.

Ahmad was gentler still. "I do cry your pardon, my lord. From the moment I saw her, I loved her. She was not pleased that you offered her elder sister as my bride, nor, at all, that I would entertain the offer. She—"

"*That* long?" Richard flung up his hands. "Christ and the leper! Was I blind?"

"Not particularly," said Sioned. "We didn't mean to deceive you; the time was never right, and what could we say? It didn't make sense then to offer me instead of Joanna when he was still a sultan's right hand. Then there was the matter of the war, and Assassins, and too many preoccupations all at once."

"But now," Ahmad said, "it's an eminently satisfactory solution, is it not? I do love her, with all my heart, and she seems inclined to tolerate me. I'll be quite effectively snared, and quite happily, too, when we come to the end of it."

Richard's head shook, somewhat more in amazement than in exasperation. His temper had cooled; he was beginning to see the humor in it. He had already seen the use of binding this prince of Islam in kinship. "You played me, you two. You played me like a lute. If I didn't need you, I'd kill you."

"Certainly you would," Ahmad said. "And we do deserve it."

"Ah," said Richard, tossing off the whole of it: his temper, Ahmad's veiled apology, even Sioned's conspicuous silence. "I can't kill you now. That would be fratricide. In my family, brothers may hate each other cordially and do everything in their power to trap and betray and maim the rest both singly and together, but we don't commit the sin of Cain. You're safe from that, at least."

"Indeed I am grateful," Ahmad said.

His eastern grace was all the more striking in the face of Richard's Frankish bluntness. And yet, Sioned thought, they were not as different as one might think. They were alike in spirit: proud men, strong-willed, and fiercely loyal to those they loved.

Well then, so was she. A fine nest of eagles, they, and a fine war they had waged—and, no doubt, would wage again. Peace never endured for long in the City of Peace.

Today was enough. Tomorrow would look after itself. She sat between her brother and her lover, and took a hand of each, and was—no, not content. That was too tepid a word. She was happy. Gloriously, brilliantly, extravagantly happy. And if the gods begrudged it, then they were poor envious things, and she would find other gods to worship.

Richard would never understand why she laughed. Ahmad would when she told him of it—later, when they could be alone, with no more secrets. No more hiding. And that was best of all.

AUTHOR'S NOTE

The story of Richard the Lionheart, Saladin, and the Third Crusade is one of the great adventure stories of history—but unlike the fictional stories which it otherwise so closely resembles, it dribbles away at the end. There is no satisfying conclusion, not even a grand defeat. Richard gave up his war in the very moment when he might have won it. Saladin lived to claim the victory, but he was exhausted, in many ways a broken man. He died not long after Richard sailed back into the west, leaving heirs who could not maintain the empire that he had built.

Richard for his part was shipwrecked on his way home and captured by the Grand Duke of Austria, whose enmity he had won during the Crusade, and held for ransom. His kingship, like his Crusade, frittered itself away into nothing, until he died as a result of a foolish attack on a minor castle.

Alternate history relies on turning points—on moments of multiple possibilities. There were many such in the Third Crusade, of which one of the most crucial was the battle of the Round Cistern, when Richard captured Saladin's great Egyptian caravan. He could have forced matters then and taken Jerusalem—if he had not simply thrown it all away.

Certainly he had his reasons. His brother John was causing considerable difficulties in England and Normandy, and the King of France, who was no friend at all to Richard, was egging him on. Queen Eleanor in fact had left Richard in Cyprus before he set sail for Acre, and turned back toward home, in large part to keep John under control. Richard was in very real danger of losing his western possessions unless he hastened home to defend them.

Suppose that John had somehow been restrained, and Philip of France with him; suppose that Eleanor, with her powerful will and her relentless pursuit of her favorite son's advantage, had gone with him on Crusade. Suppose further that the Old Man of the Mountain had succeeded in assassinating Saladin, who was his avowed enemy. The way would then have been clear for Richard to win his Crusade.

I am indebted to a large number of sources for the background of this book. Most important however are the following: on the side of Islam, Malcolm Cameron Lyons and D. E. P. Jackson, *Saladin: The Politics of the Holy War* (Cambridge, 1982), and on the side of the Crusade, Geoffrey Regan, *Lionhearts: Saladin, Richard I, and the Era of the Third Crusade* (New York, 1998).

Judith Tarr is a World Fantasy Award nominee and the best-selling author of the highly acclaimed novels *Pride of Kings* and *Kingdom of the Grail*. A graduate of Yale and Cambridge Universities, she holds degrees in ancient and medieval history, and breeds Lipizzan horses at Dancing Horse Farm, her home in Vail, Arizona. You can find her on the Internet at http://www.sff.net/people/judith-tarr.